LAZARUS:
THE SAMARITAN

KATHERYN MADDOX HADDAD

OTHER BOOKS BY THIS AUTHOR

HISTORICAL NOVELS
Series of 8: They Met Jesus
Ongoing Series of 8: Intrepid Men of God
Mysteries of the Empire with Klaudius & Hektor
Christmas: They Rocked the Cradle that Rocked the World
Series of 8: A Child's Life of Christ
Series of 10: A Child's Bible Heroes
Series of 8: A Child's Bible Kids
Series of 10: A Child's Bible Ladies

HISTORICAL RESEARCH BIBLE
for Novel, Screenwriter, Documentary & Thesis Writers

TOPICAL
Applied Christianity: Handbook 500 Good Works
Christianity or Islam? The Contrast
The Holy Spirit: 592 Verses Examined
The Road to Heaven
Inside the Hearts of Bible Women-Reader+Audio+Leader
Revelation: A Love Letter From God
Worship Changes Since 1st Century + Worship 1sr Century Way
Was Jesus God? (Why Evil)
365 Life-Changing Scriptures Day by Date
The Road to Heaven
The Lord's Supper: 52 Readings with Prayers

FUN BOOKS
Bible Puzzles, Bible Song Book, Bible Numbers

TOUCHING GOD SERIES
365 Golden Bible Thoughts: God's Heart to Yours
365 Pearls of Wisdom: God's Soul to Yours
365 Silver-Winged Prayers: Your Spirit to God's

-SURVEY SERIES: EASY BIBLE WORKBOOKS
→Old Testament & New Testament Surveys
→Questions You Have Asked-Part I & II

Genealogy: How to Climb Your Family Tree Without Falling Out
Volume I & 2: Beginner-Intermediate & Colonial-Medieval

SPECIAL ACKNOWLEDGMENT

Of the following men for spending hours teaching me about Copper Mining, both Deep Vein and Open Pit ~

MAX COMPTON, 10 YEARS EXPERIENCE

CHARLES STEPHENSON, 20 YEARS EXPERIENCE

RAY STEPHENSON, 40 YEARS EXPERIENCE

CONTENTS

1 ~ THE ROAD

AD 7
Road Camp between Mounts Gerizim and Ebal, Sychar, Province of Samaria, Palestine

"Who's there?"

Gersshon, on the ground, jerks his head up, grabs his sword, and leaps up to a crouch. The blackness of the night surrounds him. He peers through it, turning in a circle to find the intruder.

He kicks Chaanan without taking his eyes off the inky unknown. "Sir! Someone's out there."

Chaanan, superintendent of the road gang, jumps up with his own sword.

Back-to-back now, the two men turn through the sinister blackness, staring out into the night-time unknown.

"There it is again," Gersshon warns. "It's straight ahead of me. Do you think it's a mountain lion, sir?"

"No. It sounds like a man. Or men. Keep on the alert."

Gersshon turns and stands side by side with his superior, and together they move forward, one shuffle at a time.

"Who's there? Gersshon repeats. "Whoever you are, you don't have a chance. We're heavily armed. Come out now while you can."

One step at a time, challenging but not knowing who. Or what.

"Uh, sir, were you talking to me?" The muffled voice is deep.

"Come out and show yourself," Chaanan demands.

"Well, uh, sir, okay."

Chaanan lowers his sword. "Zarus, is that you?"

"I'm over here. Did I disturb you?"

"What in the world are you doing, Zarus?"

"I knew you were under deadline to get this new road to Sebaste. I wasn't sleeping anyway, so thought I'd work on getting this boulder out of the way."

"Gersshon, the next time you go after strange noises in the

night, don't wake me up," warns Chaanan, turning to walk back to his blanket on the ground.

"Hey, pipe down," a voice in the darkness calls out.

"Everyone shut up so I can go back to sleep," another voice demands.

"Well, sir," Gersshon announces, "everyone seems to be awake. We may as well get an early start."

"Gersshon," Chaanan replies, "remind me never to hire you again, so I can get some rest. All right, men, you may as well get up and get back at it. Gersshon has managed to wake up the entire crew."

"You would have been thanking me if it had really been an intruder—or a mountain lion."

Yawns. Groans. Grunts.

"With men like Zarus and Gersshon who never seem to sleep, we just might get to work and maybe arrive at Sebaste ahead of deadline," the superintendent mumbles.

As a faint hint of dawn appears in the gray east, Gersshon walks over to his long-time friend, his eyes adjusting to the darkness.

"You worked on that boulder half the day yesterday, ole boy."

"Yeah, I was dreaming about it during the night, so just got up and went back to work on it," Zarus replies. "I hope this iron bar doesn't break before I get it out."

"Gersshon, I'm going to get you for this," a crewman calls out.

Zarus pulls out a handkerchief from his sleeve, wipes his brow, and sits on the ground.

"Here, let me help you," Gersshon replies. "I've got a strong board to wedge under the boulder after your iron bar gets a groove started down there."

"I don't need any help," Zarus responds. "My iron bar and shovel are working just fine."

"Why don't you let me handle your iron bar while you dig?" Gersshon says.

"Well, you can't, because the iron bar is the handle of my shovel. Besides, it's almost as long as you, buddy. Of course, you could put that sword of yours to good use under the boulder," Zarus teases.

The two men sit together a few moments longer, waiting for a little more light on their project.

"You're not going to get this boulder out without my help one way or the other, because you've always needed my help, even when we were kids," Gersshon says, standing back up and stepping closer to the boulder.

"Watch out!"

Zarus' warning is too late. Gersshon falls into the shallow pit dug around the unmanageable chunk of granite. He stands and brushes off his knees. "Stubborn rock, I see," Gersshon says with a grin. "How deep do you think it goes?"

"We could go down three or four more hand-spans before we see the bottom of it. Maybe more."

"Well, get back to work, Zarus," Gersshon orders. "We don't have all day."

Used to Gersshon's take-charge ways, Zarus smiles and resumes his work.

The two men, one tall and thin, the other short and ample, circle the stubborn and deceptively-large boulder digging, prodding, poking, leveraging, to get it out of the way for the next section of roadbed.

"Why don't we just take the road around this monster?" Gersshon asks.

"You know how those Roman surveyors are. They want their roads straight as an arrow."

They continue working in silence.

Though still early morning, perspiration drips off the men's foreheads until the salty sweat stings their eyes, and they have to pause long enough to tie a band around their head.

Everyone with their own job to do. Teamwork. Everyone pulling together to get the job done for Rome.

"Auhhh!" It is Gersshon.

Purple and white light flash in his head. A sensation of being struck by lightening immobilizes him. A hand shoots up to cover his eye. He leans over as though his head has become too unstable to hold up. Now the light is gone. All light. Only a heavy blue blackness left. And the sharp pain of being stabbed by a million needles.

"What? What happened?"

"Auhhh! The board broke. Part of it is in my eye," Gersshon replies.

Zarus grabs Gersshon's shoulders and guides him out of the trench and over to the blankets not yet picked up from the night before.

"Water, someone," Zarus shouts.

Chaanan rushes up with his water skin. "Hold his head back."

Zarus leans his friend's head back and pulls his hands away from his eyes. Chaanan pours water over them while Zarus holds his lids open.

"Ahhh."

"What's going on here?"

It is a feminine voice. While still holding his friend so water can flush his eye of the splinter, Zarus looks in the direction of the voice.

Her heart-shaped face is framed with long, flowing black tresses and a pale blue shawl. Though the ground all around them is rocky and uneven, she seems to float above it all. Behind her head, the glow of the gradually rising sun gives her a well-deserved halo.

"Be careful where you're walking, madam," Chaanan warns," his water skin now empty. "Lots of holes and stumps out here."

Devorah reaches the three men on the blanket.

"Good thing I brought some supplies to treat injuries along with food for your breakfast," she says, smiling at Zarus and motioning for him to give her his place next to the wounded man.

Her touch is both warm and cool on Gersshon's face.

"Try to quit blinking so I can see what got into your eye," she urges with her sweet voice.

"Hmmm. That is a big splinter. If you can hold still, I think I can grab it with my fingers."

Zarus kneels on the other side of his friend while Superintendent Chaanan holds Gersshon's arms down.

Devorah holds Gersshon's eyelid open with one hand, and with deftness, takes hold of the large splinter with two fingers of her other hand, and pulls it out."

"Ahhh!" The stinging again. The needles again. The white light again. He grabs at his eye. "Ahhh!"

"Okay, I have some bands in my basket I can wrap around your eyes."

Gersshon, shorter than many men in the world, blusters back. "Oh, no, you don't, missy. You can put the bands around my bad eye, but you're not going to make me blind. I've still got work in me."

"Whatever you say," Devorah replies. She works fast while Gersshon tries to get his mind off the pain by concentrating on her gentle touch.

"There you go. One eye covered, and one eye only."

Zarus stands and helps Devorah to her feet. She looks up into his unusual blue eyes. "Thank you, kind sir."

Their gaze lasts more than it should between two strangers. *She is as beautiful as a pearl.*

Devorah looks away to break the spell she knows she should be ashamed of.

"Now, I've got to distribute breakfast to all these hungry men."

Gersshon looks up at the two with his one good eye, momentarily oblivious of the pain, and manages a grin.

"Hey, do I get breakfast first? I think I deserve it."

"Indeed you do," Devorah says, reaching into her basket for a small loaf of bread and two figs. "Don't eat too fast," she warns. "And stay down on that blanket. You don't know how much damage that wood did to your eye. By the way, there are only scrub bushes here. Where did the splinter come from?"

"A board," he replies. Since she has already turned away, he doubts she hears.

Devorah makes the rounds of the road crewmen. As she does, she notices Zarus is gone. She looks around and sees him by himself bowed prostrate in prayer. But he is facing the wrong way. He is facing Gerizim, not Jherusalem. He is a Samaritan.

She leaves his share of food nearby without disturbing him. She makes her way back over to her Egyptian horse, lowers a stool off the bridle, steps on it, flings herself over the Egyptian's bareback, pulls the stool up, and leaves.

"Well, I've got to go into Sychar to get another load of sand," Chaanan announces. "It was supposed to be delivered a few days ago from the Aravah Desert, where Devorah's father has a copper mine."

"Yes, sir," Gersshon replies. "What can I do while you're gone? I'm injured but not helpless."

"Well, you like to boss people around, you may as well be boss while I'm gone. But your only job is to make sure everyone keeps working in my absence, and that's all. Am I clear?" Chaanan demands.

"Perfectly," Gersshon replies while looking in Zarus' direction. Prayers now completed, his friend comes alert at the mention of Devorah's name.

"Okay, ole pal, your prayers are done, and the lady is gone. Get your head out of the clouds and back to work."

Zarus obeys out of habit. Gersshon, though much shorter than Zarus, has been bossing him around since they were kids.

Gersshon leans on his sword, grows tired of standing, and sits a while, watching each of the crewmen with his one good eye. Most work slowly, but they are steady and do their job well enough.

Now and then, he dozes. No one pays attention to him. To keep from falling back asleep, Gersshon stands and paces, despite the fact he is developing a small headache. He walks around the men, sometimes telling someone to do something differently, though still, no one pays attention to him.

He goes back to his original perch to survey the crew. His eye settles on Zarus, who is now rocking his boulder back and forth.

"I see you've got it about out," Gersshon calls out.

"Yup," Zarus replies, the muscles in his big arms, legs, and torso straining. Blood vessels pop out on his forehead. His face is red. He grits his teeth.

"Here, let me help," Gersshon says, approaching the boulder. He puts his hands on the boulder, pushing Zarus out of the way. "This is how it is done, ole boy," he says.

"No. You're half-blind with that injury from the board. You can't see things right. Go sit down," Zarus counters.

Without warning, Gersshon grabs Zarus' crowbar shovel and pulls dirt out of the way in the direction the large rock is leaning. It groans and breaks free of its centuries-long confinement and begins a slide down the hill.

"Watch out below!" Gersshon shouts, delighted with his accomplishment.

"Watch out below!" Zarus echoes.

Men at the bottom of the gully chiseling gravel out of larger stones look up, eyes wide, brows furrowed, mouths opened, and catching the dust. Immediately, they jump out of the way.

The unrelenting monster of , for them. Sliding, bouncing, careening.

Gersshon himself is thrown off balance and follows the boulder down the slope.

Both land. The boulder and Gersshon.

The gravel chiselers at the bottom of the gully stand and rub their eyes in all the dust. When it settles, and they can see better, they begin looking around for Gersshon's body, but still rubbing their eyes.

"Over here, guys," Gersshon says, standing and leaning against the now-settled boulder, the band over his injured eye still in place. "The boulder landed exactly where I intended for it to."

"Man, you almost killed us. Then you blind us with all that dust," one of the men calls out.

"Well, if you had been more alert, you wouldn't have gotten all that dust in your eyes in the first place. Just put some water in them, and you will be fine."

"We can't. All the water we have is for drinking."

"Well, you can have my water." Gersshon takes the water skin still attached to his rope belt, pulls the plug out, goes over to one of the men, reaches up to pull his head back, and the man loses his balance.

Medad begins to fall backward and swings his arms to regain control. He descends off the cliff at the far edge of the gully. The sky turns upside down. His muscles strain. He grabs what little brush he can to break his fall.

By this time, the road superintendent, Chaanan, is back and has been watching the turmoil from the top of the hill. "Get a rope to the men so they can get down to Medad."

A rope is thrown down, and the gravel chiselers tie one end around Zarus' boulder and throw the loose end down to the trapped man."

"Hey, Medad. Are you okay?"

"Medad! Medad!"

They look in the direction of Gersshon with his band still over his one eye. "He'd better not be dead!"

One-eyed Gersshon shrugs his shoulders and turns his hands up. "I was just trying to get the dust out of his eye."

Down at the bottom of the cliff, Medad raises one hand, then lets it fall again. There is blood on his head, legs, and hands.

"Can you wrap this rope around your waist, Medad?" Superintendent Chaanan calls down to him.

The injured man turns over and crawls in the direction of the rope. He does not get far.

"I can't reach it," he groans.

"Okay, one of us will come get you," Chaanan responds.

One of the chiselers pulls the rope back up and ties it around his waist. He repels down the cliff until the rope will not go farther. With the rope still around him, he reaches for Medad, but the injured man is not close enough.

"Medad, can you crawl over to me?"

Medad crawls a short distance, but cannot continue. The pain stabs at his bones, and his muscles cry out in anguish. He reaches exhaustion almost immediately. Every part of his body objects to any further torture.

"Okay, Medad. I'm going to go back up and figure something else out. Will you be okay?"

"I think so," he groans.

"Hang on. We'll be back for you."

The crewman climbs back up the cliff. He talks to the other rock chiselers and looks up at their superintendent.

"What'll we do?"

"Too bad, we can't throw Gersshon and his splinter over the

cliff and let him trade places with Medad."

"I think I can help." It's Zarus. "I'm the tallest one of anyone out here. I think I can reach him."

Zarus is handed the rope and ties the end of it around his waist. He walks to the edge of the cliff, turns around, and repels down its straight wall. When he reaches the bottom, he unties the rope, walks over to Medad, and kneels.

"How are you doing, Medad? You're pretty messed up. Do you think you broke any bones?" he asks as he probes the injured man's arms and legs.

"I don't think so, but I hurt all over."

"Here, I brought some bands to wrap your head in. And here's some water. Take a sip. See if you can sit up."

Zarus helps Medad to a sitting position. "Okay, now, Medad. I'm pretty strong. I'm going to wrap the rope around my waist again. Do you think you can hang on to my back?"

"I don't think so."

"Okay, let's think this through." The two men sit at the bottom of the cliff with Medad leaning over on Zarus strong shoulder. Zarus has his arm around him to keep him from slumping down. The other men watch from above.

"Okay, let's try this," Zarus says. "I will put you over my shoulder. Do you think you could handle that?"

"I can try."

"Okay," Zarus continues, "I'm going to carry you over to where the rope is, and you can sit on the ground while I tie the end around my waist. Then I will pick you up again and put you on my shoulder. Do you think you can hang on to my neck from that angle?"

"I'll try. I think I can."

"Remember, I'm strong. I've lifted a lot heavier than you in my twenty years here on earth. Once you are on my shoulder, I will begin climbing back up the cliff. There will be men pulling at the other end, but they'll need my help."

"Yes, sir. And, if I don't make it, sir, thank you for trying. And, one more thing."

"What's that, Medad?"

"Tell my wife I love her."

"That, my friend, I am going to make sure you tell her yourself. Here we go now, Medad. Jhehovah bless us both."

"Ahhh…"

"I didn't mean to hurt you," Zarus says in almost a whisper. "Hang on now."

Medad, now over Zarus' broad shoulder, hangs on to Zarus' neck.

Zarus' muscles strain as he fights for strength. He puts one hand over the other. They are now off the ground. Each muscle, each sinew, is called on to become mighty. Now the other hand reaches up. And the other.

He tries putting his feet flat on the edge of the cliff for better leverage but finds Medad is less steady when he does. He lets his feet dangle, and stretches the muscles of his other arm to reach up. *Don't stop. Don't think about it. Keep going. Keep the momentum going.* One hand, then the other, and the other.

The men from above the cliff watch in astonishment as young Zarus works his way up the cliff with their injured comrade. They grab hold of the rope where it is attached to the boulder and add their own strength to it.

"Pull!"

"Pull!"

"Pull!"

One hand at a time at the top of the cliff. One hand at a time on the edge of the cliff. Closer to safety. Life-saving safety.

"Pull!"

"Pull!"

"Pull!"

Once at the top, and the rope is untied from his waist, Zarus shifts Medad around so he is in his arms, and works his way up the hill. He lays Medad down on the same blanket he had laid Gersshon on a few hours earlier with his eye injury.

The dust is now settled. He looks around for Gersshon, but does not see him.

Instead, over where the newly laid road ends are two men dressed in finery. They watch Zarus a moment longer, turn, and walk toward the gates of Sychar, the well, and the home of Devorah.

"Why do you look at the speck of sawdust in your brother's eye and pay no attention to the plank in your own eye?

How can you say to your brother, 'Let me take the speck out of your eye,' when all the time there is a plank in your own eye?

You hypocrite, first take the plank out of your own eye, and then you will see clearly to remove the speck from your brother's eye." (Matthew 7:3-5)

2 ~ THE ARABIAN

AD 7
Road Camp between Mounts Gerizim and Ebal, Sychar, Province of Samaria, Palestine

*T*he rain comes down hard and fast. It fills the half-laid , and washes away the sand so that only the gravel below it remains. Some of the surveyor's pilings marking the proposed road's border loosen and float away. Work on the road comes to a dead halt.

"Gersshon, I think I'm going to go see my family for a few days until the rain lets up and the ground dries a little. Do you want to go along?"

"You know there's nothing for me in Sebaste any more, Zarus, especially with my father now in prison."

Except for his friendship with Zarus, Gersshon's childhood had been anything but happy. His father had made him dress in rags and sit on a street corner with a bowl begging for alms. His father would always say, "If we don't do it, someone else will." His reward was to keep five percent of the take for himself, a pretty good wage for a boy.

"By the way, when you get back from Sebaste, ole boy, I've got an idea on how you can meet Devorah again. Oh, don't think the whole camp didn't notice the way you looked at her. Now go on to your family, and I'll be here when you get back."

Sebaste, Province of Samaria

The farmhouse comes in to view. It is not the house of a pauper, neither is it the manor of a rich man. It is larger than some, as each of Zarus' three older brothers added their own family living quarters on before their respective marriages.

Reuven, the oldest, has a family—a wife and four children.

Shimeon, the next, has a wife and two children. Levii—their father was enamored with the twelve sons of Israel—just recently married. Though with no children yet, his apartment is more elaborate, a feat he likes to brag about when his older brothers make fun of his relative youth.

Zarus has two sisters who do not live at the farmhouse anymore. One is married to a silversmith in the heart of Samaria, and the other is married to a trader who never stays in one place very long at a time.

Then there is little sister Estar. Being the baby of the family, most everyone dotes on her. When they don't, she does whatever is necessary to get their attention and win their favor. It is not as though she doesn't deserve it, and she is not quite spoiled—not quite—but she does enjoy her status. Estar is the one Zarus is looking forward to seeing the most.

And his brothers? Will they accept him this time? Their jealousy is thick. It drips from their every word, their every stare, their every movement when they are around Zarus.

He watches the servants out working in the barley field. They look like ants from so far away. But, then, his brothers do their best to make him feel smaller than ants.

Why did our father will his prize-winning Arabian horse to me? I could have survived without it.

He is close enough to the farmhouse now that he can make out a few more details. There is the ladder leading to the roof, which, of course, is always pulled away at night. He can see where some of the stucco has been replaced by fieldstone of various colors.

It's not as though his brothers need the money the Arabian would have brought them. Reuven, of course, has inherited the entire farm in accordance with Israel-Samaritan law. Shimeon was put in charge of the finances, and Levii in charge of the hired hands. Reuven made sure his brothers were well paid, being that he could always trust them and couldn't strangers. There was no job for Zarus. Being their father's favorite was his pay.

His older brothers always had known he was the favorite. Of course, it was just because he looked most like their beautiful blue-eyed mother who had died when Estar was born seventeen years earlier.

Zarus approaches like a bird wanting to make friends with a cat. He knocks on the familiar gate, which now is elaborately covered with copper. A servant answers it, and Zarus identifies himself, reverting to the ancient Hebrew spoken among Samaritans. Estar is nearby preparing the mid-day meal and recognizes the visitor's voice.

"Zarus! Is that my favorite brother, I hear?" She jumps up and rushes into his arms. He hugs her back, then holds her at arm's length.

"You are more beautiful than ever, Estar!"

She pats both his cheeks with flour-filled hands and laughs. "And you are more handsome than ever, you big lug."

"What are you doing here, Estar? Your new husband is okay, isn't he?"

"Yes, he's okay, but he's gone to Tyre to look at more fabric samples for our shop, so I decided to stay here while he is gone."

"Is everything else okay with you two?"

"Well," she whispers now, "Reuven, Shimeon, and Levii don't like him. I don't know why. Maybe because he's got a successful fabric shop. Seems like they make a habit of being jealous."

"So, how is he handling these guys?"

"We're thinking of moving to Sychar."

"Sychar? That's where I'm working—at least for now. It would be great having you nearby."

A man of average height, brown hair and graying beard walks into the courtyard.

Estar leaves off her conversation with Zarus, puts on a big grin, and calls out in a sing-song voice, "Reuven! Are you here? Guess who just arrived? Our long lost brother, Zarus!"

"Well, well. What have we here? Come back, begging for a job? You're not getting one, so don't even ask."

"Look, Reuven, I didn't come here to cause anyone any problems. And I don't need a job. I have a good one. It's good-paying and I have a lot of friends that I work with."

"You with friends? That's a laugh," Shimeon adds, joining them in the courtyard."

"Hey, everyone," Estar interrupts. "Our mother and father would be ashamed of us talking to each other like this. Let's get along just this once for...how long did you say you were going to be with us?"

"I think I'd like to be here a couple days until the rain passes up in the mountains."

"You working in the mountains? What are you doing up there?" It's Levii, the brother Zarus most closely gets along with.

"I'm part of a crew putting in a road between the pass at Sychar and Sebaste."

"Working for the Romans, eh?" Reuven responds. Just like you to work for the enemy."

"Okay, guys, I'm about ready for dinner," Estar interrupts. "Everyone sit down."

The men seat themselves. Estar brings over rolls, goat cheese, grapes, and a sauce for the bread. Reuven leads the family in a prayer of thanksgiving to Jhehovah. As they eat, the brothers chat among themselves. They do not include Zarus. He eats in quiet.

The meal over, the brothers adjourn to the roof to enjoy the evening breeze and look over their crops just before the sun goes down.

The three older brothers talk among themselves. Zarus watches them. *What can I ever do to get them to stop hating me?*

Now and then, one of the older brothers stops talking, looks over at Zarus, then turns back to the other brothers. The hatred in their eyes never leaves. He knows they wish he would leave. Or better yet, die.

After a while, Zarus gets up from his cushion and goes back down to the courtyard where Estar is finishing her cleanup.

"That bad, huh?" Estar says. "Come over here and sit down. I made some honey cakes and was going to serve them for dessert, but they were treating you so ugly, I decided they wouldn't get any. But you can have all you like, big brother."

"Thank you, Estar. One is sufficient for me. I don't eat all that much at the road camp and don't want to get in the habit of being spoiled by your good cooking."

"So," Estar says, seating herself beside her brother, "got any women in your life?"

"Women? Who has time for women?" he replies, chuckling.

"Oh, c'm on now," she says, ruffling his brown hair that goes with the blue eyes of their mother. Surely you have your eye on someone."

"Well..."

"I knew it! What's her name, and what does she look like?"

Zarus is caught off guard. "Uh, well, her name is Devorah." He takes another bite of honey cake to collect his thoughts. *Our meeting was so short, she probably doesn't even remember me.*

"And? What does she look like?"

"Well, she has black hair, black eyes, and a little peak of hair on her forehead."

"Yes. And what else?"

"Her fingers. They were some of the most delicate fingers I have ever seen."

"What about her family?"

"I heard her father owns a copper mine, so they must be pretty rich. I'd be a fool to think I had a chance with her."

"Oh, Zarus, don't give up before you even try. If she's the one for you, you should pursue it."

"I don't know."

"Married life is wonderful. I love every moment of it. If you can find true love, you should marry too. Do you think she could be the one?"

"I loved her the moment I laid eyes on her. But I don't think I'll ever be able to get her to notice me."

"What are you two talking about?" Levii asks, entering the courtyard from the roof.

"Oh, nothing," Estar says, wrapping a curl around one of her fingers.

"Oh, uh, Levii, how is my horse doing?" Zarus asks.

"The Arabian? Spirited as ever. But no one takes him out for exercise. I'm afraid he's going to lose some of that spirit soon."

"I have been thinking of taking him back with me," Zarus says, "but I don't know where I'd keep him. It wouldn't work for him to be around that road crew. They're okay as friends, but a lot of them I don't trust."

"Well, I think I heard Reuven and Shimeon talk about selling him once."

"Thanks for the warning. That settles it." Zarus stands and turns to his sister. "Thanks for the honey cake. I think I'm going to leave in the morning. Is my old room still available?"

"Yes. I even put clean linens on your bed and took freshwater in for you to clean with."

"Thanks, sis. I'm going to turn in now."

———

"He did what?"

"Someone planted weeds among our barley. We don't know who. Now there are as many weeds or more than the barley. Sir, I don't know how it happened. We've never had so many weeds before."

Reuven is seething. Veins stick out on his forehead. He clenches his fist and punches the wall. "How could this be? Levii, get out here. What have you let happen? Levii! Get up!"

"I'm here, Reuven. And what did I let happen?"

"Weeds. Our fields are full of weeds!"

He stares at his oldest brother, his forehead furrowed down

toward his eyes. He squints as though looking through the darkness.

"That's impossible. Sure, there are always a few weeds, but I had them plant the barley thick enough, weeds wouldn't have much of a chance."

"Well, it's happened anyway." Reuven paces. He looks at the foreman. "Are you sure barley is all you planted?"

"I'm sure, sir."

"Where did you buy your seeds, Levii?"

"With the same man, I buy them from every year. He's reliable. He wouldn't mix weed seed in with legitimate seeds."

Reuven stops pacing. "Unless… Unless… Our enemies. Which one of our enemies would do this to us?"

"I don't know, Reuven. People who we think are our friends sometimes hate us without us even knowing it. No telling who could have done this."

Zarus walks out to the courtyard. "I couldn't help but overhear. That's tragic what happened."

"I'll bet you think it's tragic. You probably are enjoying this. Maybe you're even the culprit who planted the weeds just to get back at us."

"Stop this very moment!" It is Estar. Her hand is on her hip as she points her finger at Reuven. "Don't get started thinking like this. You know your brother did not plant those weeds. Just leave him alone."

"Well, if he didn't, who did?"

"The main thing we've got to think about right now is how to get all those weeds out," Levii says.

"I have one suggestion that might save you a lot of work," Zarus says.

"Well, spit it out," Reuven says.

"Leave the weeds there and…"

"I would expect you to say something like that."

"No, wait," Zarus continues. "If you leave the weeds in, then when you harvest it, you can separate the weeds and throw them into the fire."

"Hmmm. He's got a point there," Levii says.

"Well…" Reuven mutters. He looks over at the foreman who shrugs diplomatically. He looks over at Levii, who tips his head to one side and raises his eyebrows.

He does not see Estar wink at Zarus.

"Well, guys, I guess it's time for me to leave," Zarus says.

"Not before breakfast," Estar replies.

"Look! You may have had a good idea this time, but this doesn't mean you're ever coming back to work on the farm. You're not wanted here." It's Reuven.

"I just want you to know, Reuven, that I have never resented you or Levii here, or Shimeon. You're my brothers and always will be. I hope someday you'll be able to forgive me for whatever it is that I did."

"The fact that you exist is what you did. Now, get out of my house, Zarus, and don't ever come back."

Estar links her arm in Zarus'. He looks down at her. Amidst her tears, she tries to smile at him.

"It's okay, Sis. I was going to leave this morning anyway."

"I'll walk you out," she replies.

They go outside, and she pulls him down closer to her level. "You're leaving without even taking a look at your horse? Take your Arabian with you. I don't know how much longer they're going to wait to sell it. Take it now."

Zarus takes a deep breath, bites the inside of his cheek, and looks up at the innocent white clouds drifting by.

"But I don't know where I could keep him. I don't have just one place to live. I follow the road."

"You'll think of something. You've got to do it now. This may be your last chance."

The two walk toward the stables. They hear a neighing inside. "He knows it is you, Zarus."

He quickens his steps, and Estar lets go of his arm with a grin. "Go on. He's waiting for you. A long time he's been waiting. Go to him."

Zarus reaches the stable gate and swings it open. His Arabian neighs shakes his head and prances in place.

"Hello there, my friend. It's been a while. Did you miss me?" Zarus reaches out and touches the Arabian's head, patting him with renewed enthusiasm. The horse lets out a deep breath and pushes his muzzle into Zarus' chin. He laughs and opens the stall gate.

"Hey there, big guy. I missed you too."

Estar catches up and smiles while they have their moment.

"You know what?" Zarus says, looking at his sister. She does not answer. "I feel a kind of peace when I'm with him. Peace is valuable, you know. I'm going to change his name. From now on, my friend," he says, looking back at the Arabian, "I shall call you Shalva, Peace. Do you like it?"

The Arabian nods its head and sputters its agreement.

"Better hurry before the guys get in from the field. Now get a saddle on him and get out of here."

"Don't need a saddle. All I need is a bridle. The one on this peg will do just fine."

Deftly, Zarus puts the bridle on his Arabian, leads it out of the stable, swings his great frame up, and sits proud and tall on his steed.

"Goodbye, Sister. See you in Sychar."

"Indeed, you will."

"Now, with Shalva again, I have peace again," he says as he turns his horse and breaks into a gallop.

The earth beneath the hooves shakes. Shalva stretches his long legs and settles into a race with the wind.

But Zarus is worried. What will he do with his Arabian once they get back to the road near Sychar? How can he protect it from thieves? How can he keep it out of the harsh weather of the mountains? How will he feed him? The mountains at the pass are barren. What will he do for food?

"The kingdom of heaven is like a man who sowed good seed in his field.

But while everyone was sleeping, his enemy came and sowed weeds among the wheat, and went away.

When the wheat sprouted and formed heads, then the weeds also appeared.

"The owner's servants came to him and said, 'Sir, didn't you sow good seed in your field? Where then did the weeds come from?'

" 'An enemy did this,' he replied. "The servants asked him, 'Do you want us to go and pull them up?'

" 'No,' he answered, 'because while you are pulling the weeds, you may root up the wheat with them.

Let both grow together until the harvest. At that time I will tell the harvesters: First collect the weeds and tie them in bundles to be burned; then gather the wheat and bring it into my barn.' " (Matthew 13:24-30)

3 ~ THE EGYPTIAN

AD 7
Sychar, Province of Samaria, Palestine

Elii is thirty-two years old and brilliant. He is also a Levite, and therefore among the privileged few allowed to enter the sacred temple in Jherusalem.

The atmosphere in the synagogue—the Samaritans have their own synagogue elsewhere in town—is solemn. God is surely with the congregation as members file in one at a time, their heads covered in somber respect. The men split off from the women to go to their separate sections, each with the required head covering.

Further, Elii's father is a member of the elite Sanhedrim headquartered in Jherusalem. Adding to all this is the fact that Elii is alleged to be the tallest Levite serving at the temple in this generation. He is the prime candidate for the new rabbi position in Sychar. A natural-born leader.

Although not everyone has arrived yet, the cantor sitting in one of the elders' seats on the platform begins chanting a psalm of the revered sweet psalmist of Israel, King David. Everyone knows the psalm well and joins him in melodious strains.

When young Elii walks in, he pushes his head forward ahead of his body, stoops his shoulders, and walks kind of like a chicken. Some say he is shy. He is seated on the podium.

The psalm draws to a close. It is time. The cantor's seat is next to Elii. Another one of the local elders steps forward to the edge of the platform.

Levite Elii is worth serious consideration because he comes recommended by Priest Caalev, founder of this synagogue back when he was a missionary to pagan territories. Furthermore, the priest is the uncle of Devorah's mother, and therefore, associated with the local elite.

"Brothers of Israel, today is a special day for us. I believe at the end of our service, you will agree that our long search for a rabbi will be over. But first, I would like to present to you our illustrious founder, Priest Caalev."

Elder Joshiash motions with his hand for Priest Caalev to perform his hallowed duty. The priest is seated on one of the three chairs to one side of the podium.

Priest Caalev rises with hallowed dignity, delight unhidden in his eyes. He is about the height of the average tall woman, and with a girth near equal to his height.

He gathers up his robe and tunic. The esteemed one then walks over to the podium and turns the scroll with his bent fingers to the next place to be read.

He growls out the scripture in great solemnity to the point that some of the children poke their parent and whisper, "He sounds like a bear," to which they are appropriately pinched and given the evil eye to settle down or face consequences later at home.

Still seated in the speaker's chair, Levite Elii twists, puts his elbows on the exquisite carved arms, takes his elbows off, rolls his neck around, puckers his lips in and out, takes a handkerchief from his sleeve, and wipes his brow.

"Thank you, Priest Caalev," Elder Joshiash says. He escorts Priest Caalev to the front row on the main floor, then returns to the platform.

"Now, the moment for which we have all been waiting. It is my utmost pleasure to introduce to you Priest Caalev's personal protégé, Levite Elii." With that, he returns to the main floor to sit with Priest Caalev.

Young Elii is now alone on the platform. He closes his eyes, opens them, and admits to himself that the crowd has not gone away. Indeed, all eyes are on him like furs on a Norseman in the barbarian far north.

The Levite mentally checks his knees to make sure they will hold. As he stands, he rises higher and higher. Higher than anyone, the congregation has ever seen anyone stand. His head is just two hand-spans from the ceiling. They are duly amazed and are confident God has surely brought this man to lead them. But why does he not stay seated in the speaker's chair like other speakers do?

He looks above their heads and opens his mouth. He changes his mind and clears his throat. He opens his mouth again. "Oh, mighty men of Israel," he declares. *No one is leaving.* "This is the day the Lord has made. Oh, Praise Jhehovah, Creator of the heavens and the earth." *So far, so good. But what am I to say next?*

"Blessed are they whose ways are blameless, who walk according to the law of the Lord...."

The audience smiles.

"....How can a young man keep his way pure? By living according to your word...."

One of the men nods his head. "Amen!"

Levite Elii notices.

"....You are my portion, O Lord; I have promised to obey your words...."

Two more amens from the audience, one from the cantor.

Levite Elii warms up to his subject.

"....Do good to your servant according to your word, O Lord...."

"Yes! Yes!"

"....Your hands made me and formed me; give me understanding to learn your commands...."

The women nod their heads in approval.

Levite Elii settles into his subject, at last confident of his decision.

"....My soul faints with longing for your salvation, but I have put my hope in your word...."

A child squirms and is disciplined.

"....Your word, O Lord, is eternal; it stands firm in the heavens."

A man nudges another man next to him and winks."

Levite Elii's voice strengthens.

"....Oh, how I love your law! I meditate on it all day long...."

Heads on both sides of the aisle bob in approval.

"....Your word is a lamp to my feet and a light for my path...."

Women turn and smile at each other.

He takes a deep breath and billows forth his next words.

"....I hate double-minded men, but I love our law...."

"Say on!" one of the men toward the back calls out.

"....I have done what is righteous and just; do not leave me to my oppressors...."

More children squirm in their seats.

His voice deepens in a sudden decision to sound more like Priest Caalev.

"....Your statutes are wonderful; therefore, I obey them...."

The young women look up at Levite Elii with adoring eyes.

"....Righteous are you, O Lord, and your laws are right...."

"Amazing," someone mutters under his breath.

Speak on, Levite Elii. It's working. Don't stop now.

"....I call with all my heart; answer me, O Lord, and I will obey your decrees...."

"He's the one," Elder Joshiash whispers to Priest Caalev.

"....Look upon my suffering and deliver me, for I have not forgotten your law...."

"This is who we have been looking for," one of the women whispers to her neighbor.

Elii lifts his hands heavenward in grand gesture.

"....Rulers persecute me without ease, but my heart trembles at your word...."

"We need look no farther," the cantor whispers to the elder.

"May my cry come before you, O Lord! Give me understanding according to your word....Seek your servant! For I have not forgotten your commands!"

Silence.

Awe.

Disbelief that merges into belief.

Levite Elii turns and takes three long strides back to the speaker's chair he had left earlier without ceremony, and sits. He takes his handkerchief out of his sleeve and wipes his face and brow. He realizes now that his heart is racing. He concentrates on slowing it down. His hands are sweating and trembling. He holds them in his lap. *What's wrong with me? It's done and over with.*

Priest Caalev and Elder Joshiash both step back up to the platform to congratulate the candidate as their rabbi.

"I've never seen anything like it," the elder says. "You quoted the entire 119th psalm of David and never hesitated. It was brilliant. Absolutely brilliant."

Levite Elii smiles, partly at the compliment, and partly that his "interview" is over.

He hops down off the platform without taking the side steps and walks toward the exit.

As he approaches, Avigail, Devorah's mother, whispers to her, "Be nice. He is coming to our house for Sabbath dinner and will be spending the night. Tomorrow, you will get to know him better."

———

"Devorah," Avigail announces the next morning, "there is a new fabric shop in town. It used to be in Sebaste, so I'm sure the quality will be the best around. I am going to see what they have to offer. I will soon have the best-designed clothes in all of Sychar. And maybe even Samaria itself."

Avigail is nearly a span shorter than her daughter and is generous around her girth. Her face is oval with the point on her forehead formed by her black hair that she bestowed upon her daughter at birth.

"I want you to entertain Elii—Levite Elii, that is—until I am back. Uncle Caalev will be chaperoning you."

"But, Mother, I was planning to go riding on my horse this morning."

Avigail wears tasteful eye makeup, but which Devorah thinks should be saved for special occasions instead of worn every day. Her mother has copper ornaments hanging from her ears.

"Well, you'll either have to get a horse for him, or go riding tomorrow."

"But, Mother."

Avigail puts her hands on her daughter's cheeks and looks straight into her eyes. "You are sixteen years old. It's time you settle down and be a wife."

"Well, I've been thinking about that, and, the other day I met…"

"They don't come any better than Levite Elii."

"What? You're trying to match me up with that giant?"

"He's got connections. He's approved by Uncle Caalev, his father is a member of the Supreme Sanhedrin, and he has an excellent education. Besides, with him becoming Sychar's rabbi…."

"They hired him?"

"Yes, they hired him. So, as I was saying, being married to him, you won't have to leave home. We can get an addition built onto our manor during your betrothal."

"It's not fair, Mother. I don't love him. I don't even know him," Devorah objects.

"You don't have to know or love him. I didn't know or love your father until our betrothal, and look how good our marriage turned out."

———

"So, what shall we do first today, little Dev," Priest Caalev says, entering the room with Levite Elii in his tow.

Devorah has decided she must go along with things, at least

for now. Maybe the excitement will blow over, and her parents will change their mind.

"Would you like to see my horse, Elii? Should I call you Elii or Levite Elii? Or maybe Rabbi Elii?"

Eli clears is throat, squints, and ekes out a shy smile. "Just plain Elii is fine. After all, if we're going to be..."

"Ah, yes. Elii it is," Devorah interrupts. "So, would you like to see my horse?"

"Of course," Elii replies with some little enthusiasm.

The two walk toward the stables, Priest Caalev, between them.

"So, when are you and your parents going to come see me in Jhericho?" Caalev asks, already beginning to huff for air, but remaining cheery.

"I don't know, Uncle Caalev. This is the first time you have come to our house since I was ten years old."

"It's been that long? Well, I must say, you've grown into a fine young lady since then."

"Here we are," Devorah says. "Pesachya, I need you. Pesachya, where are you? Oh, there you are. Pesachya, get a harness and bridle for my horse and one other horse—the largest one you have."

"Yes, mistress," Pesachya replies. The stable hand is middle-aged with weathered skin. He is thin and slight and good with horses.

"Come this way, Uncle and Elii. I want you to see my prize Egyptian horse."

Smells of fresh hay and manure reach their nostrils the moment she opens the door to the stable, but it is not strong, as Pesachya cleans it a couple times a day. They follow as she leads the way to the stall with her Khemoh in it.

She pats her Egyptian on the nose, who in turn, nuzzles into her hair. Devorah giggles.

"May I introduce you, men, to Khemoh? Khemoh, as both of you know since you know ancient Hebrew, means worthy or valued. I believe all people are deserving to an equal degree. So, whenever I am with Khemoh, he reminds me of that. Don't you think it's clever, Elii?"

Priest Caalev clears his throat. "Well, I suppose. But some men are more worthy than others. Isn't that right, Levite Elii?"

Elii nods his head yes at the man he most admires—more than his father—and the woman that, more and more, he wants to make his own.

Pesachya approaches with the bridles and harness for Khemoh, and a horse a hand span larger than Khemoh already bridled and harnessed.

"Elii, let's go riding," Devorah says, shaking her hair back in anticipation.

"Uh, well, I've never been on a horse. Most Jews ride mules—white ones if we can. Even King David and King Solomon rode white mules. They're better for the hot climate."

"Egyptian horses are raised to endure hot climate too. Let's go riding."

"I don't know," Elii replies, eyeing the horse and trying to get his hands to stop shaking.

"Look, we can just ride around in the fenced circus my father made to train his horses for chariot races."

She looks over at Uncle Caalev. He shrugs his shoulders at her. She looks over at Elii, who is not budging, then back at Uncle Caalev.

Her great uncle scrunches his mouth to one side and rolls his eyes heavenward. It is a signal.

"Well, maybe we can do it another day," she says. *This suitor of mine is going to be boring.*

The larger horse is escorted back to its stall, and the trio leaves. As they walk toward the door, Devorah brightens.

"I know! We can play latrones. Did you ever play latrones, Elii?"

"Uh, well, tell me about it. Maybe I have and didn't know it by that name."

"It's a board game. It's like a war between two sides," she says, delighted that she has thought of a substitute for horse riding.

"War games?" Eli responds. "I don't like war. I think everyone in the world should try to get along. Look at King Solomon. He never went to war, and he expanded David's kingdom beyond his wildest imagination. He managed it with diplomacy and both sides trying to get along."

Devorah looks at her great uncle. Her brow is furrowed, her eyebrows draw together, and she lowers her head with only her eyes looking up. "Huh?"

Caalev once again shrugs his shoulders.

They enter the courtyard, and Penina, Devorah's personal maid, comes out with mugs of cool lemon juice.

"Well, let me see. How about trochus?" she asks, sitting on the edge of a fountain in the middle of their ornate courtyard.

"Trochus?" Levite Elii repeats.

"Oh, I'm sure you played it as a little boy. "Eshachk," she says, calling toward her father's personal servant walking through. "Go fetch a couple of trochuses for us. Bring them both out. And if the sticks are with them, bring them too."

Soon Eshachk returns with two large hoops almost as high as a horse, and two long sticks.

Devorah takes one of each, stands the hoop on edge, pushes it forward, and runs behind it, keeping the hoop going with the stick until she runs into a wall. She turns.

"So, let's do it. We'll go outside where we have more room. We can have a race. Isn't this exciting?"

Elii agrees, and they go out the gate. She runs circles around Elii as he tries to get his trochus started rolling upright.

Devorah stops, stands inside her upright trochus, and stares at her guest and possible future husband.

"What *can* you do, Elii?"

As they re-enter the courtyard of Baaruch's manor, Devorah repeats, "Elii, what can you do?"

"Well, I can recite all 600 regulations in the Law of Moses."

"What's that?" Priest Caalev asks, looking back and shading his eyes. "That cloud of dust. Who could be stirring up all that?"

Elii and Devorah turn and look in the same direction.

Soon the rider is close enough to recognize. It is Zarus on a fine Arabian. He slows as he draws close to the manor. His horse is in a slow trot by the time he reaches them. He stops his horse, looks down at Devorah, their eyes lock briefly, and he urges his horse toward the stable.

4 ~ THE COMPETITION

AD 7
Road Camp between Mounts Gerizim and Ebal
Sychar, Samaria, Palestine

"Well, did it work, ole boy?"

Zarus walks up to the tent Gersshon has set up for them to share for the night.

"Ha! I can tell by the silly grin on your face it did work. You got permission to board your Arabian in Baaruch's stable. I was right, wasn't I?"

"Yes, you were right as always, Gersshon," Zarus says as he settles himself on the ground outside their tent.

"So, how much is Baaruch going to be charging you?"

"I didn't actually see him. I saw Devorah…"

"Ho, Devorah, is it? You know her name? Did you tell her yours?"

"Had to. Her father wasn't there, but she said she handles his business sometimes and knows he would give me permission to board Shalva with their horses. She just asked for my name and the name of the horse."

Gersshon hands his friend a piece of jerky to chew on.

"So, how much is Devorah going to charge you?"

"She said it is free unless her father decides different."

"Free? Oh, she has it bad for you, Zarus."

"No, she doesn't. She's nice to everyone. You saw how she brought breakfast to all the guys that morning."

"That morning. Yeah. Don't remind me of it," Gersshon says, touching a fresh band around his still injured eye.

"It wasn't the best day you've had in your life, that's for sure, friend."

"Okay. Okay. So my bossiness gets me in too deep sometimes. I know that." Gersshon grins. "But it sure is fun—bossing other people around."

He punches Zarus in the arm.

"So, what's the next step in capturing the heart of the love of your life?"

"Well, I guess I can go out there and give Shalva some exercise."

Zarus picks up a fist-sized rock and turns it several different ways, observing the different colors in it.

"But the timing. The timing has to be right," Gersshon resumes. "Look, tomorrow after work, I'll go to see Baaruch and ask him about driving one of his chariots in a race for him. While I'm there, I'll casually ask when Devorah goes riding, whether morning, evening, or both. I'll think of a way, so it isn't too obvious."

"Let's hope it's evening. We have to start work first thing in the morning."

———

"It's been a week since you boarded your horse in her father's stables. Time to make your move," Gersshon urges.

"You don't think it's too soon, do you?" Zarus asks, picking up a boulder the size of a lion's head and moving it out of the way.

"Now is the time. I'll cover for you so you can quit work a few moments early and go to that well at the gate of Sychar and clean up."

"Thanks, pal, Zarus responds with a grin."

The day passes as though each moment is an hour, and each hour a lifetime. Zarus moves small boulders out of the path of the new road along the route the surveyor has laid out for the next two stadium.

His muscles strain. His heart beats fast within his chest. Perspiration falls down his bare chest until it wets the stones themselves.

His thinking clouds, and he puts his mind on automatic. Every stone he lifts has Devorah's face on it. Every leaf he sees has Devorah's exquisite feet on it. Every piling driven into the ground on both sides of the proposed road is Devorah's slim form. At last, the sun begins to lower itself.

"Okay, ole boy. The superintendent isn't around. Time to take off to the well, and get cleaned up for your first date with Devorah."

Zarus grins widely. "How can I thank you, Gersshon?"

"Don't thank me. Just go."

Zarus grabs a clean tunic, headband, and sandals, wraps them in a clean loincloth, and heads to the well outside of Sychar wearing only his loincloth and carrying clean clothes.

With his strong body and long legs, it takes only moments to arrive at the well. He lowers a leather pouch with a rope that stays at the well, jerks it onto its side when he hears it hit water, and brings it back up, water spilling out of it.

He looks around. No one coming from any direction that he can see.

He hurries to remove his dirty loincloth, soaks it with water, and wipes his body down to get the dirt off. That done, he lays it on the ledge of the well to dry and hastens to put on his clean loincloth. He leans over and pours the rest of the water over his head. He slings his hair around to get most of the water out, smoothes it back with his fingers, and ties a band around it to keep his long hair from getting in his face. Now his clean tunic. Finally, he sits on the edge of the well, wipes the bottom of his feet, and dons his sandals. He looks down into the well to see his reflection to make sure everything is right, but the water is too far down in the darkness to do that.

He grabs up his dirty, partially dry loincloth and carries it in his hand. He will use it to rub down Shalva after he arrives.

Zarus takes a deep breath. "Okay, Devorah. Will I pass inspection?" He says a quick prayer to Jhehovah, and heads up the hill toward the city.

Sychar, Province of Samaria

He walks through the main gates and hails the guards, men he has made friends with over the past months since starting on the road. He passes the forum, the market, and a small circus, perhaps built for Baaruch and his chariots. On the other side of the circus is another market.

"Hey, Zarus!"

He looks around, but there are so many people in the market, he cannot make out who is calling him. *Maybe I misheard.*

"Hey, Zarus. Over here!"

"Estar?"

Recognizing the voice, he turns in a circle trying to find his little sister. He sees a young lady waving at him. "Over here!"

Zarus laughs and heads over to the shop.

"What are you doing here?" he asks.

"We moved here right after you left. Our brothers are out of control. They hate everyone, and I sometimes think they even hate themselves.

"Oh, Zarus, meet my husband, Akiva. He was already in the fabric business when we married."

"We didn't want any part of the family feud," Akiva says.

"So, here we are. Sychar is a rather quiet city, not like Sebaste. There were no other fabric merchants here, so it was the perfect spot."

"I'm very happy for you, Estar. You too, Akiva."

"And we're going to have a baby. Everything is just perfect."

"That's great. Well, I need to be going."

"What are you all dressed up for, brother?"

Zarus does not reply. He grins.

"Oh, I see. That girl you were telling me about. Well, good for you. I'm anxious to meet her someday."

Zarus says goodbye to his sister and brother-in-law and hurries on up the street.

Now through the city, he goes out the back gate, it being closest to Devorah's home in the outskirts. He alternately prays she will not be there and will be there.

As he nears the manor and stables, he looks around to discover just who sees him. His heart speeds up. Devorah is not there. He goes into the stable, picks up a hand full of barley grain at the door, greets Shalva with the treat in his hand, and harnesses him. Shalva plays with Zarus nuzzling him in the shoulder, forcing Zarus to work harder to get the harness on the moving head. That completed, he opens the stall gate and leads his Arabian outside.

Though his horse is taller than the Egyptians he has seen in other stalls in the stable, Zarus is tall himself and throws his torso up with ease, mounting Shalva in one bound.

"C'mon now, Shalva. Let's race the wind."

With that Zarus eases up on the reins and lets Shalva determine his own speed and his own destination.

The wind blows Zarus' hair back and rushes through his tunic as though covering Zarus in itself. Shalva's nostrils flare, his mouth opens for deep gulps of air, and his long legs reach for the ends of the earth.

The rocks and rills race past. The hills turn into valleys, then back to hills as Shalva escorts his beloved master through the endless vistas of Sychar's surroundings.

On, and forever on. Horse and rider as one. One with each other. One with the earth. One with the universe. Zarus has never seen Shalva race so.

Ahead, he sees what Shalva has been after: The Egyptian. Shalva strides up beside Devorah's Khemoh and slows.

With that, Devorah stares at Zarus, laughs, and kicks the side of her horse. Khemoh lunges forward with the grace of an Egyptian and takes the lead.

Shalva cannot let the prissy Egyptian get the best of him, so leaps with broader strides ahead and is once more in the lead.

Khemoh, though smaller in size, is anxious to show off her silky mane in the wind and surges forward.

The two horses are neck and neck.

Zarus and Devorah look over at each other, laughing. It is a tie. Zarus pulls back on his reins,, and Devorah does the same. They bring the horses to a walk and guide them toward one of many rain troughs scattered around the Baaruch property.

Zarus slides off his mount, lets go of the reins and walks around to Devorah. He reaches up and helps her down from her delicate Khemoh.

"How did you catch up with me?" Devorah laughs.

"I didn't. My Arabian did. He knew what was waiting for him at the other end of the trail.

"By the way, my name is Zarus. I don't think we were ever formally introduced."

"And my name is Devorah, kind sir," she responds.

The two sit down in the grass and stare in silence at the rocky hills beyond for a few moments.

What a pearl she is.

"Sorry I didn't bring along some dried dates or something," Zarus says at last. "I could sure use a snack about now."

Devorah holds her chest a moment and winces. Zarus notices.

"What's wrong?"

"Oh, nothing. It happens sometimes. The humors in my body sometimes object to my exercising," Devorah explains with a forced grin. "They don't stick around very long."

She takes a deep breath.

"See there? All gone. Now, what were you saying about dried dates? Oh, you said you would like one but didn't have one. Well, how about some dried figs?"

Devorah reaches for the sash around her waist, pulls it around until she comes to a soft leather pouch tied to it. Unfastening it from her waistband, she opens it and hands two figs to Zarus.

"You think of everything, Devorah. Like the morning you came by with breakfast for us and had bandage and ointment on hand in case of accidents. Man, were we needing you that day.”

“I noticed you praying while the others started eating their breakfast. You weren’t facing Jherusalem. You were facing Gerizim. So, I guess that means you’re a Samaritan.”

“Yes, I guess I’m one of those dirty Samaritans you Jews hate. You are Jew, aren’t you?”

“Yes, I am. My great uncle was a missionary in his youth and started synagogues in several pagan places, including Rome and here in Sychar.”

“So that’s how you ended up here. You know there aren’t that many differences between us Samaritans and you Jews.”

“Really? I always was told we were worlds apart. But watching you pray that morning got me to thinking.”

“Well, we pray three times a day, the same as you Jews. Only difference is that we face Gerizim, and you face Jherusalem.”

“What do you pray about?”

“Well, we only believe in the books of Moses. So we praise God every day for Avrahaam, his son Izhaac, his son Yakov, and his son Yosef. Just like you Jews do.”

“Hey, you got too many figs,” Devorah objects with a grin. She jumps up, grabbing a fig out of Zarus’ hand as she does, and begins throwing it up in the air. I’ll bet you can’t grab it before I do. I may be smaller, but I’m swifter.

“Oh, yeah. Watch me!”

Zarus lunges at a date in mid-air, but she grabs it before he can, and circles the horses with it.

“See there. I’m as swift as my delicate and gorgeous Egyptian.”

“But not as hardy as my big and powerful Arabian.”

She moves around to Khemoh’s muzzle and stuffs the fig in the horse’s mouth, much to the animal’s delight.

“You’re in trouble now,” Zarus declares with a laugh. “You’re not getting by with it that easy. He circles both horses, then lunges at Devorah. He grabs hold of her arms, looks in her eyes, then stops.

“Oh, I’m sorry, Devorah. I didn’t mean to…”

“I know you didn’t. It’s not all your fault. If I’d not been playing around… Well, let’s sit a while longer until the sun is a little lower. Then we can head back to the stable.”

“I’ll sit over on this boulder.”

“But I thought all Samaritans worshiped idols as well as Jhehovah.”

“I know that’s what you’re told, but it’s not true. You know how you Jews have three sects—the Pharisees, the Sadducees, and the Essenes? Well, we Samaritans have three sects too."

"I didn't realize that," she says.

You know Aaron, Moshes' brother, was the very first high priest. Well, he had two sons that lived—Eleazaar and Ithamar. Eleazaar had a son named Phineas. You with me?'

"Yes," Devorah says, watching Zarus with new admiration for the intelligence he is showing.

"Well, a descendant of Ithamaar and a descendant of Phineas had a big feud. The descendant of Ithamaar declared himself high priest and set up a tabernacle at Shiloh.

"So, those following the false high priest started worshiping on Shiloh, while those following the true high priest continued to worship at Gerizim."

"You said there were three sects."

"Yes, the third one is those who accepted the false gods brought here by the Assyrians centuries ago. But back to the feud.

"The high priest who moved the tabernacle to Shiloh later moved it to Nod near Jherusalem. Finally, it was set up in Jherusalem. That is the high priest you Jews follow."

"But our history tells it the other way around," Devorah interjects, standing and walking over to the horses a moment. She turns around. "The high priest who led worshipers to put the tabernacle in Jherusalem are the true worshipers."

"And therein lies our differences," Zarus says, summing up the whole Jew-Samaritan thing. "You call yourselves Jews, but we call ourselves Israelites. You no longer speak the ancient Hebrew, but we speak it when we are among ourselves."

"We true Israelites descend from Yosef's two sons—Ephraim and Manasseh—and we also have some who descend from Benyamin and Ashur. Of course, we also descend from Levi, the priest tribe."

"So you Samaritans, er, uh, Israelites, descend from five of the twelve tribes—almost half of them. Well, as informative as this has been, the sun is getting low. I guess we'd better head back before Father sends someone out to find me and finds you here too," Devorah says.

"Why don't you ride on back alone, Devorah, so there are no undue suspicions?"

"Good idea. I guess I'll see you the next time I take breakfast out to the road crew. Father likes for me to do it at least once a week."

"Tell him we appreciate his generosity."

Zarus helps Devorah back on her horse and watches as she

ambles back toward the manor.

He waits until it is almost dark, and rides his horse back to the stable. The stable hand is not around. He unhitches his horse, gives it a pail of water and another pail of barley, and leaves.

As he nears the back gate of the city, he realizes it will be closed for the night. When he approaches it, he calls up to the guards. Do they remember him? After a few clues, they do, and let him in. He walks in the darkness past the market, the miniature circus, the other market, and the forum to the front gate of the city. His friends let him leave. The moon comes up, and he whistles as he walks toward the road camp.

———

Just as Zarus crawls into his and Gersshon's tent just outside of Sychar, Devorah finishes up her evening meal. She sees her father, Baaruch, leave to walk outside the compound. She follows him out.

"Father, you understand me the most. There's something I need to tell you. I'm in love, and it isn't with Elii."

"Don't tell me you've found a Samaritan."

"Father, it isn't as bad as you think."

"Well, it will never happen, so you'd better get that rebellious female mind back under control. You're marrying Elii."

5 ~ SABOTAGE

AD 7
Sychar, Province of Samaria, Palestine

Devorah comes out of her father's study with scroll in hand.

"Where's Father?" she asks Eshachk as he passes the door.

"I saw him leave and head toward the chariot house, mistress. Maybe he's getting ready to take it out for some training. There's another chariot race in Sebaste next week, as you may know."

"Thank you, Eshachk."

Devorah goes down the stairs and into the courtyard. She leaves out the side gate and walks toward the carriage house.

"Interested in a chariot ride with me, Devorah?" she hears from behind one of the Egyptian horses hitched outside the stable.

"Father, could I talk to you?" she replies.

"Let's do it out on the track. Will that work for you, my dear, impatient daughter?"

"You won't be going fast, will you?"

"No, I'm just checking the wheel to see if it is perfectly round and balanced."

Devorah, never much for wearing tunics that she has to take special care of, walks around the horse and sees beyond it the chariot.

It has some gilding on it along with filigree of silver. The chariot itself is overlaid with the lighter copper that will not slow it down during races.

Baaruch had grown up in a racing family, his father teaching him and his brother how to handle a chariot and get the most out of it, and the horse harnessed to it. Baaruch had made a pretty good living in chariot racing but had to be away from home too much. So, when he won a private race, and the surprised loser had nothing to pay off his bet with, Baaruch said he would settle for ownership in the man's copper mine down in the Arabah Desert just north of the Red Sea.

Baaruch had been surprised at how willing his opponent was to sign the mine over to him. It wasn't until he visited the mine that he heard the stories of the dangers within, and eminent collapse. Baaruch hired a mining engineer who led the miners in shoring up the ceiling of the mine to make it safer. But he is having trouble finding strong men to hire, willing to work under such dangerous conditions.

"I'll have it hitched up in a few moments, then we can have that chat you want."

"Well, I'll take the scroll back to the house while you do that. We can look at it later. Be right back."

Now, having returned, Devorah steps on board the chariot—her father's prized possession—and hangs on to the sides. Baaruch, with expertise, directs the horse to the practice field while Pesachya opens the gate and closes it behind them. A comfortable pace is set.

"Now, what is it, my dear favorite daughter?"

"Well, since I'm your favorite and only daughter, I need to convince you to understand something."

"Let me guess. It's about your Samaritan friend out on the road crew."

"Oh, Father," she says, punching him in the upper forearm. "How did you know?"

"Because you are most like me, and I know I wouldn't take no for an answer until I heard some compelling evidence."

"Okay, I've got some evidence for you. First, there are three sects of Samaritans."

"Yes, I know that, Devorah."

"Well, Zarus is a member of the sect that does not believe in the idols brought here by the Assyrians centuries ago."

"Okay. But that doesn't change the fact that he is a Samaritan."

"In the chronicles of our nation, it says that, when our King Josiah rebuilt the temple, money was donated by the people of Manasseh, Ephraim, and the entire remnant of Israel. Manasseh and Ephraim were the sons of Joseph, who the Samaritans descend from. Zarus claims he descends from Joseph. Well, Sychar, where we live, was part of Ephraim. So, in King Josiah's time, they were accepted by the rest of the Jews."

"Okay, I see your point, daughter. Anything else?"

One wheel of the chariot hits a rock that has appeared since the last big rain a few days ago. Baaruch looks over at the wheel and decides he'd better stop and check it out.

"Whoa, there."

While he inspects the wheel, Devorah walks around and pats the horse on the nose.

Soon they are back in the chariot and working their way around another lap.

"Jeremiah wrote about eighty men from Shiloh and Sebaste who brought offerings to the Temple in Jherusalem," Devorah continues.

"Uh, huh," her father grunts, loosening his grip on the reigns.

"The Samaritans claim some of them descend from the legitimate priests that the king of Assyria sent to their ancestors not taken into captivity. So doesn't that mean the Samaritan Israelites are the same as the Jewish Israelites?"

"My dear daughter. That feud has been going on since the days of Joseph himself. His brothers were jealous of him and sold him into slavery. Centuries later, their descendants got back together under Moses, and all formed our nation. Since Joseph's descendants got twice as much land as anyone else, they covered most of the northern half of our country. When King David faced opposition, it was from the northern half of our country. When there was a civil war after King Solomon died, it was between the northern and southern half of our country."

"Well, well. You know a lot more about the Samaritans than you've been letting on, oh father of mine," Devorah says, with a grin.

Baaruch goes off the path and heads for the gate.

"I'll get the gate, Father." She leaps off the chariot and runs to open and close it. When Baaruch gets close to the carriage house, he steps out and begins to unhitch the horse.

"What can stop the feud, Father?" Devorah asks, as she grabs a rag on a hook outside the stable and begins to wipe down the horse.

"Even the good Samaritans like Zarus who believe in and follow the Law of Moses with meticulous care, fall short because they don't believe in any of the prophets. I don't know what will stop the feud."

"Nothing?" Devorah says, wrinkling her forehead.

"Well, something could unite us: A third offshoot that both we Jews and Zarus' Samaritans both respect. That would do the trick."

"But who could unite people who hate each other so much? It

would take a miracle."

"Then, you must pray for a miracle, my dear daughter."

"Father, Zarus is a good and kind man. And a strong and hard worker. Would you even consider him? After all, they believe in life after death, and not even our own Sadducee sect does that."

"Strong, you say?" Baaruch pauses and looks over at his daughter. "Hmmm. I tell you what I'll do. I'll ride over to where they're working on the road and see how good of a worker he is."

"I suppose, but..."

That's it. That's all I'm willing to do. And, if I were you, I would not say anything about it to your mother or brother, and..."

Baaruch grabs his chest, his face twists, his eyes narrow, and he grits his teeth.

Devorah turns to hear what else he has to say and notices her father bent over.

"Oh, Father. Not that again. Not the chest pain."

Moments later, he stands upright and smiles. "It was just brief. I'm all right. Now go on in the house and help get supper started."

———

"Darling, the mayor of Sychar is having a dinner party, and we have been invited. Isn't that marvelous? Let's see. What will I wear to it? I bought some silk last week from that new fabric shop in town. I suppose we have to buy from the Samaritans sometimes, even though we don't like them."

Avigail and Baaruch are in their room, getting ready for bed. "It's emerald green." She explains. "You like that color, don't you, darling?" She goes to a basket, pulls out the fabric, and holds it up in front of her ample figure.

"Yes, it's fine, Avigail," Baaruch responds.

"I guess I'll have to go back and buy some linen for you to have a new toga."

"I told you, I don't like togas. Just get something for a new mantle. I'll wear it over one of the tunics I already have."

"Whatever you say, darling. But keep in mind that there is an opening on the infrastructure committee, and you'd be the perfect person to fill it. It should be no problem for you to work yourself up to the chairmanship. Then, who knows from there."

"Avigail, I love you, but you are too ambitious for me. Between my horses and the mine, and being on the finance committee of the synagogue, I don't have time for anything else. Why don't you design the dress you're going to wear to the dinner party and see if you can build up your little design business?"

He kisses her, climbs into bed, and blows out the lamp. "By the way," he adds in the dark, "our daughter is getting more serious about that Zarus boy who works on the Roman road."

"What?"

Avigail, still holding her green fabric, opens their bedroom door to let some of the light in from lamps in the hall kept burning all night.

"Never!"

Her neck stiffens, she lowers her eyelids while ducking her head forward, and pumps her arms down by her side as though hitting invisible tables on each side of her.

"Never will she marry that pagan. I'll disown her before she gets a chance."

"You can't disown her, dear. All our holdings are in my name."

"Well, I'll think of something. Having a Samaritan in the family will be our ruin."

Avigail has a sleepless night. She tosses and turns, then gets up and paces. She walks out to the kitchen to get a goblet of warm milk left over from earlier in the day and wanders back to their bedroom.

She still cannot go back to sleep, so goes out to the courtyard. She climbs the steps to the roof and looks over toward the walled city. Some lamps and torches are still lit and seem to twinkle across the city. How she hates Sychar.

She decides to give sleep another chance and returns to her bed. Finally, it is daylight. As soon as Binyamin enters the courtyard to greet his mother and learns when breakfast will be served, she takes him aside. She looks around to see if any other family members or even hired help are nearby.

"What is it, Mother?" he whispers.

"It's that Samaritan. What's his name? The one who works on the Roman road and has his horse stabled here."

"Oh, you mean Zarus?"

"Yes, that's the one. He's got to go."

"What are you talking about. He's not here."

"He is trying to inch his way into our family so he can marry Devorah, get rid of you, and take over."

"Never! I refuse to have a Samaritan as a brother-in-law."

"Son, you've got to figure out a way to get rid of him. Make him disappear. I don't care how you do it, and I don't want to know how you do it. But get rid of him."

"Yes, Mother. I'll ride over to the road and watch a while. A good plan should emerge."

"Good. Now, here comes your father. Go sit at the table. I'll bring your meal to you shortly."

Avigail serves generous amounts to her hefty husband and son.

"That's right. Eat all you can. Don't know when you'll get your next meal. Gotta keep your strength up. Here, have another wedge of goat cheese."

Both men are happy to obey as Avigail walks toward the kitchen area, eating her own wedge of cheese stuffed in a barley roll on the way.

Breakfast consumed, Baaruch stretches.

"I think I'll ride over to the Roman road and see if they need any more sand," Baaruch announces.

"I think I'll go with you, Father."

He pats his son on the back. "Since when did you become interested in the new road, Binyamin?"

"I think it would be good education for me to learn how to build a good road. Maybe we can do the same thing for your...er, uh, our...practice track.

"What big plans you have, my son. Well, come along."

They ride out of the city and stop at a rising just above the road. They sit on their horses and watch. Benyamin looks for the biggest man on the crew. He zeroes in on him and watches his every move. So intense is he, that he does not know his father is doing the same thing.

As Benyamin comes to understand what Zarus' job is, and what the other crewmen do, he formulates his plan to get rid of Zarus. For good. How he hates him. The Samaritan.

———

"Zarus!"

"Zarus!"

"You are being summoned, ole boy," Gersshon says, poking his friend sleeping not far from him. "I wouldn't wait to put on my sandals. Sound like you're in for it."

Zarus jerks awake and rushes to Superintendent Chaanan.

"Yes, sir."

"I told you to get rid of those rocks in the next section. We're ready to start pouring gravel on it, then the sand. But you didn't touch a single rock. What did you do all day yesterday?"

Zarus looks over at the section he had cleared the day before. He squints and his brow furrows. He walks over to it as though slipping up on something in secret. He grits his teeth and tightens his hands into fists. He looks it over, then turns back to Chaanan.

"Sir, I cleared it all off yesterday."

"You may think you did, but it did not happen."

"But, sir..."

"What did you do with your time yesterday? Sneak off to see that girl? Or maybe your horse? I'm going to dock your pay. I already paid you for yesterday, so you will get none for today."

"Sir, I know I cleared it. But I'll get started on it right now and do it again. I won't even stop to eat until it is done."

"You are right about that, Zarus. No pay for today. No food for all of today. Water either. And it had better be done by the time the sand arrives around noon. If it isn't done, you're fired."

Superintendent Chaanan glares one last time at Zarus, turns sharply, and walks away just as Gersshon arrives with his friend's sandals.

"I heard what he said. Everyone did. Want some help?"

"No, I have to do this myself. I don't want you getting into trouble by not doing your own work."

The sun rises higher, food is brought out for everyone's breakfast. Everyone except Zarus.

As always, the sun beats down on the men as they do their respective jobs, pausing now and then for a swig of water or to wipe the salty, burning sweat off their brow and neck.

Now and then, one of the other men walks near Zarus when Chaanan is not looking and gives him a swig of water from their water skin. It is not often that Chaanan's head is turned away from Zarus.

His stomach taunts him, but he knows the pains will go away eventually. Still, the salty sweat stings his eyes.

Without warning, his blood turns cold. Under one of the larger rocks is a thick brown snake with orange spots along its back. The viper is venomous. Zarus throws a rock at it, but the viper only coils itself, ready to attack. He grabs it by the tail and behind its head, wishing he had his sword nearby. He throws it on the gully side of the road, but it turns around and heads back toward him. Then swishhhh! Its head is off.

Zarus turns and sees his superintendent. "Can't work you if

you're dead," he says. "Now, get back at it."

Zarus thanks Chaanan, then bends over to pick up the rock again that the snake had been under. He does so slowly in case the snake has any relatives.

"I'm going into town to get some more sand, men," Chaanan announces to his crew. It won't take me long, so no slacking while I'm away."

As soon as he is gone, one of the crewmen comes over to him. "Sir, I'm Medad, the one you saved after I fell over the cliff. Let me help you. You'll never get done before he is back."

"Both of us working together won't get it done. What's the use?"

"I can help too," Gersshon says.

"Me too. I can help," another crewman says.

"Count me in," says yet another.

Before a sundial can cast a shadow from pointing north, then five degrees beyond that, the roadbed is cleared. As they hear wagon wheels and an oxen rumbling nearby from the direction of the well, they return to their own jobs and leave Zarus to help shovel out the sand upon its arrival.

"Chaanan looks at the roadbed now cleared and realizes what happened. He rages, "What's going on here?" then stomps over to where baskets of gravel are waiting to be poured onto the roadbed. Behind his beard, he is smiling.

The crew continues to work on the cleared roadbed, and by sunset, the gravel and sand are in place, and crude concrete is laid over that. Everyone is now ready for their rest.

The next two days are back to normal. They do not notice when Benyamin sits on his horse and watches Zarus from a rise on the other side of the roadbed. They do not notice when he slips away after their evening meal, and they head for their tents. They do not notice when he returns in the dead of the night.

Though portly, Benyamin has learned to walk with stealth. Tonight he walks through the camp of the road crew. He looks around for the finest tent, approaches it, then changes his mind.

He looks at some of the iron bars and shovels left in a pile near the campfire that is about to go out. No, not that either. Then he spots it: The fine sword laying on the ground near, but not in, the hand of Superintendent Chaanan. With deft hands and eyes that dart around him, Benyamin picks it up and turns it around. A fine sword.

He turns and looks over the tents. He notices Zarus is not sleeping in the open air tonight like he does some nights. He peeks inside several tents until he finds the one Zarus is in, lifts one side of it between two pegs, and slides the sword under it.

Morning comes. Benyamin has been long gone. One by one, the men open their eyes, yawn, sit up, and stretch, though not always in that order. Someone wanders over to where the fire had gone out during the night and begins to build a new fire. They will use it to make flatbread on hot rocks. A few other men walk back toward the well, which is now several stadia behind them, to fill their water skins and that of a few friends. Others take down their tents, roll them up with their other belongings, and tuck them in the shadow of a boulder beside the road, or one of the sparse bushes.

"My sword! Where's my sword?" Chaanan stands where he slept the night before, looking along the ground and at the bedrolls of those who slept nearest him.

"Search the camp, everyone. Search the camp! You, you, and you. Everyone else come stand by me until the search is over."

Surrounded by all the crewmen but the ones headed for the well and the three searching the camp, Chaanan stands with his hand on his hips and feet wide apart.

"I will not tolerate thievery in the camp. Whoever did this will be turned over to the authorities and imprisoned."

"Here it is, sir! I found it!" The crewman brings over a sword to Superintendent Chaanan.

"No, that isn't my sword. I wouldn't wear a thing like that. It's bent. Is this a joke?"

The crewman returns to where he found it when another calls out. "Here it is, sir. I found it!"

Superintendent Chaanan walks forward to inspect the newly-found sword. "Yes. This is mine. Now, where did you find it?"

"Well, it was in this tent right here."

"All right, men," Chaanan calls out. "Who owns this tent?"

Gersshon walks forward. "I guess I do, sir. But it is impossible for your sword to have been in our tent last night."

"Our tent? Who else belongs to this tent?"

"Well, I suppose Zarus, sir."

"Zarus. I should have known. Where is he? Zarus, show yourself."

"He's gone to the well to get water for the day for several of us."

"He'd better not be headed into town and that girl."

"No, sir. He won't be long. He's got long legs and can walk twice as fast as me. He won't be long."

"The rest of you men get to work. No breakfast for anyone until figure out who the culprit is. It had better not be a new ring of thieves. I'll stop it before it starts."

He watches Gersshon leave.

"On second thought, Gersshon, you stay here by me. I don't trust you all that much."

Gersshon sits on the ground and waits until Zarus returns.

"Hey, Gersshon, what are you doing sitting instead of working?" Zarus calls out as he re-enters the camp and spots his friend.

Gersshon stares at Zarus with his head down and puts his fists up to his mouth. Zarus recognizes the signal. His smile disappears, and he walks up to Superintendent Chaanan.

"Something wrong, sir? Can I help?"

"You've helped quite enough, Zarus. I am placing you under arrest."

Zarus creases his brow and tenses. He fights an urge to flee from Superintendent Chaanan, the whole road crew, and the road itself. But he cannot flee Sychar.

"What did I do, sir?"

Chaanan holds up his sword. "This is what you did. You thought you could take it and hide it from me, but you made the mistake of leaving the camp, so didn't have time to stash it under a rock."

"Your sword, sir? I can use a sword, sure. Most everyone can. But I prefer the bow. I was trained at the bow like most men in Samaria have been. I would have no use for your sword."

"You could sell it. No, you cannot excuse yourself and get out of it this time. I've caught you."

Zarus looks up into the heavens and says a prayer.

"Sir," says Gersshon.

"Don't bother me now."

Superintendent Chaanan calls over one of the men he uses as a nightguard. "Arrest this man."

The guard hesitates.

"I have the authority of Rome to protect this road and any necessary equipment. Arrest this man."

"But sir, I took your sword."

"It's not working, Gersshon. I know who took it, and it was Zarus."

"No, sir. I took it. You see, I never told you, but my father was a sword maker. One of the finest. He traveled everywhere making swords for the best of warriors. You probably never heard of him because of all his travels. Why, he traveled as far as India; and one time, he was summoned to go all the way to China. The emperor of China demanded the best, and my father was the best."

"So, what's that have to do with my sword?"

"Sir," Gersshon continues, encouraged by Chaanan's ignorance, "I have the finest tools for sharpening swords. I was planning to sharpen it for you during the night, but I fell asleep. I swear it by the temple that this is the truth."

"By which temple?"

"Whichever temple you want me to swear on, sir. I swear it is true. I put my hand on my head and my heart and my thigh. It's the truth. I am willing to face God himself, and will tell him the same thing."

"Well..."

"Let me take it to my tent now and sharpen it for you. It will take me a half day, but it will be worth it."

"I lose half a day's work out of you? Forget it, Gersshon. Now you and Zarus get to work. Release Zarus!"

For the next week, the road work goes smoothly. Zarus and Gersshon work extra hard in order to smooth things over with their superintendent.

Late one afternoon, a soldier of the Sychar guard shows up at the camp.

"May I help you?" Superintendent Chaanan asks.

"There has been a murder in Sychar."

6 ~ THE VERDICT

AD 8
Sychar, Province of Samaria, Palestine

"Zarus, you have a visitor," the prison guard announces as his keys rattle, and he unlocks the cell's iron door. He opens it, sets a small stool just inside, and lets a woman in. She is tall and slim, wears a simple tunic, holds a handkerchief over her mouth and nose, then takes it away.

Estar falls into the arms of her brother. "Oh, Zarus, I know you aren't the one who killed my husband in that brawl. You seldom go to taverns; you're too exhausted at the end of each day from lifting all those boulders to go to town. Besides, you've always been all work. You never played much."

The iron door slams shut, and the keys once again rattle

Zarus holds his sister, though he is aware of the putrid dungeon smells that permeate his skin and what is left of his rotting tunic. His heart aches for her. She is too young and innocent to be going through all this.

"I lost my husband," she continues, speaking in their native ancient Hebrew, "and now I have to lose my brother?" She pulls back, moving her hands from his tunic through which she can feel his bones, and looks in Zarus' hollow eyes.

"No, I will not let them kill you too."

"They have eyewitnesses," Zarus responds, smelling the lily scent on her hair. He steps back from her to give her tender sensibilities some reprieve.

"I've been trying to get in to see you, but they wouldn't let me. They said the magistrate had to give his permission, and he has been in Rome for three months. He just got back."

Zarus motions for his sister to sit on the stool brought in by the guard. He remains standing.

"So, the trial will be soon. I do not think it will last very long. I heard the witnesses say they were all personal friends of Akiva."

"I don't see how they could be. Akiva stopped at a tavern after work sometimes, but never stayed very long—just long enough to have one quick mug of ale. If I had to do any last-moment shopping elsewhere in the market on my way home, that's what he'd do so he could get home about the same time I did. It just doesn't make sense, Zarus. He had no drinking friends like they claim."

"Have you heard anything from Devorah?"

"Oh, I did meet her at our booth. She's as pretty as you said. Doesn't much look like her mother, though."

"Avigail? I've never seen her mother."

"Well, for one thing, Devorah is tall and her mother short. She must take after her father."

Zarus shifts to his other leg and gets their conversation back on track.

"So, Devorah knows where I am? Did you tell her?"

"Actually, she came alone to our booth after she realized I am your sister, and asked if I knew why she hadn't heard from you in a long time. I had thought you had advanced so far down the road that you couldn't get to town in the evenings."

Zarus smiles, but his eyes do not, and he looks up at the dank ceiling, heavy with poisonous mildew.

"After Devorah said she hadn't heard from you either, I started asking around. I even went to the city council and asked if anyone had reported an unknown dead body. That's when one of them told me the name was right, but that you were being held for murder."

"Oh, my dear sister."

"When I asked him who you were supposed to have murdered, he said my Akiva. I was shocked." She stands. "That's when I started making requests to come see you."

"Well, the guards told me yesterday the magistrate is back," Zarus replies, "so I suppose I'll be called up for trial any day now."

He looks over at his sister with a tear in his eye.

"Estar, if I don't ever see you again, I want you to know that I love you, and you have been the best sister any man could ever ask for."

She steps closer to her brother and takes both his hands in her own. "Don't talk like that, Zarus. I won't let them execute you."

"Guard! My visitor is ready to leave. Guard!"

"I pray for you every day, Zarus," she continues. "God will set you free. I don't know how, but he will. He can do miracles."

Once more, the keys rattle, the cell door opens, the stool is taken up, and the lady walks away from the condemned.

Zarus sits back down in a corner crawling with maggots and rats. He pulls up his knees, and sets his folded hands on them. In the ancient Hebrew that he uses to worship, he prays.

"Oh, Jhehovah God. I am lost. There is no hope for me. If you have a miracle for me, even though I am unworthy, I ask for it now."

Something crawls across Zarus' foot. It no longer matters.

"But if not, take my soul to the habitat of Avrahaam, Izhaac, Yakov, and Yosef. I know I am not worthy to be in their presence. But much more unworthy am I to be in Your holy presence..."

Moments later, Zarus jerks awake. His head is in the slimy stench of the cold stone floor of his cell. His eyes are stinging, and he lifts himself to a sitting position again.

What has my life been for? I have accomplished nothing of value. But, Jhehovah, watch over my family. Perhaps in my death, my brothers will finally love me.

And my sisters, especially Estar, protect them. This world is so cruel. Well, it's not always cruel, because you are here too. And do you think I'll be able to see my mother and father when I arrive? I wish so much they were here. I need them...

Once again, exhausted, Zarus is brought back to wakefulness by a rat sitting on his hand. He looks down in the dim light from the moon peering through a small window up by the ceiling.

"Well, Mr. Rat, it looks like we are in this together. Only difference is that you can leave any time you want. The next time I leave, it will either be to a swift trial and stoning, or a slow trial, insults, lies, and then the stoning."

The rat dips its head and skitters away. Zarus leans his head against the back wall and dreams of his childhood and his father's prized Arabian horse, and his mother's sweet cakes, and his old friend Gersshon. *I wonder what Gersshon is up to these days. No one much liked him but me. But life wasn't very fair to him. He always needed me. Who will he have now?*

He looks up at the small window. The moon has moved on, but he thinks he detects a little gray taking over the sky. He watches it, working to make his mind a blank, but which always settles on thinking of Devorah. Pink shows up next, and he remembers her halo from the first time he had seen her.

The small door, in which is the peek hole of his cell door,

rattles. "Here, come get your breakfast. Eat it quickly. I'm going to make the rounds of the other cells, then I will be back to get you into the bath."

Zarus reaches up and takes a small cloth knotted by all three corners, and walks back to his corner to watch the sun turn from orange to gold. He squats and bites into the stale bread—no doubt left from the guards' dinner the previous night—chewing each bite with care in order to prolong his meal. Then he remembers his orders and devours the rest in two more bites.

He hears the rattle of keys at his cell door and stands.

"C'mon. It's bath time. Your sister—that was your sister wasn't it?—brought a clean tunic for you, and new sandals."

The guard puts chains on Zarus' wrists to match the ones on his ankles and prods him with the brunt of his sword down the corridor. A prisoner looking out through the peek hole calls out, "Hey, you're going the wrong way."

"He's headed for the baths," says another prisoner on the other side of the corridor. Bad news. It only means one thing."

"Trial. That'll be a laugh. Since when do they try anyone based on the truth? He's getting all cleaned up to meet his Maker. If there is such a thing as a Maker."

At the end of the corridor, the guard tells Zarus to take off his clothes, even if he has to rip them off to get past the chains on his wrists.

Zarus now steps into the putrid water. It is cold.

"Now, go all the way underwater to get the lice out of your hair. Most lice don't live through this."

The prisoner does what he is told, squinting his eyes as tightly as possible, clamping his mouth shut, and holding his nose so as to keep vermin out of his body cavities. He comes up out of the water and stands in it.

"Here is your old tunic. Use it to rub yourself down and get as much filth off you as you can."

The prisoner obeys.

"Now, get out and put on this tunic and your sandals."

"What about a loincloth?" He asks.

The guard grins and prods him to head back up the corridor. Zarus shuffles his way back. When they arrive at his cell, Zarus pauses to let the guard unlock it. Instead, he is prodded to keep going. They pass through the guards' quarters, then outside. Zarus squints and holds his hands up in front of his eyes.

People have already begun gathering at the forum, but the two men pause just before arriving.

"Stop here," the guard says. He knocks on a door near the forum.

"Enter."

"Sir, this is the prisoner. I leave him in your hands."

"Please give me the keys to his chains. I intend to get him freed."

The guard does, then leaves. The short, portly man rises from his table. "Hold out your hands so I can get those chains off you. We'll have to leave the ankle chains on for now."

Zarus rubs his wrists, and flicks off some of the vermin he picked up in the bath that were caught under his iron cuffs.

"May I introduce myself? My name is Daniyyel. I am your lawyer."

"But I didn't hire a lawyer," Zarus objects.

"Your sister did."

"Estar? How could she afford you? She is recently widowed."

"Number one, she must be a good businesswoman and kept her trade going. Number two, she isn't that good, because she just hired me to represent you in court without doing any investigating of the facts in the case herself. Have a seat. Court will be in a few moments. We don't have much time."

Once again, Zarus obeys.

"Now, did you kill him?"

"No, I did not kill Akiva."

"What's your defense? How can you prove you didn't?"

"First, I was working on the road that day, and went straight into my tent to go to sleep as soon as I got off work."

"Can you prove you stayed in your tent all night?"

"Yes, my tent mate, Gersshon, will testify on my behalf.

"Where is Gersshon?"

"I'm sure he's out working on the Roman road between here and Sebaste."

Daniyyel etches something on a tablet, stands, and opens an inside door. "Uh, Selig, go out to the Roman road going toward Sebaste and fetch this man."

He hands the clay tablet to his servant, then sits again. "Let's just hope Selig can get him here before the trial ends."

"Now do you have any other witnesses?"

"No, I guess not."

"Do you have any character witnesses? We might try that."

"Well, my sister will vouch for me. She will tell you I got along well with her husband."

"What does her husband have to do with this?"

"That's who I am accused of killing."

Daniyyel leans back in his chair and holds his stylus up to his hairless chin. "Hmmm. That's a new twist. Anything else you think will help you?"

He pauses and listens to a trumpet out on the street. "Well, that's it. Court is coming into session. We must leave. I don't think there will be time for your Gersshon to show up. I think it's going to be a short trial. But we'll give it our best."

Daniyyel takes the steps onto the forum platform with Zarus following him. They sit on one side of the platform where three chairs have been arranged. It is the plaintiff's side.

They wait in silence. Moments later four men walk up and take seats on the other side of the forum—the accusers' side.

Zarus stares. He sucks in his breath and his eyes widen. His heart beats faster and the veins in his forehead stick out. He does not know three of the men, but the fourth is Benyamin.

Benyamin returns his stare and grins.

The magistrate walks up and takes his seat in the center. Everyone rises out of respect. His name is Magistrate Yigal.

Lawyer Daniyyel rises first.

"Most Excellent Yigal, I intend to prove that my client, Zarus of Sychar, was not anywhere near the scene where Akiva was murdered. I also intend to prove that my client was friends with the deceased and had no motive to kill him."

He sits and Benyamin rises.

"Most Excellency, I have three witnesses putting the defendant, Zarus, at the scene of the crime. It will be the word of my three witnesses against the defendant's none. I will also prove that Zarus had everything to gain by the slaughter, for he planned to take over his brother-in-law's business once he got him out of the way."

"Benyamin, you may call your first witness."

"I call...

Zarus stares in disbelief as all three witnesses swear an oath that they saw Zarus and Akiva together at the inn where he was murdered, and saw Zarus pull out a knife and kill Akiva.

Why is he doing this? What does he have to gain?

"Most Excellent Yigal, I could have given you a dozen witnesses. However, by law, only two witnesses are required," Benyamin explains. "I have provided three. The defendant has not proven he was not at the inn. He has not even produced witnesses proving he was elsewhere at the time of the murder. That is because he has none. That is because he is guilty. That is why he deserves stoning for this vicious crime. Or beheading, whichever you prefer, your lordship."

"Most Excellent Magistrate," Daniyyel says, rising. "May I call a recess of one hour. There seems to be a delay of my client's witness."

"No, you may not. You say you have another witness. Call that one to testify on behalf of your client."

"In that case, I call Estar to testify as a witness for the defendant."

Estar stirs in the audience, and walks up the steps to the forum platform. She faces Zarus' lawyer.

"Your name is Estar and you are both the widow of the murdered man and the sister of the accused. Is that correct?"

"Yes, sir."

"Now, what can you say that proves your brother did not kill your husband?"

"They have been friends since we moved to Sychar a year ago. There was never a cross word between them. Besides, Zarus is a gentle man and could never do such a thing."

"Is that all you have to say?" Magistrate Yigal asks.

"Yes, Most Excellent one."

"Since the defendant has no more witnesses, I am ready to render my verdict."

"Uh, sir. Magistrate Yigal. My lord."

Everyone turns in the direction of the voice. It is a woman. She walks up the steps to the forum platform and stands before the magistrate.

"Do you, young lady, have a good reason for interrupting these proceedings?"

"Yes, I do, my lord. I am here to testify on behalf of the defendant. I am the defendant's betrothed."

Zarus' head jerks forward, his heart pounds, his brows raise, his eyes widen. Devorah looks over at him and smiles.

Lawyer Daniyyel stares at Devorah a moment, then looks at his client. "You didn't tell me about her."

He stands and speaks. "Most Excellent Magistrate Yigal, this is an unexpected turn. May I have a few moment to confer with my client and the new witness?"

Benyamin grabs both arms of his chair on the opposite side of the forum platform, glares, grits his teeth, and rises. "My lord, this is most irregular and cannot be allowed."

"It is not irregular, Benyamin, so sit down," he says with a growl. He turns back to the beautiful young newcomer to the trial. "Go ahead. I will have a goblet of wine while you confer. When I am done, you are done."

The three leave, hurry to Lawyer Daniyyel's *officium* as fast as they can with Zarus' ankles still in chains, and close the door after them.

"What's going on?" Zarus asks, not daring to touch Devorah for fear she is just his dream.

"I overheard Mother and Benyamin talking this morning. He told Mother he had promised the witnesses he would pay them double what he originally promised them if they testified in open court that they saw you kill Akiva."

"Oh, my sweetheart. But how were you able to go against your mother?"

"I hurried to tell Father what I'd heard them say. But he was out on the practice track with his chariot. By the time he got back, I explained everything, and we returned to the house, Benyamin had already left. But Mother was still there. She confessed, and told Father she would never let a Samaritan into our family."

"God has sent me his miracle."

Lawyer Daniyyel grins.

"But what about being my betrothed?" Zarus asks.

"It seems Father has been talking to your road superintendent who told him he thought Benyamin was trying to get you fired. So Father went out to the road several times to watch you. Guess what? He said you were a strong and hard worker and would be a good addition to our family and his business."

"Go ahead and kiss her, Zarus. Then we've got to get back to the court. The magistrate must be finished with his wine."

Lawyer Daniyyel opens the door and motions for Zarus and Devorah to follow him. He pauses. "Oh, may as well take those ankle chains off too," he says as he takes out the key given him earlier by the prison guard. He squats and unchains his client.

Devorah reaches down and touches the bloody chafing around his ankles as a result of being chained for over two months. Her touch is like cotton on rusty iron.

The three walk back out, over to the forum, up the stairs, and over to the chairs set out for them. He motions for Zarus to be seated and Devorah to walk with him to stand before the magistrate.

"Sir, this woman states that the prosecutor is her brother. Madam Devorah, did you indeed hear your brother confess that he bribed the witnesses to testify against your, against the defendant?"

"Yes, sir, I did."

The magistrate looks over at the three witnesses. "Now is the time for you to change your story, or you will be trading places with the defendant in his prison cell," he tells them.

The three jump up, glare at Benyamin, run down the side steps to the street below, and disappear into the crowd.

"Is there anything else anyone has to say? No? Then I am ready with my verdict. This man, Zarus, is not guilty. Everyone is dismissed. Now, someone, get me another goblet of that wine."

Zarus shakes hands with Lawyer Daniyyel, then is grabbed by one arm by his beloved Devorah, and the other arm by his sister, Estar.

As they work their way into the crowd, they are approached by Baaruch. He is grinning.

"Well, well, my son—or almost my son—I am pleased to welcome you into the family. We will have the betrothal tomorrow. You will be indentured to me to earn my daughter's hand. Immediately after the betrothal ceremony and before you are married, you will go down south to the desert and work in my copper mine for a period of four years."

7 ~ JOURNEY'S END

AD 8
Sychar, Province of Samaria, Palestine

Zarus stretches his arms heavenward and turns in place in a

circle. He notices rays of sun coming down from distant rain clouds and, for a moment, imagines himself climbing those rays to heaven itself. The sun seems brighter this morning. The flowers along the inside walls of the courtyard seem more vibrant. The mosaics underfoot seem more amazing. Never has Zarus seen such a morning.

Baaruch walks out to the courtyard toward Zarus. "I trust your stay in the stables last night was comfortable and that you have now washed away in your bath the rest of whatever may have attached itself to you in the dungeon," Baaruch says, waving his hand in front of his face as though whisking away a mosquito. "You smell a whole lot better too." He winks.

"By the way, that bath also doubled as your ceremonial betrothal immersion."

Zarus nods his agreement with everything his future father-in-law has just said.

"Now, as soon as I confirm Devorah has had her ceremonial immersion, the betrothal ceremony can begin."

Zarus takes a quick glance at Benyamin, who is now standing one pace behind his father. He notices the glower from his soon-to-be brother-in-law.

Servants rush around the courtyard decorating for the ceremony. They hang a canopy of reeds between four pillars, then drape red gauze from the top of each pillar to the tiled floor.

"Sir," Zarus says, still gaunt from his ordeal in the prison, but now with a genuine smile on his face. "I just want to tell you, while I have the chance, how grateful I am for your trust in me to care for your daughter. I promise she will be allowed to follow your Jewish customs because your religion is almost the same as my Samaritan religion—at least my sect is. I also promise to always protect her and..."

"That's enough of that, Son. Save it for the betrothal ceremony. I assume my agreement for you to indenture yourself to me at my copper mine for the period of four years in exchange for my daughter is agreeable to you."

"Yes, sir. When will I have a chance to tell my superintendent at the road I will not be returning?"

"I've already taken care of that." Baaruch turns toward Benyamin. "Now, my son here is in charge of the mine and will be taking you to it. He has been away from it more than long enough. You will answer to him. Is that clear?"

"Yes, sir."

Zarus looks again toward Benyamin, who is one step behind his father. He mimes someone stabbing himself, then points at Zarus.

"Master, Devorah is ready for the ceremony to begin." It is Penina, Devorah's personal maid.

The men turn toward the back entrance to the courtyard and smile.

Devorah stands motionless, her hair still damp from the ceremonial immersion. Ribbons made up of copper threads form a headband. Matching necklace and earrings glisten around her neck. She wears a blue silk tunic and red shawl over her head. Her cloak is stripes of blue and red.

Zarus' head swims at the thought of marrying this Jewess with a heart of gold and eyes only for him. Two miracles in two days. *God, I am not worthy.*

Behind Devorah is her mother. Avigail—though dressed in her best white gauze tunic, mantle of blue gauze flowing behind her, and two priceless pearls adorning her ears—does not smile.

Next to Avigail is Estar. She is dressed in green linen with a royal blue shawl.

Baaruch walks over to his daughter and takes her hand. Next, he reaches over to Zarus and takes his hand.

"Bring forth the document," Baaruch says to his servant, Eshachk.

Eshachk walks to the three with a small table and scroll. Behind him is Penina with a bottle of ink and a pen. Everything in its place, Baaruch unrolls the scroll and reads.

"Number one: Zarus of Sebaste promises to support and

protect Devorah of Sychar from the day they are married until the point of their death."

Baaruch looks over at Zarus. "Is this correct, sir?"

Zarus' solemn reply is strong. "It is correct."

The old man resumes reading.

"Number two: Devorah of Sychar brings into this marriage one Egyptian horse, one pearl of great value along with lesser pieces of jewelry, and her desire for all people everywhere to love and accept one another." Baaruch looks up and over to his daughter. "Who added that last part? That isn't what we discussed. Did you add it, Devorah.?"

"Yes, Father," she responds with a sheepish grin. "I couldn't help myself."

Baaruch looks over to Zarus. "Well, pretty soon, she'll be all yours, and you can be the one to try to anticipate what she will say or do next. Now, let's get back to the ceremony."

Zarus looks over at Devorah and winks. *Indeed, a unique and priceless pearl she is.*

"Now, I believe Zarus has something to say."

Zarus steps forward. His world is now a golden globe in a sun-dominated sky. Everything is roses and lilies. Everything is a rainbow after a storm. All more than he had dared ever dream.

"I, Zarus, have no money to give Devorah's family in exchange for her hand. But I offer my body and my life for her. I hereby indenture myself to her father at his copper mine in the Arabah desert for four years. I give this with my own free will and upon the vow of my very soul."

Eshachk dips the pen in the alabaster bottle of ink and hands it to Baaruch, who, thereupon, signs his name. He dips it again, hands the pen to Zarus, who follows suit with his own signature.

"Hey, don't leave me out," Devorah announces. "Give me that pen, Eshachk." The servant looks over at Baaruch, who grins and dips his head in a "go ahead" signal. "I am signing my own contract, too," she says.

"Okay, everyone," Baaruch announces, clapping his hands, "we have a meal fit for a king and queen waiting for us at the other end of the courtyard."

Zarus and Devorah do not respond. They stare into each other's eyes, though careful not to touch and speak with their heart. The courtyard, with all its people, fades away. It is just the two of them. Their new love lifts them up, and they drift among the stars.

"It's time to go!"

"Huh?"

"It's time to go," Benyamin repeats. It is at least one hundred fifty leagues to the mine. We need to be on the road within the hour."

Devorah goes over to her brother. "No, Benyamin. I deserve my betrothal meal."

Zarus looks over at Baaruch. "Okay," Baaruch announces, "Benyamin is right. They need to get started, so they can get there before the worst of the summer heat arrives. It will take them at least ten days."

Ten days? Zarus thinks. *Ten days if we walk, but Benyamin has his Egyptian horse, and I have my Arabian. It shouldn't take us more than three days to get there.*

Wait!" Devorah calls out. I have something to give Zarus." She rushes out of the courtyard and up the stairs to her room. "Where did I put that copper pendant? She looks inside a coffer, under her bed, and in a basket holding her clothes. "Estar!" she calls down the stairs. "Never mind, Estar. I found it!"

She rushes back down the stairs and into the courtyard, but it is now deserted except for the canopy of reeds, red gauze curtains blowing in the morning breeze, and a table at the far end with most of the preserved food gone. The fresh food is still there.

"Zarus? Father? Benyamin? Mother? Estar? Where is everyone?"

She turns in a circle in the middle of the courtyard, looking around, and hoping they are just playing a betrothal-day game on her. Still, no one. She opens the front gate and looks around. In the far distance, she sees a dusty cloud. She sinks to the ground.

"No. He can't go that way," she says, lifting up her head and rushing toward the stable.

"Wait, Devorah," Estar calls out, coming around the side of the house.

"No time," Devorah says.

Estar rushes over to the stable. "No, Devorah. Let them go."

Devorah pauses and looks in her new sister-in-law's eyes with tears in her own. "But..."

"Let them go," Estar repeats. "It will just make it harder for Zarus."

Devorah's shoulders slump, and Estar takes hold of her hand. They walk inside the stable.

"Do you have an Egyptian for me?"

Devorah leads her new best friend to a stall. "This one is gentle."

———

The wind rushes through Zarus' brown hair. He races with time as though, the faster he goes, the faster the four years will pass. The horse beneath him flies above the ground, and Zarus is transported to his new world of hope, and dreams come true, and despair turned to joy ethereal.

Rather than slow down by going through the city of Sychar, Benyamin and Zarus ride around it, then on to the city well where the Roman road passes.

Benyamin reins in his horse by the well, and Zarus follows suit.

"We let them rest, give them some water, then leave again at a slower pace."

"Hand it over!"

"Huh?

"Hand over the Arabian."

Zarus turns in the direction of the gruff voice.

"Yes, you! Hand me the reins."

Zarus looks over at Benyamin.

"Better do what he says."

Zarus hands the reins of his horse over to the stranger with a scarf over all but his eyes. "What about his horse?"

"Egyptians are too small. I need a racehorse."

The stranger grabs the reins, still on his own horse, and leads it away.

Zarus looks back at Benyamin. "What do we do now?"

"I ride. You walk."

"Huh?"

Benyamin drops a lasso over Zarus' head and wraps the other end of the rope over a horn in his saddle. "Get going."

Zarus turns toward the pass between Mounts Gerizim and Ebal.

"Looks like it's going to take ten days, after all, friend," Benyamin says.

Already weakened by his stay in prison, it does not take long for Zarus to tire.

Ha! Where's his arrogance now? "Samaritans are all weak, you know," says Benyamin. "You may have been able to embarrass me in public once, but you'll never do it again. Actually, you'll never live long enough to embarrass my family or me ever again."

"I never intended for you to be embarrassed, Benyamin. No one wanted to embarrass you. We just wanted the false witnesses to change their story."

"Shut up. Just shut up and walk."

On they continue. Zarus walking and sometimes stumbling. Benyamin riding and sometimes chuckling.

They cross the southern border of Samaria and into Palestine.

"Home again," Benyamin muses. "Ah, yes, home. Away from those Samaritans I hate so much. Mother tried to talk Father out of it, but it didn't work. He claimed land was cheaper in Samaria. Devorah was four years old when we moved there. She doesn't know any better."

They stop for the night near where a caravan has stopped. Benyamin yanks a blanket off his saddle spreads it beside the road, pulls out a small basket from which he takes a wedge of cheese and hand full of apricots.

"Don't look at me," he commands Zarus. "Lie down over there; you need the sleep."

Morning. A bright morning, but one that conceals the shadows in Zarus' heart. Back on the dusty road.

"You're lasting a lot longer than I thought you would. Well, at least you're someone to talk to."

The sun moves higher in the sky. He stops at a roadside well. He pours himself a drink. He fills a bowl attached to his saddle so his horse can get a drink. He looks over at Zarus.

"Oh, yes. I guess you want a drink too. Sit there, and I'll get you one."

Benyamin lowers his water skin back into the well and pulls it up full. He walks up to Zarus, who reaches out hands that tremble. Benyamin tips the water skin so that its contents run out on the ground.

"Oops. There goes your half. You weren't fast enough. Well, you had your chance."

A bystander notices them. Benyamin looks up and grins. "He's just a Samaritan," he announces.

The bystander nods in agreement and walks away.

Benyamin refills his waterskin, attaches it to one of the four horns on his saddle, and mounts his horse.

Back on the road, following the Jordan River. The air getting hotter. Thicker. Harder to move through because Zarus' legs now sometimes buckle.

"Get up there and act like a man," Benyamin scowls from atop his horse.

The hills run together like the boulders he used to wrestle free and throw in a pile. The valleys choke and sputter like the gully Gersshon sent his boulder to in deceitful triumph. The river gurgles and invites like forbidden fruit that the eternal trickster, Satan, has made him imagine he sees.

One step, then another. Zarus feels like a bird with its wings clipped and being chased by a fox. He feels like an animal turning into a snake, doomed to crawl the rest of his life. He feels like a half-human and half insect being stepped on by fate.

Days growing hotter. Oh, to stop and rest. But nights are colder because he has no blanket, no food, little water. Nod asleep and dream of better days. Dream of Devorah and longing to see her. But, for now, he cannot protect her, he cannot make her happy. He can only love her from afar.

One step at a time. Stumbling. Wavering. Faltering. People staring on the road. Benyamin announcing that he is just a Samaritan.

Past the Jordan River. Past life and non-life. Struggling to go into the fire. Hotter. Hotter. Now desert. Dust. Choking. Strangling. Surviving to die a little at a time once again. The Dead Sea appears.

"Jherusalem is a few *milles* to the west," says to break the monotony. I have a great uncle who is a big shot priest there. Bet you didn't know that. Of course, you wouldn't. You're a Samaritan. Our family has connections with the Jewish hierarchy. He lives over in the Jhericho Valley, which is where we are now. I should stop in and say hello to him, but he's probably taking care of some important job at the temple.

Struggle. Don't struggle. Wrestle. Do battle to survive so another nothingness can reign.

"Elii has connections with the temple too. He is my great uncle's protégé. His father is on the Sanhedrin. Devorah was supposed to marry Elii until you showed up and ruined everything. Well, once I'm done with you, she can go ahead and marry Elii. Then maybe we can move out of Sychar, say good riddance to Samaria, and live in Jherusalem among our own kind."

Lizards, Scorpions. Snakes under rocks. Hissing. Taunting. Daring.

Between life and death. Take the next step. Stepping into a future full of red hot blackness. Burning. Chafing. Scorching.

Now far south of the Jordan River. Now far south of any important city. Wilderness. Desert. Mountains of desert. Valleys of desert.

Dry. Scorching. Bereft of normal life. Ruled by lizards, scorpions, tarantulas, vipers. In a world of kill or be killed.

As Zarus walks, he dares to dream and hope beyond hope. He imagines being in the arms of his beloved Devorah. He comes back to reality with a start. His silent shout penetrates the murkiness of his night. *Devorah! I shall survive. I shall live again. We will marry, have children, and grow old together. I promise, Devorah. I promise...*

Eilat, Port City on Red Sea, Arabah Desert, Idumea

"We're here, Zarus. Your lucky day. You get to start work tomorrow. Can't start tonight. It's too dark and I'm too tired.

"Father had a manor built here in Eilat. In some ways it is nicer than the one in Sychar. When I'm here, I'm master of the manor.

"You get to sleep in the stable. There are servants here to keep the house in good shape. They'll guard you to make sure you don't run away. Of course, if you did try to run away, I would have an excuse to execute you. It isn't illegal to execute run-away slaves, you know.

That night Zarus cries. Cries as he has not cried since a little boy. Now no comfort. No consolation. No hope.

Morning arrives and Benyamin takes Zarus to the place he will live in, breathe in, agonize in, and survive in for the next four years.

Copper Mine, Timnah Valley, Aravah Desert

Benyamin has changed horses. Zarus still walks, a rope around his neck. As they draw closer to the mine, Zarus is struck by a vague beauty. Barren hills that rise and fall with grace. Odd-shaped rock formations that sometimes look like dancing dolls. A desert floor with sparse shrubs scattered here and there like mysterious dark spots on an agate moon.

"Is Noach around?" Benyamin asks when they arrive at the mine.

Zarus looks around. They are at the top of a rocky hill. He searches for the entrance. Instead, he sees some men gathered around a well.

"Oh, Noach, there you are," Benyamin says, dismounting and leading Zarus by the rope. "I have a new mine worker for you today. This is Samaritan Zarus. He is going to be our slave, well, as long as he lasts."

Benyamin hands the rope to Noach.

"Now I'm going back into the city before it gets to be too hot out here. Let me know if you have any problems with our new recruit. But don't bother me unless it is urgent."

"Let me take that rope off from around your neck, Zarus. That's no way to treat a human being."

"Thank you, sir," Zarus replies.

"My name is Noach and I am the superintendent of Baaruch's mine. At first you will be working alone. Later, you will join a crew and one of them will be your foreman. Now, have you had anything to eat today?" Without waiting for an answer, "I'll bet you haven't had anything to drink either, have you?"

Zarus eases closer to the well and looks down.

"Oh, the water isn't down there. That's the mine shaft. That's how we get down into the mine. Here, Caalev has brought you some water and some cheese. Caalev will be your foreman."

Zarus takes them both and tries to restrain himself so he doesn't look like a savage chunking down everything at once. He takes a long draw of water, then a small bite a cheese. He hasn't eaten anything other than dried bread for months. He has heard of starved men eating too much all at once, then doubling over with excruciating cramps. He cannot afford cramps.

He takes his meal slowly, while looking over at Caalev to see if he is going to disapprove. "That's okay, son. I know what you are doing, and that is wise. Besides, we need to fatten you up and rebuild those muscles. You used to be fairly strong, didn't you?"

"Yes, sir," Zarus says, just before taking another swallow of water. "I worked on a road crew and was in charge of clearing boulders out of the roadbed."

"You haven't wasted completely away, so I have confidence you will get your strength back. Are you through eating now? Let me take you to where you will be working."

Caalev leads Zarus down a slope about quarter of a *mille*. "This is where you start. Initially, when the mine had its original owner, a shaft was chipped through the rock straight down until no more copper was found. That, then, was the mine floor. Inside the mine, workers have carved out a stope the size of an amphitheater with rich copper. It's the largest and deepest stope I have heard of in the entire world.

"They need more air shafts," Caalev explains. "If you walk over that way about ten paces, you will see where an earlier air shaft was chipped out of the mountain. You will make yours about the same size. That air shaft goes in about forty paces. Since this mountain is mostly sandstone, you should be able to clear away one pace in about ten hours. At that rate, it will take you about forty days to break through.

Zarus, as tired as he is, feels renewed energy as his mind slowly comprehends his new adventure into unknown worlds.

"At first, it will only be as wide as your body. Later on, if we don't need any more adits created for air, you and someone else can widen it so we can use the air shaft to send supplies to the men.

"Yes, sir. I will do the best I can. I'm sure my strength will return."

"Here is an iron gad for you and a hammer."

Zarus takes them and hefts them to get a feel for their weight and balance.

"Once your initial hole is carved out, you will work on your back. Also, you will not have any room for light in the shaft, so you will be working in the dark. Since chips of stone will be falling all over you, you may as well tie your kerchief completely over your head. It will also keep the chips out of your nose and mouth."

"You won't be sorry you chose me to do this."

"Well, it's everyone's least favorite, but has to be done, and since you are the newest man on the crew..."

Caalev walks away, leaving Zarus alone to tackle his first job to make Devorah his wife.

On his knees, he gets the hole started, wraps his kerchief around his head, lies down on his back and begins his venture into the mountain. Hours go by, but he does not care as long as he can dream of his Devorah.

"Hey, in there!" Caalev shouts while hitting on Zarus' foot. He shakes it to make sure Zarus understands he is not a wildcat. "Hey! Want to take a break for lunch?"

Zarus begins to back out and realizes he has made more progress than he had thought. He wiggles and some of the rock chips find their way off his chest to his side. Once out, he sits up, unties the kerchief from his head, and blinks in the bright sunlight.

"It's not much. Just a single roll of barley bread. Benyamin is not the most generous boss in the world. You can come up the mountain where the rest are, stretch, and meet more of the men.

As he eats, Zarus stretches and realizes his arms are beginning to ache. He forgives the ache, for it will make him strong again.

Lunch over, Zarus excuses himself. "It's been good meeting all of you. I'm sure you will be good friends, and I hope I will be a good friend to you."

As he walks off back down to the new adit, the other men watch him. Before being out of hearing distance, he hears them mutter to each other.

"An odd sort, he is."

"Whoever heard of a cheerful slave?"

"Ain't natural."

Back at his job site, Zarus gets out an old piece of wool he found blowing around the hills and puts it on the ground for his noon prayer. He faces north toward Gerizim. It is also toward Jherusalem, but he decides he can let his prayer do double duty—part on behalf of himself, and part on behalf of his beloved Devorah.

Prayer done, he sits and ties his kerchief over his head, and scoots back into his tunnel. As he works, feeling his way farther into the mountain and deeper into the mine, he returns to his dream world of Devorah.

No one is going to take her from me. Not Elii, not Benyamin, not anyone. He feels a bulge in the ceiling and raises his hammer and gad, and the bulge goes flying.

We are officially betrothed. She'd have to divorce me now, and that she won't do. She has too much honor.

The new hole is now several hand spans beyond his head. He sets his tools down, rolls over on his belly, and chips away at the stone on the lower half of his tunnel. *Besides, she loves me. My pearl loves me.* He returns to his back.

Once his body is heavy with the chips, Zarus turns over on his belly and begins to back out. As he goes, he uses his arms to pull the rock chips along with him to the outside.

He decides perhaps he'll try to take a basket in with him to save his arms from getting cut so much. Then he changes his mind and thinks a piece of wood might work to scoop the chips along. He'll have to request one or the other in the morning when he returns to work. Also, he needs a long leather apron to protect his legs. *But will they allow me to have any of this?*

As the day grows hotter, he is glad for the coolness of his tunnel.

Back to work he chisels away at the rock above him and below him. Gradually he has to crawl farther and to get out.

When the air outside begins to cool off, he continues his work. *The sun is going down, but if I could just go in one more time...*

Another pile of sharp rocks is taken out. And another. Zarus no longer knows he is tired.

"Hey, you in there! What are you doing?"

Zarus hears Caalev's voice and crawls out. He takes off his kerchief and notices the sky is black and the moon is high.

"It's nearly the middle of the night. Come down into the valley with us. We have tents set up unless you prefer to sleep in the open air. You've got to stop so you can start over tomorrow. Man! I've never seen anything like it. You must have gone in nearly two paces. Don't you ever tire?"

"Sir, I did not realize it was so late. Yes, I guess I'd better go with you and get some sleep. I just did not realize."

The men work their way down the desert mountain. As they do, the mountain begins to moan. Another invasion. The mountain moves slightly again, settles a while, then moans once more. Protests once more.

Be on guard! Be alert ! You do not know when that time will come.

It's like a man going away: He leaves his house and puts his servants in charge, each with his assigned task, and tells the one at the door to keep watch.

"Therefore keep watch because you do not know when the owner of the house will come back--whether in the evening, or at midnight, or when the rooster crows, or at dawn.

If he comes suddenly, do not let him find you sleeping.

What I say to you, I say to everyone: 'Watch!' " (Mark 13:33-37)

DEEP VEIN COPPER MINE

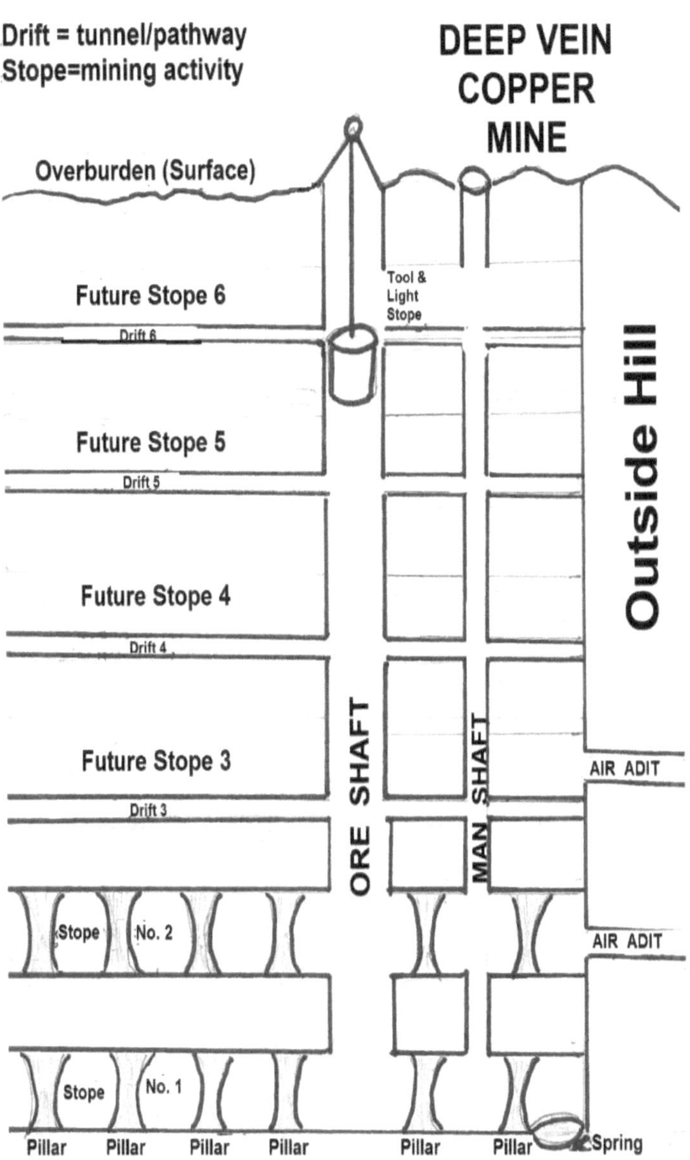

8 ~ THE MOUNTAIN

AD 9
Eilat, Port City on Red Sea, Arabah Desert, Idumea

"Well, well. If it isn't my spoiled sister come to see how the real world lives."

Devorah laughs off her big brother's barbs.

Benyamin backs away from the copper-plated gate so the servant can open it wide enough to let Devorah, her maid and their luggage through.

"Where do you want our horses?" she asks.

"My servant here will take them around to the stable. I see you still aren't using a saddle."

"No, they hamper me too much. A blanket is all I need. Is my room upstairs in the back as always?"

"Of course, dear sister. I was just getting ready for a mid-afternoon snack. Let your maid put everything away so you can join me."

"Well, we haven't eaten since breakfast, so I'll be happy to."

Devorah leads the maid up the stairs and down to her bedroom. There is an adjoining closet large enough to hang clothes on a peg. It has a small mat in it for the maid. One of Benyamin's maids follows them in with a large bowl and a pitcher. She pours the water into the bowl, leaves two towels which she had tucked in her belt, and leaves.

Glad for an opportunity to get the dust off her, she removes her traveling tunic, kicks off her sandals, and washes her face, neck, arms, and legs. Penina takes the cloth out of her mistress's hand, rinses it in the basin of water, and slowly wipes Devorah's back. Then she unbraids her hair and runs the cloth down from her scalp to the tips several times until the visible dust seems gone.

"Oh, that feels so good. Without all that dust on me, I even feel cooler. I don't know how people handle the heat down here."

The maid pulls out two tunics. "Which one do you prefer, mistress?"

Devorah chooses. Then the maid sets the basin of water on the floor in front of a stool. Devorah sits on the stool and Penina washes her feet, then puts her sandals back on her.

"You go on now, mistress. I've got work to do up here."

Refreshed, and anxious to visit with her brother, Devorah dances down the hall, descends the tiled stairway, and skips across the courtyard to where Benyamin waits for her.

The courtyard has blue tile mixed with orange and yellow tiles. Careful not to form an image with the tiles, they have been laid in a geometric pattern, though sometimes Devorah thinks they ended up with an image of the sun.

"Come, sister. It's been a long time. Catch me up on the news."

"Well, Zarus' sister, Estar, remarried a few months after you left. His name is Berel. She had her second baby just last week."

"Second? I thought she didn't have children by the first husband."

"She did. They had a good maid, and the maid took care of it whenever Estar was gone from home. Besides, we were never around Estar enough to know whether she had children."

"And, how about Father. Is he well?"

"He's about the same, except he has those pains in his chest more often. Mother is worried about him, but he says he's had them for years and will for years to come. They come and go, so they must not be serious."

"Don't worry about him," Benyamin urges, throwing another date in his mouth. "He's too stubborn to die." He laughs and holds his stomach as he does.

"Have another date."

"I've eaten five. I'm completely full now," Devorah responds.

"Don't get full yet. We're getting honey cakes after this."

"I'll just sit and watch you eat."

"Suit yourself," he says, ringing a bell for the servant to come refill the bowl and bring in the honey cakes. "Any other news?"

"Well, Estar, had kept the fabric business going, so her new husband decided to take her first husband's place and is apparently doing well."

Devorah has been looking over at the flowers growing along the wall, and when she turns back, realizes Benyamin is gone.

When she finds him, he has a honey cake in one hand and a fan in the other. "Where are my slaves? They're supposed to be fanning me. Fanning you too. It's going to be very humid and hot today. I don't know what I'd do without my fanners."

"Benyamin, when can I see Zarus?"

"Ha! I wondered when you were going to bring that up," he says twirling around to face her. "Well, not right away. He's needed in the mine, you know. And it is the mine that is paying for all your clothes and jewelry and perfumes and horses."

"But it's been nearly a year since I last saw him."

"Oh. Well, I suppose I could spare him in a few days. I could let him come here for dinner one evening, as long as he doesn't let it go to his head and he starts acting better than everyone else. Especially at the mine it cannot be tolerated."

Benyamin pops the rest of the honey cake in his mouth and heads back to his table to get another.

"Where are the fanners?" he calls out. One comes running and he sits down. "That's better. Oh, about Zarus, I guess I could have Caalev bring him over in time for dinner without him knowing ahead of time. That way he wouldn't have a chance to tell the other miners. I'll have to figure something out to keep his mouth shut afterward."

"Benyamin, I'm ashamed of you," Devorah responds, following him over to the table. "He's your brother-in-law."

"Not yet, he isn't. In a little while, I'm planning to go down to the docks to talk to a sea captain about transporting the next supply of copper to Egypt for refining. Would you like to go along?"

"Actually, I'd like to visit Ezion Geber where King Solomon had his ships for importing and exporting all over Africa, China, and India," Devorah responds.

"That is fine with me. You can ride there in my gilded litter. Two of my servants will carry it while a maid will ride along and fan you to keep the heat and humidity under control. No one will bother you."

Benyamin reaches into a purse tied around his waist and hands his sister two silver coins. "Just in case you see something you want to buy," he explains.

"Now, I need to get that sea captain to sign a contract for me. I've raised the price a little, but the quality of my copper is far superior to others."

Copper Mine, Timna Valley, Arabah Desert

"He's done what?"

"Benyamin cut down on our rations," Caalev repeats. "We now get only two meals a day."

The six men and four slave boys gathered around their foreman are mad.

"That's not right." Nisaan objects, putting his hands on his hips.

"We work hard for him," Fishel complains, jabbing his fist into the air.

"He can't do that to us," Issur adds, swinging his long arms at his side as though deciding what to punch. Or who.

The three miners couldn't be more different. Nisaan has gray hair, being the oldest of all the miners, and is big all over. Fishel is a small man but works fast. Ishur looks like a gorilla and has a temper, but it usually does not rise to the surface. Caalev hopes it doesn't now.

"He says expenses of running the mine are getting out of hand, and he has to cut something," Caalev continues. "So, back to work."

"No thanks for all we do?" Tzvi, says. Tzvi is the one who protects his looks because he considers himself the most handsome of anyone he knows.

"Give that man ten lashes!"

Benyamin's unique high-pitched voice is unmistakable. He walks over to Tzvi, stares him down, and turns to Caalev. "Do it now. Or must I do it myself?"

The other miners back away. Caalev takes out the whip he keeps in his belt, motions for Tzvi to lower his tunic or have it ripped up, then chains him to the permanent whipping post nearby.

He raises his arm. The whip falls on Tzvi's back, and he cries out. Again the whip finds its mark. And again. The other miners stand by, looking at the ground.

"Look at him," Benyamin demands. "Look at him, or you are next."

The men obey and watch the last eight lashes.

Shimson, who lives in a tent on the desert with his family, goes up to Tzvi, unchains him, and lets him slump into his arms.

"Come on," he whispers. "You do not want to lose your job. The pay isn't that good, but it's a job. If you think you can hang on, I'm strong enough that I can put you on my shoulders and get you back into the mine. You can resume your crying there."

Chaanon, who lives on a boat in the harbor, notices Benyamin is now gone. He turns to his charges, the slave boys, and tells them, "Time to go back down. Break time is over. Pretend you ate something."

Dov refuses to budge. "I ain't going nowhere," he says.

"Am I going to have to beat you, Dov?" Chaanoch challenges. "Get down there!"

"Hey, boys. First one to reach the mine shaft entrance gets a ride on my back when we get down there," Zarus announces.

Ariel, always wanting to have fun, especially when there is sadness to overcome, wins the race.

The slave boys prefer to take the side route to the mine below, so cut around the hill to the horizontal air shaft carved into the mountain by Zarus the year before. It is smaller across than the main shaft, but not as dangerous. "Ever hear of someone falling sideways?" Dov is wont to say.

The main shaft—the entrance of which casual passersby mistake for a well—is half a pace wide with niches carved on the sides to accommodate either footholds or handholds. It is the depth of sixty stucco houses piled on top of each other.

Chaanoch is the first to begin the descent because he is in charge of light down in the mine. "Okay," he calls up. "All clear. Who's next?"

He moves away from the small sunspot that reaches the bottom of the shaft and moves into the blackness beyond. He feels his way around a quick corner away from any draft that may descend the shaft to where the blackness is interrupted by a single flame that dances as though it invented light and is the darling of every man, woman, and child alive,

Nisaan is next. About halfway down the shaft, the light above him disappears. He locks his knees and calls up through the sudden darkness, "Okay, whoever is in the shaft, cutting out my light, go back up."

Above, Nisaan hears the voice of their foreman, Caalev. "Fishel, get back up here. You'll be last down because of that stunt. And you'll be last back up at the end of our shift. Fishel, did you hear me?"

"Yes, Sir," Fishel replies, just reaching the surface again.

One by one, as the miners arrive at the bottom of the shaft, they attach a small candle to the side of their head—whose drippings will land on a piece of leather attached to their shoulder—or a small olive-oil lamp to their forehead with a leather strap. Chaanoch lights them up with his master olive oil lamp.

Once all are accounted for, the men in Caalev's crew disburse down one of the five drifts that lead miners to whichever gallery and stope they are working in.

Zarus turns to the right, walks slightly downhill for twenty paces, and enters a large opening ten paces high and forty paces broad. He heads to Caalev, who collects tools when the men leave and doles them out when they report back to work. He picks up his one-pace-long iron chisel and a hammer as heavy as a five-year-old child.

He heads for the spot where he left off working before the last lunch break they will ever have. He settles back to work.

Although there are several other men and slave boys in the stope, he does not now see anyone else. The small candle on the left side of his head only lights an arm length or two in front of him.

He finds a spot with a little bit of rock jutting out and puts the point of his chisel in place with his left hand. With his right hand, he slams the head of his hammer home, and a piece of the mountain flies out of its place and onto the floor.

He settles into his routine and dreams of Devorah.

Eilat, Port City on Red Sea, Arabah Desert

"My trip to Ezion Geber was very interesting, Benyamin," Devorah says as she enters the manor built by their father but mostly used by the son. To think of all the gold, silver and silks King Solomon imported through there, and all the copper, dates and olive oil he exported on those same ships.

"Did you stay relatively cool, my dear?"

"Yes, your maid did a fine job. However, when I realized how much cooler it would be to just open the curtains and let the sea breezes in, I didn't need her services anymore."

"You let her do nothing? And you exposed yourself to being identified and kidnapped for ransom? Where in the world would I find that kind of money to buy your freedom?"

"Don't be too hard on the maid. I found her delightful company. Not as much as my own maid, Penina, who I have known most of my life, but we had some interesting conversations."

"What did you talk about?" Benyamin asks.

"Oh, nothing much."

He grabs her arm. "I said,, what did you talk about?"

"Benyamin, you're hurting me. Let go. We just talked girl things. That's all."

He walks a few paces away, then calls over his shoulder, "Dinner will be soon.

"Will Zarus be with us tonight?"

"No, he's busy."

Devorah goes up to her bedroom where Penina is doing needle-point work on the bottom of a tunic Devorah purchased just for this trip."

"Ahhh!"

"What was that?" Devorah asks?

"What do you mean, mistress?"

"That scream. It's a woman's scream."

Penina goes to the door leading out into the corridor, and the next scream is louder.

Devorah rushes out of her room and down the stairs, calling her brother. "Benyamin. Did you hear that?"

Moments later, Benyamin joins her in the courtyard.

"Who was screaming?"

"Oh, one of the maids was stung by a bee," Benyamin says. "Silly thing screams and wouldn't stand still so she could be treated. Are you ready for dinner? I am serving a new kind of wine imported from Italy."

"Will Zarus be able to join us tomorrow?"

"Maybe. Probably. Well, maybe."

Copper Mine, Timna Valley, Arabah Desert

Morning once again. The last of the night crew emerges from the mine. "It's all yours, Caalev."

One by one, the day miners arrive and descend the shaft, get their candle or lamp lit, head down the drift out into the large stope, and return to their spot where they left off the day before.

Chaanoch calls out to the slave boys. "Ariel and Carmi, go over to where Shimson is working and get those rocks out of his way and into a basket. Dov and Gidon, you go to Issur and do the same for him. And I don't want you slacking today. Do you hear me?"

"Yes, sir," each boy replies. They move almost by instinct around the galley because of the low light. "And when you come to a lull, go along the wall to each nitch and refill the lamps with oil," Chaanock calls after them.

"Yes, sir. But what about the cable up the shaft? It broke yesterday, and we couldn't send our baskets up. So they're full, and we can't put any more chips in them."

"Carmi, don't worry about it. It's been fixed. Send those baskets up to the top. There are some empty ones at the bottom of the shaft. Now go!"

"Yes, sir."

Except for the clanging of the chiselers' hammers, there is no other noise in the mine. At least, none out of the ordinary.

The rocks. The rocks always falling through the mountain. They rattle and bounce and echo from one hollow place to another. Is the mountain playing with them? Or toying with them? Is the mountain angry at the invasion of the miners, or happy for the company? What is the mountain thinking this time?

"Issur! Where are you?" Foreman Caalev calls out.

"Up here," Issur replies. "Over by the center pillar."

Caalev holds out his larger lamp and walks toward the center of the stope. The sandstone of the mountain has been left intact every three paces in all directions to hold up the roof of the stope. Niches are up one side to aid in climbing them.

"More loose rock?" Caalev calls up.

"Afraid so. This is a big one. I've got to get it loose before it loosens itself and comes crashing down on someone's head.

"I need help, Caalev," Issur calls down. I can't do this job by myself. It's too dangerous. What if I hit an air pocket and the whole ceiling comes crashing down? I need someone to support the loose rocks so we can pull them out slowly and not disturb what is around them."

"Be quiet, Issur. I've already requested a partner for you or even an apprentice, but the owner's son says he can't afford it. Now stop complaining before someone hears you and reports you."

"I guess you're right. Still, things are going to get more and more dangerous. And besides, Chaanoch has discovered a new crack."

"Chaanoch!" Caalev calls out in the darkness. "Where are you?"

"I'm over here. I want to show you something." Caalev walks in the direction of Chaanoch's voice. When he arrives, he stoops down next to the man he placed in charge of light and water.

"Hmm, water seeping in here," he says as he holds his lamp closer to the wall.

"Pretty soon, we're going to have to find some more slave boys to bail out the water."

Caalev climbs the shaft to the top. He walks toward the stucco mine *officium* where Saabhu and Noach work.

"Saabhu," Caalev says as he walks in, "things are getting more and more dangerous down there. As mine engineer, we need you to figure out how to get things in control, and tell Benyamin he needs to provide the funds to fix things."

"You know I can't do that. He will have me flogged for complaining. I've tried, and I've got the scars to prove it."

"Look, Caalev, I know the problems down there," Noach replies. "We all do. But, if we complain too much, you know what will happen."

"And if we don't complain, he could lose everything."

Caalev leaves and walks around the grounds. It is hot on the surface in the desert, but it is hotter below in the stope. What can he do? They're going to lose the mine and everyone in it.

Another hour passes, and Caalev goes back down the mine shaft, picks up his large lamp, and heads for the part of the stope where he hears the drip. He stoops down, holds the lamp closer to the crack, and is alarmed that it is larger then it had been before.

Eilat, Port City on Red Sea, Arabah Desert

"Benyamin, I think I'll try to hire a barge for a little cruise today. What do you think? I can take your maid again."

"I think you would be happier with your own maid from now on. But you can take my two servants again."

"Why don't you come with me, Benyamin? You work way too hard. You need something to get your mind off your troubles, at least for a little while."

"You're right, I am overworked. But such sacrifices have to be made to keep food and clothing supplied to our family. You go on and enjoy yourself."

"Well, suit yourself. Oh, and what about Zarus? I've been here nearly a week. Surely you can spare him at the mine for a few moments."

"I think maybe you're right," Benyamin says. "Now go on. I'll see you tonight."

Copper Mine, Timna Valley, Arabah Desert

"Zarus! You're wanted up top!" one of the slave boys calls out.

Zarus hears his name in the surrounding blackness and

immediately wonders what he has done wrong.

Through the shadows, he calls out for Foreman Caalev. "I think I'm needed up top. I need to turn my tools in to you. Where are you?"

"Over here, Zarus."

"Zarus approaches the pinpoint of light belonging to his foreman. "Do you know why I'm being called up top?"

"I have no idea. Would you like me to go with you?"

"No, I'll be okay. I'll be back soon."

"I'll make sure one of the boys collects the rocks in your workplace so it will be cleared off by the time you return."

"Thank you, sir."

Zarus turns and walks toward the one constant source of light in the stope—where the shaft is. He climbs up.

At the top, he sees Benyamin.

"Come over here, son," he tells his brother-in-law. His words are slurred. "We need to talk."

Benyamin teeters some but controls it by leaning on a copper staff he has had made with an opal on top.

Zarus smiles and walks forward. Benyamin leads him to the stucco building the superintendent and engineer work out of. "Excuse me, gentlemen, but I need some privacy."

The two men leave.

Zarus, still smiling, follows Benyamin into the *officium* and sits down.

"Did I tell you that you could sit?"

Shocked, Zarus immediately stands, hands at his side, back stiff.

"Your betrothed, my sister, is in town and would like to see you."

"Zarus fights to control a smile."

"Yes, sir," Zarus replies.

"I'm going to let you come to the manor for dinner tonight."

"Thank you, sir."

"But, you will pay a price." Benyamin takes a small flask out from a white leather purse, takes a draw, and continues without putting it away. "I cannot allow the other miners to know what is going on. You do not have to accept the invitation, which would be better for everyone. But if you do, there will definitely be a price to pay."

"Anything. What do you want me to pay you?"

"Oh, it's not money. You will pay with your back."

"My back, sir?"

"I'm going to have you flogged twenty lashes right now. Tomorrow morning I am going to have you flogged twenty more lashes for running away. That is the story you will tell the others. Am I clear? Are you in agreement?"

Zarus shudders. But to see his beloved, he would do anything.

"Yes, I am in agreement, sir," Zarus responds.

"Furthermore, if you bend over and show any signs of your beating while you are at my manor tonight, you will meet with a serious accident and never see my sister again. Am I clear about that?"

"Yes, sir."

"Good. Now walk out ahead of me and go to the whipping post. I have recruited Foreman Caalev to do the honors."

Benyamin puts his flask away. They walk outside, and Zarus spots Caalev. He has the whip in his hand, but his eyes lower when he sees his victim. When Zarus walks over to the whipping post, Caalev whispers, "I'm sorry, Zarus. I'm truly sorry."

"Zarus looks at Caalev, smiles, and holds out his wrists to be chained.

Zarus leans on the post without being tied to it. Caalev steps back one pace and once more lifts his arm to bring down the first blow.

Zarus fights off the desire to cry out. He grits his teeth instead.

Once again, the lash falls. And again. And again. Zarus' blood is on the whip. For his beloved. His blood.

"What's going on here?"

"Father! What are you doing here?"

"I thought I'd surprise you," Baaruch says, glaring at his son. "Looks like that's exactly what I have done. Stop the beating, let Zarus loose, get him cleaned up, and allow him the rest of the day off."

"But, Father. He..."

"I don't care what he did or did not do. You do not beat your subordinates."

Baaruch walks up closer to his son.

"I think it is time for you to do some traveling. I've already got someone picked out to take your place."

"Who?"

"Who then is the faithful and wise manager, whom the master puts in charge of his servants to give them their food allowance at the proper time?

It will be good for that servant whom the master finds doing so when he returns.

I tell you the truth, he will put him in charge of all his possessions.

But suppose the servant says to himself, 'My master is taking a long time in coming,' and he then begins to beat the menservants and maidservants and to eat and drink and get drunk.

The master of that servant will come on a day when he does not expect him and at an hour he is not aware of. He will cut him to pieces and assign him a place with the unbelievers.

"That servant who knows his master's will and does not get ready or does not do what his master wants will be beaten with many blows.

But the one who does not know and does things deserving punishment will be beaten with few blows. From everyone who has been given much, much will be demanded; and from the one who has been entrusted with much, much more will be asked. (Luke 12:42-48)

9 ~ THE ASCENT

AD 9
Eilat, Port City on Red Sea, Arabah Desert, Idumea

"Please don't take the mine from me, Father. Everything I did was for you and Mother."

They are back at the manor. A servant closes the gate behind them. Baaruch bristles swings around,, and points a finger at his son.

"I come down here to enter a chariot race and enjoy the sea breeze at my southern home,, and I find you drunk and beating people. What is wrong with you, Benyamin?

"I am not drunk, Father. This is a special wine and you cannot get drunk on it. It's an absolute impossibility."

"Give it to me." Baaruch waits. "I said give it to me. Now!"

Benyamin obeys and tears come to his eyes as he watches his father pour the remaining contents of the vial in a flower bed at the edge of the manor courtyard. He walks over to a fountain in the middle of the courtyard, sits on the ledge, and slumps down.

"I'm sorry, Father," he mumbles. "But I am lonely down here. Other than the city, everything is desert and there is nothing to do."

"Well, I'm going to give you something to do," Baaruch announces walking to an ornate iron chair with linen cushion of green. He sits, but leans forward.

"You are going to Egypt and tour all their smelters. You are going to collect samples of their work, and negotiate with them on a price per quadrant, which is about how much a shipload of rough copper ore is. You are to report to me either here or Sychar or where ever I happen to be when you are done. If you cannot find me in one place, you will look for me in the other. Is that clear?"

"Yes, sir. Thank you sir."

"Thank you for what? When you get back, I just may send you to China for something. Or Britannia. I am ashamed to call you my son."

"Ashamed? Ashamed, Father?" Benyamin bristles. "What about Devorah? Now there's a rebel. She tries to dress like a man, she rides horses like a man, and even gets by with signing documents that are none of her business."

"Like her betrothal contract?"

"Yeah, like that. She had no business signing it. She's the one who is the family embarrassment. And why that dirty Samaritan? She's embarrassed the whole family and you let her get by with it."

"That dirty Samaritan, as you call him, is more of a man than many I've seen in my day." He opens his mouth to say more, but closes it again. He is silent a moment. " Now don't push me, or I will say things that you will regret."

Baaruch stands, coughs, and grabs his chest. Benyamin is not looking, and for that Baaruch is grateful.

The spell passed, Baaruch walks toward his son. He takes him by the shoulders and quietly says, "I'm doing this for your own good, Son. You will thank me someday." *If I live long enough.*

"Open up!"

"That must be Zarus and the two miners I had bring him here.

"You brought him..." Benyamin catches himself and leaves the rest of his sentence unsaid.

"Who's at the door? Oh, Benyamin, you're back. And Father, when did you get here?" Devorah rushes over to her father and embraces him. He returns the embrace. "Penina and I were upstairs playing that new board game Benyamin showed me, and I guess we got engrossed in it."

"Benyamin, man up! Answer the gate!" Baaruch growls.

"But we've got servants to..." Once again he leaves the rest of his sentence unsaid. He arrives at the gate just as his servant does, and steps back. When it is opened and he sees Zarus, he turns and walks upstairs to his room.

"Zarus!" Devorah calls out. "Oh, Zarus, how I've missed you," she says as she hurries from her father to the gate.

She floats through a dream, the dream she has had over the past year since their betrothal. Her eyes bright and wide, her cheeks pink, her lips parted in joy.

Devorah stops. "What? You've been injured. Where can we put him Father?" she says, turning to her elder. "Is there somewhere down here? He can't make it up the stairs."

She looks back at Zarus and the men on each side holding him up. Zarus, though only half-conscious, hears the voice he has longed for. Her angel voice. Has he died? He forces himself alert and looks up. His angel. His angel is here. Oh, to touch his angel.

"This way," Baaruch announces. He leads them through the courtyard and toward the first room on the left. "This is our guest room. Someone, throw a sheet over this bed. There should be one in that basket. Hurry!"

Devorah rushes into the room ahead of them, finds the sheet and throws it over the bed. Just as she tucks one side under the feather mattress, Caalev and Noach arrive in the doorway. At the end of the bed, they put their arms under his chest while Baaruch and Shay take his upper legs and the four men gently put him down on his side.

Devorah gasps as she sees his back for the first time. "Oh, my darling, what have they done to you?"

"It wasn't they, my dear. It was him," her father explains. He looks into his daughter's eyes without saying more and she acknowledges his unspoken words.

Everyone leaves the room except Devorah. A servant brings in one of the iron chairs and sets it by the bed of her beloved, then leaves.

She sits and holds Zarus' hand, and brushes the hair out of his eyes. There is dirt and debris in his beard; she gently clears it away. Next, she turns him over on his stomach and puts healing olive oil on his back.

"Darling, I'm going to let the oil soak in, then I'm going to pat your back with a cotton boll in a few moments and the dirt from the whip and dust from the desert will come up with it."

Zarus opens his eyes, looks up at his angel, then closes them again. Devorah smiles briefly as she fights back the tears.

"Now I'm going to put some wine on your back. I'm going to do a little at a time so you can rest between treatments. When you say you're ready to put wine on another part of your back, let me know. We'll go slow. Now, here goes the first. I will pour it directly from the vial so nothing will touch you but the liquid. Ready?"

Zarus does not respond. He is unconscious. She pours some wine onto his back, he flinches and groans, but does not open his eyes.

"Is it okay for me to put more on?" she asks. He does not reply.

Although she asks permission between applications, he never responds. Slowly she pours the contents onto his back. That done, she pours another layer of protective olive oil out, then places her hand back onto his.

"Darling, it is prayer time. We pray to the same God. We believe the same things. Even though you do not believe in the prophets we Jews do, we have enough in common for now. I will pray for us both."

In the midst of her prayer, she weeps.

The rest of the afternoon Devorah sits and hums sometimes, works on her needlepoint sometimes, reads aloud from the Torah sometimes, and lays her head down near his and dreams with him. The first few nights she sits up with him, though sometimes Baaruch or Penina or one of the manor servants comes in to give her a break.

"How long have you been there?" Zarus says one morning.

"You're awake," she says, sitting upright in her chair and smiling. "How do you feel, my darling?"

"My back feels like it's been chiseled away."

"Well, I guess part of it was. Caalev said how sorry he is."

"I know. He was just doing his duty. Where am I?"

"You're in the guest room at Father's manor in Eilat."

"Is your father here?" Zarus asks as he twists around in his bed.

"Yes, and you need to lie still."

"I don't want to lie still. I want to sit up."

"Wait a moment. I'll call Father and one of the servants."

Moments later Baaruch and Shay enter the room.

"So you're awake, Son. That's good. You've had a fine nurse. Devorah said you want to sit up. Would you like to sit up in bed or come out to the courtyard?"

"I'd like to try to sit out there," Zarus responds.

Baaruch goes to the side of the bed, helps Zarus turn over without touching his back to anything, swings Zarus' legs around to the floor, sits on the bed next to him, and Shay sits on the other side. Gently they pull Zarus' arms over their shoulder, lift him to a standing position and slowly work their way out to the courtyard. They lower him onto a backless bench.

"Sir, I want to go back to work."

"Very admirable of you, Zarus. In time, Son. In time."

Devorah brings a bowl of dates to Zarus. "These will help. They're full of things that are good for you and will help heal you from the inside."

Zarus smiles at her, then takes a date.

"Have you heard from my sister, Baaruch, sir?"

"Yes, I've been waiting for the right time to tell you."

Zarus wrinkles his brow and squints. "Tell me what? Is she

okay?"

"I'm sorry to say that her second husband, Berel, contracted a fever from a caravan from Syria where he was trying to sell some of his fabric. He died two weeks later."

"Oh, no. This cannot have happened. My sister is too young to be a widow again. Jhehovah help her."

No one says anything for a while. "What is she going to do?" he finally asks.

"She still has the fabric business willed to her by her first husband," Devorah explains. "She is still energetic. She can continue with it."

"Zarus, in a few days when you feel better," Baaruch interjects, "I am going to take you back to the mine."

"That's great," he replies with a grin. "I'm really behind on my work on that wall."

"You're not going back to the wall. You're going back to take Caalev's place."

"No. Caalev is a good man. What will happen to him if you fire him?"

"Oh, I'm not firing him. I'm just putting him in charge of the night crew. Some of the men are blaming him for beating you, even though my son didn't give him any choice from what I've heard. Directing the night crew will get him away from the criticism a while.

AD 10
Copper Mine, Timna Valley, Arabah Desert

"Chaanoch, I need you to show me the new crack in the stope on Level Two. Is it as big as the one you found last year?" Saran says.

"Not yet. But I'm worried about it."

"Well, you managed to stuff last year's crack with concrete and mud. It's still holding."

"This one seems to be more aggressive."

The two men walk through the stope whose expanse has grown by several paces in the past year.

Zarus never gets over being awed by the copper pillars that extend down from the crude ceiling, each one thicker than a man is tall.

They rise out of the floor as though the mountain is saying, "I shall keep a part of me here to guard you. But treat me right. Otherwise, I will self-destruct and take you with me."

The moment any miner's light hits the pillars, they sparkle with their golden gift to mankind. "Take what you need," the mountain calls out from the pillars, "but let me stay here for eternity."

Zarus and Chaanoch listen carefully for the sounds of stone cutters squatting on the floor, chipping away at the larger chunks taken from the mountain until everything is gravel size. The slave boys stay nearby, ready to fill their baskets with the gravel and send them up the shaft to the top. Zarus and Chaanoch also listen for the slapping of the boys' feet on the stone floor so they do not trip over them.

Even with the brightest light, one can not see more than a pace in front of him.

It is an eerie darkness to some, with the lights shining from scattered places in the blackness like hovering wild animals ready to pounce. It is beautiful to others, especially the old-timers. To them, the little candle lights in the distance remind them of stars.

"I'm going to need some acacia wood unless you plan to use the slave boys to start pumping water out of the mine," Chaanoch says. "I will fill the cracks the best I can, but it may not hold, especially during the night when the moon is full. So, what I'm thinking is to build a wall at the bottom of the crack with wood, then piling rocks all around the wall to make a kind of pool to catch the water if it breaks through during the night."

"Good thinking, Chaanoch," Zarus says. "Have you ever done this before?"

"Once in a mine that ended up collapsing. No one was in that part of the mine when it went, so we were safe, but a lot of us quit working it."

Will that happen here? I've been told there was a collapse in this mine, but no one seems to know where it happened. It must have been in another stope that's since been blocked off. I'll have to remember to ask our engineer.

"I see what you mean," Zarus says aloud. "The rift is wider than the others we have had. Well, keep me posted. Oh, and Chaanoch. I know you used to be over me in the mine, and I appreciate your cooperation. Being older than most of the other guys, you have influence over them, and I appreciate your getting them to respect me. I know it hasn't always been easy."

Chaanoch holds out his hand to his new boss. "I've always respected you."

AD 11

"Sir, Master Zarus, you are wanted up top," Gidon, the shyest of the slave boys, calls out.

Zarus heads for the shaft, moves aside the cable rope normally hanging on it to take baskets of rock up, and grabs hold of the grooves in the wall with each hand. He works his way up with both his feet and hands in the grooves.

Once at the top, he hears a horse's neigh. *Strange. People don't normally take their horses out in this heat.*

He hears the neigh again. *Huh?* He turns in a circle trying to locate the animal. He hears hoofbeats. The animal is galloping toward him.

The earth shakes as the thunderous hooves pound on the sand and rock. The tail raises itself proudly. The mane flutters and flies.

Closer it comes. Zarus can hear its breath as it blows and snorts.

"Shalva?"

A familiar scent.

"Is that you?"

The horse slows and stops next to Zarus. It nudges its nose under Zarus' chin.

"Shalva! It is you! Oh, Shalva. Where have you been? How did you get here? What's going on?"

Emotion wells up in Zarus, and he does not know which to give in to. Laughter? Tears? Cheers? Shouts of triumph?

He pats the horse's nose, then runs his hands across its body.

"Hey, ole boy. I couldn't keep him away from you."

"Gersshon? What are you doing down here?"

The two life-time friends rush toward each other and embrace. Now at arm's length, they look into each other's eyes with grins wide enough they each could swallow a pomegranate whole.

"I finally found out what happened to you after the trial. I ran into your sister a few weeks ago, and she told me you had indentured yourself at the mine for four years to marry Devorah. Now that's love, ole boy."

Zarus tips his head sideways in agreement. "What can I say?"

"I thought I'd find you down here dragging around chains and skinnier than the last time I saw you. Instead, you look normal. Better than normal. You've filled out again and got your muscles back. Well, except they are bigger than ever."

"But, where did you find Shalva?"

Right after you disappeared, a horse trader came by our road camp, wanting to get rid of a horse that was acting lame. Said he'd take any fair price for it. I took one look at it, watched it limp, and knew it had to be Shalva. Smartest animal I've ever known."

Zarus, though still listening, is back to patting his beloved Arabian. "Hey, someone. Are there any apples around here?" he calls toward the mine *officium* where the superintendent and engineer can usually be found.

"Anyway," Gersshon continues, "I bought him and have been taking care of him since. He didn't limp after I got him, but he was listless. I'd ride him sometimes to give him exercise, but he wasn't his old self. You know, he didn't have that old spirit in him."

"Where did you board him? Baaruch and Devorah never said anything to me about him."

"We were too far from Sychar by that time. I found a farmer halfway between there and Sebaste and boarded him there. By the way, you owe me for two year's boarding; well, a year and a half."

"Are you working anywhere?" Zarus asked.

"Nope, the road work has been completed."

"How would you like to become a miner?"

"Well, if men end up looking healthy and happy as you, sure. Why not?"

"Then, you're hired."

"You got that much power?"

"Well, I'm the foreman, and the superintendent will take my recommendation."

"Okay, I'm all yours. I brought our old tent. Mind if I take a few moments to set it up and get settled?"

"That would be perfect. That will give me time to take a ride."

"Where should I set up?"

"You can go over to the side of this mountain wherever you can find some protection from the sun and wind and set it up there. Now, Shalva and I are going to get re-acquainted."

Noach comes out of the mine *officium*. "Did someone call for an apple?"

"Hey, yeah, Noach. I need one for my horse."

"Your horse. I didn't know you had a horse."

"My father left him for me when he died seven years ago."

"Fine looking animal, Zarus. Arabian, isn't he?"

"Indeed, he is, and he loves apples."

"Oh, yeah. Almost forgot. Here you go."

Zarus takes the apple and holds it up for Shalva to enjoy.

"Now, big fella, let's go for a little walk."

Zarus swings his legs and torso up, takes hold of the reins, and urges Shalva into a walk."

"You don't need to be running out in this heat. You'd drop over quicker than a bear can grab a fish out of a creek up in Samaria. That's right. Easy does it, Shalva.

"Oh, by the way, I'm getting married. Did I tell you? You'll like her. She's the one with that prissy Egyptian horse I saw you eyeing in the stable.

"I like it down here in the desert. Never thought I would where it is so hot. But you get used to it. Besides, Eilat isn't that far from here. It's a port city with lots of activity. You've never seen an ocean before, have you? Eilat is right along the shores of the Red Sea. Sometimes you and me can go for a run along the shore south of there. Would you like that?"

Shalva shakes his head and neighs.

"Well, we don't want to wear you out. Let's go back to the camp. I'll see if I can find some shade to put you in. Maybe I'll even slip you in the mine *officium* if Saabhu, the mine engineer, isn't there. Or," Zarus chuckles, "we could put you in Gersshon's tent. That might work. I suspect you two have become buddies in the past year or so. Did you thank him for being there for you while I was gone?"

Shalva nods his head up and down and snorts.

"Here we are. Hey, Gersshon! I see you've got a place picked out. It's in the shadows in the afternoon, and that's good. That's when the sun is hottest. Care to have a roommate?"

"Where do you think he's been staying on our trip down here, old buddy?"

"No! Really?"

"Couldn't take a chance on horse thieves."

"Well, tie him up, and let's go down into the mine."

They walk toward the opening to the mine shaft.

"Have you seen my sister lately?" Zarus asks.

"Yes, I stopped and saw her on my way down here."

"Is she still selling fabric?"

"Yes, and doing quite well with her new husband."

"Oh, she got married again? I really felt sorry for her when she was widowed a second time. She's too young to be a widow. She needs protecting and cared for."

"Well, I don't know how much she has been cared for. Her new husband, Micha, is not only helping her with the fabric business, but he has added silver-threaded silk to their stock."

"I'm happy for her. I've been really worried."

"Did I tell you she now has a third child? Looks just like his father."

"Here we are."

"This well?"

Zarus smiles, remembering his own first impression of the mine shaft when he arrived two years earlier.

Actually, we now have two shafts. This one is for the men. The one over there where the camel is walking to and from a tripod is for the ore.

"Now you have your choice how you get down into the mine. You can go down this smaller one; just put your hands and feet on the niches on both sides. Or you can climb in that ore basket with the hook on top and attached to this pulley. Which is your choice?"

"Well, I'm not as tall as you. Do you think I could reach all the way across?"

"Our slave boys can."

"Well, in that case, I'll climb down. You go first."

Zarus leads the way. Gersshon starts to climb down too quickly after Zarus and blocks the sun. Zarus says nothing.

They go down one level. Gersshon grins. "That wasn't so far."

"We're just at the light and tool stope. We need something to light our way. Would you like a candle strapped to the side of your head or an oil lamp on your forehead?

"I think I'll take the oil lamp. I don't relish hot wax falling on me."

Zarus attaches an oil lamp to his own forehead first, then one to Gersshon's. He picks up a larger oil lamp for Gersshon and one for himself to carry.

"You ordinarily wouldn't be able to have two lamps because you'll have tools in your hands. But you need to get to know your surroundings. And I'll introduce you to the other guys.

Gersshon looks around. He sees acacia beams around the opening of the shaft, keeping it from collapsing. He notices splits in some of the beams and wonders how much strain they can take from the earth above.

"We have six stope levels in the mine. Each one is about as high as twenty men standing on each other. Right now, the miners are working in Stope Level Two. It's down the height of one hundred and thirty man-lengths to Stope Level One."

"I've heard of deep mines but never heard of one this deep. Are you sure it's safe down here?"

"As safe as any mine. There are always dangers underground."

As the men's eyes grow used to the darkness, Zarus goes on to explain what they will do next.

"There are two ways to get down the rest of the way. We can either walk it on a zigzag path or go down the fast way used for transporting the copper by getting in a basket."

Gersshon chooses the basket, though, once they are on their way, the cable rocking their basket back and forth suspended so high from the bottom makes him wonder whether he chose wisely.

Zarus picks up a copper wand tied to the basket and hits a bell five times. "This is to tell the man at the top we are at Stope Level Five." Periodically as they reach another drift, Zarus hits the bell four times, then two times. "I told the man at the top I wanted to stop at Stope Level Two. That's where we are now. We are one hundred and thirty man-lengths down."

Zarus climbs out of the basket and steps onto the drift, a path that will take them to the work area on that level. Gersshon follows Zarus into a room with a high roof.

The first thing Gersshon notices is the smell. "It's metallic smelling down here. Dusty and musty too. And humid and sweaty. How can there be water down in this hole out in the middle of the desert?" he asks.

"There's water even in deserts if you dig down far enough. Desert doesn't mean there's no underground water; it just means it doesn't rain much."

"It's as hot as a furnace. How can that be so far from the heat of the sun?"

"Well," Zarus explains, "the average temperature on the surface of the Aravah Desert, day and night, is seventy-five degrees. For every two man-lengths, the temperature rises ten degrees."

Gersshon fans himself with his hand.

"We don't know why it gets hotter down here. But, personally, I think it is something about volcanoes. When volcanoes blow, fiery lava comes out of the ground. Maybe that's what is below us. Anyway, the fact is, mines are hot."

"If we are a hundred and thirty man-lengths down, temperature should be around 165 degrees," Gersshon surmises. "No human could stand that."

"We were lucky. We found some underground springs, and they have cool water in them. That's what makes the temperature bearable down here."

"Well, how do you get air?"

"Cool air adits. I'll explain more another time. I want to show you around.

The two friends walk a few paces and enter a large gallery.

"This is called a stope," Zarus explains before Gersshon has a chance to ask.

"The top is very high," Zarus explains. "We have a man who climbs up to there and makes sure we don't have any surprise rocks falling on us."

"Sounds dangerous."

"It's the most dangerous job we have. Everyone admires the man who does it."

"Well, how far is it across?

"You mean the stope? It's as broad as a hundred men."

"I had no idea the rooms—the stopes—in mines were so large."

"If you've got a good solid vein of ore, they do."

Gersshon notices with the small light on his forehead that they are standing next to a wide pillar of rock. He looks up and cannot see the top. "Does it go all the way to the roof?"

"Yup. The death penalty awaits anyone chipping away at the pillars. The only one allowed to do that is the man who patrols the roof for falling rock; he is allowed to chip hand and footholds in it all the way up to the roof. Eventually, we mine the ore in the pillars when we collapse the roof."

"When you do what?"

"I'll explain it another time," Zarus says as he leads Gersshon through the darkness away from the pillar.

"Here, I want to introduce you to Chaanoch. It is his job to keep water from flooding us out, and make the lights available to us every day."

The men nod in acknowledgment, and Zarus leads Gersshon away.

"I want to introduce you to Issur, who keeps falling rocks off of us. He works along the walls, but he also uses his scaling rod to get at the roof if it reaches far enough. In places the roof is too high, he scales the pillars to the top. He inspects the ceiling all the time. If he finds loose rocks—and he does every day—it is his job to hammer or jab them loose, so they go into a controlled fall. Can't introduce you yet because he's up there now. See that pin of light? That's Issur. Hey, Issur! How's our ceiling today?"

"Same as always." Comes the reply. "I'm getting ready to drop a slab right where you're standing," he calls down. His voice echoes through the hollow of the mine. "I'd move if I were you."

They walk over to a nearby wall, and Gersshon nearly trips over a man on the floor.

"Hey, there, Nisaan. Are the men keeping you busy?" Zarus asks.

"Yup. By the time I chip one rock down to gravel, they've got two more for me."

"Well, this is Gersshon. I'm not sure where I'll be putting him yet, but he is working for us now."

Nisaan looks up and acknowledges Gersshon with his eyes, but continues in his squat position to hammer out the pieces of rock.

"On the mine walls are Shimson, Tzvi, and Fishel. I used to be one of the chiselers, so we're short one man. That's another possibility for you. The shift will be over soon. We will go back up the shaft, and you can meet them when they get there."

"It's a small crew, isn't it?" Gersshon asks. "You could work a hundred men in this room if it's as big as you say."

"Yes, we could, but it's hard to find men to work here."

"Why's that?" Gersshon.

Zarus does not answer.

They pass a smaller passageway.

"Where does that go?"

"It's only another drift. There are a lot of them. We don't even know where all of them go. They take the men from one stope to another. The man Baaruch got the mine from refused to give him any maps, so we're having to make our own as we discover new drifts and where they go."

"Have there been any deaths in this mine?" Gersshon asks.

10 ~ THE UNWANTED

AD 12
Sychar, Province of Samaria, Palestine

"Mother, Penina, and I are going into town to distribute our baskets of food."

"Devorah, you aren't taking my good market basket to give away."

"No, Mother. I'm giving away the contents, not the baskets themselves."

"Well, be careful, and don't go into the dangerous part of town."

The two young women leave out the gate and head for the dangerous part of town.

They pass through the neighborhood with the fine homes, then the middle-class homes, and into the market.

"Okay, Penina. Throw that tattered mantle over you. I've got one for me."

Devorah reaches down and rubs her hand in the dirt on the street. "Here, get your nose dirty," she laughs as she smears it around on her nose and forehead.

Her maid does the same. They giggle.

"Well, Penina, do you think we fit in now?"

"Do you think we'll run into anyone we know down here?"

Devorah does not answer. Instead, she walks over to a basket booth.

"If we buy two more baskets so we each have two, we can have twice as much food to give away."

They purchase their two, then pick up bread rolls, cheese and figs, and proceed down the street.

The rats are the size of squirrels. The water thrown out into the street from windows above is partly from night-time chamber pots.

Penina pulls a handkerchief out from her sleeve and covers her nose.

"Put that away, Penina. Do you want to act better than them? We want them to accept us, not run away from us or beat up on us to get money and our baskets."

"Sorry, my lady. I will try to think of roses or lilies."

They approach a wide place where the street intersects with an alley. Devorah walks over to a woman walking in the opposite direction.

"Well, Atara," Devorah asks her, "what are you doing out today?"

Atara has a white streak in her hair which makes her look dignified, were it not for her crutches and missing right foot from the broken water vat accident.

"Hello, Devorah. Oh, I thought I'd walk around and get some sunshine after all that rain last week." A strand of hair falls over one eye, and she flips her head back to get it out of the way.

"Do you ever hear from your son?" Devorah asks.

"No, he's probably still at sea." *I wish she wouldn't keep asking about him. He's not coming back.*

"I have some food for you to share with your friends," Devorah explains. "You can have half of what I have in my basket. Do you have something I can put the food in?

"Not really. You could tie it up in my shawl since my hands are busy hanging on to these crutches."

"Why don't I just follow you home?"

"Oh, here comes my friend. Dafna!"

Dafna, just coming out from the alley, stops and turns when she hears her name being called.

"Atara? Is that you?"

"Yes, it's me. I'm over here. See? I'm waving."

"Oh, there you are," Dafna says, walking up to the three other women.

"Dafna, do you remember Devorah? She comes down here once a week to share with us. She doesn't have to; she says she just enjoys it. Isn't that right, Devorah?"

"That's true, Atara. Good to see you again, Dafna. This is my maid, Penina."

Dafna is a slight woman with light brown hair that is thinning considerably. Her husband died of typhoid fever three years earlier, and she has no children or other relatives to help her. Being shy has not helped her situation. She rents the corner of a room at a boarding house where ruffians hang out. The owner protects her because she works off her space by cooking the meals.

"Hello, Dafna," Penina says. Dafna responds warmly.

"Ladies, it is a good thing I ran into both of you at the same time. Here."

Devorah hands one of her baskets to Dafna. "You and Atara can split the contents of this basket."

"But I do the cooking for my keep at the inn," Dafna objects.

"Forgive me if what I say is offensive, but it doesn't look like they let you eat much of that food."

"Well, I am allowed to eat what is left behind on the guests' plates."

"That certainly isn't much. You could do to put a little weight on. Now, go ahead and take this basket. Divide what you have. Give Atara the basket because she has nothing to carry her share in."

"There is way too much for us in the basket," Atara objects to Devorah.

"Then share it. Do you have friends who don't get much to eat? Invite them over to where ever you normally gather and have a picnic. It will be fun."

"Well, there is no grass around here, but we'll think of something."

Atara and Dafna smile, and as if on cue, they both begin to cry. "God bless you," Dafna whispers.

"Now go on, you two. We have more baskets to give away."

"Okay, where to next, my lady?" Penina asks.

"I think we need to go farther into this neighborhood."

"Forgive me for reminding you what your mother said."

Well, I didn't tell her I'd stay away from the dangerous places. I just didn't answer. Yeah, I suppose I lied to her by making her think I agreed. May God forgive me. Now, let's go down this street."

"Yes, my lady. Whatever you decide."

The two women duck their heads down and are glad they tied their shawls to their heads before venturing out.

"That's mine! You took it from me. Now give it back."

"Hillel takes a swing at Pesach but misses. Pesach moves aside to defend himself and sticks out his left fist to punch Hillel. A crowd begins to gather."

"Over to your left, Hillel. You can get him."

"Better duck, Pesach, he's got a mean swing."

Laughter builds as the onlookers watch the blind man and the man with his arm broken attack each other.

Hillel is a small man with a small head, but long arms. Pesach is tall and thin. His yellowish eyes dart everywhere at once.

"You stole the money from my begging bowl," Hillel calls out, swinging again and missing again.

"No, I didn't. It was still empty," Pesach says, darting away from where he was a moment earlier.

"I heard coins drop in it," Hillel says, swinging in the direction Pesach used to be.

"It was your imagination," Pesach says, sneaking up behind Hillel and clomping him on the head, but not hard.

"I know what I heard," Hillel says, turning around.

"Hey, guys."

The two men turn in the direction of the feminine voice. They stand in place with arms down at their side—except for Pesach's bad arm—as though being called forward by a parent.

"Having a rough day, I see," Devorah continues.

"Well, he…"

"It's your lucky day, guys," she interrupts. "Where is your mat, Hillel? We can sit on it and talk.

"Not with Pesach. He's a th…"

"I am not!"

Okay, first, here's a copper coin for each of you, a peace offering. If you take it, that means you agree to be friends again."

"Well…"

The two men squat near Hillel's mat. The two women squat on the other side of it, unsure what it may be crawling with.

"I have a basket here for you two men to share. Pesach, why don't you tell Hillel what is in it."

"Well, bread, cheese, and…and are those figs?"

"Yes. How does that sound, Hillel?"

"I could stop begging for the rest of the day."

"Longer than that," Pesach says. "As little as you eat, you could rest for four or five days."

"Thank you, Mistress Devorah," Hillel says.

"Yes, thank you," Pesach repeats. "With my broken shoulder, I can't pick fruit or do anything to make a living. It's been like this two months already and doesn't seem to be healing very fast."

"I can do a little first aid," Devorah explains, but I do not know how to set bones. Did you get it set properly?”

“Dunno. Hillel here did it.”

“Well, my doctor lives over on the camel street,” Devorah says. “Go there, and I will have your fee covered.”

“Well, okay. Hillel, here is your money back.”

“I knew you took it.”

“I was hungry.”

“Well, you guys don’t need to be hungry,” Devorah discretely interrupts again. “At least, not for a while. Penina and I need to go on now. We have two more baskets to give away.”

The women stand and turn to walk away.

“God bless you,” Hillel says.

“Yeah, God bless and keep you safe,” Pesach says.

“I hope you go on home now. This is no place for a fine lady like you,” Pesach calls out.

They do not hear him.

“Okay, where should we go next?”

“If my lady thought we should leave this neighborhood, I would not object,” Penina replies.

“I have an idea. We can go out the city gate to see if anyone left a caravan and can’t find work.”

Penina smiles and gets her handkerchief out. Devorah does the same.

Eyes watch them with a mixture of curiosity and hatred. Sometimes the eyes seem to be peering at them from the very walls themselves.

The two women, now with one each, cover the contents of their baskets with their handkerchiefs and pull the bottom of their shawls around so that they cover their faces. They rush, but not fast enough to attract attention.

Back up the street from whence they came, the two women try not to look toward the left nor to the right. Devorah begins to hum under her breath. Penina joins her.

Finally, back into the market place. Penina looks behind them. “No one following us, my lady.”

“Okay, let’s go over to the city square in front of the gate. There may be some men looking for work.”

They take off their tattered mantles and give them to a beggar, then enter the city square.

“Ma’am. Do you need to hire someone for your house? I can do almost anything as long as I can do it sitting down.”

Devorah looks down at the man. Both legs have been cut off.

"I'm sorry, sir. I don't need anyone right now, but I do have a basket of food for you and a friend. May I be so bold as to ask what happened to your legs?"

"Mining accident, ma'am. I was working in a copper mine down by the Red Sea, and a big slag of rock loosened itself and shot out at me. I couldn't get out of the way in time. It cut off both my legs."

"Oh, I am so sorry. What a terrible things to live through."

"If you can call it living. Not long after that, the shaft collapsed when a bunch of the men were riding up in a basket to get to the surface. Killed everyone in it. I heard the owner dug a new shaft, covered the old one over with the bodies still in it, then sold the mine."

"How horrible. Surely no one wanted the mine."

"You're right about that. Heard he got rid of it in a bet on a chariot race."

Devorah sucks in a guttural breath and grabs her chest.

"Are you okay, ma'am?"

"Oh, I just had a pain in my chest, but it's gone. My father has them, and he's lived a long time." She turns back toward the man on the ground. "We may have something at our house you can do. Can you write?"

"Some, ma'am. But I can work with numbers really well."

"I will talk to my father and come back tomorrow. What is your name, sir?"

"My name is Yair. If you hire me, you will never be sorry."

"Do you have a family?"

"Yes, I have a wife and four children; they have all moved in with my wife's parents down in Eilat. My father-in-law put me in a wagon in a caravan and hired someone to take care of me on the road. The man wasn't going any farther than Sychar, so that's how I ended up here.

"I came up here to find work that wasn't in mining. Or at least find a new trade. Do you think your father would be able to help me with a new trade? I do numbers really well."

"I think there is a real good possibility of that, and your being able to support your family again."

"Thank you, ma'am. You are an answer to prayer."

"By the way, I have a basket of food here. Do you have any friends in the square you could share it with?"

"Yes, I have Rafael."

He looks around. "Hey, Rafael. Come here."

Rafael is a big man but stooped. He is forced to look at the ground perpetually because of a birth defect in his back.

Rafael follows the sound of his friend's voice and joins Yair on the ground.

"Rafael, this is, uh, I didn't get your name."

"My name is Devorah. It is nice to meet you, Rafael."

"Devorah says she has a basket of food. If we can't eat it all, she said for us to share it with some of the other guys out 0here looking for work. Isn't that right, Devorah Ma'am?"

"Yes. That's right. Now Penina and I have to be on our way. We still have one basket of food to give away, and want to check outside the gate."

"You won't forget me to your father, will you?" Yair calls out after her.

She turns and waves.

"Okay, Penina. Let's see if there are any caravans out here. Or maybe someone down at the well."

The two women walk out the city gate.

"No one here at all except merchants, Roman soldiers, and others who seem to know where they're going. Let's walk on down to the well."

"They named the well after our forefather, Jacob, you know," Penina says.

"Yes, and it's a good well, It's been here nearly two thousand years. I guess it will be here another two thousand. Do you see anyone down there?"

"Yes, I think there are two women sitting on the edge. They don't seem to be doing anything but sitting, though."

Devorah and Penina approach the well. It is three paces across. Many people could draw water from it at the same time and probably do in the mornings. For now, there are only two women.

"Hello there, ladies. Do you need help getting water up from the well?"

Gila and Hinda look over at Devorah approaching them. Hinda stands and helps Gila to a small tree over to one side where she sits, then returns to the well.

Devorah stops at the edge. "Penina, why don't you set the basket down here?"

She looks at Hinda. "Is that your friend over there? Is she sick."

Hinda has very curly black hair and dainty features. Her eyes are the same blue as Zarus'. Devorah thinks of him, purses her lips, and takes a deep breath. "Is your friend okay? Is there anything we can do to help?"

"My friend is blind. I was afraid she would fall into the well.

She would drown, of course, because it is so far down, and she wouldn't be strong enough to hang on to a rope."

"Well, my name is Devorah. It's kind of late to be drawing water. Are you having company at your house? Or is it for an animal?"

"Neither. I'm going to sell it. Gila and I are both widows. We earn a little bit of money each day by taking water to the city gate where people are headed home after work. We sell to people who are thirsty, and some to people at the nearby market who plan to have a feast and need extra water."

"At the end of the day, we split the money, I walk her to a farmhouse where she rents a room, and I go to my own place. It's in a shed where a milkmaid stays, and she lets me sleep there. The next day we start over again."

"I see. Well, I'd like to help you out. I don't need any water. But I do have this basket of food. Take it. There is enough for both of you. If it's too much for you and you have friends who could use a little help, share with them."

Devorah looks over at the late afternoon sun.

"I must be going now. God bless you both."

"How are you going to explain where you have been to your mother?" Penina asks.

11 ~ THE GUESTS

AD 12
Sychar, Province of Samaria, Palestine

"There you are, Devorah. You've been gone for hours," Avigail says, greeting her daughter at the gate into their manor. She walks over to a table in the courtyard and hands a small scroll to Devorah.

"I've got to talk to you. Look at this list. Is there anyone else you want to be invited to your wedding with that, that, well, you know."

"You mean that Samaritan?"

"Yes, well. We will just have to make the best of it. Now, is there anyone I have left off?"

"These are all Jews, Mother. Aren't you inviting any Samaritans?"

"No, they're not all Jews. The mayor is a Samaritan. I am inviting him and his wife. Also, the two magistrates on the list are Samaritans. Other than that, I don't really know any Samaritans.

"You know Estar, Zarus' sister, and her husband, Micha. You go to their fabric shop all the time."

"Well, yes, I do. They have a fine selection. I have created some pretty amazing designs using their fabrics, I must say. Yes, yes. They are Samaritans, and we shall invite them. You see, I am being broadminded. Now, who else?"

Devorah looks over the list and sets it back down on the table without comment.

"Now, what about your wedding attire? I think you should wear a stolla. It is all the rage in Rome."

"No, Mother. I plan to wear the traditional floor-length white tunic and deep yellow floor-length shawl."

"Well, okay. That's what I wore when I married your father. Now how about your hair? You have to have those six braids done and then piled on top of your head."

"No. I'll wear flowers in my hair, but don't want anything fancy. The tunic and shawl will be plenty."

"Let's go to the fabric shop tomorrow and pick out what you want. How about silk?"

"Gauze. I want gauze."

"Oh, Devorah, you are so hard to please."

Avigail takes another fig from a small, ornate bowl, several of which are always disbursed throughout the house. She savors the morsel, then looks back to her daughter.

"Maybe the rabbi can come over and say a few words at your wedding."

"No. The parade through town will be plenty. Well, we can have prayer before the parade. That's all. The main ceremony was at my betrothal. All that is left is confirming our marriage with friends."

"At least you are not doing away with the wedding feast. Now I've got some new recipes, and..."

"That's fine, Mother. Your recipes will all be perfect, I'm sure."

"My lady, there is someone at the gate to see Devorah."

"Oh, it's Zarus! He has arrived. Thank you, Eshachk."

Devorah rushes to the front gate and greets her Zarus. Their eyes touch. She feels her mother watching them. "I see you have recovered from, well, you know."

"Yes, I've not only recovered, but your father made me foreman of my crew."

She steps aside so Zarus can enter. "He told me about that. How did it go?"

"I got a lot of guidance from Caalev, whose place I took so he could take the night crew. Noach, the mine superintendent, and Saabhu, the engineer, backed me up. So it went pretty smoothly."

Silence. Neither one speaks further. The mine isn't what they want to talk about. Standing two paces apart is not what they want to be doing. They want to touch and speak of their love for each other. They want the wedding to be over with. And the feast. And saying goodbye to parents. And to be together forever. That's what they want.

"Is your father here?" Zarus finally asks.

"Yes, he's probably out at the stable or in the chariot house."

"Good-bye for now," Zarus says. "The next time I see you, we will finally be married. Then life will begin for real."

"Good-bye, my l...my Zarus. Until then."

The servant, still standing by the gate, unbolts it and lets Zarus out.

Zarus walks around the outside wall of the manor house and over to the stables. Baaruch is outside polishing his chariot.

"Isn't that something for your stable hand to be doing, sir?"

"If it isn't Zarus! How are you doing, Son?"

Zarus is shocked at how much Baaruch has aged in the two years since last seeing him.

"Here, let me help you. Do you have another cloth for me?"

The two men settle into polishing Baaruch's prize.

"I hear you did a good job managing the crew after I left."

"They are good men."

"Do you have any ideas for increasing production?"

"Maybe. But I do have some suggestions for better safety."

"Well, Benyamin will be going back down. You can discuss that with him."

"Sir, I don't believe…"

"Don't worry about Benyamin. He's a changed man. He'd better be, or I'll keep my promise to send him to China, or even Britannia next."

Zarus does not look up.

"So, you have fulfilled the indenturement," Baaruch continues, "and done it with honor. I am proud to welcome you into my family and hand my daughter over to you for protection. And of course to give me grandchildren. How many in your family will be coming?"

"I've invited my brothers and sisters. I never heard back from any of them except Estar. You know Estar. She and her husband will be coming.

"Well, I guess this time next week, regardless of who comes, Devorah will be mine."

"The servants have been decorating the banquet hall all day," Baaruch says. "We are going to have a feast fit for a king. By the way, where will you be staying at night?"

"At the home of my sister here in town."

———

The night before the wedding, Devorah does not sleep well. Long after everyone else has gone to sleep, she walks out into the courtyard. The moon is full. She gazes at it a long time. *If Zarus is awake, he may be looking out his window at the same moon.*

She goes back to bed, and the next thing she knows, Penina is speaking to her.

"Good morning, my lady. This is your wedding day. By tonight you will belong to Zarus, and he will belong to you."

"Devorah opens her eyes, smiles, turns over on her front, and hugs her pillow."

"My lady," Penina repeats with a singsong voice. "The sun is up. Your mother is up. I am up. Zarus is probably up. And it is time for you."

"Good morning, my daughter," Avigail says, prancing into the room. "Today is your big day. Let's get ready. First, you will bathe, then I will help you in to your wedding dress. This is the only time you will ever wear it, so you may as well wear it all day."

"Yes, Mother."

"After your bath, why don't you come out and see how we have decorated the banquet hall. You will love it. It has red and yellow gauze hanging from all the corners and over the table where you and Zarus will be."

The bath and tour over with, Devorah allows her mother to help her dress. First comes her long white tunic. Next comes her long deep yellow shawl, draped from the top of her head to the floor. It is secured on her head with a red ribbon that will be replaced just before the wedding with a fresh garland of flowers.

Avigail and Baaruch dress in their finest. They wait. They double-check the banquet hall. Everything is perfect.

The day drags by. Devorah had expected her girlfriends to come over and help her pass the day. They do not come. However, Estar does come. She has a garland of flowers for Devorah's bridal crown.

"C'mon, girl. You are going to have the most special wedding a girl has ever had. I promise," Estar says.

"Your maids are probably getting a special surprise ready for you, dear," Avigail reassures nervously.

Baaruch paces. Avigail walks between the banquet hall and the courtyard incessantly.

"Did you know he calls me his pearl?" Devorah says to whoever is nearby.

Early afternoon arrives. It is time for Zarus to come to her house with all his friends and pretend to snatch her away from her parents.

Devorah sits and listens for the parade to reach her home. She is happier than she has been, but the tears always seem to be near. *What if he has changed his mind?*

Finally, she hears a knock. She stands, and her mother puts Estar's garland on her head.

She is ready. The gate is opened.

Zarus stands alone except for his brother-in-law on one side and Gersshon on the other.

"Well, are you going to let us in?" Gersshon announces. All things are ready. May I present to you, the groom," he announces with a flair.

The three walk in with forced smiles. Devorah, her parents, and Estar smile back.

"Well, we need to begin the ceremony," Baaruch announces. "Everyone into the banquet hall."

In addition to the red and yellow gauze drifting down from the ceiling to the floor at each corner, more has been draped across the ceiling as though they are in a tent. Runners of red and gold grace each table. A harpist's strains begins to fill the room with melody as soon as they enter.

Everyone sits at the head table, which has trays of fruit on silver platters spaced about five handbreadths apart. Baaruch motions to his head steward for the feast to begin.

Wine is poured into a goblet for Zarus and for Devorah. The happy couple expresses to an empty banquet hall their intention to take care of each other the rest of their lives. The rabbi seems to have forgotten to come. Baaruch leads them in a Jewish prayer. Gersshon leads them in a Samaritan prayer.

Zarus and Devorah are now officially married.

Devorah feels a stabbing pain in her chest and doubles over. *It must be all the excitement.* The pain leaves as quickly as it came. She looks her groom in his blue eyes and smiles the smile of brides.

They smile to the empty banquet hall

Baaruch disappears to the courtyard. He calls all his servants and maids.

"My daughter is not going to be insulted like this for marrying a Samaritan more godly than most of those hypocrites. Go out and bring the guests in. Here is the guest list. Divide up and get to them all."

Baaruch returns to the banquet hall and whispers to Gersshon. Gersshon rises.

"Attention everyone," Gersshon says, addressing the empty banquet hall. "I have been asked to say a few words about my old buddy, Zarus. Would you believe, when we were ten years old, Zarus and I decided to not show up for synagogue school? Ha, ha, ha.

Instead, we decided to go up in the hills and look for snakes. Ha, ha, ha. You should have seen him when we finally did find a snake. Ha, ha, ha. Then there was the time...."

They hear the gate open and close. Baaruch excuses himself and goes to the courtyard.

"Sir, we went to the mayor's house. He was there, but not dressed for a celebration. We thought he forgot, but he said he had just bought a field and needed to go see it to make sure he got his money's worth before the seller got too far away from here."

As he is speaking, another servant returns.

"Well?" Baaruch asks.

"I went to the magistrate's house. He said he had just bought five yoke of oxen for his new venture of hiring them out to get merchandise across the pass between the two mountains."

Baaruch's face reddens. "He chose today to buy them?"

"He said he already had some clients and needed to go get his oxen."

While he is yet speaking, Avigail's maid returns.

"Did you know there was another wedding in town this morning. You invited the groom to come to Devorah's wedding. Of course, he said he couldn't come."

"Hmmm. That may be where all our guests are." Baaruch paces. He hears weak laughter coming from the banquet hall.

"My daughter's wedding is not going to be a laughing stock. Just because it's a mixed marriage, it doesn't mean they deserve this.

"Everyone, go down to the neighborhood on the other side of the market. Invite the poor people who will appreciate my invitation enough they will cancel all other plans and come here. I don't care if they are Samaritans or Jews. I don't care if they can't see or can't walk or can't talk. Tell them to come and bring their friends.

"And you, Bayla, here is my purse. Go into the market and buy fifty or sixty robes fit for a wedding. Buy out every shop in town if you have to. If you can't find enough, robes, get some large tunics. Hire someone to help you bring them back here. Hurry."

Baaruch returns to the banquet hall and re-seats himself with a smile.

"....And in conclusion," Gersshon says with gusto, "I would like to say to Devorah, the bride, living with Zarus will be anything but dull."

A weak applause.

Zarus and Devorah, sitting side by side, smile at each other. They are oblivious to anyone else in the hall. Their eyes absorb one another.

Micha stands. "I believe my wife has a few words of advice for Devorah."

Estar rises. "I haven't known Devorah all that long, but I think I've got her figured out. You, Zarus, my dear brother, will probably never figure her out. But that's just because you are a man. Men never understand women. That's part of our charm. Now, about Devorah, she is more at home on a horse than in the kitchen. That reminds me..."

"Wait!" Baaruch announces. I hear something."

He rushes out of the banquet hall to the gate and opens it. There his servant stands with twenty-one people of all sorts. Most are dirty, but that can be remedied. He has wedding garments ready to cover them, and maids to wash their faces and feet and comb their hair.

Baaruch returns to the banquet hall and announces that some of their guests have arrived and will be in shortly. As they walk in, Devorah recognizes four of the twenty-one.

"There's Atara with her crutches and Dafna." She looks again. "Oh, my! There's blind Hillel and his friend, Pesach."

She leaves the wedding party table and rushes over to her friends. "Welcome! Welcome! Have a seat. Eat all you want. Are these your friends?"

"Some of them are," Dafna replies. "The rest are friends of those two men over there."

Devorah rushes over to Hillel and Pesach. "Welcome to our home and wedding. I see you have wedding clothes on, probably provided by my father. Have a seat over there with your friends."

"Now that's more like it," Gersshon says with a wide grin.

Once again, Baaruch slips out of the banquet hall and into the courtyard. Once again, he takes Eshachk aside.

"That's not enough. We've got to fill the hall. Is this all you could find on the streets in town?"

"Yes, sir. Some didn't want to come, some said they were busy, some said they wouldn't attend a wedding between a Samaritan and a Jew, and some said they didn't believe the invitation."

"Okay, then. Go outside of town and find more there to recruit—you know, maimed people, people with birth defects, blind people, poor people. I don't care who or what they are. Tell them to bring all their friends. Bring them all in."

Once again, Baaruch goes to the banquet hall and, instead of seating himself, stands behind the head table. "Attention, everyone. I am glad you were finally able to come to the wedding of Zarus and my daughter, Devorah. We were worried because you were so late. That does not matter. You are here. Now eat."

Talk resumes at the head table. Things are better now. But not good enough for Baaruch. He walks over to the door leading to the courtyard. Nothing. He walks among the new guests, then back to the door. Still Nothing.

Then he hears the latch to the gate. He rushes out, and there stands Penina with twenty-two guests. They walk into the courtyard, have their feet and heads cleaned, and don wedding garments.

Satisfied, Baaruch returns to the banquet hall and calls out to get everyone's attention. "The rest of our guests have arrived. Perhaps they had the time wrong. Well, they're here now. Come on in, my friends."

As they do, Devorah recognized blind Gila and her friend Hinda.

"Welcome, Gila and Hinda. You are so very welcome," she calls over to them.

"We brought some of our friends," Hinda replies. "They think you are beautiful."

Devorah blushes, then turns to Yair, and the man with his back bent low, carried in by Rafael. "I haven't forgotten you. I have just been so busy with the wedding and all. In a little while, I will introduce you to my father and my husband. They may have work for you."

She returns to the table and surveys the room full of happy celebrators, talking, eating, and making their own memories.

Baaruch rises. "Attention, everyone. Today is a fine day to be married. I would like to present to everyone, my daughter, and now the wife of Zarus."

Applause. More musicians come out and provide entertainment. Now, at last, everything is perfect.

Zarus is happy beyond words, but a gnawing feeling momentarily creeps over him about the mine. Will anyone live through it?

Jhesus replied: "A certain man was preparing a great banquet and invited many guests.

At the time of the banquet he sent his servant to tell those who had been invited, 'Come, for everything is now ready.'

"But they all alike began to make excuses. The first said, 'I have just bought a field, and I must go and see it. Please excuse me.'

"Another said, 'I have just bought five yoke of oxen, and I'm on my way to try them out. Please excuse me.'

"Still another said, 'I just got married, so I can't come.'

The servant came back and reported this to his master. Then the owner of the house became angry and ordered his servant, 'Go out quickly into the streets and alleys of the town and bring in the poor, the crippled, the blind and the lame.'

" 'Sir,' the servant said, 'what you ordered has been done, but there is still room.'

"Then the master told his servant, 'Go out to the roads and country lanes and make them come in, so that my house will be full.

I tell you, not one of those men who were invited will get a taste of my banquet.' " (Luke 14:16-24)

12 ~ The Victory Mask

AD 14
Copper Mine, Timna Valley, Arabah Desert, Idumea

"**T**he **mine down on Stope Level One is getting more unstable,**" **Zarus tells Saabhu, the mine engineer.**

Saabhu is shorter than the average man, has long arms, and is darker complexioned than most men in Palestine. His father, a mine engineer in Maghara, Egypt, raised his son there. Saabhu had been formally educated in Memphis, where he was head of his class, then was apprenticed to his father. "I learned from the best," he is often heard to say. Saabhu is now forty years old and respected by everyone in the mining industry.

Zarus continues. "Issur is trying to contain falling rock from the ceiling and walls with chains hooked together in several rows. Sometimes he can use strong rope, but a lot of the falling rock is sharp. He used to be able to make the rounds on Stope Level One in a day. Now he has to try to do it twice a day, and it is too much for him. I hired an assistant for him, but the assistant isn't very experienced."

"How about the water situation?" Saabhu asks.

"We have a love-hate relationship with the water. The temperature on Stope Level One should be 180 degrees. But the cold-water spring there keeps it down around a bearable 120 degrees."

"Yes, I know that. But is the water level under control?"

"It is starting to come in through fissures in the wall. Actually, there is just dampness in those cracks. But it is only a matter of time before water starts seeping all the way through. If the water just comes from the spring on the other side of the wall, we can provide Chaanoch with boy slaves to bale water out. We can have large vats lowered from the surface for the boys to fill. It would save us bringing drinking water in for the men and the camel that works the pulley. Or we could use the water to help cool Stope Level Two."

"On the other hand," Saabhu says, "if it is a strong underground river, once it begins to break through, it could displace all the rock on that wall and cause the mine to collapse."

"That's what I'm afraid of," Zarus responds.

"How are things on Stope Level Two?"

"Hardly tolerable. Drift Two above Stope Level One is ready for our men to go in and mine, but it's too hot. We're chipping from Stope Level One into Drift Two to bring up some of the cool air from the spring. It's almost done. Then we can start mining the floor and walls in Drift Two, and it will become Stope Level Two.

Saabhu stands and walks around. He looks at a map on the wall showing all six drifts, each one man length high. The unexcavated rock above and below each drift is twenty man-lengths.

He studies the map, looks over at Zarus, sits a few moments, then goes back to his map.

"Once we've got everything out we can from Stope Level One, we can go in and collapse the pillars holding up the roof, and extract the copper from the pillars. We can hire extra gravel chippers to go down into Stope Level One and do that while the experienced miners can get started expanding Drift Two into becoming Stope Level Two.

"What about the spring?" Zarus asks.

"We'll have to protect it. We won't pull the pillars down on either side of the spring. Then we'll take the roof off so that it is completely open to the new Stope Level Two above it."

"I think I understand everything you said," Zarus says, running his hand through his hair.

"Tomorrow, I want to meet with Issur, who controls the falling rock, and with Chaanoch who controls the water situation," Saabhu continues. "We'll tour Stope Level One together."

"Yes, sir. How do you think Benyamin and his father will take the news?" Zarus asks.

"Oh, I think they will like it. Collapsing the pillars is an easy way to break up the rock with no manpower and get to the ore. We always have a real windfall when we do it."

"It'll be dangerous, though," Zarus adds.

Saabhu sighs. "Everything about mining is dangerous."

Zarus stands to leave. "Well, I'm going to go down to the light-

and-tool distribution stope and leave messages for Issur and Chaanoch to meet us here tomorrow morning. Then I'm going over to the manor in town and tell Benyamin about the pillar collapse and opening up Stope Level Two. See you tomorrow, Saabhu."

"Yeah," he says, looking back at the map on the wall. "See you in the morning."

Back on the surface, Zarus walks over to a shallow cave he has had created to shelter his Arabian from the desert heat. There, he takes off his sweaty tunic, throws a splash of water on his face from a barrel, and puts on a fresh tunic. He gives Shalva a deep drink of water, puts a harness on him, mounts, and heads toward the city, less than a *mille* from the mine.

He lets Shalva walk at his own pace in the desert heat, which, at the moment, is well over 100 degrees. As they progress, he looks out across the desert with its sparse low scrub brush. He looks up into the foothills and wonders how many other copper mines are out there. He looks up at the gigantic columns majestically formed out of a mountain by the wind and imagines King Solomon mining copper there.

As he rides, he remembers it is prayer time. He does not get off his horse. Although headed straight east, he looks toward the north and prays toward Mount Gerizim. As always, he prays for there to be a way for his beliefs about Jhehovah to be united with Devorah's beliefs. But how is it possible?

Eilat, Port City on Red Sea, Arabah Desert

Arriving at Baaruch's' manor, Zarus hands the reins of his horse to a stable boy and knocks on the gate to the house. When the gate is answered, a servant greets him warmly and tells him Benyamin is in his bathhouse sitting in cool water. Zarus knows the way there.

"Greetings, Benyamin. The water looks grand."

"Come join me then. I don't mind bathing with a genuine Samaritan sometimes. See how liberal I have become?"

"Forgive me, but I need to go on home," Zarus says, careful to laugh at his brother-in-law's joke. "I just wanted to tell you what may be happening at the mine in the next week or so."

"Okay. Then take a seat while I continue my bath, and tell me all about it."

"Engineer Saabhu is going to inspect Stope Level One

tomorrow along with Issur who is complaining there are too many rocks falling from the ceiling, and Chaanoch, who is afraid the spring may grow out of control and flood Stope Level One."

"Stope Level One is at the bottom of the mine, isn't it?"

"Yes. I've had some adits carved from Stope Level One up to Drift Two in order to cool it enough men can work there. That should be completed any day now. Then, Saabhu thinks we should collapse the columns holding up Stope Level One."

"Is that good?"

"It's good if we do it now before someone is killed by falling rock from the roof by accident. There is a lot of copper in those pillars. Once we collapse them, they can be mined easily because the rock will already be broken up for us by the fall."

"And you can start work on Drift Two to extract the ore and expand it into Stope Level Two."

"Exactly."

"Okay. If you and Saabhu think it's a good thing, then you should do it."

Zarus wonders about Benyamin's change. Now that he cannot control everything, it is as if he does not want to control anything.

"Well, I need to be getting on home now."

Zarus goes back out the front gate, takes the reins of Shalva, mounts him, and heads for home and his Devorah. They have been married two years now, and he wonders how the two years could have gone by so fast.

As he draws closer to their rented house, he urges Shalva into a trot. The Arabian raises his tail proudly and happily accommodates his beloved master.

Once home, he takes his horse to the stable where his servant takes over and goes through the gate.

"Devorah, I'm home."

His wife comes out to the courtyard, and they embrace.

"I never get tired of looking at your beautiful blue eyes," she says.

"And I never get tired of looking at your beautiful smooth skin, your pink cheeks, your pointed chin, that little dip of hair on your forehead, and..."

"Oh, by the way, I have a surprise for you."

"A surprise? You're not..."

"No, not that. But just as good."

"I can't imagine what that could be."

"Hello, Son."

Zarus looks up when he hears the familiar voice. "Sir, when did you get here?"

"Well, I got here about noon. I wanted to check on my daughter to make sure you have been living up to your promise before going over to my manor," Baaruch says with a wide grin.

"Which promise? Seems like I gave you several."

"Well, we'll get to those later. The promise I'm most interested in is about my daughter. She assures me you have been treating her well, and you are both happy. That's all that matters."

"Can you stay for dinner before going on to the manor, Father?"

"If we can eat before dark."

"It's ready right now."

They sit down to eat, and Zarus asks his father-in-law to lead the Jewish prayer of thanksgiving. Then Baaruch dips his bread in the plum sauce and takes a bite of cheese with his bread.

"By the way, sir," Zarus says, "we're going to be having a meeting in the morning at the mine with Saabhu, Issur, and Chaanoch. Please join us."

"Indeed, I will. That's the second thing I wanted to check on. By the way, the third thing I plan to check on while here is entering a chariot race in Eilat."

"Oh, Father, are you still into that?"

Copper Mine, Timna Valley, Arabah Desert

"Has everyone arrived?" Saabhu asks. "I'm glad you are here, Baaruch, sir. We have a major decision to make today."

"Benyamin too. He needs to know what is going on," Baaruch adds. "Right, Son?"

Benyamin nods.

One by one, the team members lower themselves into the mine shaft. When they arrive at the supply stope, they each take a lamp or candle according to their preference. Then by two's, they enter the basket that will lower them down the larger shaft to the bottom of the mine, Stope Level One.

According to plan, one of them strikes the bell five times at Stope Level Five, four times at Stope Level Four, so the man on the surface in charge of the pulley knows how far they are. Once they reach Stope Level One and strike the bell, the pulley is stopped.

Baaruch, as always, is struck by the metallic smell along with the smell of sweat, urine, and silicone dust, and pulls a handkerchief out of his sleeve the cover his nose. He notices a rat scurry away.

"Okay, Saabhu, give us your conclusions," he says.

The engineer leads the way.

"You will notice the adit over here. It provides adequate fresh air to Stope Level One, so is not a problem.

"The pillars are another matter," the engineer continues. "We have air holes running through the pillars, so each section is well supplied. That part is okay.

"But now look up at the top of this pillar. Well, you can't see it, but it has a break line. It is not stable up there. Rocks continue to fall around it. If we have a rockburst, the pillar itself will be threatened and could bring disaster. Isn't that right, Issur?"

Issur steps over to the pillar and looks up, then back at the others on the team.

"Yes, that's right, sir. I have help keeping the rocks under control, but it is getting so that even two of us cannot do the job properly."

"What do you suggest, Saabhu?" Baaruch asks.

"I think we need to start cycle mining. We mine what we can for half a day, then we switch to Drift Two to start brushing it to expand the headroom and prepare for extricating ore from there."

"But the temperature is too high in Drift Two," Zarus says. "We are still working on an adit from the spring down here up into Drift Two."

"When will it be completed, Zarus?" Issur asks.

"I think by next week."

"What about the soundness of the mine walls down here in Stope Level One?" Baaruch asks.

"We have a growing fissure close to the spring," Chaanoch says. "So far, it is only damp, but I fear water is going to start breaking through soon, and we don't know how threatening the water will be."

"Watch out!" Benyamin shouts. Trained to rely on instincts rather than reason, everyone rushes out of the way, then hears a crash where they had just been standing. They cover their noses so as to avoid breathing too much of the float dust from the fallen rock.

"Okay, that's just a sample of what we've been having to put up with," Zarus explains.

"What do you suggest?" Baaruch asks the engineer.

"I suggest that, as soon as the adit leading from the cold-water spring is completed to Drift Two, we switch to retreat mining."

"How will you pull the pillars down?" Benyamin asks.

"We'll attach chains around the middle pillar of Stope Level One at one pace apart, Saabhu explains, "and attach them to the pulley coming down the main shaft. We normally have one camel on the surface, but I suggest that, instead, we have two oxen for the pulley."

Baaruch slaps his hands together. "Then let's do it. And let's get out of this unbearable, stinking heat."

The next day, Baaruch and Benyamin return to the *officium*. Saabhu brings him up to speed. "Okay, sir. We're ready. Everything has been prepared in both Stope Level One and Drift Tunnel Two. We're ready to pull down the middle pillar in Stope Level One. Once it begins to collapse, the others will too."

"Then we wait for the dust to settle. That won't happen until tomorrow. Once we can get back in, we can evaluate the quality of copper that was in the pillars. If it's good, all we need is chippers to break the rocks down into gravel and send it to the surface. The rest we leave down there for backfill and will add to it from waste rock in Stope Level Two.

Besides, chippers, we won't need any other miners for the project. Monetary profit will far exceed what we normally get when we also have to pay for miners to chip the ore from the walls and roof."

"In other words," Benyamin says, "This time tomorrow, Father and I will be richer than we ever dreamed. Isn't that right, Father?"

Eilat, Port City on Red Sea, Arabah Desert

Baaruch has a restless night. *Did the pillar fall like it was supposed to do? Did it only jar loose the other pillars, or did the whole mine collapse? Surely Saabhu is a better engineer than to let that happen.*

Finally, it is morning. A maid calls him to breakfast. Benyamin is already there. They eat in quiet. Had they made the right decision?

"I think I'll go on into town to check the schedule for their next chariot race," Baaruch says. "I want to enter it."

He is, indeed, able to enter. The race is scheduled for three months from now. Then he walks down to the waterfront and watches the ships. He sees one that he normally uses for delivering copper to Egypt for smelting, then on to Italy. That afternoon, he returns home.

It is nearly dinner time. He joins Benyamin in the courtyard. They still do not speak much, letting their minds crawl over all the pros and cons of their decision to collapse Stope Level One.

There is a knock on the gate. Shay, a servant who has been with the southern manor since it was purchased, answers it.

"There is a message for you, sir," he says to Baaruch, scroll in hand. Baaruch grabs it, breaks the seal, unrolls it, and reads the message.

"It couldn't have gone any smoother, Son," Baaruch tells Benyamin. "They've inspected the crumbled pillars and say there is good copper in nearly every rock. In fact, they're bringing up the rock so fast through the shaft, they can hardly keep up. They've hired more loaders to get the rock into the wagons. And they've lined up more wagons and oxen to get them to the warehouses."

"Sounds like things are really going our way. That's great news."

"Let's go out there now. We can eat when we get back."

Copper Mine, Timna Valley, Arabah Desert

"Sir, we've filled all the warehouses but one," Zarus says upon arrival of the two mine owners. "What are we going to do? It's a real windfall.

"There's only one thing we can do," Baaruch says. "We must tear down these warehouses and build bigger ones."

"I'll line up carpenters and masons tomorrow, Father. We'll have to get the ore out of here and onto ships as soon as possible, so we can empty the warehouses."

"I saw an empty cargo ship this morning. I'll go see the captain first thing in the morning.

"And I don't want just anyone building our warehouses. It's got to be Moshe. He built both of my manor houses—the one up in Sychar and the one here. In fact, he built these warehouses.

"Nothing but the best, We, my dear son, are now the richest mine owners in the entire Timna Valley. We've arrived, Son. We've arrived!"

Now let's go over to the *officium* for a few moments before we go back to the city. It's too hot out here in the desert."

Zarus gives his father-in-law a drink from the water skin he always carries with him.

"Thank you."

They walk slowly toward the *officium*—Baaruch, Benyamin, and Zarus.

"I can't wait to tell Avigail. Now she can build the biggest house in Sychar up on the highest hill around just like she always wanted."

Baaruch walks just a little slower.

"And I'll be able to take her to Rome like she always wanted. Then down to Alexandria. She'll love that."

Baaruch walks still slower.

"And I'll be able to buy her a necklace of the most costly pearls in all of the Roman Empire."

Baaruch stops. Benyamin and Zarus stop with him.

"At last, I'll be able to make her happy."

Baaruch, grabs at his chest, doubles over, grows limp, and dies.

Sychar, Province of Samaria

The funeral occurs within hours of arriving back in the Sychar manor. The Jewish rabbi is out of town. They contact Estar to see if she can ask the Samaritan rabbi to come. He does.

Others in town come if they receive word in time. Among them is Moshe, the contractor who built the manor house.

Everyone gathers around Baaruch's casket. The Pentateuch is read for him the last time. At the end, Avigail, with son Benyamin holding one hand, and daughter Devorah holding the other hand, leads the procession to the cemetery. They walk. There is no hurry. As they walk, they chant the song of Moses and David's last psalm.

Lawyer Daniyyel reads the will. Benyamin gets the mine and southern manor house. Avigail gets the Sychar manor and all the land. Son-in-law Zarus gets the four Egyptian horses and the chariot. Devorah gets ten silver ingots and the pearl that had once belonged to her father's mother.

"But I can't live alone. Where am I supposed to go? What am I supposed to do?"

Everyone leaves and Avigail sits down and cries.

And he told them this parable: "The ground of a certain rich man produced a good crop.

He thought to himself, 'What shall I do? I have no place to store my crops.'

"Then he said, 'This is what I'll do. I will tear down my barns and build bigger ones, and there I will store all my grain and my goods.

And I'll say to myself, "You have plenty of good things laid up for many years. Take life easy; eat, drink, and be merry." '

"But God said to him, 'You fool! This very night your life will be demanded from you. Then who will get what you have prepared for yourself ?'

"This is how it will be with anyone who stores up things for himself but is not rich toward God." (Luke 12:16-21)

13 ~ The Beast Within

AD 15, Day One
Copper Mine, Timna Valley, Arabah Desert, Idumea

Always something falling. Zarus hears the falling rocks that he cannot see within the scattered cavities of the mountain. He prays that the mountain does not fall in on itself, at least, not while he and his men are in its grasp. Sometimes when things are especially quiet, he hears the mountain groan. The agony of the mountain. Zarus promises his men will be gentle.

He and Gersshon climb out of the basket in the shaft. "Good luck today," Zarus says.

The heat hits Zarus like a furnace, but he has trained his mind to immediately move into neutral and refuse to acknowledge it. Is the mountain feverish today? Will it just lie down and die? Mountain, don't die.

One by one, as they arrive for their shift, each miner takes hold of his chisel in one hand with fingers strong as steel, and hammer in the other, his muscles straining to show what they can do. Each miner begins the daily routine of prying pieces of rock from the inner skin of the mountain. Does it hurt, mountain?

Pillars on each side creak, and the miner asks forgiveness.

This morning, though, there is an eeriness. Zarus senses the mountain moving more than usual. His feet are subtly unsteady. Is it his imagination? The mountain always moves. Perhaps it is just swaying to music. Perhaps because it has lost its equilibrium. Which is it mountain? Are you weeping today, mountain?

Issur seems especially busy this morning. Worry on his face as usual, but more so. "Look at that squeeze on the roof," Issur tells his assistant. I can't seem to get it under control. I can't break it apart and ease the pressure."

"Grab that slate bar, Eitan, and scale the pillar, See if you can loosen the rock. You're younger than me. Maybe you can do it."

"Sir, have you told the engineer about it?"

"Yes, I have. So has Zarus. He says we need to get out of Stope Level Two and follow the copper vein in a completely different direction. He says a collapse is inevitable. But he can't get Benyamin to spend the money getting it done.

"Now get up there and see what you can do with the bar. I had the blacksmith put a new iron tip on it."

The other men gouge the mine wall, the chippers on the floor chisel the rocks into gravel, the slave boys gather up the chips into baskets, and all are aware of what is going on. They do not talk. Talk is useless over the striking of steel mallets onto stubborn walls and the constant smacking of hammers on unsteady stones.

Still, in the darkness, they listen. Listen beyond their own clatter to the unknown. Are you playing games with us today, mountain? Are you mocking us?

A rock falls from the ceiling. The men jump in surprise, but not surprise. More, in suspicion.

Back to work, with muscles hardened by constant tough use, the men swing mattocks at the face of the mountain. The mountain obliges by dropping a tear of rock down its cheek.

"Something's wrong," Fishel calls out across the blackness, the flickering candle on his head all that is moving.

"Shut up," Tzvi calls out in his corner of the shadows. You're casting a spell by talking like this.

"The evil eye," Shimson mutters loud enough everyone can hear through the ever-present blackness.

"Wait. Listen. Did you hear that?" It is Gersshon.

"I didn't hear anything."

"Me neither."

"You're crazy, Gersshon."

"Stop it!" Chaanoch shouts. "I've got to check what's going on with the spring down on Stope Level One. I think I hear it."

"Oh, sure," Fishel says.

Chaanoch takes a ladder down the winze leading to Stope Level One, now nearly solid with backfill except where the cold-water spring is.

He takes the olive oil lamp out of the nitch in the wall and holds it closer to the spring. He thinks he sees movement. He watches. And waits.

"C'mon, show yourself, you devil, you fiend. I dare you," Chaanoch says. He sits on his haunches.

Half an hour passes. An hour. "You're not fooling me," he says, glaring at the waters of the spring, his brows furrowed and shaking his fist at it. He stands and surveys the water.

A crack in the wall behind the spring shutters and spews out a few drops of water from behind the wall.

Bats come out from their hiding place, flap their mysterious wings, and slap the air.

Rats scurry out of hiding and run in circles.

Then the shudder. At first, just a shudder. Then a ripple.

Color. The water changing color. No longer clear to the bottom. Now hazy. Now gold. Now brown. Black.

Humming. From the walls. A low hum like the wail of a distant wolf. Now like a dog's guttural warning growl.

Shuddering.

Trembling.

Quaking.

Nerves overloaded.

Straining.

The humming still.

Then quiet.

The mountain heaves,

    gags,

        and throws up.

Earth shattering and blasting and detonating.

Rocks.

Flying rocks.

Down the shaft.

Flying.

Crashing.

Rushing to their doom.

Head on.

Wind.

Sudden wind. Wind like a cyclone in a desert. Growling. Swooshing.

Now the roar.

The mountain bellows and heaves. Charging. Attacking. Violating its own peace pact with the miners.

A blast of disarming dust. Gray. Brown. Black.

Nowhere to go. To run. To hide.

Bodies flying backward.

Zarus and the others are bodily picked up and pushed against the nearest wall by a force stronger than a bull camel, more mighty than a tidal wave rushing in to reclaim the shore. Pushed against the wall, unable to fight back, incapable of breaking free.

Now down on all fours. Heads ducked and covered with rough hands. Protecting that which cannot be protected.

Crawling. Crawling like cockroaches scrambling for the protection of cracks in the wall.

The floor. Rolling. Swaying. Heaving.

Still, the roar. The roar of the beast inside the mountain. Screaming. Piercing. Shattering.

A few lingering rocks looking for a place to invade. Bouncing, rolling, careening.

Landing. Sliding. Settling in.

Then silence.

Nothing.

Darkness.

Awe.

Slowly, each miner lifts his head. He feels his bones. No breaks.

Zarus looks around, but all he sees is more blackness.

Listening.

Listening for the rocks to return.

Listening for the replay of the moan.

Listening for the shriek as the mountain, tired of always being the giver, now becoming the taker.

"Does anyone have a light that didn't blow out?" Zarus bellows through the dust he has swallowed.

"How many of you are by a wall?" This time it is Chaanoch calling out into the cavernous stope. His voice echoes.

"I am."

"Me too."

"I am."

"Okay," Chaanoch continues, still with as loud voice as he can while choking, and even while the airborne dust continues to find places to settle. "Feel along it until you come to a fair-sized nitch." He waits. "I put a bow drill in each one." Once more, he waits, trying not to breathe in the dust scratching his nose and mouth.

"I think I found one."

"Is that you, Fishel?"

"Yeah, it's me."

"Have you ever used a bow drill? Do you know how it works?"

"I know how it works, but never used one. Wait. I think I can get a spark out of it."

They wait. Soon they smell smoke. Some see a glow. The sawdust has caught fire. Fishel reaches up, takes hold of his candle, and holds the wick next to the ember.

"Hey, over here, Fishel. Can you light my lamp?"

"Can you light mine next?

Zarus feels along the wall to try to figure out where his body has landed after being thrown across the stope by the blast. He realizes he is next to the shaft. He calls out, "Helloooo up there! Can anyone hear us? Helloooo! Anyone? We're alive. Help us. Hello!"

He decides to climb the shaft using the hand and foot niches. "The people above must learn we are still alive," he tells whoever may be nearby in the blackness. *Devorah must be told.*

Stretching.

Straining.

Pushing himself forward.

Pausing now and then to call for help. "Helloooo! Helloooo up there! Can anyone hear me? We need help. Helloooo!"

And listening.

Zarus does not go very far before his head runs into a barrier above him. He feels the barrier to determine what it is made of. Hopefully, it is just the bottom of the two-man basket. It is not. It is rock. Solid flat rock.

His one hand still holding on to the nitch in the shaft wall slips. He grabs hold with both hands and begins his descent.

Once at the bottom, he sees flickers of light on the far side of the stope. He calls out. "I need light. I need light over here!"

"Do you still have your lamp on your head?"

Zarus reaches up and finds it still there. "Yes, I do."

"Well, keep talking so we can find you."

"No use wasting your breath looking for me. I see your lights. Or are they something else?"

"Those lights are us," Rafael calls out.

"Keep coming toward the lights," Fishel says."

Moments later, Zarus joins the others, and someone lights the candle on the side of his head.

"Is anyone injured?" Zarus calls out, "other than minor scratches?"

No one answers.

"Praise God, we've all been saved. Now we've got to get organized, The first thing we need to do is let the men on the surface know we are still alive, and where we are.

"Now we need two or three to call up the shaft. We need two or three to call through the air adit. We need two or three down by the Stope Level One spring if it is still there, just in case someone on the outside can hear us there."

"What about getting ourselves out?" Issur says.

"Good idea," Zarus says.

"I'll take the rest of you around on an inspection of the walls," Issur continues. "Whenever we feel a fissure, we'll climb up as far as we can to see if it leads to an opening somewhere. Our candles burning brighter in those places will be an indication of outside air."

The men scatter. The little pin of light each man has that penetrates the hazy blackness of the mine is the only indication where anyone is. Dreading the aloneness and desperation of being buried alive, each man depends on the light of the others for his only comfort.

Hours pass. There is no more sense of time or even of day or night. But they know it has been hours. They are tired. And hungry.

Will their candles last? And their food?

"Men," Zarus announces in the blackness, "it's time we stop and take a break. We need to conserve our energy. See my light? I have taken it off my head and am waving it in a circle. Come to the circle of light."

Gradually the men stumble their way to Zarus. They sit on the floor, stare into their tomb, blow out all of their lights but one, and mercifully fall asleep. They dream of their loved ones. Zarus dreams of Devorah.

In the blackness, the fever in the mountain continues to rise.

Day Two

"Anyone got any food? I'm getting hungry," someone says.

"I have a few figs."

"I have two rolls."

"I have a piece of jerky about the size of my hand."

"Well, we need to consolidate all our food. Anyone else?" Zarus asks.

"Remember, if you stay alive and the rest of us die of starvation, you'll be stuck down here by yourself," Gersshon adds.

"Well, I have a wedge of cheese."

"I guess I have three rolls."

"I've got two fish, but they're small."

"Anyone else?" Zarus asks.

"Okay. Do you trust me to keep it and divide it up equally? I think we should eat once a day."

"Fine with me."

"Me too. Other than climbing and calling for help, that's about all we'll be doing."

"I'm going to go check on the spring," Chaanoch says. If it was saved, good. If it wasn't, maybe we can pull the rocks out, blocking it."

"Watch out!"

The men scatter as far as they can run in the darkness. The sharp boulder crashes down and splits into three pieces bouncing and sliding along the mine floor.

"I've got to get up there and see what's going on," they hear Issur say. Eitan, come with me, and anyone else who knows how to climb."

"I'm going to check to see if the air adits on this level and Stope Level One are still open," Nisaan says. I'll send slave boys to go as far as they can and call for help. Then maybe they'll work on their end to get fallen rocks out of the way, so we don't run out of air.

Zarus agrees. "I'm going to climb the shaft as far as possible again. We've got to let people know we're still alive so they won't desert us. He climbs as far as the barrier, then calls out.

"Helloooo! Anyone up there? Can anyone hear me? Helloooo!"

He pauses and listens.

He hears voices below in the blackness and calls down. "Quiet, everyone. I think I hear something."

The men below grow silent. Each man prays. Each man grits his teeth, or presses his lips together, or clenches his fist. Each man, in his own way, waits for his miracle.

"Helloooo! Anyone up there? Can anyone hear me? Helloooo!"

A muffled voice finds its way through from the other side of the mountain. A familiar muffled voice.

"Zarus? Is that you?"

"Saabhu?"

Day Three

Issur and Chaanoch waken about the same time but do not know it. The candles and lamps need to be relit. Since they cannot tell daylight from dark, they have decided to stop and sleep as soon as their lamp goes out, lamps having wicks that last eight or ten hours.

Now it is *morning*. At least, morning for the trapped miners.

They have slept on the mine floor. Some have taken off their leather aprons to use for pillows. They had left their tunics on the surface as always. The temperature has soared during the *night*. It is hotter than the surface at the hottest part of the day.

"We've got to keep doing what we ourselves can to survive until they get to us," Zarus says, wiping his brow before putting his leather apron back on over his loincloth.

"You mean if they get to us," one miner says in the unrelenting blackness.

"And before it finishes collapsing on us," another says.

"First, we need to make fire for today, Chaanoch says, "so we can see each other and inspect this level a little more."

As the men wake up to the voices, they cough and blow their noses to get rid of some of the dust that has settled on them during the *night*. They look into a blackness that can never be penetrated and remember where they are.

Speaking into the blackness, Zarus says, "Today, we must do two vital things. If we don't, we won't survive the day. First, we have to get more air in." He coughs and clears his throat. The slave boys will resume their work on the air adit.

"The other vital thing is to uncover the cold-water spring at the bottom of the winze. If we don't cool off in the next few hours, we will die of heatstroke."

"While you men are doing that, as soon as I have my head lamp lit, I'm taking Eitan to help me inspect the roof and all the walls," Issur says.

Gradually, each miner's candle or lamp is relit.

"How about some breakfast?" Gersshon asks. "We had a big stash of food yesterday. I want my share."

"We ration it," Zarus warns. "Each of you gets a fig or a date for your breakfast."

"Is that all?"

"We may be down here for a week or more. We must be careful and ration the food."

The ten survivors wait their turn and are given their one piece of fruit then scatter to whatever job Zarus has assigned them to.

Air and water to cool down must be found to survive in the next few hours. If they only accomplish one, it will do no good. They must succeed with both or die.

Silently they shuffle through the familiar mine that used to be their sometimes friend and has now become their enemy.

Silently they grope as through a black fog of dampness threatening to boil.

They walk across a mountain floor, shedding its own sweat and mocking their will to survive.

They walk. Like black ghosts through a world in which they do not belong, and which is now trying to punish them for their invasion.

No noise except the constant falling of rocks beyond their present habitat, falling, falling down the cheeks of the weeping mountain. In their darkness, some of the miners also weep.

Day Four

"We can't do it anymore," Shimson says. "It's too tight in the air adit, and the heat is too bad. It's impossible to get more air. We're going to die in our sleep tonight."

"And water to drink. We're almost out."

"I'm out of water, Nisaan says. How about the rest of you?"

"I ran out last *night*," Gersshon says. "We can't live without water. We're dead men."

"I'm going to check on the water crew," Zarus says as he walks in the direction of the spring.

"We've gone down one man length. We've got to find the spring," Chaanoch says.

Hour after hour they work, pulling rocks out of the way of the spring Chaanoch is convinced is still there. Zarus helps, remembering his days on the Roman road.

"Stop, everyone!" Chaanoch says, getting down on his knees and putting his face to the bottom rocks. "Hand me a candle, someone. I think I hear something."

The men wait and watch in silence.

"There! I hear it. Take those three rocks out of the way," Chaanoch says.

Three of the miners move the rocks out.

"Water! Black and red water, but it's water," Chaanoch says.

"Water!"

"We've reached water!"

"We'll live!"

Despite their weakened condition, the miners shout in celebration, then stop suddenly. They dare not let their voices start another rock slide. Instead, they pat each other on the back, dance, jump up and down, or turn in celebratory circles, arms raised in thanksgiving to God.

Devorah, didn't I tell you I'd get out. It's close, Devorah. It's close.

Chaanoch gives them their directions. "Okay, line up."

One by one, the men get down on their knees, cup their grimy hands, and bring up water to their cracked lips, then splash it on their head, their arms, their chests.

Water.

Water to quench their thirst.

Water to cool the air.

Water to keep them alive another day until their rescue.

They fill their water skins, then go up the winze to Stope Level Two.

"We still have no additional air unless Issur has found a crack in the wall that goes to the outside," Zarus says.

"I haven't," Issur says, just arriving to join the others. "What I did find is a very unstable roof and walls that are bulging. I don't know how long the mountain is going to withhold its full fury against us.

Silence.

Thinking of survival.

Thinking of living until they can be rescued and return to their loved ones. *Devorah, I'll be back. I promise. I'll be back.*

"How much food do we have left, Zarus?"

"Enough for one more meal—one bite of cheese. Then no more food."

Zarus passes the rest around. The miners eat their last bite, their last meal.

They stare.

Their stares are hollow.

They stare into their imminent deaths.

The slaves boys move close to the men for comfort.

What will get them first? No air or no food? Will it be painful?

Day Five

"We can't break through the air adit," Nisaan reports. All we can do is wait and hope the men above ground get through to us before we run out of air."

"Everyone, we're going to have to conserve our lights now," says Chaanoch.

"No air, no food, now no light?"

"As long as we are together as a group, everyone will put out their candle or lamp, and we will rely only on one lamp."

"You're right. We don't know how long we'll be trapped down here," Issur says.

"Maybe forever."

"We only need lights to check the stability of the roof and walls. Well, and to go down to the spring."

Darkness.

Blackhole.

Staring, but asking why.

Wondering.

Thinking.

Praying.

Standing and stretching.

Sitting back down.

Scooting down to the floor and leaning against a rock.

Dreaming.

Wishing.

Remembering what it is like to see.

"I hear something." It is Gersshon.

"I don't hear anything," Tzvi says.

"I'm next to the wall. The sound is coming from the wall."

"Have they reached us?"

In their blackness, they hear scrambling of feet. A squeak. And a "Gotcha."

"What is it, Gersshon?" Issur asks.

"A rat. Food."

"No," Issur says. "Get rid of it. It'll bring diseases."

"Not if we eat it right away."

"Gersshon, you must be out of your mind," Zarus says.

They hear a loud squeak, then something thrown up against the wall.

"Chaanoch, I need to light my lamp. His head is off. All I need to do now is to take off his fur, and cook the rest."

"Against my better judgment, you can have a light to cook that creature. But I will never eat anything unclean."

"Okay, so it's against the holy Law. But there are always exceptions. Starving to death is one of those exceptions."

The men grow quiet again as they watch the little flame cook the rat, then Gersshon sinks his teeth into it.

"You couldn't pay me to eat that rat."

"That's what you think now. Wait until you haven't eaten for a few more days."

Is this what life is all about? Zarus thinks. *Surviving so we can die in the bowels of a black hell?*

Day Six

Quiet.

Thinking.

Listening to the rocks crumble and fall through unknown, unseen crevices of an angry mountain.

Dazed.

Coughing.

Eerie groans of the mountain.

Cracking.

Crawling through an abyss of the soul.

Sometimes ascending the blocked shaft just to see if a sound of muffled voices can be heard from the top side, the side of the living.

For reassurance.

For a reminder, they are not being left for dead.

For human contact above where life is normal.

Harder to breathe now. The end is surely near. Trying not to move and use up extra air.

Stillness in the midst of heart longing. To see loved ones just one more time before giving in to the mountain and dying.

Oh, Devorah, my sweetheart. Do not cry. Be brave. God will bring us back together.

Anyone hungry? I've caught two more rats."

"Shut up, Gersshon."

"No, wait, I think I'd like one," Shimson says.

"What will you give me?"

"I don't have any money on me."

"That's okay. I'll take something in trade."

"I don't have anything. Just things at my home in the city."

"That'll do. What do you have that I may want? How about a nice robe?"

"I'm a mine worker. I don't have nice robes."

"What kind of animals do you have?"

"Well, I just have a mule."

"That'll do. I'll take your mule."

"That's too much."

"Take it or leave it."

Shimson thinks a while. His mind stays on his stomach and how hungry he is.

"Well, if I die in here, I won't need my mule. Okay. You can have my mule."

"Get your fire lit, and I'll finish killing it for you," Gersshon says. "I'll wring his neck off. Is that satisfactory with you?"

"Yeah, as long as the blood is out."

"No, Shimson. Don't do it."

Shimson gets a light off the master lamp. Gersshon walks toward him, holding on to the rat by its tail and with a small, smooth rock in the other."

"I've etched out an IOU. Put your mark on it, and the rat is yours."

Shimson obliges Gersshon, gets his rat, cooks it over the low flame, and eats it.

"Not bad. A little stringy, but not bad. I certainly feel better," Shimson says. "The rest of you guys ought to give it a try."

"Forget it, Shimson. You and Gersshon are crazy."

"Did you say you had two?" It's Fishel.

"I did, indeed. Interested?"

"Depends on the price."

"What do you have I want?"

"My wife has a ruby ring."

"That's fine. I'll take it."

Silence.

Breathing.

Choking.

Vomiting.

Another light. Another roasting of the creeper. Another miner's stomach satisfied. Temporarily.

Again the quiet.

Gagging at just how far a human will go when desperate.

Wondering, each for himself, what his limit will be.

After rats, then what? Or who?

Dampness back. Now that the spring has been exposed and is cooling the men off, the humidity is up. Sweating. Reeking of body odor. Smelling death all around.

"What was that?" Fishel asks.

"What?"

"Sounds like metal hitting rock. There it is again."

"Quiet. Listen. Do you hear it?"

"Chaanoch. Bring a light over here. I hear it too," Zarus says. "It's over by the blocked air adit. Let's get closer."

"It's them! They're breaking through," says Fishel.

"Shhh…"

Clang.

Scrape.

Silence.

Clang.

Scrape.

Silence.

Clang.

"Sounds like a metal bar. But how can it break through the rock without unsettling the mountain?" Nisaan asks.

"I know how," Issur says. "They're pounding it. I've heard that rhythm before. That's the rhythm of a battering ram. Instead of a wooden pole, they're probably using a metal pole with a tip on the end, or a metal tube."

"No one can be so accurate that they hit the same hole over and over. Can't be done," Chaanoch says.

"By the sound, I think they're doing just that. They're pounding a small air adit for us."

Grins once again.

Hope once again.

Life once again.

The men wander back over to their rock seats.

Thinking.

Dreaming.

Anticipating.

Trying not to think of the roof of the mine stooping lower and lower onto them, threatening to crush their life away.

I'm coming home, Devorah. I'm coming home.

Oh, to breathe again. Deeply. Fully. Happily.

Time to sleep. Each man scoots down onto his damp bed on the mine floor, his rotting leather apron once again cushioning his head.

Each dreams. Of knocking. Knocking on a gate. Knocking of a door in the wind. Knocking of their hearts beating against their chest.

Exhausted. Fatigued. Weak.

Lungs overworking. Heart overworking. Chest muscles overworking to bring in the air that is becoming more and more scarce. They dream of breathing again.

Day Seven

Zarus does not sleep. All *night* he listens as the clanging noise gets closer. As he does, he dares to think of Devorah. Now there is hope. *How is she doing? She's probably working her way through all the families who have probably come out to await our rescue.* He smiles.

Suddenly the clanging noise is so close, he has to block his ears. The others awaken, block their ears, and stumble in the darkness toward the sound.

"Chaanoch, get a light lit and come over here,"Zarus says.

In a few moments, a single spark of hope is seen in the blackness of their tomb. Or is it a tomb after all? Chaanoch lights his lamp and works his way over to the sound. He holds his lamp up to the mine wall and sees rock crumbling just over their heads. As other miners go to him with their candles and lamps, he lights them, and hope grows.

They wait.

Only the clanging.

More waiting.

Closer.

Then it happens.

 "They're through."

"They're through!"

I see daylight. They've made it."

Zarus calls through the tube. "We're all alive. All ten of us. Come get us!"

The men take turns standing in front of the tube to breathe fresh air.

"Oh, no. It went black. A rock blocked it. We're doomed," Gersshon says.

"Wait," Zarus says. "There's noise inside the tube. They're pushing something through it to us."

Soon, a small bottle drops out of the hole, and a long pole protrudes from the tube opening. Zarus picks up the bottle, takes the stopper off, and tips it. A piece of parchment falls out. "Bring me more light, Chaanoch," Zarus says.

"This is a note. It says they will send us food through this hole, and asks if we have water. If we have no water, we are to keep the note. If we do have water, we're to send the note back."

Zarus puts the note back in the bottle, pulls the pole out of the tube, and pushes the bottle back to the outside world.

The men wait. Now smiles. Now hope. Now expectation.

The pole is pulled back to the outside, and once again, the men take turns breathing in the fresh air.

Blackness again and scraping of the pole.

"Food at last for all of you men," Zarus says.

When the bottle arrives and is tipped, it only contains another note.

Zarus reads it aloud. "Now that we know where you are, we have begun a rescue operation on the other side of the mountain. It should take us four or five more days, but we will get you out. Listen for us."

Once again, the waiting. Will rescue really come? Will it be in time? Will the mine fall in on itself first?

Waiting.

Hoping.

Praying.

Pacing.

Running in place.

Down to the spring and back again.

Devorah, keep praying.

Day Eight

The men develop a routine. Now that they have food and air, most shuffle back and forth across the mine to give themselves exercise and something to do.

Day Nine

It does not take them long to begin hearing activity on the other side of their wall.

Day Ten

Day after day, Zarus and his men wait. Some stay by the air-and-food tube. Others work their way through the blackness to the other side of the mine.

Day Eleven

Periodically Zarus calls the men together to pray.

Day Twelve

Then it happens. They hear the voices of rescuers. Frantically, they remove rocks from the bowels of the mine.

Daylight!

"Moshe, is that you?" Zarus calls out through the hole.

"At your service, friend. I brought my crew, and we have been shoring up a shaft as we go. I have Estar with us, and her husband, Micha. Now, we don't dare remove any more rocks than necessary. We don't want to destabilize the mountain more than it is already.

The miners push to be the first through. "First, we get the slave boys out." Zarus instructs, "then the rest of you."

One by one, the miners climb through the hole of escape and are greeted on the other side by a line of rescuers helping to get him across their pile of rocks and to the arms of loved ones.

"Tzvi," Zarus says. "I haven't seen Tzvi. Did he get out?"

"No, he's not out yet."

"Tzvi!" Zarus calls out. "Tzvi! Are you still in here?"

Rocks falling from the ceiling. More than before.

"Yeah, I"m here. I just had to go back and get something."

"Tzvi, hurry! Get out. The mine's going."

"I'll be right there, as soon as I..."

The mountain rumbles.

"No, Tzvi. Now!"

"I can't seem to find it."

"There's no time left. Tzvi. Run!"

A rumble. Shaking. Trembling.

"Hurry, Zarus," Moshe calls to him. "it's barely hanging on. Hurry!"

Cracking.

Groaning.

Shrieking.

The mountain screaming in pain.

Falling in on itself.

The mountain takes one last breath, howls, and bursts.

Zarus hoists himself up and twists through the opening. Rocks rain down on both sides of the opening. Micha rushes up to help him the rest of the way out of the collapsing hole. He grabs hold of Zarus' arms, and as he does, a large rock, the size of a lion's head falls on him.

Micha crumbles to the ground. Zarus pulls himself the rest of the way out of the mountain's clutches. He struggles to get the rock off his sister's husband. He hears Estar screaming. Beyond human strength, Zarus rolls the stone off, lifts Micha into his arms, and rushes him out of the shaft just as it collapses completely.

People running. Shouting. Screaming.

Devorah calls out. "Over here, Zarus. Over here!"

A thick cloud of red-gray dust blasts out of the mountain, blowing people to the ground, and blinding, choking, deafening everyone in its way. The merciless particles settle thick on each person in its wake.

Estar sits on the ground with her beloved's bleeding head in her lap. She bends over to protect him from the fury in the mountain's final tears. Devorah and Zarus draw closer.

And Micha dies.

No one lights a lamp and puts it in a place where it will be hidden, or under a bowl. Instead, he puts it on its stand, so that those who come in may see the light.

Your eye is the lamp of your body. When your eyes are good, your whole body also is full of light. But when they are bad, your body also is full of darkness.

See to it, then, that the light within you is not darkness.

Therefore, if your whole body is full of light, and no part of it dark, it will be completely lighted, as when the light of a lamp shines on you." (Luke 11:33-36)

14 ~ THE REPRIEVE

AD 15
Eilat, Port City on Red Sea, Arabah Desert, Idumea

"*T*he mine is destroyed. Benyamin has sold what was left of the copper in the warehouses and his manor house and gone to Egypt. Saabhu has gone back to his hometown in Egypt. Noach has gone to sea. Everyone is gone. What are we going to do now, Zarus?" It is Devorah.

They are in their rented house in Eilat. Despite the heat, but because the sea breeze makes it tolerable, Zarus and Devorah sit in their courtyard at a table made of acacia wood. Devorah runs her hands over the beautiful finish.

"We've collected some nice pieces of furniture to go in the house you were going to have Moshe build for us, but those plans are dead now too."

Zarus sits slumped in his chair, looking at the floor. "I'm sorry, Devorah,"

"It wasn't your fault. It just happened." A tear comes to her eye. "I feel so sorry for Estar. This is her third husband to die. No woman should have to bear so much."

"He was a good man. But she's a survivor." He looks over at his beautiful wife. "We will survive also. I will go out job hunting tomorrow.

———

"Zarus, you're a good man. You know the mining business, but

I don't need anyone else in my mine right now. I'm sorry."

"Zarus, you are strong and healthy. I can't use you, but maybe someone down at the docks could use someone like you to carry cargo to and from the ships."

"Zarus, we have slaves to load and unload the ships. You are too smart to be doing something like that."

"Zarus, I heard a cotton farmer is looking for help sowing seeds for the next crop. I know it's beneath you, but it could tie you over until you get on your feet."

"Yes, Zarus, I do need help. The job will last two weeks. I know it's not much, but it's all I can offer you right now."

"Thank you, sir."

"And, Zarus, I'm sorry about what happened in the mine."

"No one is more sorry than I am."

"It wasn't your fault, you know. Can you report in before daylight tomorrow morning? Can't work you guys too long in this hot sun."

"Yes, I'll be here."

———

"Here's your pay for the two weeks of sowing cottonseed, Zarus. It's not much compared to what you are used to getting."

"Thank you, sir. This is exactly what my work is worth."

"By the way, Zarus, I heard about a horse breeder who needs some more hands. He breeds Arabians. Don't you have an Arabian of your own?"

"Indeed, I do. I love Arabian horses. Where is the ranch?"

"It's over in Arabia."

"I'd like to breed Arabians someday myself. Maybe this is my chance to learn the ins and outs of it."

"Well, it's at Qaryat al-Fāw."

"I'll find it."

Zarus hurries home to Devorah and gives her the money.

"Devorah, I have found another job. But it's over in Arabia. I don't know how long I'll be gone."

Devorah is dressed in a simple tunic and preparing fresh vegetables for their lunch. She does not light the oven except in early morning while it is still fairly cool.

"Zarus, there is something I have to tell you." Devorah is serious.

"You've been sick lately, haven't you? Forgive me for not

paying more attention to you. Is it serious? I'll find a doctor for you, even if I have to sell some of this furniture to pay him."

Devorah's expression changes, and she smiles. "Yes, it is serious. But not a bad serious."

She walks over to him and sits in his lap.

"What's going on here?" he says

"We are going to have a baby."

Zarus stares at Devorah a moment, then breaks out into a broad smile. "That's the best news I've heard in ages."

"I know it is a bad time financially. But..."

"But we'll work things out. I must leave in the morning for Arabia and will send money back to you. There should be enough to hire Penina back to help you around here. By the way, would you see if you can locate Pesachya, your father's old stable hand? If you can, ask him if he might be available to work for me and take care of your Egyptian horses while I'm gone."

AD 16
Eilat, Port City on Red Sea, Arabah Desert

"Your husband has been in Arabia three months now, mistress. I wish he would come back before your baby is born."

"Penina, you worry over me too much," Devorah tells her maid.

"That has always been my job since you were a little girl, so how am I supposed to change?"

"Well, I guess it's nice to have someone worry over you. And, of course, it would be nice to have Zarus back. I don't know what I would have done without you."

"Oh, someone is at the gate, Penina."

Penina answers the gate.

"Oh, master Zarus. We were just talking about you. Mistress Devorah missed you terribly."

"I've tied up my horses right outside the gate. Were you able to find Pesachya?"

"Yes, master."

"Tell him he has two more to look after."

"He has two more what to look after, my darling?" Devorah rushes to the gate, arms wide open, a broad grin gracing her delicate face. "Welcome home, my love," she says, falling into his arms.

"I thought you would be in Arabia longer than this."

"Oh, so you want me to go back?"

"Quit teasing me and kiss your wife," Devorah says.

They embrace and grow quiet, not talking, just absorbing one another in each other's arms.

Zarus holds her at arm's length. "Let me see you now. Well, our baby seems to be progressing well enough."

"Master, it is good to have you back," Pesachya says. "I see you now have two Arabians. Congratulations, Master."

"It's good to see you, Pesachya. The years have treated you well.

"My old bones are rather brittle now, and my knees don't work like they used to, but other than that, I feel pretty good."

"You have another Egyptian now. A filly."

"Yes, isn't she something? I earned her as a bonus for nursing her after she contracted tetanus. She was so young, no one thought she would live through it, but she did."

"Well, come on in and tell me all about Arabia," Devorah says, the couple walking arm in arm toward an inner room that is cooler than the courtyard this time of day."

Penina brings two mugs of lemonade.

"I mostly broke in the horses so they could be ridden."

"Oh, my. You didn't break one of your bones, did you?"

"No, I'm fine. And now I am going to start my own horse breeding business."

"That's going to take time, Zarus. What will you do in the meantime?"

"I heard they are building a road between here and the old port of Ezion Geber. I'm going to apply to be foreman if they'll take me. The Arabians want the road put in as much as anyone. Two port cities here wouldn't hurt at all."

"You're acting a lot different from when you left to go to Arabia."

"Those were hard times, I have to admit. The mine closing forever, Saabhu and Noach leaving, the death of the one miner who didn't get out in time, and of course Micha being killed. I couldn't have made it without you, Devorah."

"I married you to spend the rest of my life with you, no matter what the future holds. We will always have each other."

"Tomorrow, I'm going to put the word out that Shalva is available for breeding. That should bring in some seed money for our new business. Then I will talk to some magistrates to see who is in charge of the new road. I'm back, Devorah. I'm back and will never leave you again."

"We finished the road in four months instead of the expected six," Zarus tells his wife, coming in through the gate one afternoon with a big smile. "I got a good bonus, and that should help us while we wait for the breeding business to pick up."

They sit in the courtyard with a goblet of pomegranate juice served by Penina. Both take a sip, but that is as far as it goes.

"I'm worried," Devorah says. "Shops are closing up at the market. People are beginning to move away."

"I didn't realize it was that bad. The drought. I guess it's hurting the town more than I thought it would. We don't get much rain, of course, but we always get enough for what is raised here."

"Not this year," she replies with a sigh.

Zarus' smile is gone. "Things change so fast. Why did I raise my hopes, Devorah? What am I going to do? You are eight months pregnant. How am I going to support you?"

"Sweetheart, we just need to ride it out. Rain will come back someday. Look, I see some clouds already."

"But droughts sometimes last ten years, and I don't trust those clouds. They'll just blow over. I'm going to take Shalva out for a walk by the old mine. It will do him and me both good to get out of the city for a while."

He stands and strides toward the door leading to the stables. "Pesachya, why don't you get the filly and my horse ready and go with me for a ride out into the desert."

"But, why, master? There's nothing there anymore."

"Those were good years, Pesachya. I need to go out to where I had good years."

The horses are readied. Neither man uses a saddle. Zarus helps Pesachya up onto the filly, then leaps up onto Shalva.

Timna Valley, Arabah Desert

Slowly the horses take the two men through town. They go through the market, and Zarus is shocked at how many shops have closed down. He tries not to look at them. Instead, he looks up at the gathering clouds. Their presence does not make sense. They are in the midst of a drought.

Shalva, oblivious to it all, sniffs the wind, raises his tail proudly, and begins to prance through the streets of Eilat.

"Whoa there, big boy. Can't have you using up all your energy before we even leave town," Zarus says, leaning forward, pulling back on the reins and patting Shalva on the cheek.

Shalva slows down but swishes his tail in protest.

"The wind has been blowing for two days. Just stirring in circles. It has been a nice relief to the heat," Pesachya says.

All flowers and trees immediately disappear as soon as they go through the city gate, just like the smiles Zarus has shown are now gone. *What am I going to do? Sometimes there is an oasis in the desert of life, but they are so far from each other.*

They notice little swirls of dust dancing along the ground here and there. The breeze is picking up. It feels good.

Zarus thinks about the many times he got up in the morning and headed toward the mine. Hard work, but good work. Got to work with brave men. Not just any man is willing to risk his life every day, entering the mountain in hopes that the mountain will let him leave again a few hours later.

No more. No more copper mine, no more brave men, no more job, no more hope.

He looks at the hills surrounding the Timna Valley. He recalls the times in the early evening when he left work and watched the sun give them a rosy golden glow. Some people say deserts are ugly, but desert people are the first to dispute that. Zarus had always said a little thank you prayer for the beauty of the desert whenever he saw the hills thus adorned.

But now, Zarus sees only a dry desert with nothing to offer. The desert gives, and the desert takes away. Cursed be the desert.

A swirl of dust along the ground lifts itself, grows, and becomes a miniature whirlwind. It dances mockingly above the desert floor, then disappears.

The men draw closer to where the old mine used to be. Benyamin had deeded it over to Zarus, but it meant nothing except to be the recipient of any lawsuits that might follow.

Zarus squints as he looks at the mountain, now disfigured with its side blown out. Blowing sand has filled in part of the crevice.

The big man gets down off Shalva and leads him closer to the old mine. He looks along the ground for the old shaft, stepping carefully, lest he fall into it. He is sure he knows where it was, but perhaps it has now been filled with the desert, like everything else in Zarus' life. All aspirations filled with dryness and now dead.

Shalva neighs. Zarus looks up at the sky. The clouds seem to be merging and becoming a brownish gray. Still, the wind they are stirring up feels good. It's actually a little cooler than it was when they left home, though it is mid-day.

Unable to find the old shaft, Zarus works his way around to the side of the mountain that is still intact. He looks for the adit he had hewn out of the rock when he had first arrived at the mine as an indentured servant to Devorah's father.

I had more energy then than I do now. What a difference six years make. Or maybe it was enthusiasm. Oh, how I wanted Devorah as my own. I became the luckiest man in the world when I was betrothed to her. I need to remember to tell her that more often.

Zarus looks through fallen rocks and amazingly finds the adit. *It never was very large. I wonder how far into the mine it goes now. Probably not very far. The old stopes and levels have all collapsed like every plan I ever had for myself. All gone.*

He and Pesachya lead their horses to the other side of the mountain, the side that collapsed in on itself. Part of Moshe's shaft is still standing. *Moshe always did good work.*

"This is where Estar's husband was killed. He was helping me crawl out, and a falling rock got him in the head." *Why did it have to happen? What do we accomplish in life, anyway?* "He was a good man, Pesachya."

"Yes, I met him while I was still in Sychar. He did well with Estar's fabric booth."

"That's right. I forgot."

The horses neigh again. Zarus notices birds flying in and huddling under sparse brush that scatters around the desert flood.

Pesachya looks around. The wind picks up. "Something's about to happen, Zarus. We'd better take cover. Do you think this mineshaft will protect us?"

Zarus begins to cough. The old miner's cough that he'd thought he'd gotten rid of.

"Look!"

Pesachya points in the direction of Mount Timna. There, towering over it as though the mountain were a toy, looms a cloud of dust crawling in like a giant monster.

Zarus and Pesachya lead their horses into the rescue shaft Moshe had made nearly a year earlier. The gray-brown clouds are now brown and beginning to be absorbed in the swirl rising above the mountains.

The wind stirs and the overhead beams of the shaft creak and groan.

Just like before.

Suddenly they are in the midst of the unending brown monster. The wind swirls around them. They make the horses lie down next to them, facing toward the back of the shaft. Zarus and Pesachya crouch, put their heads down, close their eyes, and wait. Wait for the assault to turn another way.

On it comes like a dry wave of ocean. On it comes like a lion in the mountains surrounding Sychar. Like an army bent on destroying the enemy.

Still, the men and horses crouch. The sand now stinging as it swirls relentlessly around the useless copper mine and into the rescue shaft. Now in their noses. They breathe it in. It makes its way to their mouths. Grainy to the taste. Stinging the eyes, though they are closed tightly. Stinging whatever skin is exposed.

On the sand comes. Billowing, rushing, threatening. A giant bent on overcoming the mountains and anything in its way. Advancing like a moving wall.

They do not know how long the dust storm ravages. They hear the roof fly off of one of the warehouses left deserted by Benyamin the year before. They hear another crash and guess it is the old mine *officium* where Saabhu and Noach worked such long hours.

Swirling relentlessly. Out to compel whatever is in its way to move.

Zarus' miner's cough grows worse. He hacks. But each time he does, more dust gets in his mouth, and the more he hacks. Pesachya moves around to where Zarus is and places his body between the outside and his master.

Zarus is ashamed. It is he who should be protecting Pesachya. The horses remain still, eyes closed, head and tail down.

The sand becomes part of Zarus' being. Sometimes he dozes, and the sand becomes his dream. He wakes with a start and knows the sand is still ravaging him and all that he used to hold important.

Devorah. Is she okay? Did she and Penina get everything off the roof and out of the courtyard in time? Are they now safely inside with the gate and inside doors shut and the windows tightly shuttered? What would I do if I lost Devorah?

The sand slowly moves on. The men open their eyes and blink the dust out of their lashes. The orange sun shows faintly through the sandy cloud. It has been three hours.

They wait a little longer, and blue appears. The blue of the sky had been there all along, though unseen through the monster wall of sand. Now, as the beast moves out to sea, blue sky reappears as though it, too, had had its eyes closed for a while.

Zarus blinks again, stands, and coughs again. Pesachya stands too. "Are you all right, master?"

The two men take off their head kerchiefs and tunics, shake the sand out of them, and put them back on. The horses get back up and shimmy to get the sand off of them.

They look around. The entire shaft where they had been staying has been filled in except where the two men and their horses had been. They step out and look up at the mountain that used to hold their mine. It is gone. A giant sand dune has covered it. A passer-by would never guess what it had been.

Their water skins are still intact, as well as the bowl they carry on their horses when in the desert to give them a drink.

Zarus remembers the shallow cave he had made to shelter Shalva whenever he kept him at the mine. He had a small well there. Could he find it again? He looks around, thinks he sees it, then decides he does not.

They walk out farther, keeping Mount Timna in their sight for a landmark. The desert floor has been exposed, having donated all its sand to covering up the former mine and its mountain.

The men feel eerie as they walk out onto the desert floor to a strange new world. It is now solid rock. They walk slowly as they lead their horses.

It is late afternoon. Normally the desert floor reflects the orange of a soon-setting sun. Indeed, it does. But not everywhere. There are places where the sun is...

No, it cannot be.

"Pesachya, come look at this."

Pesachya joins his master, and they look down on a place on the desert floor just now revealed by the monster storm.

"It's green, Pesachya. Doesn't it look green to you?"

"Indeed, it does, master."

Zarus gets down on his knees and looks closer. He runs his hands across it. "Pesachya, hand me my water skin."

"You are wearing it on your belt, master."

"Oh, that's right." Zarus feels for his waterskin, not taking his eyes off the green spot on the desert floor, takes out the cork, and pours the rest of it out.

"It's still green, Pesachya." Zarus looks up at his comrade. "What do you think? Is it green to you?"

"Indeed, it seems so master."

Zarus stands, walks several paces away, bends down, and

cleans off another spot. He repeats himself several times.

His heart beats faster. Tears come to his eyes. His hands tremble. He looks up at the blue sky and whispers, "Do I dare hope?"

"Come here, Pesachya. Does that look green to you too?"

"Oh, yes, master. Very green. And coppery too."

Zarus stands, raises his arms heavenward, and shouts. "Copper! A huge vein of copper!"

He dances in circles, waving his arms at his side as though he were a soaring eagle.

"Hurry, Pesachya. We have to get back into the city and to the magistrates' *officium* before it closes. I have to find out who owns this land. I've got to buy it.

Zarus kneels in prayer facing Gerizim and Jherusalem, thanks Jhehovah God for his blessings, and rises.

"Wait 'til I tell Devorah."

"The kingdom of heaven is like a treasure hidden in a field..."
(Matthew 13:44a)

15 ~ REBIRTH

AD 16
Eilat, Port City on Red Sea, Arabah Desert, Idumea

As Zarus and Pesachya approach Eilat, they see a giant sand dune pushed up against the city wall. The gates had been closed during the storm, so once reopened, those passing through must either climb the sand dune—a precarious proposition considering the lack of density—or shovel his way through. They choose the lowest part of the dune and carefully climb it.

They ride through the market, or what is left of it. Canopies have collapsed. Booth counters have been torn away. Produce is scattered around the streets, and all is covered with sand.

Progress is slow because stirring up the dust left behind is like walking through the ashes after a fire. A new path is created by horse hooves and steps of man.

Once back home, Zarus gratefully sees the gate still intact. He knocks loudly and calls for Penina to unbar it.

"Are you okay, master Zarus? We were so worried about you," she says as she opens the gate.

"Yes, we were lucky to find shelter. Where is Devorah? I must see her. There you are, my dear. Go with me up to the roof. I have something important to tell you."

Devorah's hair is down in her eyes. There is dust all over the courtyard. Zarus does not notice.

"What's wrong, Zarus? What happened out in the desert?" she asks as she takes her husband's arm and heads toward the ladder leading up to their flat roof.

"Oh, I forgot I had Penina take everything down just before the storm hit," she says.

"That's fine. We'll sit on the ledge."

Zarus helps her up the sturdy ladder by staying close behind her. They arrive and sit side by side. He looks at her as though he has been reborn.

"Devorah, the most wonderful thing has happened." He pauses to tease her a little. He stares at her, making her wonder what he is up to.

"I have found a new vein of copper."

She stares back at him, brushing a wisp of hair out of his eye. "A what?"

"A new vein of copper. And it is right on top of the ground. It will not require burrowing under a mountain."

"Are you teasing me, Zarus? If so, it isn't funny."

"I'm not teasing you. It's the truth. Get Khemoh out, and we'll ride out into the desert. I'll show it to you if you need proof."

"You're serious, aren't you?"

"I've never been more serious. But there is one catch. It's not on the same land as the mine your brother deeded over to me. Close, but not on it. We've got to buy the land."

"How much will it cost? We have no money, Zarus."

"I am on my way to the magistrates' *officium* to find out who owns it. If the owner lives here, I will go to his home tonight."

———

"Hector?" Zarus responds to the clerk. "The owner of that land is Hector? A Roman then."

"Yes."

"Where can I find him?"

"He is a ship captain. The *Celox*, I believe," the aging clerk says.

"Do you know if the ship is in?"

"That I do not know. Why don't you go down and look?"

"It's running late."

"I doubt the captain goes to bed very early. If you do not find him on board his ship, try the taverns."

Zarus stops in the market to buy a torch since the sun is fast going down. He proceeds to the harbor and looks for the ship, *Celox*.

His heart races as he spots it and walks up the plank. "Permission to come aboard," he says to the sailor on guard duty.

"State your business."

"I am looking for your captain, Hector."

"He is not here. He may be at one of the taverns."

"What does he look like?"

"He's a big man. Bulky too, but it's all muscle. He has red hair. Are you a spy?"

"No, I'm not a spy. And even if I were, it sounds like he could take care of himself. Thank you, kind sir."

Zarus walks back down the plank and looks for the nearest tavern. He knows there will be plenty in this part of town. At each place, he describes the captain, and at each place, he is told Hector is not there.

Finally, at the fourth tavern, he sees Hector. He is sitting at a table with five other men and laughing heartily. He finishes his drink and slams his mug down upside down with a thump and a guffaw.

"There! You see, I can out drink all of you," he pronounces.

Zarus approaches but says nothing.

Hector looks over at him. "May I help you, sir?"

"Yes, I understand you own some land out in the desert. May I talk to you about it?"

"Okay, men, time to get lost. I have important business to take care of. And don't drink too much while you're gone."

The five men grab their mugs, laugh, scoot their benches back, and saunter to another table.

Zarus seats himself.

"Your men seem to really like you, sir."

"Yeah, I think they do. Kind of like a father figure, though I can't imagine why."

"Do you have children at home?"

"Actually, my wife just gave me my first child just before I left on this voyage. A son. Named him Livianus. Got red hair just like his father. You have any kids?"

"My wife is due to deliver any day. We live here in the city. Now, what I came to talk to you about..."

"Yes, let's get to the point. The night is yet young, and I have plans."

"I understand you own some land out in the desert."

"That I do, but cannot imagine why anyone would want to own a desert. I inherited it from my uncle. Seems his own sons didn't want it. Don't blame them. All I do is pay annual taxes on it."

"Well, I may be interested in buying it."

"What in the world for? Not that I doubt your sincerity, but why?"

"I used to work out in that desert at a copper mine. It collapsed, and that sand storm yesterday covered most of the mountain completely. My brother-in-law signed the worthless thing over to me and went to Egypt. I had good friends when I worked there. I just want to have something adjoining it to remember the good times," Zarus lies. "Who knows? I may even build something out there."

"Are you crazy, man? Out in the desert?"

"Well, I have several ideas for it. Anyway, would you be interested in selling it, sir?"

Captain Hector scratches his clean-shaven chin and looks up at the ceiling with his green eyes.

"Well, sir," he finally says, "you'd have to buy the whole parcel. It's ten *acgers*. I would need 100,000 denari for it."

Zarus flinches, then calms himself. "Well, I don't have that much money right now, but I'm sure I could raise it. How long will you wait for my decision?"

"Two months. That's how long it will take me to return to Greece, get rid of my cargo, and be back here."

Smiling, Zarus holds out his hand. "Agreed." The two men shake hands, and Zarus stands. It is a pleasure doing business with you. I assure you, I will have the 100,000 denari ready for you upon your return."

"By the way," Zarus says before leaving, "what is your usual cargo?"

"Copper."

———

Zarus receives a light for his torch from the innkeeper and heads for home. As he walks through the narrow and dark streets, he has the feeling he is being followed. *But why would anyone follow me? Everyone knows I am out of work.* He looks back, sees no one, and rushes on toward home.

"Sweetheart," Zarus tells Devorah once inside their home. "Come back up to the rooftop. I need to tell you what I learned."

Once again, they wade through the sand on the rooftop and sit on the ledge.

"I found the owner. He is a sea captain. It is in a parcel of ten *acgers,* and he is willing to sell it if I buy all ten."

"How much?"

"One hundred thousand denari."

Devorah's eyes widen, and her mouth drops open. "What did you say? We don't have that kind of money."

"We will sell whatever we have to buy the field."

"We would have to sell everything."

"In that case, that is what we will do."

"What will we start with?"

"I think the chariot your father left me. It was already down here when he died since he'd come to enter the chariot race. I haven't ridden in it. I think I can get 10,00 denari for it."

"Where will you find a buyer?" she asks.

"Don't forget they have chariot races here once a year. Remember when your father came down to enter?"

"But that's not for seven more months."

"Well, I can get names. I'll find whoever is in charge of it this year and get the names and cities of all the last participants."

———

The prospective customer knocks on Zarus' gate, and Penina answers it.

"I'm here about the chariot."

"My master is around the other side at the chariot house. He said you couldn't miss it."

Avigdor walks around and sees a tall young man with blue eyes running a cloth over a chariot.

"I believe this is the chariot you have for sale?"

"Yes, sir. I inherited it from my father-in-law. Isn't she a beauty?"

"Well, she was in her day, I'm sure," Avigdor responds, running his hands across the silver filigree. "Looks like there is a little rust over there. That would have to be repaired."

"Perhaps I could repair it for you," Zarus replies.

"No, I need an expert."

"Then you're interested in it?"

"Depends on the price."

"For you, I can let it go for 25,000 denari."

"Oh, I can't go that high. I'm getting it for my son as a birthday present. He's been watching chariot races since I started taking him at age six, and always wanted one of his own."

"Well, since it's his birthday, I could lower the price to 24,000 denari.

"Agree to 14,000 denari, and you've got a deal."

"Oh, I couldn't possibly go that low. Look at all the silver on it. There's even a little gold somewhere. Would you give me 20,000 denari?"

"How about 16,000 denari?"

"Would you give 18,000 denari?"

"It's yours," Zarus tells Avigdor, proud of his negotiating skills. *Got more out of it than I thought I would.*

"Do you have a horse?"

"I've got three Arabians. Would you like them? They are 5000 denari each," Zarus replies, excited over his good luck with just one customer.

"No, I only need two. Let me see them, and I'll think about it."

Zarus walks Avigdor around the outside of the building and back in through another door leading to the stalls. There he keeps his Arabian horses, thanks to the mating of Shalva the previous year with a local mare and having twin colts.

"Well, two of them are pretty young. How about the big one?"

"He's not for sale. He was my father's prize, and he willed it to me. I can never sell him."

"He's a fine animal. I can see why you wouldn't want to sell him. I don't think I'm interested in the two yearlings. They're not broken yet, are they?"

"No, not quite yet."

"Well, how much for the twins?" Avigdor asks.

"I'll take 4500 denari for each of them,"

"I'll give you 3600 for each, and you break them for me."

"Sold. I can have them broken for you by next week. I used to break Arabians for a living," Zarus says with a broad grin.

"Fine. Go with me to the bank, and I'll pay you the 18,000 denari for the chariot now."

As they walk toward the bank, Zarus thinks how much closer he is to owning the copper deposit.

"Have you lived in Eilat long?"

"Not long to the locals who were born here, but I've been here going on eight years," Zarus replies.

"Haven't I heard of you before?"

"I don't know, but you probably knew my father-in-law Baaruch of Sychar. He was the owner of the chariot I am selling you, and used to enter the annual races here."

Arriving at the bank, they take care of their business. Avigdor gives Zarus the 1800 denari. "Here you are, my boy. By taking this, you also promise to save the two Arabian yearlings for me. You get the rest next week. When I come back, I'll expect the two Arabians hitched to the chariot and ready to go."

"Yes, sir. Do you want me to sign something?"

Avigdor hands Zarus two small clay tablets about the size of a woman's hand with the prices and items listed. The men etch their signatures, and each man gets one tablet for his records.

"Sir, it has been a pleasure doing business with you. I will see you at my house a week from today."

"Yes, you will. And I will be bringing my son with me. On that day, he will turn twenty, almost as old as you if I am guessing correctly."

Zarus walks back to his house. As he does, he prays thanksgiving to Jhehovah God. And, as always, he prays that something or someone will come along to unite him and his wife in their faith.

Before entering his house, he walks around to the stable where Pesachya stays. "We've got to start breaking these two Arabians first thing in the morning."

"Where will we do it?"

"Why, out in the desert, of course. If we leave just before daylight, the temperature won't be unbearable."

"Yes, master," Pesachya says.

Zarus walks back to his front gate, knocks, and is let in by Penina.

"Devorah," he shouts. "Are you here, Devorah?"

"There you are," she says, walking to the courtyard, barefoot, her dark hair in one pigtail down her back, one hand on her lower back, and the other over her womb. "Where have you been all day?"

"Making money for our very own you-know-what," he replies, glancing at Penina. "You haven't told anyone have you?"

"No, it's just between the two of us until you have it in your name. So how much did you get and what did you sell?"

"I got 18,000 denari for the chariot, and 7200 denari for the two yearling Arabians."

Zarus swings Devorah around in a circle. "Stop that! Your baby is going to become all twisted!" she says, laughing.

"Oh, I forgot."

"So, you sold two Arabians. What about the Egyptians I inherited from Father?"

"You wouldn't mind if we sold them?"

"As long as you don't sell my Khemoh."

"Okay, I'll see what I can do tomorrow."

———

The next day at mid-morning, Zarus heads back to the municipal *officium*. There he takes a parchment out of his leather bag and posts a sign: FOR SALE THREE EGYPTIAN HORSES, PERFECT FOR THE LADIES. SEE AT HOME OF ZARUS ON PALM STREET.

He is gratified to see two men reading it as he leaves.

Next, he goes down to the waterfront and posts a sign.

Then he walks over to the market place and looks around for a booth selling horse feed or horse equipment. He sees the latter and walks over.

He pulls out another parchment and shows the owner of the booth. "May I post this sign at your booth?"

"Sure. Why not? How long do you want me to leave it up?"

"Until I come to take it down, hopefully in the next few days. And thank you, sir."

"Hmmm... I think I'll try the city well. Perhaps there is a post near where the women line up to get their day's supply of water. Zarus is duly rewarded. Both the post and women are there. Some cannot read, but those who can immediately tell those who cannot read what it says, and excitement grows among them.

Finally, he goes to a booth at the market, selling fine jewelry, and receives permission to post his sign.

When he arrives home, there is a litter in front of his gate with four servants at the end of each poll, standing at attention, and one standing next to the litter. He walks forward.

"Are you the one who posted the sign for Egyptian horses for sale?"

"Why, yes, I am," Zarus replies with a grin.

"My mistress is interested."

With that, the servant opens the curtain of the litter and helps the lady out.

"Madam," Zarus says as he tips his head in a gesture of respect.'

"My name is Aida."

"Before you go any further, may I invite you into my home for some refreshment?"

"I am afraid I am in a little bit of a rush. I am visiting here from Arabia. Of course, all the horses you see there are Arabian. I rather like Egyptian horses. Though they are somewhat smaller than Arabians, they are more delicate and fancy. I have two daughters. I would like to purchase your three Egyptians if they meet with my approval."

"Yes, madam. If you will follow me, they are in the stable over there."

Rather than get back in her litter, the exotic lady who Zarus takes to be a princess of some kind, follows behind Zarus, her arm through the arm of her spokesman.

They arrive at the stable, and Zarus leads the three Egyptians out. Aida looks inside the stable and sees a fourth Egyptian.

"Oh, she is exquisite. I know I would like to have her."

"Forgive me, madam, but that is my wife's horse, and I could never sell her. I hope you understand."

"How refreshing to meet a husband looking out for his wife's interests instead of money. Well, how much do you want for the three you brought out to me?"

"I thought of 3000 denari for each one."

"That is fine, young man."

Zarus' eyes widen. *She didn't even bargain with me.*

"Abu, pay the man 9000 denari."

The transaction is completed, Princess Aida—Zarus is convinced she is a princess—and her entourage leave, Abu now walking behind the litter holding the reins of three Egyptian horses.

Zarus starts to knock on his gate to get in when it is opened by Pesachya.

"I hope you don't mind, master, but I was listening with the gate ajar. Come in. I'm sure Mistress Devorah will want to hear your good news."

"Devorah," Zarus says, forgetting to acknowledge Pesachya's comments and walking toward the kitchen area.

"Devorah, Jhehovah God is with us."

They walk into their bedroom and sit side by side on the bed. "I have just made another 9000 denari."

"How?"

"I sold three of your Egyptian horses."

"Oh! You didn't sell mine, did you? Tell me you didn't."

"I didn't. I have kept back your Khemoh and my Shalva. They will always be ours."

"So, now, how much do we have toward buying the ten *acgers*?"

"Well, we will have 34,200 denari by next week after we complete the sale on the two yearling Arabians."

"We're one third there, but it's not enough," Devorah says. "We have run out of things to sell. Where are we going to get the rest of the 100,000 denari? It's impossible."

Devorah suddenly feels a sharp pain in her chest. She turns her back on Zarus, looking down at the floor, and clutches at the pain."

"What is it, Devorah, my pearl?"

"Oh, nothing. I was just praying."

"The kingdom of heaven is like treasure hidden in a field. When a man found it, he hid it again, and then in his joy went and sold all he had...." (Matthew 13:44)

16 ~ SWEPT AWAY

AD 16
Eilat, Port City on Red Sea, Arabah Desert, Idumea

"*I*f we think it through, we can find the other 75,800 denari."

"Well, I hope you're not thinking of getting rid of Penina and Pesachya," Devorah responds. "I couldn't bear it. They've been with my family nearly my whole life."

Devorah stands and walks as quickly as she can into the courtyard. Zarus follows and embraces her.

"Oh, my love, I'm not thinking about that. If Jhehovah God wants us to have the treasure land, he will help us."

Devorah leans her head against his chest and weeps.

"What's wrong?"

"I don't know. You've sold all but one of the horses I inherited from Father. I don't regret that you did; I know you had to. But, they were kind of a tie for me to my father. His memory is growing so dim, and, well…Ohhh!"

"What? Devorah, are you okay?"

"Ohhh!" she says, holding her bulging abdomen. "I think my birthing pains have begun."

"Penina," Zarus calls out. "Penina, where are you? Come quickly."

"Master, what… Oh, bless us all," she says, smiling with a sympathetic twinkle in her eyes, "it has begun."

Penina walks over to Devorah, gently nudges her from her husband, and puts one arm across her shoulders and the other at her elbow. "Let's walk around the courtyard. It will hasten delivery."

"How long will it take?" Devorah groans, fear in her eyes."

"Well, it could take until midnight, or this time tomorrow. I suspect the wee one will be born by morning."

"What can I do," a confused Zarus asks, standing alone.

"I'm not a midwife, but I know about childbirth. Wait until her birth pains are half an hour apart, then go get the midwife. You do have one picked out, don't you?" she inquires of Zarus.

"Yes, we do."

"Oh, Zarus, that's just another expense," Devorah says,

"It is an expense I am prepared for," Zarus says with a wide grin. "Apparently, midwives like to be paid in fine fabric, so I wrote my sister to send down enough linen to make one full-length stola."

"Still, that's an expense we couldn't afford."

"She gave it to me. Kind of as a birthday present."

"Oh, Estar, she is such a jewel. How I miss her," Devorah says, sitting down to rest.

"So, my dear one," Zarus says, sitting next to her, "that is one thing I forbid you to worry about."

"Oh, silly. I should have known." Devorah lays her head on her husband's shoulder. "Ohhh! Ohhh!"

"There goes another one," Penina says with a sympathetic grin. "Poor baby. Poor girl. But it will pass, and this time tomorrow, you will be holding your own precious son or daughter. Now, let's get up and walk some more."

"We don't have a birthing stool," Devorah objects as she begins her third lap around the courtyard.

"The midwife will bring one with her. Now, don't you go worrying about all this. You just concentrate on bringing that wee one into the world."

She makes a few more slow laps around the courtyard, then sits next to her husband to rest.

Once again, she lays her head on Zarus' shoulder and closes her eyes.

He puts an arm around her. "I'm so proud of you, my pearl," he whispers.

An hour goes by. Another hour.

"Oh, I almost neglected your dinner, Master Zarus," Penina says. "After Mistress Devorah's next birth pain is over, I will go prepare something for you. We can't neglect the father, you know."

Three more hours. Zarus has eaten, and alternately holds his wife during her times of rest, and tells jokes or quotes from the song of Moses whenever she goes into birthing pain or whittles a stick of acacia wood whenever she walks in her circle in the courtyard.

"It's time," Penina finally says. Her pains are close enough. Go get your midwife, Zarus."

Zarus lights a torch and heads out into the dark street on his mission to at last become a father. He runs into a Roman patrol.

"Halt! State your business."

Zarus freezes in place.

"Uh, sir, my wife is about to deliver."

"I've heard that one before. The truth. Why are you sneaking around in the middle of the night?"

"I swear by all that is holy, that is what is happening."

"State your name. Where do you live?"

"I am Zarus of the Baaruch Copper Mine."

"I heard about that. Collapsed and killed a man."

"That's right, sir. I am the brother-in-law of Benyamin. He deeded the worthless mountain to me and went to Egypt. Now, may I continue on? My wife, Benyamin's sister, is..."

"Where does the mid-wife live?" the suspicious soldier asks.

"Please, sir. She is due to deliver any time."

"If you are who you say and doing what you claim, I will accompany you to the midwife's home and wait until she comes out. You will have to my count to fifty to get her out on the street with a birthing stool."

"Yes, sir. Follow me, sir," Zarus tells the soldier, breaking into a run, the soldier following.

They arrive, and Zarus knocks rapidly on the gate. The midwife comes out, and the soldier glances at her. "Follow me," he says, leading the way for the two to get back to Zarus' home.

"Thank you, sir," Zarus says upon their arrival.

"The soldier salutes and with a wink responds, "Good luck."

"Ohhh! Ohhh! Ohhh!" they hear while wrapping on the gate.

Immediately Pesachya opens it. "Time is getting close," he says with a grin.

"Ohhh!"

"Zarus, I think you and I need to go out to the stable," Pesachya say.

Zarus stands still, looking in the direction of the bedroom.

"But my wife..."

"The women will take care of her. We will just be in the way."

Finally, it is dawn. Zarus has whittled eight pieces of acacia wood down to nubs.

"Sir," he hears. It is Penina. "You are a father. I will let your wife show you what you have sired."

Zarus rushes into the house and to their bedroom. There Devorah lies in the bed with Zarus' child in her arms.

"What is it?"

"A boy, my love. You are the father of our baby boy."

He kneels at the bedside, kisses his wife, then takes a peek at his baby. "We shall name him Amram," he whispers. "After my father. Take the cover off of him so I can see everything about him."

"Devorah hesitates,"

"Quit teasing me. Take the blanket off him."

Slowly she moves it away from their son so Zarus can see all of him. He becomes confused. He stares at his son and then at Devorah. He reaches over and touches Amram's little club foot.

"We will love him," Devorah says.

"I shall find the best doctors for him. I've heard they can straighten babies' feet while their bones are soft."

"We don't have money for doctors, my sweet," Devorah says. We'll be okay. He will learn to walk just like any other little boy."

"I will find another job. I heard they are getting ready to expand the circus. They'll need strong men to lift the stones onto the new wall."

"They have machines to do that."

"Not for everything. I will go within the hour and get paid tonight. Our baby will have a doctor by tomorrow.

———

"It has been another month, and we are no closer to buying that land with the copper buried in it," Devorah tells her husband. He is by the gate, ready to head to work with the stonemason at the circus.

"I know. Perhaps it was a dream far beyond our reach. Captain Hector will be sailing into port any day now. I can't do it. Our treasure is as good as lost."

"No, my darling," Devorah says, nursing Amram. "You deserve it. You are smart. You know the copper business. You've been working for other people all your life, even though you are smarter than your bosses."

"Now, wait a moment, wife. Everyone is smart in their own way. I'm certainly not smarter than other people," Zarus objects.

"Devorah glares a moment at her husband, her head down, brows lowered, and eyes looking upward menacingly. "Move away from that gate and sit," she demands, her child suckling happily in his own little world.

"Yes, ma'am," Zarus responds half startled and half-amused.

"Just what's going on behind the most beautiful dark and mysterious eyes in the world?"

"I've been thinking about this for a long time," she says. "I have money. Remember the ten silver ingots my father left me?"

"Yes, I know you do. But your father left them to you to buy something special for yourself."

"Well, they aren't doing any good sitting in my coffer. Besides, what if someone finds out about them and they are stolen? No, they are safer if I spend them on something."

"Now, wait a moment," Zarus objects. "You are not thinking of…"

"Yes, that's exactly what I am thinking. You need—we need—to spend them on buying the *acgers* where the copper is."

"I forbid it," Zarus says.

"You can't forbid it. They're my ingots."

"No."

"Yes. Now, each of those silver ingots is worth 5000 denari. So all ten would be worth 50,000 denari. That would give us 84,200 denari. Then all we'd have to come up with to reach our 100,000 denari is another 15,800. Zarus, I've made up my mind. Go into our bedroom and bring out my coffer.

Zarus stares at his wife. He shakes his head. He looks over at one of the walls, then up at the sky open above the courtyard. Now back at his wife, he sees her smiling.

"It's what I want. There is such a little bit I will be able to give you in my lifetime, I want to do this."

"But, it will show that I need a female to help me."

"That's talk of young, foolish men. You, my husband, are wiser than that. You are not asking for it; I am giving it."

"But…"

"That's enough of that male foolishness. You are going to take my ten silver ingots, or I am planning to pout the rest of our married life, and that's a long time. You've never seen me in a major pout. You don't want to either. No, go get the ingots while I'm still smiling."

Zarus rises, goes into the bedroom, picks up his wife's cedar coffer, and brings it out to her. She hands baby Amram to his father and takes the coffer in her lap. She opens it with pride, her eyes gleaming.

She is so beautiful, Zarus thinks as he watches her.

"Okay. Here we are. Give the baby to Penina. Penina! Come here, please, and take the baby."

Penina rushes out and takes her new charge.

"Come sit beside me, Zarus."

He obliges, though still feeling awkward.

"Hold out your hand. One. Two. Three. Four. Five. Six. Seven. Huh? Eight? Nine? That's all? Where is the tenth one? Zarus, we've been robbed."

"Oh, I'm sure the other one is around here somewhere."

Trying to remain calm, she says, "Well, on our way out the gate, will you send for Pesachya? We've got to find that missing coin."

Zarus leaves for work, and soon Pesachya has joined the two women.

"Pesachya, I am missing one of my silver ingots."

He shuffles and looks at Devorah, his forehead wrinkled and brows drawn together. "Mistress, I did not take them. You must believe me."

"Of course, I believe you, Pesachya. I want you to go out to the stables and look for the ingot. Maybe the coffer fell open when I got home from the funeral, and one dropped out when I took it from my leather bag."

"Yes, Mistress. Right away."

"Well, maybe I'll go with you."

The two go out to the empty stables. She had not been in them since Zarus had sold the two Arabians and three Egyptians. Only two horses left. So empty.

"Pesachya, you take the stalls on that side, and I'll take them on this side."

"Please, oh God, help me find the ingot," she whispers as she bends down to look through the hay. She knows the hay that was there when they arrived home from the funeral has long been gone and replaced many times. She pulls as much of it up as she can to expose the bare ground under it.

"Pesachya, hand me a hand spade. I want to scrape along the top to see if they've been trampled over."

Pesachya hands it to her and goes to the other end of the stable to fetch another one for himself.

Half an hour passes. An hour. Two.

Pulling aside hay. Scraping the ground beneath it. letting the hay drop a little at a time in case logic is defied by reality, and perchance the ingot has been caught up in the new hay.

Knees aching but still searching.

"We've covered the whole stable as well as the carriage house. It is not out here, Mistress."

"You're right. Surely we would have found it. Let's go back to the house. It has to be there somewhere."

"I need you to search through the large water and grain vats. Empty them. Turn them upside down to make sure everything is out. If the ingot isn't there, search through the grain to see if it's there."

Devorah goes to her bedroom and stands in the doorway. *Where do I start? What's going on? Why is my ingot missing, and only one of them? Why not all of them?*

She drops to her knees. "God, help me find the missing ingot." She lowers her head and looks under the bed. She crawls all the way under, feeling with her hands as she goes. To her left. To her right. Feeling and searching and seeking.

Nothing.

She backs out from the bed and goes to a table with a bowl and pitcher of water. She empties the pitcher and feels around inside of it. Nothing.

She turns to look elsewhere, and her hand brushes the bowl of water. It falls, shatters on the floor, its pieces fly. She kneels back down on the floor, crawls around, picking up the pieces, and cries.

As she does, she lifts her eyes to the ceiling. "God, why is all this happening? Is this your way of saying we shouldn't buy the land with the copper in it? God, help me find my ingot."

She stands, tears still streaming down her cheeks.

"Mistress, I heard something break."

"It's the washbowl. Can you pick up the rest of the pieces on the floor?"

Devorah leaves her bedroom, deposits the broken pottery, and sits at a table in the courtyard.

"Mistress, I've looked everywhere I can think of—jars, wineskins, floor mats, wall tapestries. Penina has too."

"What about the roof?" Devorah replies with a renewed smile.

The three rush up to the roof and check everything they see. Lifting, shifting, moving things around. Still nothing.

Devorah leads them back down the ladder. She sits while her servants remain standing. Amram cries in the next room, Penina picks him up and brings him to his mother. "He must be hungry," Devorah whispers.

Cuddling and comforting her baby, she sighs. "We've tried everything. Thank you for helping. Zarus will be home soon. Let's get ready for him."

As Zarus comes into the courtyard, he says, "I've been worried about you all day. Did you find your missing ingot?" He pauses and looks at his wife. "I guess not."

He walks over and sits in a chair near hers. He leans toward her. "Sweetheart, I'm doing pretty good on this new job. They've told me about another building project coming up, and they want me to go with them. Maybe we won't have a rich copper mine, but I can support us well with this new job."

"You're not giving up. That ingot has to be around here somewhere. I'll find it. Heed my words. I'll find it."

After their meal, Zarus walks around the courtyard picking up jars and looking under them. Checking under floor mats and wall tapestries. Bending down on his knees to search under the table. Repeating everything the others had spent the day doing, and with the same result. Nothing.

The household is quiet that evening. The parents take turns playing with the baby.

"How are the doctor treatments working with Amram? His foot looks a little straighter than it used to be. Don't you think?" Zarus asks.

"Hmmm, what?"

"The baby's foot."

"Yes. The doctor said he needs another payment."

"I'll deliver it to him tomorrow as soon as I've been paid."

———

Morning, and Devorah is humming.

"What has gotten into your pretty head, my sweet?" Zarus asks.

"Ohhh, nothing," she says with a grin. I think Amram and I will go for a walk today."

"That will be good for you. Get your mind off, well, things."

"You run off to work, Zarus. We'll be fine today."

As soon as Devorah hears the gate shut, she calls Penina and Pesachya to her.

"As you know, Zarus and I have been gathering our funds together. You may not know why. You are not to tell anyone what I am about to tell you. Zarus has found some land with copper in it, and he is trying to buy it. I'm not going to let him lose his dream. I want the two of you to go to your friends serving families in the richer parts of town. Tell them our furniture is for sale."

"Mistress, no!" Penina says. "You got some of it from your mother. The other pieces you handpicked, sometimes right off the ship that imported them. You cannot sell your furniture."

"Thank you for your concern, but my mind is made up. We have some beautiful pieces and should be able to get a good price for them. Now, do as I say and tell your friends to tell their mistresses. I will be here all day receiving prospective buyers. Go, now."

As the day progresses, one piece of furniture after another is sold to the proud new owners of society's elite in the city of Eilat.

By the time Zarus arrives home, there is only a mat on the floor in the bedroom, and a straw mat for meals in the courtyard left. Devorah has placed cushions on the floor to sit on the way ordinary people do. She greets him at the gate, wearing one of her nicer mint green gauze tunics. Her hair has a matching ribbon woven through a single dark braid going down her back.

"Sweetheart, I'm home," Zarus says as he steps through the gate. He stops, looks at his beautiful wife with pleasure, kisses her, and holds her close. As he looks beyond her, he is startled. He pulls Devorah from him.

"What happened? Where is our furniture?"

"I sold it. I still have 35,000 denari worth of silver ingots, and I made 3300 more denari today on the furniture. So, adding that 38,300 to the 34,200 we already had, and now we have 72,500 denari. We are so close to getting our 100,000 denari.

"But the ship came in today. I don't have the money to give Captain Hector. The deal is dead. The mine is dead."

"Sweetheart, the ship hasn't sailed away yet. It has to have time to unload and then take on new cargo. We still have a few days left. We'll think of something. We're so very close." Devorah looks up at her husband and smiles, though he detects a tear in her eye. "We'll think of something."

That night, they sleep on the floor.

"Remember when we used to do this?" Devorah whispers in the dark.

"Yes. I had just finished paying for you and was as poor as a beggar on the street."

"But we were happy then, even without fancy furniture."

"I suppose so, my dear." He turns over and tries to sleep. Eventually, the night is over, and he is able to rise and go to work where his mind can be kept on the structure and off his money woes.

Devorah is left alone with the baby.

Hmmm. While Penina is at the market, I may as well sweep the floor.

She begins in the kitchen end of the courtyard. She sweeps carefully around the oven. She picks up all the pots she can manage and puts them on shelves. She sweeps where they had been. She takes hold of the large vats, tips them, and rolls them on the bottom edge to a new spot so she can sweep under them.

The kitchen area done, she goes up on the rooftop. It is always very dirty up there, what with catching all the sand off the desert whenever there is a slight breeze. She picks up straw mats and sweeps under them. She moves aside pots and vats as she had in the kitchen area and sweeps under them.

That done, she returns to the courtyard and finishes sweeping it, picking up the cushions they had sat on the night before and will tonight. She picks up the straw mat that had served as a table the previous night and sweeps under it.

She goes to the bedroom of her son and sweeps under the mat on the floor that serves as his bed, and a mat with squares of wool on it used on the baby little bottom whenever they are away from home. Also on the mat are swaddling bands. Devorah sweeps under both mats.

Next, she goes into the bedroom she shares with her husband. She lifts the mat off the floor and sweeps under it. She lifts the pitcher of water and sweeps under it. She goes to a straw mat to set their shoes on under hooks on the wall for their clothes. She lifts the mat and sweeps under there.

She hears a clang. *Oh, it was just my imagination.* She sweeps the dust toward the door and hears the clang again. She looks down at the small pile of dirt but sees nothing.

She sweeps the dust as far as the doorway and hears the clanging once again. She stoops down and stirs the dust with her fingers. Something bright shines through the dust. Trembling, she picks it up, stares at it, turns it over in her hand, and clings to it tightly. Tears come to her eyes.

Thank you, Almighty God. Thank you.

She stands. "I found it! Penina, I found it! The missing ingot! It was lost, and I found it.

Once again, Devorah dresses up. This time she wears a pale blue silk tunic.

When Zarus comes home from work that evening, she greets him at the gate, grinning broadly.

"My darling, look." She holds out her hand with the silver ingot in it.

"Zarus' eyes enlarge, his mouth opens, and he stares a moment.

"My beloved," she continues. "My silver ingot was lost, and I have found it. Furthermore, I sold the pearl my father left for me. It brought 6000 denari. So, now, my dear, we have 93,500 denari."

"No, not your pearl? Who did you sell it to?"

"I sold it to the mayor's wife."

"Well then, I hope her health holds out because someday I am going to buy that pearl back for you."

Devorah smiles and whispers, "You don't have to."

Zarus draws his wife close, and they sway back and forth. "So close. But the ship is leaving in the morning. You have sacrificed everything, and we have nothing left to sell."

Changing the subject to ease the burden of the moment, Devorah says, "The baby lifted his head by himself today."

"What about his foot? What is the doctor saying?"

"He keeps saying he can twist his foot back around some, but he may be crippled the rest of his life."

Zarus grows more depressed. He sits and puts his head in his hands. "How can things be going so wrong for us? Nothing is working out right. Nothing."

"Well, after we eat a bite of something, let's go for a ride. It will be Amram's first trip outside the house."

I cannot let her see me so discouraged. Zarus lifts his head and calls out, "Pesachya, get our horses ready. We're going for a little ride out into the desert."

Shortly the horses are ready. Zarus takes the baby while Pesachya helps Devorah up on her Egyptian. He mounts his Arabian, and they head out of town.

They arrive at the city gate. Zarus knows the guard on duty.

"Sir, are you going very far? We're going to be closing the gates pretty soon."

"We won't be gone long. We're just taking our baby for a little ride."

"Did I hear baby? I see you had your baby after all."

Zarus looks over at the stranger and realizes it is Captain Hector, riding in through the gate on a fine Arabian stallion.

"Sir, how good to see you, captain. May I introduce my wife, Devorah. And this is our son, Amram."

"It is too bad we do not live closer. Your Amram would enjoy playing with my Livianus," the sea captain says.

"Indeed, they would," Zarus replies. "Oh, and about the land, I wanted to buy from you. I was planning to come to see you in the morning before you set sail. And, well, I am short. I have raised all but 6500 denari. I have run out of ideas."

"I see you ride an Arabian like I do. Fine animals, especially for desert riding. The Bedouins do a magnificent job of raising them. Hmmm. Your wife rides one of those delicate Egyptians. My wife likes Egyptian horses also. Many women prefer them."

"Yes, sir."

Captain Hector directs his horse to the side of the road. "I believe we are holding up people behind us," he says.

Zarus and Devorah follow him.

"I tell you what," Hector continues, "sell me your two horses, and we have a deal."

"What?" Zarus says, stunned.

"Sell me your two horses, and you can have the ten *acgers*. I can't imagine why you would want land out in the middle of a desert, but if you're in favor of it and can afford it, I say it's a deal. The land is yours."

Zarus looks over at Devorah. He does not know whether or laugh or cry.

She understands. She smiles. "Yes, my darling, we shall sell Khemoh and Shalva."

"May we deliver them to you in the morning, sir? We've become very attached to them."

"Of course. I understand. I shall meet you at the magistrate *officium,* and I will sign the deed over to you."

"And, sir, would you not forget us and give us a chance to buy them back, or even the offspring of our horses, should we ever be in a position to do so?"

"Good idea. I will keep you in mind and give you first opportunity."

The two men shake hands, and Zarus and Devorah continue their ride out into the desert. They are quiet.

"It's so hard to believe, Zarus. You are going to be the owner of a rich copper mine."

"But what good will it do me, Devorah? It has occurred to me that I have no way to hire workers or purchase tools, wagons, and oxen. Where am I going to get the money for those things?"

"Or suppose a woman has ten silver coins and loses one. Does she not light a lamp, sweep the house and search carefully until she finds it?

And when she finds it, she calls her friends and neighbors together and says, 'Rejoice with me; I have found my lost coin.'

In the same way, I tell you, there is rejoicing in the presence of the angels of God over one sinner who repents." (Luke 15:8-10)

"The kingdom of heaven is like treasure hidden in a field. When a man found it, he hid it again, and then in his joy went and sold all he had and bought that field. (Matthew 13:44)

17 ~ THE PARTNER

AD 16
Jhericho, Province of Jhudea, Palestine

"Thank you, Mother, for letting Amram and I stay with you while Zarus is gone. Uncle Caalev doesn't mind?"

"He loves it when I spend the winters at his home. Besides, that's what mothers are for, my dear: To rescue their daughters when their sons-in-law cannot take care of them."

Avigail and Devorah are in Caalev's mosaic-tiled courtyard. Devorah is playing with her baby son while Avigail embroideries the bottom of a new linen tunic.

"Oh, Mother. Let's not get into that again."

"Well, if he hadn't caused your father's mine to collapse, you wouldn't be in this mess."

"So, how is Benyamin doing over in Egypt?" Devorah says to change the subject. "Do you ever hear from him, Mother?"

"Not very often. He is very busy. He is determined to find a gold mine, your father's dream, you know. He plans to name it in honor of your father—the Baaruch Gold Mine."

"I wish him luck. Speaking of luck, when I was packing to come and stay here while Zarus went up north, his boyhood friend, Gersshon, came. He'd been at sea a long time. Said he knew more about sailing than any of the sea captains he had met and has decided to check into buying his own ship."

"Is that so?"

"Anyway, he needed a place to rent for a while, so Zarus let him sublet our house. It worked out perfectly."

"Well, at least one thing is perfect," Avigail says. "On the other hand, what's going to happen to poor Amram with the club foot?"

"Our doctor worked on his foot every week, and sometimes more often. He even wrapped the foot up to try to force it back in place."

"None of which worked, I must say. Poor child. Needs a proper physician."

"Do you know a good one here in Jhericho? I have a little money since Gersshon is paying a little more than our own rent is."

"As a matter of fact, I do. Would you like me to send a servant out to make an appointment for you?"

"That would be wonderful."

"And, no need to pay. Caalev gives me a liberal weekly allowance."

"Oh, thank you, Mother. You have such a good heart."

"Well, I feel sorry for that baby boy. He's going to have a hard life with a club foot. The other children will make fun of him, some of the parents won't let their children play with him because of a foolish notion that it is catching, and when he is grown, he'll have a hard time finding a job."

"Maybe Amram will grow up to be just like Father. Don't you think he looks like Father?"

"Absolutely not."

Sebaste, Province of Samaria

"So, the prodigal returns." It is Reuven. Zarus' oldest brother stands at the copper gate of the family farmhouse. He looks around. "Where's Father's horse? Dead? You never did treat him right. You didn't deserve him. Had to walk here, did you? Serves you right."

"Reuven, I did not come here to argue. Will you let me in?"

"Oh, forgot my manners, little brother." He moves out of the way, bows, and sweeps his arm toward the courtyard.

"Hey, everyone. Our idiot brother has come home to roost. Or maybe he came home to roost."

Shimeon and Levii come to the courtyard laughing and patting each other on the back. "So glad you're back, little brother," Shimeon tells Levii. "Oh, I couldn't wait to come home and ask for money," Levii tells Shimeon, mocking.

The three men sit on cushions and motion for Zarus to join them. He is not given a cushion, but joins them anyway.

"I may as well get right to the point. I have discovered a rich deposit of copper in the Timna Valley and have bought the land surrounding it."

"Yeah, right! Our brother rich? Never happen," says Levii.

"Now, what I need..."

"I knew it," Shimeon says, slapping his knee.

"Wait. It's just an investment and should come easy for you. You already have some of what we need. You've already got wagons, and you've already got oxen. We'll need those to deliver the ore to ships for distribution all over the world."

"So? You're not getting our wagons and oxen for your business."

"It wouldn't be my business; it would be our business. You would be part owners."

"And let baby brother be our boss? No way."

Hurrying with his proposition before being run off by his brothers, Zarus rushes to tell the rest. "The only money I—we—would need is to buy hammers and chisels, and for wages to the workers."

"The *only* money, he says. You would need a hundred men to work that mine, if it does have the copper you claim it has," Shimeon says.

"And of course you would control the money, and we'd get a penance back for our so-called share. No way, little brother. You're not getting a single mite from us," Reuven says.

"We have a successful farm and are not going to help you run after a crazy scheme like mining. You're the one who deserted us, remember?"

Reuven stands. "Brother, we were just getting ready to receive a broker for our barley, so you need to leave before he arrives." Reuven walks to the gate, opens it, and stands, glaring at Zarus.

The other two brothers rise but say nothing. Zarus looks around and feels the silence rise up as though to choke him. He clenches his fists. He stares at Shimeon, then Levii. Finally, he stares at Reuven at the gate and walks through it. The gate is fast slammed shut behind him. Zarus walks away.

Sychar, Province of Samaria

"Well, if it isn't my big brother. How have you been, Zarus? I know things have been rough since the, since..."

Zarus watches the ever nearby tears come to Estar's eyes. He takes hold of her shoulders and draws her close to him.

"I am so sorry. Micha was a good man. I don't know how you have handled it, losing three husbands."

Estar lays her head on Zarus' chest and weeps silently at first. Then she gives in to it and trembles in her grief.

He puts his strong hand on her head and gently weeps with her.

Moments later, she raises her head, wipes her eyes with her hands, and steps back.

"What am I doing?" she says with a forced smile. "I should be welcoming my brother, and instead, I act like a fool while he stands in the gateway. Welcome, Brother. Welcome to my home."

Zarus smiles and walks into her courtyard. He looks around. "Seems as though you have been doing pretty good. Your house looks very nice."

"It's nice enough for my kids and I. We are satisfied. The fabric business keeps us from starving. Please say you will stay. You can have my bedroom. I promise not to cry anymore."

"I would be honored to stay with you, Estar. Is there anything I can do around here for you so you won't have to hire it out?"

"Well, one of the shutters in my bedroom is coming off the hinge. Could you put it back on? And there is a crack in my oven. Could you patch it for me?"

"I'd be glad to. Did Micha leave any tools here I could use?"

The next morning, Estar asks Zarus if he is just on vacation or on business.

"A little of both, I think. It is nice to get up in the mountains after living in the scorcher of a desert down there."

"What else?" Estar prods.

"Well, I'm looking for a business partner."

"A partner? What have you gotten into now?"

"I've bought some land, Estar. It has a rich vein of copper right on the surface. But the cost of the land took everything I have. I need a partner to pay for operating costs."

"I don't think I can help you there," Estar says. "But I'll be happy to introduce you to some of my business friends."

"That would be nice. But first, I think I'd like to go out and see Baaruch's house and stables. I know his wife inherited them and the land. But I'd just like to walk around out there. That's where I got to know Devorah. We would go riding together."

"You old softy, you," Estar says with a grin. "Okay. Enjoy yourself."

Zarus remembers the way: Walk past the market place and

exit out the city's back gate to and from the city. Baaruch's manor house and pasture are not far from there.

When he sees it in the distance, he remembers back. He sees Devorah riding past him on her Egyptian, her black hair flowing behind her, back arched and graceful.

The manor is boarded up. He knows Avigail will come back during the hottest part of the summer in Jhericho.

He walks around to the back to see the stables. He stops. Next to the stables in the pasture, a house is being built. A nice house. He walks over to the construction site to get a better look at what is being built on the land of earlier dreams.

"Well, if it isn't Zarus."

"Moshe! Well, I'll be. I guess Baaruch's widow parted with it to give herself a little income. Good thinking. So who are you building it for?"

"Good to see you, Zarus. Where are you staying? How long will you be here?"

"I'm staying with my sister; you remember her husband was killed when the mine collapsed. I'll be doing some repairs for her while I'm here."

"You asked who I'm building this house for. You wouldn't know him. He's new here. But, come take a look. Nothing but the best. It will be paneled with cedar from Lebanon. It will have copper doors. It will have five bedrooms. The courtyard will have marble columns holding up the bedrooms on the second floor. It will have its own bath. It's going to be quite a showplace."

"Sounds like it. Congratulations for landing the contract," Zarus says, looking around at the walls being erected with stones from the nearby mountains and approving of their methods.

"I was hoping I'd be building a house for you someday. One even nicer than Benyamin's. Too bad, the mine collapsed."

"Well, that is something you may still be able to do for me someday after all."

"How's that?" Moshe asks, walking Zarus around the beginnings of a new manor house.

"Moshe, the most wonderful thing happened. I discovered a vein of pure copper right on the surface of some land out in the Timna Valley. I bought ten *acgers*."

"Congratulations, Zarus!" Moshe says, patting the younger man on the back. "Good for you. You're not one to stay lying down. Good for you, young man."

"But I spent everything I had to buy it and have no way to buy chisels and hammers, wagons, oxen or camels, and hire men."

"Oh," Moshe says, looking down at the ground out of respect for Zarus' embarrassment.

He walks slowly away from Zarus.

Oh, no. I've made another enemy. Why did I have to bring it up? Zarus thinks to himself.

"Well, Moshe. It has been nice visiting with you, and good luck with your latest house."

Zarus begins to return the way he had come.

"Wait, Zarus. I think I have an idea."

"Huh?" Zarus stops and turns back around.

"I've been doing well with my construction business and have been looking for a side investment. Your mine may be just the thing I've been looking for. How much would I have to be involved?"

Zarus tries to control a sudden grin that wants to make an appearance. His head becomes light as though floating above the clouds. *It's falling right in my lap. Am I dreaming?*

"Well, you wouldn't have to be involved any more than you want to be. The biggest part would be hiring men. I'd like to get up to one hundred within a year. Someone would have to supervise them, but we could hire someone to do that," Zarus says, thinking out loud.

"Would 5000 denari start you out well enough?" Moshe asks.

"Of course, 5000 could get me started. I could hire twenty men right off with that. Sir, I'll pay you back."

"Well, pay me back in copper. I can always use copper spigots, doors, and decorations in my houses. And maybe also a copper necklace and earrings for my wife who is more patient with me than I deserve."

"It's a deal," Zarus says, finally letting his grin show itself in full force, teeth gleaming in the process.

Moshe holds out his hands. "Yes, it's a deal."

"Come down and see it for yourself. Devorah will be happy to see you. Can you bring your wife too?"

Eilat, Port City on Red Sea, Arabah Desert, Idumea

"Gersshon will be surprised to see us," Devorah says with a grin as they draw closer to their rented house.

"Oh, I forgot he is there. Well, he will enjoy hearing our good news.

"I'm sorry Mother blamed you for the mine collapsing. She just can't accept that it was just an accident."

"That's okay. At least I had a place to spend the night before finishing our trip home. It was nice getting to know your uncle, Caalev, a little better."

"Great uncle. He's my mother's uncle."

"Oh, yes, that's right. Well, we're almost there," Zarus says.

"It will be good to be home again. It's been a month. I hope Gersshon took good care of it."

"I'm sure he did, sweetheart. Well, here we are."

"Zarus raps hard on the gate to their home. Moments later, Gersshon opens it."

"Well, well. If it isn't my illustrious best friend and his illustrious wife and baby. Welcome to my—our— abode."

The young family enters their home. Zarus looks around. "I see you have bought some furniture."

"Just a few pieces. I like to have a table and stools."

"They look nice," Devorah says, taking a closer look at the tabletop. "I am going to put little Amram to bed now. You two men catch up with whatever you've been doing."

"So, how was being at sea? Different than being underground and hot?"

"The sea can be either one—cold or hot. Personally, I'd rather be hot than cold. Have to buy too many clothes when it's cold. So, how was your trip up north?" Gersshon asks while going into the kitchen area.

"As you know, I went looking for a silent partner in my new mine."

"Your new what?" Gersshon swings around and walks back toward Zarus.

"Didn't I tell you? I thought I did."

"I happened to be at sea, friend. Unless you can figure out how to talk loud enough I can hear you a thousand *milles* away, you didn't tell me."

Gersshon sits down on the bench by the table. "Join me and tell your old buddy all about it."

"I found a strain of good quality copper on the desert floor. I found out who owned ten *acgers* around it, and bought the land. That's why there wasn't any furniture here. We sold it all."

"Your horses too?"

"Our horses too. We sold everything, including Devorah's inheritance."

"What a woman," Gersshon replies, grinning and shaking his

head.

"So, where is it?"

"Out in the Timna Valley."

"When are you going to start actually mining it?"

"That's what I went up north for. I found a silent partner who will put up 5000 denari to buy wagons, oxen or camels, and hire workers. How fortunate is that?"

Gersshon stops smiling and studies Zarus. You needed a partner? Why didn't you ask me?"

"Because you were at sea. Remember?"

"Oh. Well, do I have a chance?"

"To be my partner? We already shook hands on it, Moshe and I."

"Is that the name of my competition? I don't believe I know him."

"He built Benyamin's manor house and the warehouses, but that was before our time. He was a long-time friend of Baaruch, Benyamin's father. He's also the one who built the shaft that got us out of the mine just before the whole thing collapsed."

"So, how much did he offer you?"

"Moshe offered me 5000 denari. He's going to come down and see my find, then give me the money."

"So I do have a chance. No money has changed hands yet."

"I don't know, Gersshon. I told him he could be my partner."

Devorah reappears and brings pomegranate juice to the men, then goes up on the roof.

"Would you change your mind if I offered you 6000 denari?"

"Where would you get that kind of money?"

"Do you doubt me, friend? With all my talents? Of course, I have 6000. I have 2000 right now. When we were trapped in the mine, I did some favors for the other miners, and they signed sandstone IOUs for me. They were desperate for what I had, so were willing to give me anything—their animals, their jewelry, their houses."

Zarus recalls the rats and wants to vomit. "Well, that's only 2000. Where's the other 4000?"

"I will have another 2000 for you by tomorrow."

"How could you come up with so much money in one day?"

"Wait and see."

Zarus does wait. All night he tosses in his sleep. He wakens Devorah.

"What is wrong, dear?" she asks in the middle of the night.

"I've already agreed on Moshe as my partner, but Gersshon is offering more money. What should I do? Betray Moshe, or be unable to hire those men at the city square and down by the docks begging for work?"

"I don't know the answer. Try to get some sleep. You will be able to think more clearly in the morning."

Morning comes, and Gersshon is in a singing mood.

"Gersshon, cut that out. You never could sing. It's driving us insane."

"Okay. But you'll need the right kind of partner who understands insane things like selling everything you have to buy a potential mine. What if it plays out after you go down a pace?"

"It won't."

The men eat their simple breakfast of fruit and cheese. "Well, I'll be on my way," Gersshon says, wiping his mouth on the back of his sleeve.

After Gersshon leaves, Zarus looks around to see if there are any blank scrolls where they used to keep them. There is one. He goes up on the roof, taking the scroll and a piece of slate to set the scroll on, and some blackening.

He sits cross-legged, places the slate and scroll on his lap, and dips his pen in the blackener. He pauses, stares, sets everything down beside him, gets up, and walks to the ledge overlooking the already-busy street below. He looks up into the heavens, "Oh, Jhehovah God, what am I going to do?"

He returns to his spot on the roof, but instead of sitting cross-legged, he falls to his knees and puts his head all the way down, facing north to Gerizim and Jherusalem. "Jhehovah God, I worship you. I depend on you. I am in a quandary. How do I choose between betrayal and men not being able to support their families? Show me a sign so I will know what to do."

Zarus pauses before rising. "And, Jhehovah God, Devorah and I both worship you in the same way, except I go to Mount Gerizim, and she goes to Jherusalem for our temple worship. Find a way to unite us, Jhehovah God. Find a way to unite us."

He rises back to his sitting position, sets the scroll back in his lap, dips his pen and draws a line down the middle of the scroll. *Everything on the left side will be reasons to stay with Moshe. Everything on the right side will be reasons to go with Gersshon.*

The sun is high in the sky. Zarus has one by one written reasons for going both ways. His confusion does not subside.

"There you are, Zarus, ole boy."

"Where have you been?" Zarus asks, looking up from his scroll.

"To the races."

"What races? It's morning."

"Chariot races. And it's not morning anymore."

Zarus sets aside the scroll and looks up into Gersshon's eyes.

"What were you up to there?"

"Tsk, tsk, tsk. You don't trust me. Well, I bet my entire 2000 denari, and guess what?"

"By your smile, you did okay, though I could never completely rely on your smiles."

"Right you are, old buddy. I doubled my money. I now have 4000 denari.

"You said you had 6000," Zarus reminds him.

"I do. Someone owes me 2000. Now, we can use 2000 to buy equipment, wagons, and oxen. We can use 2000 to build a warehouse. And we will use the last 2000 to hire workers. Having been at sea, I know exactly where to get them."

Zarus stands. "Are you sure about all this?"

"Of course, I'm sure. Have I ever lied to you, Zarus?"

"Yes, you have. Half the time when we were kids, you lied to me."

"Well, that was a long time ago. I am a changed man. I'm as honest as they come."

Gersshon reaches into the sash around his tunic and brings out a money bag. "Here you go, my friend: 4000 denari.

"Tomorrow, you go out and buy whatever you need and get them on site. I will go down to the docks and the city square and line up men to start working for us. How many do you want to start with?"

Zarus pours the coins out of the pouch, all silver coins but one which is gold.

"C'mon. How many men do you want me to hire for you—for us—tomorrow?"

"Well, I could use twenty to start with, but want to work up to one hundred."

"Good. I will have twenty for you—for us—out at our mine the day after tomorrow.

"But what about Moshe?"

"He already has a business. He'd be putting too much work on you. I can share the load with you."

"Now, tomorrow is going to be a busy day for both of us."

———

"Captain Athos, sir, I am selling stock in a new copper mine, just discovered. No one else knows where it is except my partner and I. It has high-grade veins of copper in it. I am selling stock in the mine."

Gersshon is at a tavern on the waterfront.

"I'm not really interested in investing in a mine. Besides, I don't have the money for it."

"I tell you what I will do. You carry slaves, do you not?"

"Yes."

"Okay, for every slave you give me, I will give you 1000 denari worth of stock. What do you say?"

"How do I know they're good?" the ship captain asks.

"I'm the owner of the mine. I can guarantee your shares will be good," Gersshon replies with a swagger.

"I'd have to see it in writing," the captain replies.

"How many slaves do you have onboard for sale?"

"I have twenty-two."

Gersshon reaches into a large pouch at his side, and hands Captain Athos twenty-two sandstone plates half the size of a man's hand. "Each one of these is one share in the mine. Now show me my slaves."

They leave the tavern. The captain takes Gersshon on board his ship, and orders twenty-two slaves brought up from the dark hold.

"They look satisfactory to me. Can you keep them until tomorrow? I won't need them until then. You have the certificates of stock already, but I trust you."

———

"Zarus, what are we going to tell Moshe? You said he's supposed to come down to look at your mine next week," Devorah says.

"I'll have to get a message to him telling him I don't need him after all."

"How could you betray him like this?"

"It was between him and being able to put fifty or a hundred men to work so they can support their families," Zarus replies.

"I don't trust him."

———

Work begins on the mine. It is open-pit with little risk of

accidents. Zarus and Gersshon hire back Saabhu as their engineer, Noach as their superintendent, and legless Yair—who had returned to begging for a living—as accountant and treasurer.

18 ~ THE JUDGE

AD 17
Sychar, Province of Samaria, Palestine

"It's so good to be back in my own home, Sarach. Before you put my clothes away, I need something to eat. I sent word to Eshachk to make sure there was food in the house before our arrival. Check to see if you have enough ingredients to make baklava. I'm starved."

Avigail licks her lips in anticipation of the sweetmeat, then walks over to a gilded seat, her pride and joy, gathers up the skirt of her long, white tunic trimmed in royal blue, and sits. *You magistrates and senators and kings think you're so important in your curule seat. Well, I've got one of my own. What do you think of that?*

She folds her hands, looks at the walls and doorways leading off the courtyard, and takes a deep breath. She crosses her feet and swings her legs. Her hands become busy, smoothing out the folds in her tunic. She sees a spot of dirt on her sleeve and flicks it off.

She takes another breath and stands. She walks over to a tapestry on the wall depicting the Maccabees brothers leading the Jews to victory over occupying Greeks. She had insisted on buying it, even though Jews refuse to have images in their house, lest they be worshiped.

"Hmmm, I never noticed that before. All the Maccabees have beards in this tapestry but Jonathan. Maybe he was too young to have a beard in this scene."

"What did you say, Mistress?" Sarach asks, walking into the room with a plate full of baklava.

"Oh, I was just taking a closer look at this tapestry. I don't think I ever paid much attention to it before. It just had the right colors, so I bought it."

"Yes, Mistress."

"Do you remember how long ago I bought it, Sarach?"

"I believe it was when Mistress Devorah was about five years old."

"That long ago? Oh, bring my sweet over to the table by the couch. I shall be reclining as any proper hostess would," Avigail instructs.

Sarach pauses long enough for Avigail to get herself situated on the couch with the bronze legs in the shape of a lion's head.

"Now, you may serve me."

The baklava is quietly set on the matching bronze table next to the couch, and Sarach returns to the kitchen at the far end of the courtyard.

Avigail picks up one piece, looks it over as though it were something precious, and takes a bite. She returns it to her plate, chews, then licks her fingers. The routine is repeated until the sweet has been consumed.

"Well, that was good," Avigail says, sitting up on the couch and licking her fingers one last time. She folds her arms as though to hug herself, and wanders once again around the courtyard, pauses to look up at the very blue sky overhead, and calls Sarach.

"Do you think it will rain tomorrow?"

"I don't know. Maybe. There are clouds up there."

"Well, I hope it doesn't. I think I want to go for a horseback ride tomorrow."

"Mistress, all the horses are gone."

"I know that, silly. I will rent my neighbor's horse."

"Of course, mistress."

Avigail goes up the staircase to the bedrooms upstairs and checks them for suitability for guests. *Now that I'm back, I know my old friends in Sebaste will want to come over and visit for a few days.*

She returns downstairs, sighs, and goes out toward the stables. As she walks, she swings her body, hugs herself, smiles, and looks at her feet.

Maybe I should buy a horse of my own for whenever I am in Sychar. Yes, that would be a good idea. I could hire Eshachk, Baaruch's old personal servant, to take care of it. I don't think he got any other job after Baaruch, after Baaruch, after…

Baaruch, why did you have to die? I know it's been three years, but I am still not used to it. If you'd lived just a little longer, you could have been mayor of Sychar by now. Now all that's gone. Now you're gone, and you're never coming back to me. Oh, Baaruch, how I miss you.

Avigail reaches a bench on the outside of the stable, sits, puts her hands up to her face, and cries.

That night Avigail goes into the bedroom she and Baaruch had shared over twenty-five years. She reaches over and touches his matching feather pillow. She draws it to her and hugs it. Tears come to her eyes, she turns over and buries her face in his pillow.

"Baaruch. Baaruch," she groans. "Why did you have to leave me? It's not fair. You weren't supposed to die. Come back, Baaruch. Come back to me. Don't leave me alone."

As the days go by, Avigail finds ways to occupy her time. *There used to be so much going on in this house as long as Benyamin and Devorah were at home, and Baaruch was here. Now they're all gone. Well, I must make a life for myself now.*

"I think I'll go into town, Sarach, and check out the fabrics. I wonder if Estar still has her fabric booth." *Poor girl. She has lost three husbands. How has she survived?*

After a few days, Avigail finds her way. She visits many of her old friends and tells them she is back to designing clothes—mostly tunics and shawls and cloaks, but sometimes a stola. She has her lady friends over for lunch. Sometimes she invites the mayor and his wife and a magistrate and his wife, but it is always awkward, what with Baaruch gone. Mostly she sticks with her lady friends.

Finally, summer in the mountains is over. Avigail loads up her clothes and anything special she wants to take back to Jhericho. She hires a litter, joins a caravan, and returns south. Sarach rides a donkey at her side.

Jhericho, Province of Judah

"Welcome back."

"It's good to be back, Uncle Caalev."

"Where did you get the money for a litter all that way?"

"Remember? I sold all the land except what the manor house and stable are on. I've got the money. Don't you worry."

"Isn't that just like my niece?" He replies with a grin.

"Uncle Caalev, I know this is your home. But would you mind me being the mistress of your house? I've lived here over two years. People are used to seeing me here now."

Caalev is sitting in his chair, reading through a scripture scroll. He looks up.

"I made some new tunics for my wardrobe," Avigail says,

taking another bite of raisin cake, "while up there and would like to show them off. Maybe I can pick up some customers here. Would it be okay if I invite the wives of some of the priests one afternoon?"

"I suppose."

"If I etch some invitations on little tiles, would you give them to the husbands at work?"

"No, I won't. But perhaps Elii will. He's enthusiastic and remembers his visit to your house a few years ago. Too bad, he turned down the offer to be rabbi at the Sychar synagogue."

"I sure wish Devorah had married him. Well, she didn't, so there is no use pining over it. Besides, Zarus hasn't done bad for himself, after all. A rich copper mine owner. Yes, you can give them to Elii."

Priest Caalev returns to his scroll.

"If it goes over well, I think I will contact Zarus to see if the wives of his officers would like to come up for a few days away from the desert and look at my fashions. What do you think, Uncle Caalev?"

"That's fine, niece," Caalev mumbles.

The day comes for her first showing of modest tunics for the wives of the priests.

"Oh, I love how you combine the colors, Avigail."

"Oh, I love how you double stitch the seams, Avigail."

"I love how you make matching shawls, and in two sizes."

Before long, Avigail is inviting ladies, not only from Jhericho, but also Jherusalem, Bethel, and Emmaus to come for her lunches and showings.

———

"Uncle Caalev," Avigail says one evening while embroidering the top of a special-order tunic, "don't you think we should invite Zarus and Devorah up to show them off to the elite of Jhericho? After all, he's now one of the richest men in Eilat, if not *the* richest man.

"You have, indeed, become mistress of my house, niece, and done it well," he says, setting down a pen next to his unfinished letter. "I didn't realize how quiet this house was until you moved in with me. Who would you invite?"

"Well, the mayor, the magistrates, you know, the elite. I am sure they will feel honored to personally meet such a rich man, even if he is Samaritan."

Avigail clears her throat and presses down her tunic with her hand.

"If that's what you want to do and you think everyone will come, go ahead. You have my blessing."

Avigail spends the next two weeks planning decorations and food. She shops for new silver goblets and buys cardinal red silk for a new tunic for herself. She buys turquoise linen to make into a tunic to go with the white toga she made Caalev for his birthday.

The day before the big event, Zarus, Devorah and Amram arrive. Avigail is disappointed that her daughter is wearing such a plain tunic. Zarus is not much better. *I'm sure they brought better to wear at my banquet in his honor.*

"Oh, let me see that precious boy," she says, taking Amram out of Devorah's arms. "Looks like he has most of his teeth. Can he talk?"

"Yes, he says mama and papa. Amram, say Grandmother Avigail," Zarus urges.

"Gr*Amma* Avail," Amram repeats with a giggle.

Avigail sits and puts Amram in her lap. Amram looks up at her and gives her a kiss on her cheek. His grandmother beams. "You're such a sweet child, Amram. Now let's see you walk."

Before his parents can stop Avigail, she sets Amram on his feet. He falls.

Avigail looks at him, her brows furrowed and mouth pursed.

"What's going on? Didn't you get his foot fixed?"

"Mother, we have tried all the doctors in Eilat, and they have been exercising the foot and even putting it in swaddling bands to straighten it out. He's only two years old. Give them more time.

"Well, after the banquet, I'm taking that child to my own physician. He'll fix that foot for good."

"But Mother, we have had the best physicians."

"Well, you haven't had mine, and my physician is the best. Now, don't argue with me. I'm still your mother, even if you are rich."

Zarus does not say anything.

Sychar, Province of Samaria

Summer returns. Once again, Avigail packs her clothing, sewing supplies, and other things she considers necessities, and heads up to her manor house in mountainous and cooler Sychar.

Once again, she hires a litter which delivers her right to her door. When it stops, she moves aside the curtains and is shocked.

"What? What is going on?"

Sarach slides off the mule she has ridden next to the litter and helps her mistress out.

Tears appear as she looks up at her manor in disbelief.

"No. No. This is wrong. Men, take me into the city. I must see my attorney right this instant. His name is Daniyyel"

She forgets to wait for Sarach to help her back into the litter. "They're not getting by with this. They cannot just come in while I'm gone and lock up my manor. It's illegal, and I will prove it."

As they work their way back into the city, Avigail bites the inside of her cheek, purses her lips, and stares daggers at the wall of her litter.

"How dare they? They don't know who they are dealing with."

She clenches her fists, every muscle in her body grows stiff, and she begins to tremble.

"Here we are, Mistress," Sarach says as she slides down off her mule.

Avigail climbs out of her litter and pounds on Daniyyel's gate.

"Daniyyel. Daniyyel! Open up. It's Avigail. I've got to talk to you. Daniyyel?"

Moments later, a manservant opens the gate and lets Avigail in. Behind the servant stands Daniyyel. He has on a long, purple-edged white tunic with tassels on the hem.

"Avigail, what's wrong? What has happened?"

"My manor. That's what happened. It's locked up. Who did that? I demand you stop him."

"First, we'll have to learn more. It's too late in the day. Tomorrow I will go to the forum and find out who is behind it. Do you have someplace to stay tonight?"

"Oh, uh, well, I suppose my daughter's sister-in-law, Estar. She owns the fabric shop in the market."

"Good," he says. "You can go to work with her tomorrow, and I will meet you there when I find out who is responsible for your misfortune."

"Goodness, no. I cannot be seen acting like I'm a common clerk."

"Well, then, Daniyyel replies, "you will have to come to me. I should know something by noon tomorrow. Now go on and try not to worry."

"I can't get into my own house, and he tells me not to worry," she tells the ceiling. Avigail turns and leaves without saying goodbye.

She gives directions to Estar's house, climbs back into her litter, and cries. When they arrive, she pays for the rented litter and tells the men their services are no longer needed.

Avigail knocks on Estar's gate. "Well, hello there, Avigail. I was just thinking about you. What's wrong, dear? Why are you crying? Come in."

"All my clothes are in chests out in the street. Would you mind terribly if I brought them here?"

"Well, of course, you can bring them in. What's going on? Why aren't you at your manor?"

Avigail does not say anything, but steps in and waits for her maid to bring in her chests of clothing.

"Sarach, you can take them to the downstairs bedroom. Sorry, I don't have a man around to carry them. Now, Avigail, come sit and tell me what is going on."

They move over to some red silk cushions on a flax mat.

"Oh, Estar, it's terrible. Someone has taken my manor house from me."

"Who? Why?"

"I don't know. Lawyer Daniyyel is going to find out for me in the morning. Oh, Estar, what am I going to do? If only Baaruch were alive today. He would have not ever let this happen. What am I going to do?"

Estar shifts around so she is beside Avigail rather than in front of her, and embraces her friend. Although Avigail is old enough to be her mother, she puts her arm around her, and Avigail lays her head on Estar's shoulder.

"I'm not going to tell you not to worry. Just hang on until tomorrow when you find out what is going on with your house."

———

"It's the judge, you say? Judge Yigal ordered the house locked up? But why?"

Avigail is once more at Lawyer Daniyyel's house. She is wearing a red silk tunic with silver threads embellishing the neckline, sleeves, and hem, and a silver necklace to match.

"He has admired your manor house for years. You do know it's the envy of everyone in Sychar."

"Yes, well..."

"He has found a loophole in Baaruch's will. Your husband left you the house as your place of residence. You are down in Jhericho half the time. He claims you have forfeited your right to call it your residence."

"No! That's not right. It doesn't say how long at a time I have to live in it."

"I'm just telling you what the judge told me. I don't see how you are going to fight this. You may as well accept the fact that you have lost your house. At least you got some money out of selling the pasture land for someone to build a house on. Maybe you can sell the stable and chariot house, unless the judge finds a way to stop you from doing that."

"No! I won't let him take my home from me."

"Avigail," he says, putting his hand on her shoulder, "there is no way to stop him. He is the judge."

"Well, I will stop him. I will find a way."

She raises her head and goes toward the outer gate. The gatekeeper lets her out, she turns right, and marches toward the government forum.

Upon arriving, she goes to the clerk by the front door of the forum government *officium*.

"Sir, I demand to see Judge Yigal."

"I'm afraid he is listening to court cases all day. Perhaps he will be free tomorrow."

"No. I will not accept that. I demand to see him today."

"I'm afraid that is impossible."

"Do you know who I am, young man?"

"If Caesar himself wanted to see Judge Yigal, he would have to wait until court was over."

"All right then. Make a note on that scroll of yours that I will be here first thing in the morning, and I expect to see him."

"May I tell him what it is about?"

"Indeed, you may. He has illegally kept me from entering my own manor. He must open the house back up and leave."

"Yes, ma'am."

Avigail, her head high, turns and struts out of the *officium* as proudly as she can muster herself to look, despite the fact that on the inside, she is crying. Her maid dutifully follows behind her.

What to do with her day? The hours creep by. She finally goes to Estar's fabric booth and spends several hours pretending she is a customer. The rest of the day, she wanders through the market.

The next morning she is up early and dons her royal blue linen tunic with gold threads around the bodice and gold fringe around the sleeves. Her necklace is of gold also.

She walks over to the government *officium* at the forum.

"Sir, I was here yesterday to see Judge Yigal, and am told he will see me first thing this morning," she tells the young clerk she had spoken to the day before.

"I'm so sorry, madam, but he was called to an emergency court session. There was a murder last night, and..."

"I don't care if there were three murders last night. He agreed to see me first thing this morning, and that is what he is going to do."

"I'm sorry, but it is impossible."

"When will he be out of court?"

"That's impossible to say. It may take him all day."

"Where is the courtroom?"

"Normally, it is held out on the forum platform, but there are security issues, so they are in the courtroom down the hall."

"Then, I will wait for him there."

"You cannot. You are not involved in the case."

"Watch me!"

Avigail swings around and marches down the hall to the courtroom. She opens the door herself, sees Judge Yigal in the front, and benches for participants. She sits in the back row. Briefly, she catches the eye of the judge. As the senseless proceedings continue, her mind settles on her own problems.

Judge Yigal has been to receptions in my home. His wife has bought some of my designed dresses.

"You will be given a chance to defend yourself later," she hears the judge pronounce in the front.

Maybe I shouldn't have. He saw how wonderful my manor is, and got greedy.

"Is your client denying he killed Uriah in cold blood last night?"

It's not my fault he could not afford a house as grand as mine.

"I have heard all twenty of the witnesses. You have been found guilty, Uriah of Sebaste, and will be stoned to death. It is too late today, so we will do it tomorrow morning."

Finally, I have my chance. Avigail stands and fights her way through a crowd. *If I can get to him before he leaves...* She tries to keep her eyes on the judge who is taller than most of the others, but he disappears.

She continues on. *He's not going to avoid me that easily.* She pounds on the door he had just disappeared through. "Judge Yigal, it's me, Avigail. We have an appointment. Judge Yigal. Open up. I know you're in there. Judge Yigal?"

The courtroom empties. Only the guard is left. "I'm afraid you're going to have to leave so I can lock the door, ma'am."

Avigail leaves, walks through the hall to see if she can figure out where the judge disappeared to, is unsuccessful, so goes out into the street. She spots him. "Judge Yigal, we had an appointment!" she calls out. He turns upon hearing his name, spots Avigail, and hurries on, putting more distance between them.

It is late. Avigail goes back to Estar's house. Sarach knocks on the gate for her mistress, and Estar lets her in."

"Well, did you get your house back? I guess not. You're not gathering up your things. Maybe tomorrow will be better. Here, I have some apricots fresh from the market. Take all you want."

Avigail settles in on her cushion, and alternately eats an apricot and bawls out Judge Yigal. When she is done, she cries.

The next morning, rather than go to the government forum, Avigail goes to the home of the judge.

She knocks on the gate, and a servant answers. "May I know who you wish to see?"

"Judge Yigal," Avigail answers.

"And your business? Are you related?"

"He took my manor, and I want it back."

"One moment, madam."

As she waits, she picks lint off of her black tunic with flowers embroidered from the top down to the hem of her tunic.

"I am sorry, madam, but the judge seems to have left while I was elsewhere in the house," the gatekeeper says. I do not know where he went. Perhaps out in the country or over to Sebaste."

Avigail swings around and marches away. *If only Benyamin was here. Benyamin is friends with the judge's son. Or Zarus. He wouldn't dare refuse to see Zarus.*

Avigail walks toward the market and Estar's booth.

"What am I going to do?" she asks Estar after her last customer leaves. "I even went to his house, and he still refuses to see me."

"It looks like you've tried everything. Maybe you should take your lawyer's advice and sell the stable and chariot house and return to Jhericho. Not that I don't want you here, though."

"No! I will make him see me."

That night, she takes Eshachk, her husband's personal servant, with her to Judge Yigal's house. She takes along a heavy cloak and encourages Eshachk to do the same. And to bring a torch.

Once at the judge's house, Avigail knocks on it, and the same gatekeeper answers it.

"I know you're in there, Judge Yigal. I demand my house back. I know you're in there and can hear me."

"Madam, it is getting late. The judge does not see people this late. If you want to talk to him about your house, you will have to do it at the government *officium*."

"We shall see about that," Avigail pronounces as he shuts the gate.

She steps over to one side and sets a cushion down and sits on it.

"Your job tonight, Eshachk, is to protect me—just being a man will be enough to protect me—and to knock on Judge Yigal's gate once every hour."

"But, Mistress, he has a lot of power. What if he decides to take my house next?"

"He doesn't want your house. It isn't fancy enough for him. He only wants my house. Now, I am paying you well. Remember, every hour."

Morning and Eshachk is sitting on the ground, leaning against the gate. When the gatekeeper opens it, Eshachk's head hits the ground. Jarred awake, Avigail jumps up.

"The only way Judge Yigal is going to get rid of me is to give my manor back to me. He has no right to it."

"Madam, I believe the judge will not be able to see you today. He has business over in Sebaste."

He closes the gate, and Avigail straightens her dress. "Eshachk, you did fairly well during the night. You can go home now. I have another plan. He is not going to get by with this."

Avigail walks back over to the government *officium* and enters. She stands by the front door in her wrinkled tunic and tresses of her black hair falling down around her eyes. As people come in, she tells each one, "Judge Yigal has stolen my house from me and won't give it back."

After doing it four times, the young clerk approaches Avigail.

"I'm sorry, madam, but you must leave. You cannot bother people like that."

"Just watch me. I'm not going anywhere until he gives my house back."

The clerk disappears through a door at the other end of the corridor. He comes back out and sits in his normal seat. Now and then he looks over at Avigail

"Judge Yigal has stolen my house," she continues to tell people coming in through the door. "He won't give it back."

At noon a messenger enters the corridor from the back and speaks momentarily to the clerk. The clerk rises and follows the messenger. A few moments later, the clerk comes out and walks toward Avigail.

"The judge will see you now, madam. He is prepared to give your house back."

That's better. Now to get a manor for Devorah. They need to live in a house worthy of their station. But to get them to even talk about it...

Then Jhesus told his disciples a parable to show them that they should always pray and not give up.

He said: "In a certain town there was a judge who neither feared God nor cared about men.

And there was a widow in that town who kept coming to him with the plea, 'Grant me justice against my adversary.'

"For some time, he refused. But finally, he said to himself, 'Even though I don't fear God or care about men, yet because this widow keeps bothering me, I will see that she gets justice so that she won't eventually wear me out with her coming!' "

And the Lord said, "Listen to what the unjust judge says.

And will not God bring about justice for his chosen ones, who cry out to him day and night? Will he keep putting them off ?

I tell you, he will see that they get justice, and quickly." (Luke 18:1-8)

19 ~ THE ROCK

AD 18
Eilat, Port City on Red Sea, Arabah Desert, Idumea

"Are you glad you stuck with me, even after the confusion over the stock in my mining company?" Gersshon asks the ship captain.

"Well, I almost backed out and demanded my slaves back."

"I've brought you a lot of business, remember."

"Yes, the cargo of copper has been a boon to my shipping company. And only in exchange for slaves. It did work out well, didn't it?"

Yes, and Zarus will never miss that copper. He never looks at the tallies or books. He just comes in, gives orders, and goes back home to play with his son. Too bad he has that club foot.

Do you have twenty more slaves for me today? As the mine expands, my need for workers expands.

Copper Mine, Timna Valley, Aravah Desert

The officers of the new copper mine sit around in their *officium* tent. It is six man-lengths long and five man-lengths wide, made of goat skins, and expected to endure more desert storms than the stucco *officium* Baaruch had built for his headquarters.

Gersshon always makes sure Yair, the bookkeeper, is not considered an officer, and therefore never included in their meetings. "How much can a former beggar know?"

With a floor of camel skins and Persian rugs scattered around on it, the men are comfortable on their cushions.

"Gersshon, you've hired twenty more? What would I do

without you? I don't know how you manage to get so many men to come work for us out here in the heat of the desert."

"It's not as hot as being under a mountain and sweltering in the dark, remember," Gersshon replies with a wink.

"It still takes planning, even if you are creating an open-pit mine," Saabhu says, having been located in Egypt and hired by Zarus the previous year. "If the mine ends up covering the whole ten acres you bought…"

"Remember, I bought the equipment," Gersshon interrupts.

"Yes, yes, Gersshon. Now, as I was saying, if the mine ends up covering all ten acres, we're going to end up needing at least five hundred men. Gersshon, you are the recruiter. So you think you can come up with that many men?"

"We're talking a few years down the road, aren't we?"

"Yes, of course. It could be ten years before we get out and down that far."

"I think I could recruit that many men in five years."

"What are your thoughts, Noach? Can you organize that many men? It's a lot more than when we worked Baaruch's mine."

"Of course, he can," Zarus interjects before Noach has time to be offended."

"If we had five hundred or a thousand men, I could put them in shifts of two, working twelve hours at a time, or shifts of three, working eight hours at a time."

"What do you recommend, Zarus?"

"We would get more out of the men if they worked three shifts. Hot, exhausted men don't do well."

"These long-term plans sound good, but we have to think about right now," Gersshon says. "Since Zarus and I started chiseling the mine ourselves to get it started two years ago, we have hired fifty men. I think that's pretty good progress."

"Yair, how many amphoras of copper have we shipped to Egyptian and Persian smelters?" Zarus asks.

"Well, Noach, how long do you think it takes to mine fifty amphora?"

"I'd say a month."

"So, in the past year, we have shipped out six hundred amphora of copper."

"You know, it's no reflection on Yair," Gersshon says, "but I think we ought to bring in a professional, and I know the very man to do the job. He was a successful banker in Sebaste, and uh decided to resign so he could, uh, spend more time with his family. He wants to leave Samaria and go to uh, warmer climate."

"Do you think we can afford him?" Zarus asks. "He sounds expensive."

"He says he will take a cut in pay because it will be worth spending more time with his family."

"I'll take it under advisement, Gersshon. Right now, I have to go home."

Eilat, Port City on Red Sea, Arabah Desert

Zarus arrives home with his new Arabian horse. As he puts it in the stable, he turns to Pesachya.

"Have you been able to find Captain Hector for me yet?"

"No, but I think I'm close. Down at the docks, someone said his ship goes back and forth between Britannia and Italy now.

"Do you think you can find out what city he lives in?

"I think he lives in Greece. I'll check to see if any of the older sea captains down there know which city."

"Good man, Pesachya. Shalva and Khemoh are not getting any younger. Maybe when you find the captain, he will part with them."

"I'm sure that will be the case."

Zarus walks into the same rent house he and Devorah have had since arriving in Eilat six years earlier. He is greeted by Amram, hobbling up to him with a make-shift cane and wearing his catching big smile. Zarus sweeps down and brings Amram up into his arms.

"Papa home. I love Papa."

"I love you too, Amram, more than anyone in the whole wide world except one. Now, who is the one?"

"*Amma!*" the three-year-old says enthusiastically.

"Yes. There is no one in the whole wide world I love more than *Amma* and Amram."

Devorah walks from the far end of the courtyard to greet her husband. With Amram in one arm, he embraces Devorah with his other arm. They kiss and Amram giggles.

"I have something special to tell you, but you have to eat first," Devorah says with a twinkle in her eye.

"Aw, c'mon now. Do I have to eat first?"

"Yes you do. So sit."

Dinner consumed, Zarus suggests they all go up on the roof to enjoy the night breeze and watch the lights down at the waterfront.

"Okay, I've eaten. Now, what's so special that you have to tell me?"

"I'm pregnant again."

Zarus' head bobs forward, he leans back, grins, and slaps his thigh. "I knew it. You've been acting funny in the mornings."

"Funny, am I? Well, you have acted funny in the mornings ever since I married you. So there."

Not to be left out, Amram puts one hand on his belly and lets out a guttural "Ha, ha, ha."

Both parents laugh. Then Zarus grows serious.

"What are we going to do about our beliefs? They are so close. I believe only in the first five books of the holy scriptures just like your Sadducees do, and you believe in an additional five books of poetry and seventeen books of prophecy."

"And I keep the required yearly feasts in Jherusalem," Devorah responds, "while you keep them in Gerizim. How are we going to solve this? We can't raise our children in both religions."

"We shall keep praying that God will send something or someone to help us unite."

"If it were only possible," Devorah laments, putting her head on Zarus' shoulder while he plays with Amram at his feet.

"I keep reading where God is going to send us someone like Moses. Perhaps that will be our link to uniting."

"But, when? It's been two thousand years since that was predicted," she says, raising her head and pulling a prodigal strand of hair off his forehead.

"We shall pray that it be soon."

AD 19

"I received a letter from Mother today," Devorah says while hemming a new tunic for her husband. "I guess I forgot to tell you."

"What did she want?"

"Oh, she didn't want anything. Well, not exactly. She has decided it is time for us to build our manor, so she's coming down next week."

"Who would we get to build it?"

"She's bringing Moshe with her."

Zarus stares at his wife. "After the way I treated him by agreeing to be partners, then backing out on him and getting Gersshon instead?"

"Mother seems to have smoothed things over for you. She is

definitely bringing Moshe."

"But what about her? She thinks it's my fault for not getting better doctors."

"Well, that problem was solved when you became rich. You will be happy to know that Mother has forgiven you. Of course, you didn't do anything, but she has forgiven you anyway."

There is a knock at the gate. Penina lets him in.

"Hello, you two," Gersshon announces. "What have you been up to this Sabbath? Got any lunch made? I forgot to have my maid pre-make today's meals, and I'm starved."

"Hello back," Zarus says. "Yes, we have some food for you. You need to get married. That would solve a lot of your problems."

"Create some more, too," Gersshon adds with a laugh. "No offense to you, Devorah. You are the exception."

"So, what's new?"

Zarus looks over at Devorah and shakes his head just enough for her to notice.

"My mother is on her way down to show us how to build a proper manor."

"Oh, I didn't know you were thinking of building. It's about time. And I have the exact spot for you. It's on the highest hill in the city. You could sit on your roof and look down on everyone, both on land and at sea."

"We don't really want to go out today," Zarus says.

"Then, we'll go tomorrow."

———

"Hello, Mother. We're so glad you could come. You too, Moshe. Zarus is still at work, but he is looking forward to seeing you again. How is your wife?"

"She is fine. We have a grandchild now, you know."

"Congratulations."

"Okay, now I've brought a rough sketch of your new manor," Avigail announces, "and a list of things that must go into it."

Moshe laughs. "Don't you think we can wait until tomorrow?"

"My, my no. It's never too soon."

"Gersshon said there is a lot available at the highest point of the city," Devorah says. "Not that I care, but Mother would. I shall show it to you tomorrow."

"Now, as I was saying," Avigai continues, "you're going to want outer walls of the finest brick, and inner walls paneled with marble and cedar. Your courtyard will be lavish with mosaic tiles and marble pillars supporting the second and third story balconies. Of course, you will want a spiral staircase up to those floors. And…"

"Mother, you are wearing me out with all your plans. Let's go to the kitchen and help Penina make our supper."

"Who is this little guy?" Moshe asks, looking over at Amram. The boy with the light brown hair and blue eyes of his father hobbles past Moshe and to his grandmother Avigail."

Avigail laughs nervously. "Go play with Moshe until I'm done in the kitchen; then you and me can talk."

"*Safta, Safta,*" he says. "Kiss you. Kiss you." Avigail leans down to Amram's level and lets him kiss her on the cheek. "I love you, *Safta,*" he says.

"What did you say?" Avigail asks.

"I love my *Safta.*"

"Oh, my precious little one. Your grandmother loves you too."

"Hug you," Amram insists.

Avigail leans down a second time so that her grandson, the one with the club foot, can give her a hug.

"Well, if it isn't Moshe," Zarus says, walking in through the gate. He takes Moshe's hand, shakes it, looks into Moshe's eyes, but does not speak more.

"I know, son. It's okay."

———

Morning comes. Before breakfast, Zarus suggests they all go to the hilltop Gersshon had told them about.

"You can tell us what you think, Moshe."

Zarus puts Amram on his shoulders and leads the way for Devorah, her mother, and the building contractor.

When they arrive, Moshe walks around, kicking stones as he goes. He does not talk. He looks off at the city and the waterfront. He walks halfway down the hill, stares at its surface, then back up again. He kneels, pulls away loose stones, and stares. He rises.

"It's very beautiful up here," he says.

Zarus walks over to Moshe. "And?"

"Well, there are a lot of loose rocks up here. The hill just doesn't look that stable. I saw cracks that seem to run deep. Do they ever have earthquakes around here?"

"Yes, they had one right after Benyamin brought me… Well, right after I arrived six years ago." It wasn't bad. The earth shook a little and not for very long."

"How about that mine collapse after Baaruch died? Do you think it was caused by an earthquake?"

"I don't know. The mountains out there shift and move all the time."

"I see springs up here too. That means there are hollow places under the surface. Do you want my honest opinion?" Moshe asks.

"Of course. That's why we brought you up here."

"I don't think you should build here."

"Okay, I take your word for it. I know of a couple more lots. You up to going to see them?"

"Sure. I'm still healthy. Let's go."

They make their way down the hill and into a neighborhood that is hilly, but not as high as the one they'd just looked at.

"After looking at these two lots, I can say you would be safe building your house on either one. Solid rock down there. No loose gravel, no cracks, and the other houses in the neighborhood seem to have been here a long time."

"Thank you. Devorah, which lot do you like best? We'll get whichever one you want."

"How about the one we're standing on right now?"

"Then, it's settled. Let's go down to the government *officium* to find out who the owner is. We'll put the lot in both of our names."

Avigail smiles in approval. "I always liked you, Zarus," she says.

"If you don't mind, Avigail and I will linger a little longer here to get the lay of the land," Moshe says, "then go back to your house to make more solid plans. And rest. Our bones aren't as strong as they used to be."

———

The manor is begun, and there is a birth in the family. Zarus' second child, a son, is born.

"We shall name him Ithamar," Zarus announces.

He picks up his baby from his mother's arms. He could almost hold the baby in one hand.

Baby Ithamar's eyes shift from side to side, always searching. His arms pump up and down, and his legs act like they can't wait to start running.

"He's going to be a hand full, mistress," Penina says.

"Maybe Amram will keep him under control," Devorah says.

AD 19

"I am amazed at your precision and craftsmanship, Moshe," Zarus says. "You've been able to put everything into the house that Avigail has suggested."

"Avigail has been designing tunics for years," Moshe says with a grin. "Looks like she should go into the house designing business next. She's got real talent."

"I guess our time here is over. You've got a new house and all new furniture," Avigail says. "I shall return to Jhericho tomorrow. Moshe will be going back up to Sychar."

"I've arranged for a few men at the mine to help us move," Zarus says. "We don't need the furniture, of course, but there are a lot of personal items we want to bring with us."

Two nights later, after everyone is gone and there is only the little family of four, it begins to rain. The wind picks up. Thunder. Lightning. Winds whipping in destructive circles. It is a cyclone.

Roofs blowing off. Rains sweeping away everything sitting on everyone's roof and in their courtyard. Gates bolted closed. Windows shuttered.

Hour after frightening hour. Will the whole city be swept out to sea?

Then it is over. Devorah and Sarah walk outside. They look around. The houses in their neighborhood are safe.

"Your miners, Zarus," Devorah asks. "Were they able to find shelter?"

"Therefore, everyone who hears these words of mine and puts them into practice is like a wise man who built his house on the rock.
The rain came down, the streams rose, and the winds blew and

beat against that house; yet it did not fall, because it had its foundation on the rock. (Matthew 7:24-25)

OPEN PIT COPPER MINE

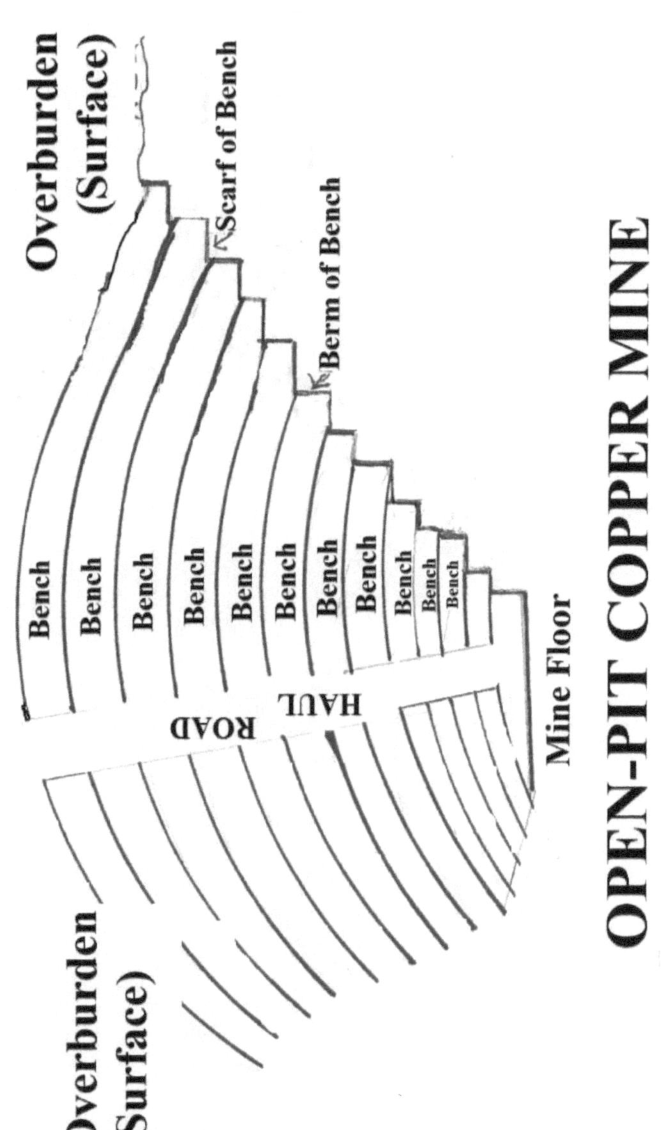

20 ~ PAID IN FULL

AD 21
Copper Mine, Timna Valley, Arabah Desert, Idumea

*I*t is an hour before daylight, the coolest part of the day. Zarus watches the men who are just starting their shift leave their tents and head to the pit.

"How are you progressing on the new shelters, Moshe?" he asks.

"I've built three so far, Zarus. Each one should hold one hundred men.

"They are sturdy and perfect for the desert. The roofs are made of acacia wood, and we are using cement posts to hold them up. As we take down the tents they formerly used, we are putting the camel skins back on the floor, and are using the goat skins as side flaps that can be secured to the roof, or let down in case of storm."

"Moshe, you are a genius and a lifesaver. I wish I had had you build these shelters before you built my house. The loss of those forty-seven men in the cyclone was devastating, not only to the mine but more so to their families. Luckily, Gersshon had kept records of where each man was from and notified their families."

Moshe does not answer. "Well, I need to get back to work. I still have three more to build before I can return to Sychar."

"You must be anxious to get home to your wife."

"Indeed, I am. She's a good woman."

"How does she handle you being gone so much?"

"It's your family that pulls me away from Sychar," Moshe says with a sheepish grin. "I built Baaruch's warehouses down here, then I built his southern manor, then I built yours, and now these barracks. That's enough for me. I'm going back to a normal existence in Sychar.

I've got my eye on some lots in a good part of town that I might buy to build on, then see if someone would like to buy them."

"You will do well, Moshe, in whatever you do. And I promise not to ask you to build anything else for me."

————

"Zarus, I need to show you something." It is Engineer Saabhu

The two men start down the angled haul road, first passing the waste rock that has been piled at the top of the pit, then down into the mine pit itself. They descend ten man-lengths almost to the floor of the mine.

"Look down there," Saabhu says.

"I see what you mean. We have hit water."

"It's coming in pretty fast."

"What do you suggest?" Zarus asks.

"A water wheel. It will have to be large enough to keep up with the flow. After the pails fill with this water on one side of the wheel, we will have men taking the filled pails off and replacing them with empty ones on the other side of the wheel. Then the men will have to carry the water up the haul road to the surface to get it out of the way."

"Hmmm. That means we'll have to dig a pit at the top to dump the water in." Zarus pauses to think. "Either that, or we could put the pails in a wagon, take them to desert encampments out here to sell them the water."

"Or, we could put them in large vats at the top and let people come to us to buy the water. Maybe we could distribute the water to sell at first until we get a pit dug. We have to do something, and quick."

"That's what I would do," Saabhu says.

"But first, we've got to get the water wheel built," Zarus says.

"I know where one is. There is a mine that shut down not far from here, and they no longer need their water wheel. I heard it's already taken apart. I can send for someone to buy it and deliver it back here in a couple of hours."

The two men walk back up the haul road. On each side of them is a series of mine benches stepping down to the floor of the mine.

"At least we haven't had a landslide yet. These benches you oversee are doing the trick, and I thank you for keeping them in good condition, Saabhu."

Once at the top of the pit, Zarus asks the first miner he runs into whether he has seen Noach. The man has not. He works his way to the *officium* tent. Inside, he asks Yair if he knows where Noach is.

"I haven't seen him yet today."

"How about your new boss, Hudas?"

"He's not here either."

"Look, Yair, I'm sorry about what happened. You know what you are doing and have kept good records. But Gersshon is my partner and thought we should have this retired quastor to monitor you."

"It's okay. He doesn't come into the *officium* very often, so I'm able to keep doing most of what I've been doing," Yair replies.

"Back to Noach, Gersshon is gone to Sebaste to visit his dying father, and he's the one who always does the hiring. Since Noach superintends everyone, I could send him into town to find men to hire."

"I just don't know where Noach is."

"No one seems to know. He's usually reliable. Maybe he's sick. Well, I don't have time to wait for him. I'll have to do it myself. I hope he's okay."

Eilat, Port City on Red Sea, Arabah Desert

Zarus arrives at the city square, slides off his horse, and watches the men standing around talking to each other, or squatting and staring at people walking by.

Chagan is a thin man. His face is drawn. He calls out to a man on the street.

"Do you need to hire a good worker? I'm your man. I could go to work right now."

As Zarus draws closer, Chagan turns to him. "Do you need to hire a good worker? I'm your man. I could go to work right now."

"Indeed, I do need to hire someone. Would a denarus be enough for you to work all day?"

"Certainly, sir. Thank you, sir."

"Okay, go through the city gate, turn left toward the cliffs, and watch for an open-pit mine. I'll need you to help set up a water wheel, then carry water."

"Will do, sir. Right away, sir."

As Chagan hurries away, Zarus looks around the square again for someone looking for a job. He sees a man sitting on a small blanket with a begging bowl over by the street and walks over to him.

"Are you job hunting?"

The man looks up and shades his eyes against the sun behind Zarus' head. "Yes, sir."

"Would you be willing to work all day for a denarus?"

"Would I ever," he replies, standing and picking up his blanket and bowl. "My name is Eitan, and I'd be happy to work for you."

"If you can start right now, you're hired. Now go out through the city gate, turn left and walk until you see an open-pit mine. You will help put together a water wheel and spend the rest of the day carrying water away."

As the man leaves, Zarus is already looking for other men to hire. Those left are talking to each other in a huddle.

Well, I'll just come back later and see if more have showed up. I think I'll go home and see how Devorah and the boys are doing.

Soon, Zarus pulls out his key and unlocks his copper gate with geometric designs etched into it.

"Where is Devorah?" he asks Penina.

"She is in the garden. She loves it out there."

Zarus walks through his ornate courtyard with tiles of many colors arranged on the floor in a geometric pattern. The tile layers had wanted to make the pattern in the form of flowers or ships, but Zarus had forbade them to put any graven image in his house.

He sees Devorah sitting on a concrete bench facing a man-sized pool with lilies and small fish in it. She is wearing a white linen tunic with no ornamentation except red fringe at her sleeves and hem.

"Hello, my darling," she says rising. "Oh, where did Ithamar go? Amram, are you watching your little brother?"

From behind a rose bush, they hear Ithamar. "Amram is beating up on me."

"No, I'm not. I'm trying to get him up out of the dirt where the violets are."

"Well, come here. Your father is home for a while."

"Amram, now six years old, hobbles out from behind the rose bushes, leaning on a miniature staff. Ithamar, three, toddles out after him.

"Papa! Papa!" Amram calls out, rushing into his father's arms. His hair is now a darker brown to match his father's, and his eyes just as blue.

"How's my little man today? Are you done with your schooling already?"

"No, the tutor hasn't come yet. So I'm playing until he does."

"Don't you like school?"

"I love school, especially counting. But I love to play too."

Zarus laughs, puts Amram down, and lifts Ithamar onto his shoulders."

"Go, Papa, go!" he shouts.

Zarus holds on to his son as he begins to gallop around the garden.

"I don't know who is more of a child—you or Ithamar."

Zarus puts Ithamar down and sits next to his wife.

"So, how are you feeling today, my sweet pearl?"

She puts her hand on her abdomen and sighs. I guess I'm doing about as well as any woman in her ninth month. So, what do you want this time? Another boy or a girl for you to spoil."

"Definitely a girl. And, while I'm at it, she is going to be as beautiful as you."

"Ithamar already looks like me. You don't want too many me's running around here."

"Ithamar, stop your bouncing. You're shaking the bench, and Mother may fall off."

"But, I'm a grasshopper."

"Then be a grasshopper on the ground."

"He is never still, Zarus. If he isn't jumping or hopping, he is running. Amram has a hard time keeping up with him."

"At least God has blessed our Amram with a sunny view of life," Zarus says. "And I don't believe he ever met anyone he didn't like."

Devorah laughs. "He even loves being around my mother. He has even figured out a way to make her smile when she is crying."

"Once people get to know him, they no longer notice his bad foot. The important thing is that he has a good heart.

"Well, I need to go back to the city square. I need to hire at least eight men for a new project we have out at the mine, and I need them today. Maybe more have showed up looking for work."

Devorah stands and reaches up to her husband to kiss him goodbye for a while.

Zarus rides his horse back over to the square. He slides off, and leading it by the reins, walks around to see if any more men have showed up. Most of those who had been in a huddle talking to each other are now gone. Zarus spots a man sitting on the edge of the square and approaches him.

"Looking for work, my friend?

Alon looks up. "Are you talking to me?"

"Yes, sir. You look healthy enough. Could you use some work?"

"You couldn't have come at a better time. My friend, Dov, is going to be here in a few moments. The ship we were working on left without us, and we are stranded."

"In that case, I will help you get money to return to your home. Would you be willing to work all day for a denarus?"

"That would help. Hey, Dov, we have a job offer already. Where do we go?" Alon asks, speaking for both of them.

Zarus gives them the directions and looks elsewhere around the square. Other than these two men, it is deserted.

Hmmm. May as well stop by Noach's house to see if he is okay.

Leaping up onto his horse, Zarus rides one slow step after another through the hot streets and arrives in his old neighborhood where he and Devorah had lived their first nine years in Eilat. He relives those years as he ambles toward Noach's house.

"Greetings, Master Zarus," Noach's servant says with a broad grin.

"Is Noach at home?"

"Yes, indeed, sir. He is. But I am afraid he is not well."

Zarus' brows furrow and he looks in the servant's eyes. "How serious is it?"

"Zarus, my friend," he hears from the other side of the courtyard. "Come in. Come in."

"Well, at least you're not dead. You're never absent from work. What..."

"I'll tell you what. I was in the market this morning buying something to take to eat at work when a donkey reared up, tipped a cart, and..."

"And the donkey fell on you?"

"I wasn't that lucky. The cart full of pottery fell on me and broke my leg. And I've got scratches and cuts everywhere."

"Your leg is all swelled up. You must be in a lot of pain."

"Like a scorpion got me."

"Take all the time you need. I'll just assign more work to the crew foremen, and cover the rest of your work myself."

"No, way. I'm not about to sit around here, eat, and get fat. I'll be back on the job tomorrow."

"Noach, how long have we known each other?"

"Well, I'd say around thirteen years if you want to count those days you indentured yourself for Devorah and was treated like a common slave. Oh, I didn't mean to bring that up. I'm surprised you survived it. But now, look at you all dressed up in fine linen. I'm proud of you, son, and will never let you down. Now, get outa here. You have twice as much work to do today."

Zarus smiles, embraces Noach, they pound each other on the back, and Zarus leaves.

May as well go back to the square and see if anyone else has shown up.

The day is growing hotter, despite the sea breeze. Zarus leads his horse back over to the town square. He sees no one, so squats on the ground. He watches the guards at the city gate, the merchants and a few farmers coming in and going out, and some children playing on top of the city wall.

"You come down from there right now!" he hears a distraught father—he seems to be their father—shout. The boy and girl clamor down and take the man's hand. He walks with them in Zarus' direction.

When they come within easy hearing distance, he hears one of the children groan. "Papa, I'm hungry."

"Shhh, child. I will feed you in a little while."

Zarus stands and approaches the man.

"Sir, I am looking to hire some men to work at my mine today. The work is easy, but it's hot out there in the desert."

"I'll do anything. My name is Yoel."

"Will you work for the rest of the day for a Denarus?"

"Will I? Of course, I will. It will be enough to feed the three of us. My wife died a month ago in childbirth, the house we were in was in her parents' name, we have been sleeping in alleys, and I have been looking for work since then." He pauses and looks over at his children.

"Oh, but I can't take my children out there. It would be too dangerous."

"I tell you what I will do. I have a son, six, and another son, three who would love to have some new playmates for the day. I will take them to my house. How old are your children?"

"The boy is 7, and the girl is 9."

Zarus gives Yoel directions to the mine. As he does, he notices another man standing nearby who seems to be listening. Zarus turns to the other man.

"May I help you, sir?" he asks.

"I have a pottery booth and had to close it up today because the potter got in an accident this morning, broke all his wares, and I have nothing left to sell. My wife is in the family way and is not doing very well. I need to get her to a doctor as soon as possible. Could I work for you too, sir? My name is Fivel."

"Then that makes two of you. Will a denarus for the day be suitable?"

"I think that is how much the doctor and his elixir will cost, so it is perfect. How can my wife and I thank you?"

"You can thank me by reporting in to work as soon as you get out to my mine. Just follow Yoel here while I deliver these children to their playmates."

Zarus does not linger at his home. He makes introductions and whispers to Penina to clean the children up and give them fresh tunics to play in.

I need more workers. I think I'll take care of some way overdue business while I wait.

Zarus leads his horse to a manor four houses down from his. He hands the reins to a stable boy but tells him he won't be long. He knocks on the ornate engraved cedar gate and is greeted.

"Good day, sir. May I help you? If you're looking for the honorable mayor, he is not here."

"Oh, I didn't come to see the mayor. I came to see his wife."

"The gatekeeper arches one eyebrow. "Wait here." He closes the gate, latches it, and disappears.

"Well, hello there, Zarus. Good to see you. Is that lovely wife of yours, okay? Does she need me?"

"May I have a moment alone with you?"

They go into the garden and sit on two ornate concrete benches.

"Several years ago, my wife sold you a pearl."

"Indeed, she did. It is lovely. I keep it in a special coffer I had made just for it."

"I have come to buy it back."

"What? You don't mean it."

"It has special meaning to Devorah. She inherited it from her father when he died a few years ago. He inherited it from his mother."

"Oh, my, it is more valuable to you than I thought."

"I will pay you anything you want. Twice as much as you paid for it. Three times more. Name your price." Zarus says.

"Excuse me."

She leaves the room, and Zarus notices the unique purple stitching that only his mother-in-law can create and smiles.

Soon she returns carrying a small coffer. She opens the top, and Zarus sees the pearl sitting on a bed of cotton-supported purple silk. It is more beautiful than he remembered.

"I paid 600 denari for it. You may have it back for 500 denari."

"No, I insist on paying at least full price." Zarus pulls his money pouch out from his sash, and takes 600 denari out of it."

"I insist. And thank you."

He leaves, leading his horse behind him, and clutching the cedar coffer in his left hand. *She will be so happy.*

An hour later, as Zarus unlocks the gate into his home, he hears Eshachk calling his name. "Oh, Master Zarus. We're so glad you are here. Your wife is in labor."

"What? Where is she?"

"Penina and the midwife are with her now."

"How long has she been in labor?"

"Since right after you delivered the poor children here about mid-afternoon."

"It's been four hours. Her time could be soon."

"Where are the children?"

"I'm afraid, sir, the duty of watching over them has fallen on me and Pesachya. Right now, Pesachya is giving them rides on Mistress Devorah's horse."

"Well done, Eshachk. Well done. Now, what should I do?"

"Nothing. It's all up to your wife and the three women with her."

"Three women? She's got Penina and the midwife. Who else is in there?"

"Forgive me, master. In all the excitement, I forgot to tell you that your sister arrived from Sychar."

"Estar?"

"Hello, brother-in-law. I'm the latest addition to your family, but about to be outdone by a little tyke. My name is Simcha. Estar and I wed a month ago."

"Oh, how nice. She didn't write me about it."

"She wanted to surprise you."

"She has done that, all right. Well, welcome to our family."

Zarus sets the coffer down on a table near the front gate and paces. Simcha joins him. Now and then, Zarus says something funny about babies—at least to him, it is funny—then returns to pacing.

Zarus stops. "I think I'm going to go for a walk into town. Simcha, make yourself at home. There is plenty of new wine and fruit. Help yourself. I won't be gone long."

Zarus mounts his horse and walks it down to where the ships are loading and unloading.

"Do you know a ship captain named Hector? He's from Greece," he asks the first person he sees.

He walks up and down the docks.

"Do you know a ship captain named Hector? He's from Greece."

He walks over to the nearest tavern.

"Do you know a ship captain named Hector? He's from Greece."

"I know him, or at least knew him."

Zarus' heart tugs.

"He has changed his route to Britannia. I live in his home town—Corinth— and see him occasionally.'

"Do you know if he still has an Arabian and Egyptian horse?

"He has several horses, but I've seen both Arabians and Egyptians. Why? Do you want to buy one?"

"No, I sold them to him a few years ago when I needed the money. I want to buy them back now. If you see him, tell him I will pay whatever he asks."

"I will, indeed, sir. I will, indeed."

Zarus leaves and works his way back up through town toward his house, then remembers another bit of business.

It's late in the day, but even at this hour, I need more workers. They could at least learn their duties tonight, then be all ready to work in the morning.

He works his way over to the city square and sees two men arguing. He squats near enough to them that he can overhear what they are yelling at each other about.

"It's your fault we got fired."

"How can it be my fault? We were both guilty, if that's what you want to call guilty."

"It was your idea to stop work and help that man up the hill."

"Well, you went along with it."

"What if he has something catching, and we die of it?"

"Then, we die. So what? We're out of work and may as well be dead."

Their voices calm. "What are we going to do, Meir?" We can't go home and admit we've been fired for helping an old cripple man up a hill so he could get home."

"I don't know, Leib. We've both got a house full of kids. You've got your parents living with you."

"How do we go home and tell our families they are going to starve to death now?"

"Excuse me, gentlemen. I was wandering through the square just now and noticed you here visiting with each other. I know you must be busy, but I am desperate to hire men for my mine. Would you take a denarus each to report to work for me for the rest of the day?"

"But the day is almost over. The sun is going down."

Zarus is startled to realize how much time has gone by.

"Listen, I'm in a hurry. If you want the job, go out through the city gate, turn left, and walk until you get to an open-pit mine. Report to Saabhu, and he will tell you what to do. And I'll need you indefinitely if you would consider it."

"Yes, sir," Meir answers.

"We'll go right there," Leib says. "And sir, God bless you. He has just blessed us."

Zarus smiles and turns toward home. He mounts his horse again and urges it into a trot. He arrives home just as the sun is dipping past the horizon."

Pesachya takes the reins to Zarus' horse, and the gate opens.

"Sir, we have been watching for you," Eshachk says with a twinkle in his eye. "Hear all that screaming? It's coming, sir! It's coming."

"Hang in there, man," Simcha says. "You're about to be a proud father three times over. How lucky is that?"

Zarus resumes pacing. Simcha happily paces next to him. Eshachk stands in the middle of the courtyard, grinning. "Reminds me of the night Devorah was born."

"Amen!" they hear coming from the bedroom. Penina opens the door a crack, sticks her head out, and shouts, "It's a girl!" then closes it back.

"Where are the children, Eshachk?"

"I believe they may be playing on your horse, master."

Zarus rushes out to the stable. He is pleased to see Alon's two children laughing and revived with good food. "Amram. Ithamar. You have a new baby sister."

"How wonderful, Papa," Amram says with full vigor.

Ithamar toddles up to his father. "Papa, can I pet her?"

Estar arrives in the garden. "There you are, Zarus. What an exciting day this has been," she says.

"You don't know half of it," Zarus says, hugging his sister. "We'll talk later."

"Of course. Now you go on in and say hello to your new daughter."

Zarus rushes into the bedroom and kneels at the bed Devorah has taken to after no longer needing the birthing stool.

"My love, my pearl," Zarus whispers.

"Here is your baby daughter."

"She is so beautiful. Looks like you just like I knew she would. What shall we name her?"

"I'd like to name her Lleah after my grandmother."

"The grandmother whose pearl you inherited?"

"Yes, that grandmother."

"That reminds me," Zarus says rising. "I'll be right back. Don't go anywhere."

Zarus takes several long paces into the courtyard and the table where he'd set the precious coffer hours earlier. He rushes back into the bedroom and once more kneels at Devorah's bedside.

"Let me hold little Lleah while you take a peek at what is in the coffer."

"Oh, a present for me?" she says weakly.

Zarus watches her eyes as she opens the lid. They widen and sparkle, and she sits up farther in the bed.

"My pearl! My grandmother's pearl. How?"

It does not matter how. What matters is that I still have my beautiful wife, and she has given me three beautiful children. Everything is perfect."

"What was that?" Devorah says, looking around the room in shock."

"What? I didn't feel anything."

"There it is again."

"Oh, it's nothing. You're just recovering. That's all. Now you rest. I will put your pearl on the table right here. I think baby Lleah may be hungry."

Zarus sits back and watches his wife and daughter. His life is perfect now.

There is a knock on the outer gate. *Who could it be this hour of the night?*

He hears Wajid's voice. "Saabhu sent me. Tell the master there is trouble out at the mine. Recent hires fighting over their pay."

"For the kingdom of heaven is like a landowner who went out early in the morning to hire men to work in his vineyard.

He agreed to pay them a denarus for the day and sent them into his vineyard.

"About the third hour, he went out and saw others standing in the marketplace doing nothing.

He told them, 'You also go and work in my vineyard, and I will pay you whatever is right.'

So they went. "He went out again about the sixth hour and the ninth hour and did the same thing.

About the eleventh hour, he went out and found still others standing around. He asked them, 'Why have you been standing here all day long doing nothing?'

" 'Because no one has hired us,' they answered. "He said to them, 'You also go and work in my vineyard.'

"When evening came, the owner of the vineyard said to his foreman, 'Call the workers and pay them their wages, beginning with the last ones hired and going on to the first.'

"The workers who were hired about the eleventh hour came, and each received a denarus.

So when those came who were hired first, they expected to receive more. But each one of them also received a denarus.

When they received it, they began to grumble against the landowner.

'These men who were hired last worked only one hour,' they said, 'and you have made them equal to us who have borne the burden of the work and the heat of the day.'

"But he answered one of them, 'Friend, I am not being unfair to you. Didn't you agree to work for a denarus?

Take your pay and go. I want to give the man who was hired last the same as I gave you.

Don't I have the right to do what I want with my own money? Or are you envious because I am generous?'

"So the last will be first, and the first will be last." (Matthew 20:1-16)

21 ~ LOST

AD 23
Copper Mine, Timna Valley, Arabah Desert, Idumea

"**I** brought **Simcha out for a tour of your mine,**" **Estar tells her brother. "We've been here a couple weeks and need to get back to Sychar before our customers forget us.**"

Estar, Simcha, Zarus, and Gersshon talk to each other in the *officium* tent. It is early morning, and Gersshon has just joined the other three.

"So, Simcha, how do you like being married to my sister? It's been two years now," Zarus asks.

"Every day, I wake up wondering what is going to come out of that little bow mouth, and where her feet with the long toes are going to take her."

Zarus smiles. "That seems to sum you up, Sis," he says to Estar.

"You've been good for her. She was a widow for six years. I'm glad you're in her life."

"She's too beautiful to not have a husband," Gersshon adds.

"What am I?" Estar asks, her hands on her hips. "A flea on a mountain lion, talking about me as though I weren't here."

"How about giving you the royal tour with both owners showing you around," Gersshon adds with a wide sweep of his hand and a bow.

"I guess we'd better get the tour started," Simcha says. "That is, if you have time for us."

"We will make time," Gersshon says. "However, I'm not so sure Estar's white tunic will survive it."

"What's wrong with my white tunic? It matches the white feather in my hair."

"Let's go, kids," Zarus says with a broad grin. "My sister has her own mind made up. No sense arguing with her."

The couple follows Zarus and Gersshon out of the *officium* tent.

"The mine is now seven years old," Zarus explains. "It started with just Gersshon and me and now employs one hundred miners in addition to officers.

He walks over to the edge of the pit. "Be careful here. As we learned when working the deep shaft mine, the earth is always moving. It shifts more at night than the day, and we don't know why. It also shifts more when there is a full moon, and we don't know why about that either."

"We're going to take the haul road down," Gersshon says.

"How deep is the mine?" Simcha asks.

"We normally go down about one man length a year. So in the seven years we have been operating, we've gone down about seven man-lengths," Zarus explains.

"Watch out!" Estar screams.

The men look behind them and see an empty wagon being drawn by a team of oxen coming down the haul road behind them. They run over to the side and stand on one of the stepped benches. As the team passes, they notice both oxen lowing as they've never heard oxen do before.

"Are they in pain? Are you working them too hard? Poor babies," Estar says.

"I don't know what's wrong with them. They usually do their job in complete quiet," Gersshon says. "Well, they're out of the way. Let's keep going."

"You will notice when the wagon gets to the bottom, rocks with copper in them are thrown into it to be taken up to the overburden, the surface of the desert. Then we have camels to carry the ore the rest of the way to the warehouses."

"Is there copper in all the rocks the miners break loose?" Simcha asks.

"No. We have other ox-drawn wagons that come down to haul that away and dispose of it in our waste dump, that mountain you may have seen between the pit and the warehouses." Zarus and Gersshon take turns explaining things and answering questions.

By now, they are near the bottom. "What's that water wheel doing down here? It's huge. Are the men that thirsty?" Estar asks.

"Well, they do get thirsty. But the water wheels are pumping water out of the floor of the mine. We've run into an underground river. Those boys you see take a filled pail off the wheel, replace it with an empty one, then carry the filled pail to the surface where each one is emptied into large water vats. People with villages out in the desert come here and buy water from us."

"Oh, no!" Estar cries out.

"Estar. Are you all right?" Simcha asks.

"I scraped up against a rusty place on the water wheel, and now look at my white tunic."

The three men accompanying her look at each other, but decide not to respond.

"Let's go back up to the surface."

As they progress, they are refreshed by a breeze. "That certainly feels good."

"Yes," Zarus replies. "The breeze starts about mid-morning and picks up through the day. It makes the heat bearable for us."

Now back at the surface, they walk to the *officium* tent. "Come on in and rest before you head back into town. Have some juice. We usually have orange, pineapple, apple, or pomegranate," Gersshon says with a grin.

"How do you get such a wonderful variety?"

"You forget, dear sister," Zarus says, "that we live at a seaport.

"Uh, I see Noach motioning for me. Are you going back into the city?" Zarus asks.

"No, we're just going to keep going north until we're back in Sychar," Simcha says.

"I don't know of a caravan going that way."

"We don't need one. I'm all Estar needs to keep her protected," Simcha explains.

Zarus embraces his sister and his brother-in-law. "God go with you and keep you safe.

When they leave, Gersshon tells Zarus, "I'm going into town. I just realized I have some very important business to take care of."

————

"Something strange is going on, buddy," Gersshon tells his partner the next day.

Zarus walks into the *officium* tent and takes off the band and kerchief from his head, throwing it onto a pile of cushions used for meetings with guests.

"You mean out in the valley? You're right." He stretches his arms over his head, arches his back, and grunts. "Do we have any juice here? I don't care what kind it is."

"There are no birds," Gersshon continues. "The few birds I've seen have been huddled under bushes and making shrill sounds. Salamanders and desert rats are running in circles. Weird."

Zarus wanders over to a table with several survey scrolls on it and picks up one.

"I hadn't noticed those things, Gersshon, but I did notice the camels at the warehouses are roaring and growling. The oxen pulling the wagons up the haul road are lowing as though their lives were being threatened. And my horse is stomping at the ground like he's trying to put out a fire."

"Something bad is going to happen," Gersshon says. "Animals know these things."

Zarus looks over at his boyhood friend and partner. Very few times in his life has he ever seen Gersshon spooked, but this is definitely one of those times.

"Did you know we hit a milestone yesterday, Gersshon? You hired our hundredth man. Just think. When we started this mine seven years ago, it was just the two of us with our chisels and hammers. Just the two of us out in the middle of the desert acting like fools."

"But now we're rich fools," Gersshon adds with a grin.

"Hey, why aren't you married by now? You're not that much younger than me."

"Never had time. Perhaps I will someday if, that is, I find one that knows how to follow orders."

"Zarus. Gersshon. Zarus. Gersshon. Sirs. Come quickly," Wajid says, gasping for air. "There's something bad wrong with the floor of the mine. Saabhu says so. Hurry."

Forgetting his juice request, Zarus grabs his band and kerchief and situates them on his head as he goes out into the direct sunlight. Being thirty-three years old, he still looks fit but is slower than when he first arrived at the mine as a slave at age twenty. Still, he is in better shape than the shorter Gersshon who likes to eat.

Zarus' long legs take him to the edge of the pit far sooner than Gersshon and Wajid. He looks down and sees a surge of dirty water bubbling up out of the pit floor. He takes the haul road down to the water.

The hundred men working the floor have scrambled and are standing around it on stepped benches carved in the inside of the pit to avoid erosion and landslides.

Saabhu is standing among them, but identifiable by his Egyptian *shendyt* wrapped around his hips instead of a full tunic.

Zarus walks around one of the benches until he stands next to Saabhu. He does not say anything, but rather stands watching the bubbly, muddy spring water come up from under the pit floor.

When Gersshon arrives, he asks the first question: "When did it break through?"

"I noticed Zarus riding in on his horse, and it happened about then."

"And it has risen this fast since then?" Zarus asks.

"I'm not sure it's all that deep. What worries me is the force with which it appeared."

"What do you make of it?" Gersshon asks.

"I have my theories, and they are all bad," Saabhu says, "but I prefer to keep them to myself right now."

Gersshon puts his fists on his hips. "Do you know just who you are talking to?"

Zarus clears his throat. "Gersshon," he says under his breath, "Saabhu was raised in the mining business. His father was a mining engineer before him. If he says he wants to wait, we shall wait. He will tell us when he knows for sure. Isn't that right, Saabhu?"

"Yes, sir, it is."

"Well, I don't guess there is anything we can do here. We need to find Noach and have him reassign the men to…Huh? What was that?

Gersshon steps back away from the water, then watches as it collapses upon itself and disappears inside the earth.

Zarus stares at the pit floor then over at Saabhu. "What does this mean?" he whispers.

"It means it is the worst of my theories."

"Has anyone found Noach yet? All you men stay where you are until Noach gets here and can reassign you. We don't want to endanger you, but give him time to figure out how best to use you out away from this danger.

When Zarus reaches the overburden at the top of the mine, he walks out into the desert alone. He orients himself and faces Mount Gerizim—though Jherusalem is in the same direction. He falls to his knees and bows his head to the desert floor. "Jhehovah God, don't let these men be in danger. If you allow the mine to be destroyed, I have started over before. But do not allow the men to be destroyed."

He rises and walks over to his horse, being protected under the shadow of a cliff, pawing the dirt as though there were a snake at his hooves. He pats the horse and speaks to it softly. "Calm down now. Stay calm. That's right. Nothing to be afraid of. That's right. You're safe."

He continues to pat the horse. As he does, he sways, and the horse's body quivers. The horse stops, its eyes darting around, and he rises up on his hindquarters.

"Easy boy. Easy."

Zarus sways again. He hears small rocks overhead. He steps back farther under the shadow of the cliff. He faces forward and hears a roar of men rushing up from the bottom of the pit.

One side of the pit loosens, cracks, and bellows. A slide begins. Slow at first, then picking up speed. As brown dust billows and flies upward, the roar grows louder.

A crack appears in the desert floor. It runs two hundred man-lengths down through the desert. It swallows up whatever is in its way.

Zarus looks back over to the pit. Brown gray dust rises out of it like a bear out of its lair, looking for something to devour.

He looks up at the sky and sees clouds turning the colors of a rainbow.

Then the quiet. Not a whisper. Not a whimper. Not a sigh.

He hears Noach's voice.

"Everyone over here. We need to get a count to see if anyone is missing."

The *officium* tent is now flattened. But the men oblige Noach and hurry to the area in front of what is left of the tent through the gray-brown dust lingering in the air and raining down on them. They stand in rows of ten as though standing before their commander.

"Men," Noach says, picking up on their desire to mean something in a world now upside down.

Yes, they are still men. Covered with a finger span of dust, their eyes the only human part of them revealed to the world. But they are still men. Men with stamina, courage, fortitude.

"Start counting."

"One. Two. Three. Four. Five...Ninety-six. Ninety-seven. Ninety-eight. Ninety-nine..."

"One hundred? Is one hundred here?" One hundred? Do it again. Count again."

"One. Two. Three. Four...."

"Still just ninety-nine. Who's missing?"

"I think it's Alon, sir. Whenever we get counted like this, Alon always stands by me."

Zarus, Gersshon, and Saabhu arrive right after the count begins.

"Okay, who was the last person to see Alon?"

"I guess that would be me," Dov says.

"You both came to work for us on the same day, didn't you?"

"Yes, sir."

"Well, we need to find him," Zarus pronounces.

"Sir, everyone needs to go home and see if their families are okay."

"Well, all right. Go on home. I will stay here and look for Alon."

Zarus begins by walking along the cliff to see if Alon had found an impression deep enough he would be safe from falling rocks above. "Alon. Alon, do you hear me?"

He has no luck, so walks over to the fissure in the desert floor. It is a man length wide and two-hundred man-lengths long. He looks down into it the whole way in case he had been swallowed up by the earth. "Alon. Alon!" He listens, but there is no reply.

He goes to the edge of the pit, something he does not want to do, but must eventually do. He is shocked at what he sees. The landslide just happened to one side of the mine. It can be salvaged. But there is something else.

The bottom of the pit has broken open. He makes his way with caution down the surviving haul road until he reaches the floor of the mine, or what is left of it.

Zarus looks down at the hole in the bottom and stares at something that looks familiar. He thinks he sees pillars around the fallen smaller rock. Pillars of copper. He stands at the edge of the gaping hole. *Alon has to be down there.*

He looks around the sides of the pit. *They seem stable enough. I've got to get in there.*

He walks to the edge, squats, and jumps down into the hole. He looks around. *Why does this look so familiar?* With daylight streaming in, he looks closer. He picks up something iron. It is a chisel. He looks nearby and sees a hammer.

This has to be another stope of Baaruch's mine. He always said the original owner didn't have maps, and he had no idea how many milles of other galleries and stopes there were that had been blocked off by earlier collapses.

"Alon. Alon? Alon," he calls out. "Are you down here?"

Zarus hears a weak groan. He walks with caution in the direction of the groan. He comes to a pile of fallen rocks. He looks around to determine whether it is safe. *I must take the chance. I've got to save Alon.*

He makes his way across the collapsed rock. On the other side, he sees skeletons. *Is this what fell and blocked the way of the miners before Baaruch bought the mine?*

He detects a shaft. It descends into blackness. He checks around for a candle or oil lamp. He finds a lamp still strapped to the skull of one of the skeletons. He removes it and looks for emergency oil and a bow drill for making fire. He finds both, works with feverish speed to create fire for the lamp, and succeeds.

He looks down into the shaft but does not see the bottom. He picks up a stone and drops it down the shaft. It takes a while before he hears it thump at the bottom.

Zarus hears the groan again. It does not come from the shaft. With the light on his forehead, he looks around. "Alon? Alon? Are you here?"

The groan again. He sees a hand appear on a rock. He looks closer and sees Alon lying on the floor of the former deep vein mine.

"I'm here, Alon," he says, leaning over the injured man. "I'm here. I'm not going to leave you. Now, where do you hurt? Alon? Come on, you need to help me."

Alon's hand slips from the rock, and he moves it to his leg. Zarus feels along his leg. "It's broken. You can't walk on it. Where else do you hurt?"

Alon moves his hand to his head. "Well, of course, your head is going to hurt. I see blood on it. Are you dizzy?"

Alon tries to lift his head but lets it go back and whispers yes.

"Okay, Alon, this is what we're going to do." He remembers back when he was twenty and did the same thing for the man who had fallen off the cliff by the road they were building.

"I'm going to carry you in my arms to the highest place I can find to get us out of here. Okay, so far?"

Alon nods weakly.

"Now, once we're at the best escape route, I'm going to put you over my shoulder and begin climbing. Don't worry. I'm still very strong. I won't drop you."

Alon blinks his eyes in ascent.

"Wait here while I get things ready."

With no more words, Zarus goes over to the hole in the roof and looks around for boulders that have a flat side. He picks them up as he had picked up boulders on the road so long ago and lines them up to make a step. He continues his work until he is satisfied they go high enough for him to grab hold of the pit floor and pull them out.

"Are you ready?" he asks Alon. Alon manages a smile.

Zarus picks up the man he had seen in the town square a year earlier, and once more rescues him.

He carries the injured man to the highest spot and sets him down. He checks where he needs to put his hands, as gently as possible, puts Alon on his shoulder, reaches up, and grabs hold of the top edge of the mine roof, now his own open-pit mine floor. With muscles bulging, he lifts his own weight as well as Alon's.

As soon as he gets his elbows on the upper surface, he swings his free leg up and scoots his body along until his torso is on his mine's floor, above the old mine's roof. He pushes his entire torso up, then slides Alon off his shoulder and onto solid ground.

He rises to his knees and looks down on his worker. "You're safe now, Alon. You're safe."

He sits down next to Alon and rests. Then Zarus picks him up in his arms and carries him up the haul road to the surface of the open-pit mine.

As he does, he hears the other men. They are lifting parts of their sleep barracks and trying to make them serviceable for when they return to work.

Zarus looks toward his warehouses. He remembers the night Baaruch had died. He turns back and walks in the direction of his horse, or where he had left it. It is safe.

He puts Alon on his horse, then slides up to sit behind him, and heads for the city.

As he does, his mind wanders back to Baaruch's son, his wife's brother, and wonders what has happened to Benyamin.

Then Jhesus told them this parable:
"Suppose one of you has a hundred sheep and loses one of them.
Does he not leave the ninety-nine in the open country and go after the lost sheep until he finds it?
And when he finds it, he joyfully puts it on his shoulders and goes home. Then he calls his friends and neighbors together and says, 'Rejoice with me; I have found my lost sheep.'

I tell you that in the same way, there will be more rejoicing in heaven over one sinner who repents than over ninety-nine righteous persons who do not need to repent. (Luke 15:3-7).

22 ~ TRICKED

AD 23
Road from Jherusalem to Jhericho, Province of Jhudea, Palestine

"**N**o! Don't hurt us. Here is my purse. You can have all our money." It is Simcha, trembling.

"The highwayman is big and thick. He has a head of red hair with a matching wild beard. He wears clothing more suitable for a barbarian from northern Italy, with a tunic of wool, a cape of boar skins, and high leather shoes.

"Buddy," he growls, "I intend to take your purse. I'm also going to take your donkeys. And your life."

"No! Don't hurt him. I'll do anything you want. Just don't hurt him," Estar cries.

The wild man looks over at the woman and smiles. "Oh, I intend to take you too, my sweet."

Simcha prods his mule into rising up on its hind legs in an attempt to trample their threat.

A second barbarian jumps down from the rocks above and lands on Simcha, wrestles him to the ground, pulls out a knife, and plants it in Simcha's heart.

"No! You brutes! Not Simcha."

"You are next, my sweet," the first highwayman says, grabbing hold of Estar and pulling her off her donkey.

"No. We were paid to just kill the man. He told us to not harm the woman."

"At least we get the money and the animals."

The two men scale the cliff at one side of the steep road and disappear.

Jhericho, Province of Jhudea

"What's keeping them?" Avigail says, walking the elegant tiled floor of the house she shares with Uncle Caalev, the priest. "They left Eilat four days ago. They should be here by now. Benyamin, see who is at the gate."

"I believe you have servants to do that, Mother."

"Do as I say," she says, her eyes flashing with anger and tears. "And bring me another plate of baklava."

Benyamin opens the gate and jerks back.

"Sir, do you know this woman? I found her sitting on the road from Jherusalem next to someone she calls her dead husband."

"Oh!"

Estar is supported by the stranger, her hair down in her eyes, blue dress torn, face and arms coated with dirt and scratches. She looks up at Benyamin but does not acknowledge him or anyone else.

Benyamin steps beside her, sweeps her up in his arms, and brings her into the courtyard.

"Mother, quick. It's Estar. Where can I put her?"

Avigail throws down her sweet and directs her son to the couch she often uses when eating meals and snacks.

He lays her down and Avigail nudges him out of the way to look her over.

"Poor, poor dear." Without turning her head, she calls out, Sarach! Come quickly and bring some water and soft towel with you. Oh, my, she's cold. Kalman, get a blanket off your bed and bring it. Hurry."

"Sir. Ma'am. Ahem."

Benyamin and Avigail look over at the gate still ajar.

"Oh, we forgot about you," Avigail says, standing and walking toward the stranger. "Please forgive our untoward manners."

"I have the body. The lady's husband's body. Will you take it?"

"What? Benyamin, go get Simcha's body."

"Not me, Mother. Get Kalman to do it."

"Kalman, come get this woman's husband's body. Take it to the kitchen area where we can lay it out and clean it up. It will have to be buried today."

"Yes, mistress," Kalman responds.

"Oh, and, Benyamin, pay the man something."

"You know I used everything I had to get here from Egypt. He'll either have to go unpaid or..."

"Oh, never mind. Wait here."

Avigail climbs the stairs, trips on her scarlet linen tunic hem, goes to her bedroom, picks up a bronze coin, and returns to the gate. "Here you are, sir. We are most grateful for what you did for us," she says as she closes the gate.

When she turns around, she notices Benyamin now has his arm around Estar as she leans her head on his shoulder.

He should have married her in the first place. "Poor girl, tell us all about it," Avigail says as she nudges Estar's legs over far enough, she can sit on the couch. "When did it happen? How many were there?"

"I don't remember much," Estar says. "There was a big man with a cape of skins. He was so big, he was able to stop both our donkeys, and...."

"Oh, sweet dear. You have been through so much," Avigail says.

"Zarus. Does Zarus know? Please get word to Eitan. I need my brother."

"Quite right, my little one," Avigail says softly. She turns and calls to Kalman. "Send a rider down to Eitan to tell her brother, Zarus, she has been injured and her husband killed. Do it quickly. Maybe the rider can get there by tonight. Camels can run in the desert."

Benyamin looks at the delicate doll leaning heavily on his arm and pats her face with his free hand.

"What are you doing, Benyamin? Quit patting her."

Benyamin obeys but finds his bulk slipping farther off the couch until he is almost to the floor. He pulls his arm away from Estar and holds her delicate hand.

———

"We came as soon as we heard," Gersshon says the next evening. "We have ridden all day. Had to change horses often because of the heat. But we're here now."

Avigail leads Zarus over to the couch they have kept Estar on so they wouldn't have to move her. Zarus kneels on the floor next to his sister.

She wakens, sees Zarus, and smiles weakly.

"I insisted on coming along," Gersshon says, standing behind her brother. "I couldn't desert Zarus like this. How are you, my dear?" he asks Estar.

Benyamin, sitting nearby, glares at Gersshon and mumbles under his breath, "She's not your dear."

Estar sits up and holds out her hands for her brother. He envelops her in his arms, and her tears come rushing out. Neither says anything.

The other three in the room say nothing but watch closely.

"They took my Simcha away from me," she finally whispers amidst her tears.

"I know. It's not fair. You've been through so much. Too much. You don't deserve this," Zarus says.

"Simcha didn't deserve it either. Why did God let it happen?"

"I don't know, except that he gives everyone free will, and sometimes they side with Satan when using their free will," Zarus responds, not sure what to say.

"Do they know who did it?" Gersshon asks.

"No one seems to have ever seen anyone like them before," Avigail interjects. "They looked like barbarians. They were barbarians."

"Oh. That's too bad. You're sure no one can identify them?" Gersshon says.

"Do you want to go on home to Sychar, or stay here a while longer?" Zarus asks.

"There's nothing for me to go home to. May I stay here a while longer, Avigail?"

"Of course you can. We have a guest bedroom you can have during the duration."

Days go by. Everyone dotes on Estar. Zarus sits by her and talks about better days when they were children and sometimes makes her smile. Avigail tells her about the important people in Jhericho and Sychar she has sold her tunic designs to and suggests she needs more fabric.

Benyamin takes her for walks to the nearest bakery and buys her sweets. He takes her arm in his and pats her hand while Avigail's maid, Sarach, walks with them to keep up appearances of respectability.

Gersshon puts her on his horse, and they ride out to see the beauty of the Dead Sea, with Kalman on a separate horse to make sure decorum is kept.

Sometimes she asks Benyamin or Gersshon to take her to the cemetery.

"Well, sister, I need to go," Zarus says one morning. "I have good officers, but cannot be gone too long. Gersshon, I regret to say, must leave with me."

"I would give anything to stay here and comfort you, my dear," Gersshon says. "But, please take this token into your bosom in remembrance of me." He hands her an alabaster box with an exquisite necklace of peridots and diamonds embedded in copper filigree.

"Even though I will be gone, my thoughts will still be with you. It is not easy being a widow. If you ever need anything, anything at all, let me know. What's mine is yours. I will write to you when I arrive home and make sure you are okay."

"Well, my dear," Benyamin interjects, "after they leave, I will take you to town to a jeweler who lets you design your own jewelry."

A week later, Estar sits on the roof, catching the evening breeze. "Avigail, you have been most kind to me. You, too, Benyamin. But I have to try my wings alone now. I need to go back to Sychar. I need to face life without my Simcha."

Tears return to her eyes. "I miss him so."

"Someday, you will put your pain behind you, and live again," Avigail says. "You have been through so much in your short life."

"Well, I will be thirty-four soon. I feel like I'm growing old too fast."

"God go with you, child."

"Have you lined up a caravan to travel with?" Benyamin asks.

"Yes. Your servant, Kalman, helped me make the arrangements. I just cannot travel alone anymore."

"I will be happy to ride out to the city gate with you in the morning."

"Thank you, Benyamin. You are very kind."

AD 24

"Mistress, a messenger has just arrived from Sychar with a letter for you."

"Thank you, Kalman," Avigail says. She is seated in the garden, embroidering the bodice of her latest tunic design with gold thread. She sets her work down, breaks the seal on the scroll, and opens it.

DEAR AVIGAIL. I JUST WANTED TO LET YOU KNOW THIS PAST YEAR WITHOUT SIMCHA HAS BEEN DIFFICULT, BUT MADE EASIER BY YIGAL. HE HAS BEEN A GREAT COMFORT AND STRENGTH TO ME. YOU MAY THINK IT IS TOO SOON,

BUT I HAVE THREE CHILDREN. I HAVE MARRIED AGAIN FINALLY.

I HAVE FEWER FRIENDS IN TOWN NOW. THEY DO NOT THINK A WOMAN SHOULD MARRY FIVE TIMES, EVEN IF SHE WAS BEREFT OF HER HUSBAND THROUGH SUCH TRAGIC CIRCUMSTANCES. I DID NOT ASK FOR THIS. SATAN IS SURELY TAUNTING ME. BUT I WILL CONTINUE TO BELIEVE GOD WILL BE MY HELP. I HOPE YOU LOVE ME STILL.

"Benyamin, a letter just arrived from Estar. I think you will be interested in it."

Benyamin comes out to the garden when he hears his mother's shrill voice.

"Yes, Mother. Did you call?"

Avigail hands the scroll to her son and says only, "From Estar."

He takes the letter and wanders over to one of the other native-stone benches elsewhere in the garden. *At last, she sees me for what I am and misses my attentions. My patience has at last paid off.*

He opens the scroll, and after a moment, throws it into a fountain in the center of the garden.

"How can she betray me like that? I've sent her jewelry, unset pearls, and diamonds to mount on her clothes or in her hair, urns from Egypt, murals from Sheba. I demand them back." Benyamin grits his teeth and hits an olive tree in the garden, winches, and draws his bleeding fist back to nurse.

He walks in circles through the garden that, to him, is now overgrown with blackness and death. "She cannot mock me. She's not an Estar at all. Never has been. She's an Istar, goddess of heaven now plunged to hell. How I hate her."

"Dear, what you need is something to get your mind off her," Avigail volunteers.

"Didn't you say you heard from someone back in Egypt wanting you to go in with him and someone else to buy a gold mine?"

"I hate her. I hate her." Benyamin yells into the air as though cursing the clouds.

"Now, Son, maybe this would be a good time for us to approach your uncle about an inheritance of some kind. He never married, never had any children. All he has is you and me. Well, he has Devorah, but she doesn't need anything; she's rich. Come on inside with me. I'll have Sarach bringing us some grapes, and we'll come up with a plan before Uncle Caalev gets home from work at the temple."

"Well..."

"Come on, Benyamin. You are too good for her."

Benyamin looks over at his mother, who has just taken his arm. "Yes, I am, aren't I? I'm too good for that, Istar."

"Come now. We will make a list of reasons why you should have your inheritance now."

Once inside, she reclines on her couch, and Benyamin sits on a bench by a table.

"Sarach, please bring us a plate of grapes or whatever you have. And Kalman, go into Master Caalev's study and bring out one of his wax tablets and a stylus."

"First, Benyamin, he is getting old and would want to control his holdings while he can rather than wait for vultures to come take it from us. Second, if you can buy that gold mine, it will honor your father, Baaruch, who had always wanted to own a gold mine. Third..."

"Did I hear my name spoken?" they hear from the gate.

"Of course you did, Uncle," Avigail replies, rising to meet her benefactor and kiss him on the cheek. Now you come right over here. I am going to wash your feet myself."

"Niece," he says with a grin. What has gotten into you? I know. You want something."

"Sit down now. I have the water and towel all ready."

Caalev takes off his priest robe and prayer shawl, grabs hold of the bottom of his tunic, and raises it a hand span before sitting on the bench.

"So, how was everything at the temple today?" Avigail asks.

"The Sanhedrin needs me. They don't know it, but they do. I could solve a lot of their problems if they'd just give me a chance. I would do anything to be appointed to the Supreme Sanhedrin of the land. It's always just beyond my grasp. I am growing old. I don't want to miss my chance, and..."

He realizes he has been lecturing the sky and looks down at his niece.

"Oh, listen to this old man ramble on. I'm sorry, Avigail. I didn't mean to put my burdens on your delicate shoulders."

"Uncle, after dinner, let's go up to the roof. I have an idea that might get you on the Sanhedrin after all."

"Avigail, you are always full of such surprises."

"Go on, now, and eat," she says,, rising with the bowl of water.

"Here, Benyamin, throw this out, and then you and Uncle can eat. I'll be on the roof meditating."

She climbs the steps to the ornate roof with flowers around the ledge surrounding it, sits and enjoys the fragrance of violets and roses. *My plan is coming together better than I thought...*

"There you are, Avigail. We have been well fattened up. So, now, what do you want to talk to me about?"

"Members of the Sanhedrin are some of the richest men in the country. Perhaps you need to join their economic ranks."

"What do you mean, child?" he answers, wiping his mouth with his sleeve.

"Would gold be enough to raise your esteem in their eyes?"

"Of course, but I have no gold, other than a purse of gold coins."

"I know you want on the Sanhedrin, and the Sanhedrin needs you. They are missing out on your wisdom and knowledge. They're missing out on hearing you speak when none of the rest of them knows what to say. They're missing out on a lifetime of experiences you can take to them. They're missing out on you."

"Well, you put it so eloquently. Do you think I'm all that?"

"Of course you are. I cannot even put it all into words. But one thing I know: You must be appointed to the Sanhedrin."

"That's fine, niece, but how?"

"Gold speaks to them, doesn't it?"

"Yes, but as I said, I don't have enough to impress them."

"You could."

"How?"

"A gold mine."

Priest Caalev laughs. "That would certainly catch their attention, but I don't have a gold mine. You know that."

"You could," she says.

"Huh? How am I ever going to own a gold mine?"

"Benyamin, would you come up and bring the letter from Egypt that arrived a few days ago?"

Benyamin takes the steps to the roof two at a time, scroll in hand.

"Okay, now, Benyamin, read your letter to Uncle Caalev."

"Well, it basically says that two of my friends have a chance to buy a gold mine from a new widow who wants to get rid of it."

Caalev stands and walks around the roof, then returns to his seat.

"You know, I like the idea of owning a gold mine."

"Well, it wouldn't quite be yours, Uncle Caalev. It has to be in Benyamin's name in order for the other partners to accept the deal."

"Hmmm....Let me see that letter. Kalman," he calls down to the main floor, "bring me a lamp."

Benyamin hands it to his elder, and the three sit in silence as Caalev reads. Avigail looks over at her son, smiles, and winks. At last, they hear the rattle of the scroll being rolled back up.

Priest Caalev lays the scroll on the table next to the lamp. They wait. He stands and walks around a while, looking down at the street below sometimes and looking up into the sky sometimes. He walks back over to his niece and great-nephew and sits back down.

"How much did they say they needed for your share? I know it was in the letter, but I don't remember."

"Ninety thousand denari," Benyamin replies.

Benyamin braces himself for the outburst that does not come.

Caalev puts his hands behind his head and sways back and forth as though counting. He squints his eyes. He purses his lips and takes a deep breath. He bites the inside of his cheek and pulls at his gray beard.

"I tell you what, young man. I will provide the ninety thousand..."

Benyamin struggles to hold back a grin.

"...if you bring me in as your partner. This will be a private second arrangement. You go in as partner to the other two men, but I will own half your partnership. Do you understand what I am saying?"

"He agrees!" Avigail says, rising to her feet. She steps over to her uncle and hugs his neck.

"Niece, you're smothering me."

She backs away, and Caalev rises. Benyamin rises too. Caalev holds out both his hands, and Benyamin takes them. Caalev pulls Benyamin into an embrace and kisses him on both cheeks. Benyamin reciprocates.

"We will go to my lawyer tomorrow and draw up papers for my partnership with you. Then we will work out arrangements to get the money directly to the widow, not those other two men. You will sign their documents, but you will deal directly with the widow for the money."

Priest Caalev walks to the steps and heads down. They hear him chuckle. "Me in the Sanhedrin. Finally."

———

Now that everything is official, Uncle, we need to have a celebratory banquet. We will invite all the important people in Jhericho and Jherusalem. We will invite members of the Sanhedrin and their wives."

"We will also invite Zarus and Gersshon to come up here for it, and Zarus' sister—he can't bring himself to say her name—and her new husband to come down for it," Benyamin says.

"What would you invite them for?"

"I have my reasons. Let me take care of them."

"All right, Son. It's your banquet, after all. If it will make you happy to invite them, go ahead, though I cannot imagine why."

Benyamin sits down at a table in the elaborate courtyard and pens a letter to Zarus, Gersshon, and Istar. Each will be sent their own letter, though they will say the same thing.

FROM BENYAMIN OF JHERICHO AND SYCHAR. I AM PLEASED TO INVITE YOU TO A SPECIAL BANQUET BEING GIVEN THE THIRD DAY OF THE MONTH OF TEVET IN JERICHO. IT WILL BEGIN WHEN THE SUN GOES DOWN. IT IS TO HONOR A SPECIAL GUEST, BUT THE HONOREE WILL NOT KNOW THEY HAVE BEEN CHOSEN UNTIL THE BANQUET BEGINS.

EVEN THOUGH YOU WILL NOT KNOW MOST OF OUR FRIENDS WHO WILL BE AT THE BANQUET, I WANTED TO MAKE A POINT OF INVITING YOU THREE. PLEASE MAKE A SPECIAL EFFORT TO COME AND MAKE ME VERY HAPPY. THIS IS MY PROMISE TO YOU: YOU WILL NEVER FORGET IT.

"Now, I have already been to a carpenter to get more tables and couches made," Avigail says, walking through the courtyard with Caalev. We will need at least one hundred couches, don't you think, Uncle?

"You do what you want. I'll just show up."

The next month is spent preparing everything.

"This kind of reminds me of Devorah's wedding," Avigail tells Benyamin. "It was such fun planning. I can use some of the same ideas I did then. Too bad, no one would come. We ended up having to bring in beggars and the riffraff of society to fill the hall. Well, it won't be that way this time."

Avigail spends days with a clay tablet listing things that need to be done.

"Now, I think we should have a color scheme of royal blue, white, and gold. We will emphasize the gold, of course, for obvious reasons," she tells her maid, Sarach.

"I want you to be in charge of the food. Everything will be elegant in the extreme. But first, you need to help me make gold buds out of gold silk. We will attach each one to a copper wire, and they will be sent to the wives of everyone attending to put in their hair.

Weeks go by. One by one, the couches are made, sent to an upholsterer, then delivered to Priest Caalev's home and stored in the stable. Kalman is fattening up five calves. Sarach is making most of the gold roses for the women's hair.

The day arrives. Avigail wears a gold silk tunic with matching hooded sleeveless cloak. It is embroidered with royal blue thread. She wears a gold necklace and matching earrings.

The guests begin to arrive. Kalman meets them at the gate. He has hired three assistants who lead them to the garden where their feet are washed, and they are given special sandals to put on for the festivities.

Benyamin stands near the gate, waiting for the special guests for whom he has planned a surprise. Estar is the first of the special ones to arrive.

"Greetings, Estar. And this is your husband, Yigal? Welcome to our home. Please go into the garden for a special perfumed foot washing. Then you may go into the banquet hall and choose your own seats."

More guests arrive. Those from the Sanhedrin with their prayer shawls outnumber the other guests. It is as it should be.

Then the mayor of Jhericho arrives with his wife and three magistrates. The mayors of Bethany and Bethlehem arrive with their wives. The mayor of Jherusalem arrives with his wife. He wears the now popular togas as an indication of his higher station in life.

The air is full of sparks and sparkles.

"Please go into the garden for your foot washing," Kalman says. "An attendant will show you to your seats of choice."

When most have arrived, but not all, Kalman answers the gate again.

"Hello, Kalman," Gersshon says with a slight bow. So good to see you again. I hope we are not too early."

Gersshon is wearing his new royal blue robe with silver-threaded sash, red tassels, sandals with pearls on them, a gold chain, and a gold ring with ruby embedded in it.

He hears noise coming through a nearby door. "Looks like almost everyone is already here. Maybe we got the time wrong."

Zarus steps up and greets Kalman also. "Has my sister arrived?"

"Yes, sir. However, I believe the table where she reclines must be full by now. I'm sure you will find a suitable place. I have been told to let you sit wherever you wish. That is quite an honor, sirs."

Gersshon and Zarus enter the banquet hall. Dignitaries with their toga and priests with their prayer shawls dominate the room, decorated by their lovely wives who are seated separately but not far from the men.

Zarus looks around the women's section until he sees his sister. "There she is. Let's go say hello."

Gersshon steps ahead of Zarus and arrives at the seat of Estar first.

"Well, there is the life of my heart," he says, taking her hand

and kissing it.

"Oh, my, Gersshon, you should not have done that?"

"Why? You know how I feel about you."

"Didn't anyone tell you? I've been married since this winter."

Gersshon steps back, his eyes squinting as though, if he closed them, her announcement would go out of existence.

"Hello, sister. It's so good to see you again. I kept your secret like you asked. You know; about your marriage.

"I didn't tell you to keep it a secret."

"You didn't directly, but I got a letter from Benyamin saying you wanted it so. Regardless, we are here. We will talk to you more after the festivities."

Zarus and Gersshon walk toward the men's section.

"Where shall we sit? He said we could choose," Gersshon says.

"There are a couple of places back here," Zarus responds.

"But look upfront. There are two empty places at the head table. They said they were going to announce the honoree after everyone arrived. Well, most everyone has arrived, and still, no one has taken those two seats. They are for us, Zarus. I know it. Benyamin just tricked us when he said there would be one honoree when there actually are going to be two—you and me."

Gersshon begins to walk toward the front of the room. Zarus calls after him.

"No, Gersshon. What if they aren't for us?"

"But they are. Don't you see? This whole banquet has been organized to honor us among the elite of Jhericho and Jherusalem."

"Well, I'm staying back here. You go ahead," Zarus says.

Zarus takes a place in the back where there are two couches left. He watches as Gersshon walks forward. He also sees Benyamin watching Gersshon. Benyamin has a wide grin on his face.

Gersshon arrives upfront and takes his place at the head table. He looks around in anticipation of an applause. His excitement is shown in his face as his eyes dart around the room as though to say, "Thank you for honoring me this day."

Zarus sees Benyamin motioning for one of the servants. Benyamin points at Gersshon and nods his head. The servant walks over to Gersshon and whispers something to him. Gersshon' face turns red. He shakes his head no at the servant. The servant whispers to him again, and again Gersshon's shakes his head no.

The servant motions to another servant. Upon the second one's arrival, each takes one of Gersshon's arms and lifts him off the couch. Zarus looks over at Benyamin, who has a wide grin and is winking at the servants. The servants wave back.

Gersshon turns his head and sees who the servants are obviously obeying. It is Benyamin. Benyamin waves at Gersshon then pulls his hand across his throat as if cutting it. He holds out his fist toward Gersshon, then sticks out his thumb and points it down.

By this time, many are watching the scene upfront. They watch also as Gersshon is escorted to the back of the room.

Benyamin motions to his uncle and Caalev stands. "Everyone, all of my esteemed colleagues, thank you for coming to our banquet in honor of my nephew, Benyamin of Sychar and Egypt, who is now owner, along with me, of a large and profitable gold mine.

When he noticed how the guests picked the places of honor at the table, he told them this parable:

"When someone invites you to a wedding feast, do not take the place of honor, for a person more distinguished than you may have been invited.

If so, the host who invited both of you will come and say to you, 'Give this man your seat.' Then, humiliated, you will have to take the least important place.

But when you are invited, take the lowest place, so that when your host comes, he will say to you, 'Friend, move up to a better place.' Then you will be honored in the presence of all your fellow guests.

For everyone who exalts himself will be humbled, and he who humbles himself will be exalted." (Luke 14:7-11)

23 ~ THE WELL

AD 27
Sychar, Province of Samaria, Palestine

"Oh, God. What am I going to do? I can't stand it. How can I endure my life? It has been cursed. No woman should have to live what I have lived through. Widowed five times."

Estar kneels on the grave of her husband. She is alone. No one comes to his funeral.

"Why did Yigal have to die? It makes no sense. I tried to take good care of him. I sent for the best of doctors. We were only married one year. He should not have died."

She leans her head over and onto the ground. Her black hair falls down onto the ground with her. Her tears turn the dust into clay.

"Did you form me just so you could mock me? No, I didn't mean to say that, God. It is unfair to you, just like it is unfair to blame me for their deaths. Forgive me, God."

She sits up and raises her eyes to the heavens above.

"God, what am I doing that is so wrong? I pray to you three times a day, I helped build the synagogue, I give alms to the poor. What is wrong with me? Why are you punishing me like this?"

Her voice is now guttural as it speaks out of the depths of her being. She brings up her knees, lays her head on them, and groans.

"It's Satan, isn't it? He's trying to get me to blame you and forsake you. Well, I may be confused, and I may be mad, but how can I forsake you?

"People in town no longer call me by my name. Instead, as soon as Benyamin and his mother came back for the winter, he started to call me Istar in public. He said I deserved it for killing off five husbands."

Estar stands, puts her hands on each side of her head, and screams. Her face is red, her nose runs, her eyes are swelled and puffed, and she wants to throw up.

"I'm thirty-seven years old. Twenty years of losing one husband after another. People blame me and call me names. I am no Istar in hell. If I'm going to be condemned by everyone in town, I may as well live down to my reputation.

With that, she walks away from the cemetery in steps so small, it is hard to tell that she is moving at all.

Once home, she writes a note. FROM ISTAR TO ELYAS, YOU HAVE BEEN WANTING TO MOVE IN WITH ME. COME ON. I HAVE NOTHING TO LOSE.

———

A message arrives at the gate. Elyas accepts it for Istar. Soon after the messenger leaves, there is another knock at the gate.

"Let me in, Elyas. I have wonderful news."

Elyas unbolts the gate, and Istar rushes in. "I got an order for four different colors of silk from the mayor's wife. Isn't that wonderful? She also wants enough gold and silver fringe to go around the hem and sleeves. I'm so excited."

"That's wonderful," Elyas says. "Now, I've got dinner ready for you."

"Wait. I want to read the message. Who is it from?" Not expecting an answer, Istar tears off the seal and opens the scroll.

FROM ZARUS, YOUR BELOVED BROTHER. AVIGAIL IS ALLOWING US TO STAY IN HER MANOR HOUSE IN SYCHAR. WE JUST NEED TIME TO OURSELVES AWAY FROM THE BUSINESS. WE LOOK FORWARD TO SPENDING A LOT OF TIME WITH YOU. WE ARE SO SORRY ABOUT THE LOSS OF YOUR HUSBAND.

A week later, while at her fabric booth, she hears a familiar voice. "Whatever Devorah wants, let her have it. I will pay full price."

Istar turns and holds out her arms for her brother. He leans over her counter and embraces her. She turns to Devorah and embraces her.

"And who do we have here with you?"

"Children, say hello to your aunt Estar. Estar, you remember Amram, who is now twelve, Ithamar age nine, and Lleah all of age six."

"Your children are so beautiful."

"As soon as we get settled in," Devorah says, "we want to have you over for dinner."

"Uh, well, there's a complication. I let Elyas move in with me."

"I didn't know you got married again," Zarus replies.

Istar stares at her brother but says nothing.

"Oh, Estar, I wish you wouldn't."

"Why not? People blame me for all my husbands' deaths and even call me Istar now, a fallen goddess."

"Well, we'll talk about it later. We still want you to come visit us at the manor house."

"I'm taking tomorrow off. I have a friend who fills in for me so I can take a break. I'll be home most of the day. See you soon."

———

Jhesus slumps down by the low wall around the well in exhaustion. He is too thin. He does not eat like he should. He pushes himself too hard. What's the hurry? He has a lifetime ahead of him.

As he sits, he watches a woman come out through the city gate and walk down toward the well. Despite her mission, she wears a tunic of emerald green and shawl of royal blue. She lives well and can afford the extravagance.

She eyes Jhesus suspiciously, then goes to the opposite side of the well from him. With care, she lowers her jar with her seventy-five feet of rope to reach the abundant waters below. She hums as she lowers it.

Jhesus, having rested briefly but enough, returns to his feet. He walks around to her side of the famous well.

"Give me a drink!" he asks in almost a whisper but looking straight at her. She has a fan-shaped face, pointed chin, and wide eyes.

His countenance seems so shrunken. His voice a little shaky. He certainly does not look or sound like a threat.

Istar is surprised to see a Jewish man in such an emaciated state. But she does not one hundred percent trust him either. She thinks she'll have a little fun with him while he is so tired.

She does not answer him but continues humming as she works. She is stunning and exotic with hair, her crowning glory, piled high like a peacock's plumes.

The jar has reached water. She stops humming a moment, jerks the rope so the jar will tilt and fill, then begins to pull her rope and the jar back up, resuming her humming as she goes.

Jhesus sits down next to a nearby tree and leans against it.

The filled jar now on the ledge, Istar turns around and answers Jhesus. She is ready to toy with her prey.

"You, a Jew, are asking me, a Samaritan woman, for a drink? You Jews think you're too good for us Samaritans. You're so holier than thou." Then she raises her water jar to her lips and takes a deep drink, much of the water spilling out onto her clothes and the ground. As she does, she peeks around the jar to see if Jhesus is watching.

"If you knew who asked you for a drink, you would have requested I be the one to give you the water—living water."

"Sir. You have nothing with you to draw water out of this deep well. So, where in the world are you going to get your so-called living water? Up your sleeve?"

Istar grins, and a glint appears in her large eyes. She puts a hand on her hip and tilts her head this way and that.

"You Jewish men think you're so superior. Don't tell me you think you're smarter than our mutual ancestor Jacob who dug this well and gave the water to his family and herds."

Jhesus puts his hands behind him, hefts himself up, moves toward her, and sits on the ledge of the well. Her water jar sits on the ledge too. He puts his hand in it, pulls up some water in his palm, then pours it back out into the jar.

"Whoever drinks from this water of yours shall become thirsty again," Jhesus says.

Istar rolls her eyes heavenward. "Why do you think people have to make this trip out here every day? Tell me something I don't know."

His voice lowers, and his eyes sparkle. He crooks his finger, bobbing it to and fro. She draws closer.

"But whoever drinks the water I give out will never thirst ever again forever!" he explains with a twinkle in his eye.

She draws back with a jerk. "Never thirst forever?"

He's got her baited. "Come back," he says. "There's more."

She leans in again toward this enigmatic man.

"The water I will give will be a fountain within you!"

"A fountain?" she responds. "Not a well? Thank God I won't have to use a rope to get it."

Jhesus knows she is toying with him. Still, she is willing to listen.

"But within me?" She draws back and puts a hand on her hip. "Well, I don't know about that."

"Yes, within you," he reassures. "And it will gush up to give you eternal life," he adds excitedly.

She puts her elbow in her hand crossed over her waist, and her chin in her other hand. She taps one finger on her lips and looks heavenward.

"You haven't discovered some kind of herb to help a person create their own water inside their body, have you? Or have you learned how to absorb rainwater through the skin like plants do?"

If he has, I could be the first one in Sychar to know about it and go into a second business.

"This is a certain kind of thirst, Istar," Jhesus responds.

"You know my name? Who are you?" She backs away, thinks a moment, then returns to the edge of the well and Jhesus.

He swishes at the water in her pail.

"Sir, I would definitely like to have this water, so I don't ever get thirsty again and have to come all the way out here to this well every day."

Jhesus changes the subject.

"Go get your husband and bring him back here," Jhesus tells her.

"Uh-oh." She tries to get the discussion back on water. "Is the jar filled with your water so much heavier than normal water that I'll need helping carrying it?"

She stares at him, curiosity in her squinting eyes. She starts to walk away, goes several paces, then turns back around.

"That water. It would be worth having. But if it's so heavy that I'll need help with it…" She clears her throat, and her words drift away.

"Your husband?" Jhesus says, bringing her back to his question.

"Well, to tell the truth, I don't have a husband."

"You think I'm going to walk off now, don't you?" Jhesus responds.

She holds her head high and struts back to the well's edge. "So, what if you do?"

"You're right about your husband," Jhesus declares.

"You know? How could you know? What's going on?"

"Well, Istar, you are at least truthful. You have had five husbands," he continues, looking her straight in the eye, "and the one you are now living with is not your husband."

"How can you, a stranger with a northern accent that's not even from around here, possibly know this?" Istar walks over to a rock nearby and sits down on it.

Jhesus says nothing. He waits.

Istar looks over at him, still standing by the well. He smiles. She looks up at the clouds. She looks over toward the city.

"Well, whoever you are, the sun is headed toward the west. I do need to get back home, you know," she blurts out. "But that water and…who are you? How do you know all this about me?"

"I just do."

Istar shakes her head and looks down at the barren ground. She pushes around some pebbles with her big toe.

She thinks back. Not used to being one-upped by someone else, she searches her memory. Has there ever been anyone else like this? Back. Searching. A long time ago. It hasn't happened for centuries. Back. Prophets. They told things that no one else knew.

She walks over to the well, looks down into the dark waters so far below.

But that sort of thing doesn't happen in our century. That was a very long time ago. Not now. These are modern times.

Hesitatingly, Istar looks up and speaks, slowly and almost in a whisper. "Are you some kind of prophet?"

He smiles again. It makes her nervous.

He seems to know everything about me—probably my thoughts too. That's scary! Besides, what business is it of his even if I'm living with a guy?

Gotta change the subject. This guy, this prophet, whoever he is, is getting just a little too personal. He knows too much. Gotta change the subject.

Istar turns and looks up at the city. "Well, my ancestors built a temple to worship God here, but you Jews claim Jherusalem is the only place anyone can worship, there where your temple is."

She turns back to face Jhesus. "Who did you say you were?"

Jhesus is not diverted. He just picks up what she says and brings it back in line with the living water thing.

"Listen to me. The time has come when you will not worship the heavenly Father on this mountain or in Jherusalem either one."

Jhesus continues. "You worship what you do not understand. We worship the God we know by name. Salvation comes only from all of Jhehovah's scriptures.

Jhesus isn't shy about saying he has the truth. Istar likes that about a person.

Istar sits on the ledge of the well, then stands. *This man, if he is a man... This prophet... What is he saying?* She walks closer to Jhesus.

Jhesus keeps talking and explaining. His words are hard.

"The time is here when genuine worshipers of God will worship the Father in truth and not just in spirit. It takes both.

"What is he trying to tell me?" she whispers, looking up into the sky as though she will find her answer there.

"The Father is looking for the kind of honest people to be his true worshippers. God is Spirit, and His worshipers must worship in both spirit and in truth."

"Both? They're not just spirit? They're not just truth? They're both?"

Istar recalls teachings taken from Moshe, the leaders of God's people out of Egyptian slavery centuries earlier. She has always believed these teachings. She recalls God telling Moshe he would raise up a prophet like Moshe and put his words in his mouth so he'll explain everything God said.

She takes a deep breath. She holds the back of her hand up against her forehead, her other hand on her waist.

"Well, I know that the Deliverer, called the Christ, is coming someday," she finally says. "When he arrives, he will explain everything to us."

"I just did, Istar. I just did."

Istar's eyes open wide. She stares. "I think I understand what you're saying."

Is this stranger sitting on the well before me the person coming someday to replace Moshe? Moshe, the new lawgiver? Moshe, the freer of slaves? Moshe, who gave up heavenly luxury in a palace for everyday people? Moshe, the creator of a new kingdom of God?

Jhesus slides off the ledge of the well and looks Istar in the eyes, prepared to make the announcement.

"I—the one talking to you right now...

Yes, Jhesus?

"...am the one Moshe predicted."

"Huh?"

"I am he."

He waits for the reaction.

Istar looks at Jhesus a moment. A moment of dawning. A moment of light rushing in to shatter the darkness. A moment of truth. She smiles. She grins. A broad grin. Suddenly two and two equal four. Suddenly words and logic equal wisdom. Suddenly God and love equal salvation!

"Oh, yes!" she shouts. "You are! You are!"

———

Istar rushes back up the hill and through the city gates.

There is a circumcision ceremony going on at the Samaritan synagogue. She hadn't been invited. But the infant belongs to an important family, so everyone knows about it anyway.

"The ceremony. That's where I need to go," she tells herself, catching her breath. "Half the city is there."

She pauses at the double doors, pats her hair back in place, brushes off her tunic and shawl, and flings open both doors at once. They bang against the back wall.

She rushes in.

"Oh, Jhehovah, we dedicate..."

"Everyone," she declares, interrupting the priest in mid-sentence.

People turn and give her the evil eye.

"You can't just barge in like this, Istar!" the priest admonishes.

"But, everyone..." Istar screeches. "Everyone..." She points in the direction of the city well. "He is here."

"Istar, I told you..."

"Who is here?" Old *Ammar* questions.

"The prophet!"

"We don't have prophets anymore, Istar," the priest declares before she can go any further. "So, just sit down."

Istar does not obey. She turns and looks at the people on the left side of the meeting room. She looks at the people on her right. She holds out both hands, then clenches them.

"But he is really a prophet! Weren't we supposed to get another prophet 'like unto Moses'? Isn't that what you older people have been teaching us all our lives?"

"Istar. Be quiet and go home." It's Hani.

She stands firm. She is used to standing firm, despite what people say.

"This man, down at Jacob's well, told me everything I ever did in my life!"

"Right."

"Sure."

"Uhhh-huh."

"It's true. He told me about my upbringing. And my husbands..."

Many shake their head in disgust.

"And my children. Everything. He told me things I never told anyone."

No one replies this time.

She turns and looks down at Saban on the end of a row of

women in the back. "You've got to believe me, Saban."

The woman looks away.

People shuffle and strain to look at this questionable woman in their city.

The priest and elders mumble among each other.

"Everything, Istar?" Hany questions.

"Everything."

"One thing we know about Istar is she never lies," Hany continues. "And didn't she donate half the money to build our synagogue? Seems like we owe her a little time to check out her claim. A prophet, you say?"

"Well, you've disrupted things so much now," the priest declares. "I can't remember what I was saying about this baby when you barged in.

"Now, where is he? The prophet?" the priest asks. He looks back at Istar. "Well, where is he? If he's outside the door, we may as well take this time while everyone is together to let him talk."

Many in the audience nod their approval. "Go ahead and invite him in."

Istar stands. "Well, he is not here. He is still down at the well. He knows all about Jacob. Moses too."

Singly, in twos, and in family groups, people begin to file out.

"Don't want to miss out on the fun."

"You know," someone else says quite loudly as he approaches the outside door, "she just might have something there. The prophet's got to appear sometime. Why not in our generation? Huh? Why not?"

"He's right. I'm going too."

Outside, the others stand talking. The sun is lowering itself in the western sky. Sunset approaches.

The priest decides to lead the procession along with Istar.

"Everyone, go home and get a torch or lamp. I'll wait for you. Go get what you need and meet me at the city gate in half an hour."

Istar rushes home to get her own lamp.

"Where have you been all afternoon?" her live-in asks.

"I met a prophet."

"Come on, there aren't prophets anymore. You know that," he responds.

"But it's true, Elyas. He told me everything about my life. He knew."

"Well, I want you home now. You've had your fun."

"I have to go back."

"You forgot to bring the water back with you, didn't you?"

"Yes, I did. But more importantly, I left the prophet behind. I plan to invite him to stay in our home for a few days so he can tell everyone the kind of things he told me."

"Like what?

"Like he is the prophet that Moses predicted. Elyas, go with me. Go with me to hear the prophet and to invite him into our home."

"Well, I don't know. Of course, it's your house, and you can do whatever you want with it."

Istar stops in her tracks and realizes what she has just said.

"Elyas, I don't guess he will stay here. Our living arrangements. It's wrong. I am going to spend the night with my brother. I would like you to pack your belongings and go somewhere else to live from now on. What we are doing is wrong."

"He has affected you that much that you're kicking me out?"

"I'm asking you to leave. I have to go now. Everyone is meeting at the city gate. Will you go with us?"

"I don't think so. I'll just stay here and pack. Besides, I need to decide where I am going."

"You have two brothers living in the city. Or, you have a good job; you could rent a place tomorrow morning. I wish you well, Elyas. I really and truly wish you well."

Istar turns her attention back to her brother at the manor house outside the gate at the opposite end of town. "I must tell him." She makes her way out through the back gate and to the manor. She knocks on the gate and calls through it.

"Zarus! Devorah! Let me in. It's an emergency. Let me in."

She hears the gate being unbarred. Zarus answers. "What's going on?"

"I've found the one Moses prophesied about."

Devorah joins her husband at the gate.

"Come quickly. He's a prophet. A real prophet. I've got to go now."

"Children," Zarus calls out. "Come. We're going to see a real live prophet."

Istar leaves and turns back to the city. "Everyone is meeting at the city gate. The whole city wants to meet him.

Within the hour, a procession has formed, and everyone follows Istar out the city gate and down to the well.

Istar shouts in Jhesus' direction. "Prophet, are you still here?" she shouts. She has brought her family. Partly-grown kids behind her.

Shouting increasing from the crowd.

"Is that the prophet down there, Istar? Which one is he?"

Istar turns toward her friends and neighbors, points, and shouts. "That's him! That's the one who told me everything I ever did! Listen to him! He's the prophet! He is the one who knew all about me!"

Jhesus waits as the townspeople arrive and settle in on the ground. Settle in to stay a while. Jhesus stands by the water. People come to the water.

Jhesus holds up his hands and quiets the crowd. He begins to speak. He speaks of the one God, the God of every nation on earth. He speaks of the one creator, the judge, the merciful heavenly Father.

Jhesus speaks late into the evening. He becomes tired again. He speaks a little longer. But his energy is about spent.

The crowd understands.

Zarus, who had been one of the last to leave the city, has heard it all. He approaches Jhesus.

"Stay here in our town. Just stay here and teach us more tomorrow. Istar is my sister. She will come too."

Jhesus agrees. He and his friends follow Zarus, Istar, her friends, and neighbors into town.

That night in the manor house where Devorah had grown up, Jhesus speaks privately with Zarus and his family.

"Jhesus, my wife and I have been praying for decades for God to send us something to help us be one in religion. I am a Samaritan like Estar while my wife is Jewish. Can you unite us? Can we now believe everything alike?"

"Yes, I have come to bring peace into the world. My peace I give to you. You and your wife can unite in me. Would you like to be baptized?"

"We have a bath in the manor. Devorah, I want to be baptized. Do you?"

Devorah steps over to her husband and slips her arm into his. Yes, I would like to be united in Jhesus." She looks up at him. "I think our prayers have finally been answered."

The Pharisees heard that Jhesus was gaining and baptizing more disciples than John, although in fact it was not Jhesus who baptized, but his disciples.

When the Lord learned of this, he left Jhudea and went back once more to Galilee.

Now he had to go through Samaria.

So he came to a town in Samaria called Sychar, near the plot of ground Jacob had given to his son Joseph.

Jacob's well was there, and Jhesus, tired as he was from the journey, sat down by the well. It was about the sixth hour.

When a Samaritan woman came to draw water, Jhesus said to her, "Will you give me a drink?"

(His disciples had gone into the town to buy food.)

The Samaritan woman said to him, "You are a Jew and I am a Samaritan woman. How can you ask me for a drink?" (For Jews do not associate with Samaritans.)

Jhesus answered her, "If you knew the gift of God and who it is that asks you for a drink, you would have asked him and he would have given you living water."

"Sir," the woman said, "you have nothing to draw with and the well is deep. Where can you get this living water?

Are you greater than our father Jacob, who gave us the well and drank from it himself, as did also his sons and his flocks and herds?"

Jhesus answered, "Everyone who drinks this water will be thirsty again, but whoever drinks the water I give him will never thirst. Indeed, the water I give him will become in him a spring of water welling up to eternal life."

The woman said to him, "Sir, give me this water so that I won't get thirsty and have to keep coming here to draw water."

He told her, "Go, call your husband and come back."

"I have no husband," she replied. Jhesus said to her, "You are right when you say you have no husband.

The fact is, you have had five husbands, and the man you now have is not your husband. What you have just said is quite true."

"Sir," the woman said, "I can see that you are a prophet.

Our fathers worshiped on this mountain, but you Jews claim that the place where we must worship is in Jherusalem."

Jhesus declared, "Believe me, woman, a time is coming when you will worship the Father neither on this mountain nor in

Jherusalem.

You Samaritans worship what you do not know; we worship what we do know, for salvation is from the Jews.

Yet a time is coming and has now come when the true worshipers will worship the Father in spirit and truth, for they are the kind of worshipers the Father seeks.

God is spirit, and his worshipers must worship in spirit and in truth."

The woman said, "I know that Messiah" (called Christ) "is coming. When he comes, he will explain everything to us."

Then Jhesus declared, "I who speak to you am he."

Many of the Samaritans from that town believed in him because of the woman's testimony, "He told me everything I ever did."

So when the Samaritans came to him, they urged him to stay with them, and he stayed two days.

And because of his words many more became believers.

They said to the woman, "We no longer believe just because of what you said; now we have heard for ourselves, and we know that this man really is the Savior of the world." (John 4:1-26, 39-42) (Not a parable)

24 ~ THE CHALLENGE

AD 28
Eilat, Port City on Red Sea, Arabah Desert, Idumea

Zarus and his family are together on the roof of their manor. It is evening, the time of the cool evening breezes, and the time they always set aside for that togetherness.

"We are together now in a way we never were before," Zarus says to his wife.

"I had no idea how God was going to answer our prayers, but he finally did twenty years after our betrothal," Devorah says. "From now on, we do not have to face Gerizim or Jherusalem either one. Jhesus said we just face heaven, and our prayers are answered."

"Amram, we don't talk about your foot anymore. But I want to talk about it now," Zarus says.

"That's okay with me, Father," the tall thirteen-year-old young man says.

"Jhesus said he can heal you. Would you like to be healed? I can take you back north and find him for you. Then you will never have to limp or use that cane again."

Amram does not answer right away. He stands and walks around. Zarus and Devorah watch him with pain in their souls for him.

He returns but does not sit.

"Father, I have a good life. I have a loving family, the best education, good friends. Just before we left Sychar, I was baptized, too; Jhesus said I was old enough to understand. So I have Jhesus too. What more could I want?"

"Son, are you saying you don't want to be healed?" Devorah asks.

"Why? Would I have a better family, a better education, more friends? What if changing my foot changes me? Will I become arrogant? I'm taller than most of my friends my age, so if I win foot races and other things because I'm both taller and healthier, will that make them like me more? Father. I am afraid of change. I want things the way they are right now."

Zarus and Devorah look at their oldest son in amazement. *Where did he get such wisdom? Surely not from us.*

Finally, Zarus speaks. "Son. I am so proud of you. Maybe when you're grown, you can go back north and help Jhesus with his campaign. Would you like that?"

"Would I? Wow! In five years, I'll be eighteen. Maybe I can help him then. That would be grand."

Ithamar, never one to sit still, turns summersaults. "Get down here, Lleah. I want to see if I can play leapfrog over you. I bet I can."

Zarus takes Devorah's hand.

"Father," Amram says, "could I go visit Grandm*Amma*? She's back in Jhericho. Can I? I promise to keep up my studies while I'm there. She is lonely. I can tell. Can I go see her?"

———

"Gersshon, I have to do something for my family."

They are walking along the edge of the pit, checking for new fissures.

"You do things for your family all the time. I'd have a family of my own by now if that Benyamin hadn't interfered."

"Not that family, Gersshon. I'm talking about the family I grew up with."

"You mean those spiteful brothers of yours? I never liked the way they treated you, just because you were your father's favorite."

"That's all in the past," Zarus says.

Gersshon stops walking and faces his partner and friend.

"It's never just in the past. It will continue. It will always be now and in the future. People don't change. They will never change. They will never stop being jealous of you. And now that you are richer than they are, richer than most people, they will be even more jealous. Mark my words, they will get back at you for being you."

"Hey, slow down. Your face is getting red."

Gersshon turns back to Zarus' side, and they continue on their rounds.

"So, anyway, I need to do something for them."

"You're crazy. If I did anything for them, I'd do something to wake them up to how they're treating you."

Zarus stops, looks at his friend, shakes his finger back and forth as though admonishing a child, then resumes his walk.

"I think I'd like to send them some nice presents. Of my three brothers and three sisters, Estar lives in Sychar, and I see her often. We're close. She accepted me when..."

"Your brothers didn't deserve her as a sister. She was, she is, above them all. Good thing she got away from them."

"As I was saying, my brothers stayed on the farm outside the city of Sebaste. My sister Chana married a silversmith, and my sister Talia married a trader."

"I knew your brothers in school. I knew you had sisters but never saw them unless I went to your farm to visit you. I admired your father. He took care of his kids, not like my father, who used me to make a living."

"Those have to be painful memories," Zarus says.

"It's been a long time now, but the memories are always there. Just like the time he made me pretend I was blind and made me beg so he'd have enough money to go get drunk.

"Ever wonder why I eat so much now? To feed us kids, my father would make us lie and go to different corners in town to beg, claiming we were orphans."

"Yes, despite all that, you've been looking out for me most of our life. Well, sometimes you went a little too far like you did on the road crew that time when you injured your eye."

"Well, I was young and foolish then. Have you noticed I am getting a few gray hairs in my beard? But, yet, I have always looked out for you, kind of like when I looked out for my father. Only you returned my friendship. We were always tight, my friend. We will be friends to the death."

"Yes, we will. Now, back to my family..."

"Just send Devorah shopping. She'll think of something."

"Excuse me, Zarus. I need to go into town to see if there are any men in the city square wanting work. I need to send a message up to Sebaste. I have a couple brothers left there. We don't see each other much, but I guess we need to get in touch sometimes.

The day continues as most days do and without incident. Thank God. And thank Jhesus.

When Zarus returns home, Devorah greets him at the gate with a wide grin.

"What is my lovely wife up to now?" Zarus says, returning her grin.

"I have a surprise for you," she says, taking his hand and leading him. "I went to town today and bought some gifts for your family."

Zarus stops and takes her into his arms. "How did I ever deserve you? You know my every thought, and even my every step before I take it."

Devorah smiles and pulls away. Now, come look at what I bought them.

As she leads her husband into the next room, the old pain comes back, and she grasps her chest. She does so in such a way that only the most observant could notice it. Zarus is behind her. The pain, as always, leaves as fast as it had arrived.

She picks up a small alabaster coffer and opens it. "Now, for your brothers, I got each of them a copper ring embedded with opals. Very unique. For your sisters, I got each of them a copper mirror large enough they can see their whole body in it. Those are just as unique. What do you think?"

"You are a genius, my pearl. But these had to be custom made. When did you order them?"

"As soon as we returned from meeting Jhesus. He said to love our enemies. I know your brothers wouldn't act like enemies if they knew you like I do."

"Devorah, you have a heart of copper."

They laugh.

"I think when I have a chance and things are running smoothly with the mine—though that could change in a wink—we should go see them."

"Yes," Devorah replies, "and we should take the whole family. Sometimes children soften hearts. You know how Amram is with his grandmother."

———

A month later, Zarus calls a special meeting.

"Saabhu, Noach, and Wajid, I have called you into this private meeting for a special reason."

Everyone else has left. Gersshon is in Egypt, checking on a new smelting operation there. Yair's grown children have come to get him at their usual time to help him home.

"We have been working together for twenty years. Wajid, you have been Saabhu's assistant for much of that time."

Is he going to retire me because I'm getting too old? Noach wonders.

Is he going to make me a partner? Saabhu wonders.

Is he going to fire me because of those three accidents last week? Wajid wonders.

"I'm going to be gone up north for a while. I don't know how long I will be gone. I have a special assignment for you three while I'm gone."

Zarus pauses to watch their reactions and is satisfied they feel up to the job.

He turns away from them and walks over to a camel skin covering something on the ground. He takes the skin off, and the men gasp.

"This gold bouillon comes from my treasury. I want it invested. Saabhu, I am giving you five bricks of gold, Noach, I am entrusting you with two bricks of gold. Wajid, you are the newest, so I am leaving you with one brick of gold."

"Sir, what do you have in mind," Saabhu asks. "This is a lot of money."

"While I am gone—and I don't know how long that will be—I want you to invest it any way you choose. When I return, you will give an accounting to me of how you invested my money."

Sebaste, Province of Samaria, Palestine

"Now children," Devorah admonishes, "You must be on your best behavior while visiting your uncles. They are your father's brothers."

"But why?" Ithamar says, riding on a donkey with his sister.

"Because they are part of our family."

"We've never even seen them, and they're part of our family?"

"Ithamar, do you have to play dumb all the time?" Amram asks, riding on his own donkey. "When Father is gone to a refining operation in Persia, and we don't see him for weeks, it doesn't mean he quits being our father. Family is family."

"Hey, I'll race you, Amram," Ithamar says.

"Whoa. No, you don't, Ithamar," Zarus warns.

"Mommy, Ithamar won't quit wiggling," Lleah whines.

"Ithamar, be still."

"I see the farmhouse up ahead. I wonder if my sisters were able to make it. I hope so."

"Yuk. You have sisters too?"

"Yes, Ithamar. Did you know Estar is my sister?"

"But I thought she was my aunt."

"Same thing, dummy," Amram explains.

"Now, everyone, let's be quiet the last part of our journey," Devorah says. "Father needs to meditate."

They near the farmhouse and memories rush to Zarus' mind. Will things be any different this time? Will they still resent him for being their father's favorite? He never chose to be. *Maybe this time they will forgive me.*

Zarus urges his horse on ahead of his family. Devorah holds the children back.

"Your father needs to greet his brothers alone first. Let us stop now and wait. He will motion for us to come on." *Please, God, may his brothers accept him this time.*

The four watch as their beloved approaches the now opened gate. They see three men come out. They are animated.

Oh, no. They're still angry.

Zarus slides off his horse and talks to them. He looks back at his family and points.

Now what? Will they send us on our way?

Zarus waves.

"Father wants us to come," Amram says.

"Yes, children," Devorah says with tears of joy in her eyes. "He wants us to come. Ithamar, you may now race your horse. But when you arrive, you must not say anything about winning or losing. Amram, you may race with him, not to win or lose, but to show your enthusiasm at meeting your uncles."

"Yes, ma'am," Ithamar says as he urges his animal into a run.

Devorah leads her horse slowly. They need time. This is a lot for them to accept. It always used to be Zarus. Now it is Zarus and four more.

She sees the boys arrive, and Zarus reach up to take seven-year-old Lleah down from the donkey. He keeps her in his arms, and the three men reach over and pat her on the head.

Ithamar slides off his donkey, and the men laugh. Devorah assumes Ithamar has taken it upon himself to tell them who he is. The men pat him on the shoulder.

Amram slides off his donkey and stands at attention. Soon the three men are shaking hands with him.

Zarus looks over in her direction. She is almost to them. She can hear him.

"And this is my beautiful wife, Devorah, the pearl of my existence. To her, I owe everything, even my very life."

Devorah arrives, waits for Zarus to help her off her horse—though she could have done it herself—and stands next to her husband.

Zarus beams.

"Welcome to all of you Zarus, you have a fine family," Reuven says. "Welcome to our home."

Shimeon and Levii each take the reins of a horse and donkey while Reuven opens the gates wider.

"Surprise!"

Zarus beams. Can things be any better?

"Hello, little brother," Chana says, rushing toward Zarus. "Wait for me," Talia says.

Both sisters rush into Zarus' arms. He looks over at his brothers as he does, and they beam.

"When did you get here?" he says, pulling them away from him so he can see them better.

"I got here yesterday," Chana says, "and Talia got here just this morning."

"Are you hungry?" Talia asks.

"We ate something not too far up the road." He notices the downcast expressions on his sister's faces. "But it wasn't that much. After we rest a while, we will be ready to eat again."

"Let's go up on the roof. There is plenty of room for everyone up there. Please forgive our shabby carpets when we get up there, Zarus," Levii says.

"Nice breeze up here," Zarus says while giving the eye to Ithamar as a signal to sit down and be quiet.

There are pillows for everyone to sit on in a circle.

"Where are your wives and children?" Zarus asks.

"We've put them away for now," Shimeon grins. "You will see them in the morning."

"We thought it would be a less hectic welcome home without so many people around," Reuven explains.

"Do you have any kids my age?" Ithamar asks.

"Indeed, we do. We've got kids of all ages."

"I noticed you didn't have Father's horse with you," Shimeon says.

"No, I sold him so I could buy the mine. I was pretty poor back in those days."

"Little did Father realize when he gave him to you that he

would be worth millions someday," Levii says, laughing.

"I've been trying to trace him down for a long time, so I can buy him back, but he is pretty old by now."

"Zarus," Reuven says with a low serious tone in his voice, "about the gifts you sent us. You didn't have to. Not that we don't appreciate them, but you didn't have to."

"Yes, I did. You're my brothers. We grew up together. We worked this farm for Father together. You are good men. They don't come any better than you."

"But, what about the times..."

"There were only good times, Levii. Only good."

"Uh, you have a lovely copper gate. Who did your etching?" Devorah asks.

"Oh, some old guy in Sebaste. He's been dead a long time."

"How can a dead man itch a gate, Papa?" Lleah asks.

The laughter is interrupted by a call from Talia. "Everyone, come down. We are ready for you to eat."

———

"Did you have a good night's rest?" Chana asks as Zarus comes out to the courtyard with his family.

"Children, we have something special for you," Talia says. "Each of you gets a roll for one hand and a piece of cheese, for the other hand. That way, you can start playing right away. Our children are out by the stable. You can join them there."

"Yuppie," Ithamar says, jumping and going in circles both at the same time.

"That will be just fine," Amram says.

"Do you have any girls?" Lleah asks.

"Indeed, we do. And here is your breakfast. Now, out the gate with you and have fun."

Devorah joins the women in the kitchen.

"Hey, guys. It's time to eat breakfast," Talia announces.

The men sit down at the low table for a simple breakfast.

"Zarus, would you like to do the honors?"

Zarus raises his hands and closes his eyes. " Jhehovah God, thank you for all the blessings you have given our families, including providing this meal for us. And, Jhehovah, thank you for Jhesus. May his movement grow and survive."

The men begin their meal.

"Who is Jhesus?"

"He's from Galilee, just north of here. He is going everywhere preaching peace. I met him. My whole family met him. He stayed at our house in Sychar. He's young, but he is wiser than anyone I have ever met. Actually, he is the prophet Moses predicted would follow him."

"If he's preaching peace, I'm all for that," Levii says before taking his first bite of cheese.

"How do you know he's the prophet?" Reuven asks, reaching for some grapes.

"He not only preaches peace, but he baptizes and can actually perform miracles," Zarus responds. "He's a Jew, but he doesn't look down on Samaritans. He travels through Samaria on his way to and from Jherusalem sometimes. Maybe you'll meet him soon. I really liked the man. If he is a man."

"There's a horse race at the circus in Sebaste tomorrow, Zarus. Would you like to join us?"

A month goes by. A month of talking and reminiscing, and becoming the family they never were until now.

"Well, I have to return home now, guys," he says one evening. "We'll be leaving early in the morning."

"What's your hurry, brother?" Reuven asks.

"I think I'll stop by Sychar on the way home and visit with our sister a while. Then I left some of my belongings with three men at home, and I need to go back and see how well they took care of them."

For it is like a man going on a journey, who summoned his slaves and entrusted his property to them.

To one, he gave five talents, to another two, and to another one, each according to his ability. Then he went on his journey. (Matthew 25:14-15)

25 ~ LIVING DEAD

AD 29
Sychar, Province of Samaria, Palestine

Nearing Sychar, Devorah reminisces. "I'll bet you children didn't know your father helped build this road between Sebaste and Sychar."

"Did you, Papa?" Ithamar asks. "I'll bet you were the fastest and strongest one of all."

"Your father may not have been the fastest, but my guess is that he was the strongest."

"Were you, Father?" Amram asks. "What was your job?"

"My job was to move boulders out of the way."

"How big were the boulders, Papa? I'll bet they were bigger 'n this donkey's head."

Zarus laughs. "Some were bigger."

"Whoa! You must have been the strongest man in the world then."

"How old were you, Father, when you built this road?"

"Well, I was twenty years old, almost as old as you, Amram. But I didn't build the whole road. My work was, well, interrupted."

Devorah laughs. "And I'm the guilty one who interrupted it. I used to come out to the road crew and feed them breakfast, and bandage up whatever cuts and scrapes they picked up."

"Is this where you met, Father?"

"Yes, it is. We're almost on the exact spot we met."

"Women! I'd never let a woman make me lose my job," Ithamar says.

"Oh, no. He wasn't fired. He worked in my father's copper mine for four years to win me," Devorah explains.

"Okay, everyone. We're nearly at the city gate. When the guard asks questions, you do not say anything. I will do all the talking," Zarus admonishes.

Once in the city, Amram asks if they will be visiting Aunt Estar first.

"I think we'll go to the manor house where I grew up first," Devorah says. "Gr*Amma* is there. Would you like to see her?"

"I like her. I'm glad she will be here," Amram says.

They walk their animals in silence the rest of the way, looking at the booths in the market place and watching the people as they pass by.

People begin pointing.

"Isn't that Zarus?" someone asks.

"He's the rich mine owner down by the Red Sea," someone says.

"He's the brother of Istar."

"Don't call her that. She is Estar, and she's trying to be a good woman."

"She's the one who told us about Jhesus."

"Papa, why are people talking about you and Aunt Estar?" Ithamar asks.

"Because your father is famous," Devorah says.

"Wow! My papa's famous," Lleah says. "What does famous mean?"

They arrive at the manor. A servant comes out and takes the reins to their two donkeys and two horses. Zarus helps Lleah down off the donkey and holds her in one arm as they wait for the gate to be opened.

Maid Sarach opens the gate, and Zarus' family files in.

"Oh, my darling children. Come see your grandmother," Avigail says. She walks forward, leaning on a cane

Amram is the first one to her, even with his cane.

"My, you look more like your father every time I see you," she tells Amram. "And look. We both have canes now."

"I love you too, Grandmother." He kisses her on each cheek.

"And how has your trip been so far, Devorah?" Avigail asks as she hugs her daughter.

"We can only stay a few days. We still have most of our journey home ahead of us.

Outside of Sychar, Province of Samaria

Not too far away up in the mountains are three caves. The larger one has men in it. The next smaller one has women in it. The smallest one is empty except when one comes near the end of life and wants to go out of this wretched world alone.

All with leprosy. Full of despair. Destitute of hope.

Some are from Jhudea and are purebred Jews. Some are from Samaria—the half-breeds. They dare to associate with each other. Society would ostracize them for such associations. But society has already ostracized them. So, in their exile, they cling to each other. To ease their survival.

It is mid-morning, and several are huddled together on a nothing spot amid other nobodies. A spot forgotten by normal humans. Forgotten by God.

"I feel so useless," Doron says. "No one needs me anymore. All I do is wander these hills with no meaning to my life. Wander and stumble and become worse. I've become a leprous nobody."

"Why wouldn't my family talk to me about my dying when we first began to suspect it?" Yigal asks. "I've tried and tried. But they changed the subject every time. I desperately needed someone to talk to."

"I wanted to talk about where I'd go when I died. But my family just kept saying, 'Oh, Father, you're not going to die. You're going to live forever.' I hated it when they lied to me." Tzvi says.

"I haven't lived a perfect life. I'm so afraid of God. Surely he can't forgive me for everything I've done. I'm so afraid. What's going to happen to me?" It's Nachshon.

"I'm so tired of being tired. I can't do anything. My mind's not gone. Just my body," Kalman explains. "I'm so weak, sometimes all I can do is sleep. I hate dying."

"What about my children?" Eitan asks, knowing the answer is unbearable. "I'll never see them grow up. And my wife. How is she managing without me? It's so unfair. I feel so guilty."

"If I could just go home one more time to really see my things, smell the flowers, drink from my old mug, and enjoy my family. Just one more time." It's Chaanoch.

"My death would be a relief," Yona says. "No more numbness. No more lumps and ulcers and stumbling and blindness. I wish I could die and get it over with. I'm so tired. I wish I could just go on to heaven. It has to be better there than here."

There are no answers. There never are—not the right ones. Though together, they are really talking to themselves.

"I heard about a new cure," Shabtai says, trying to shake the dark mood. Some wave off his comment, some turn to talk to whoever is next to him, others stand to leave.

"Now, hear me out. I know I shouldn't be running after every quack. But this man is different. He has healed people of leprosy. At least, I heard about it. He always goes to Jherusalem at Passover time. If he doesn't go through Perea on the way, he'll come through Samaria."

"Are you talking about Jhesus?" Nashum asks.

"I've heard about him. He does heal people. He's been doing it for three years. All kinds of injuries and diseases. It's been proven over and over. The priests are amazed." It's Eitan.

"Well, where is he?" Tzvi asks.

"Let's take turns going down to town until he shows up," Doron suggests. "Then, whoever hears will come back and tell the rest of us."

"But what if he never comes this way?" It's Nachshon.

"What have we to lose? We're dead already," Kalman says.

Not everyone agrees. Many go back to the hopelessness of their dark deadly caves. There are ten who decide to try. There are ten who dare to hope.

Each day someone volunteers to go down to the town. Each day that same someone comes back with no news.

Then it happens. Just as they had dared lose hope.

"He's in Tappush and working his way south," Chaanoch reports. "We'll go into town and be there when he arrives."

"Where will we sleep?" Yona asks.

"We'll decide that when we need to." It's Nashum.

Sychar, Province of Samaria

"Where is that brother of mine?"

It is morning. The adults are up, but just Lleah of the children is. She is sitting in her grandmother's lap after getting wet playing in the lily pond. They are in the garden.

"Wherrre arrre you?" Estar says again.

Zarus stands and walks toward the courtyard. "Out here, Sis."

The brother and sister embrace.

"Oh, do I detect a few gray hairs?" she teases.

"Possibly so. I'm forty-two now."

"You are getting sooo old."

"Is that you, Estar? Come on out," Avigail says from the

garden.

"You couldn't have timed being here better if you had planned it."

"What's going on?" Devorah asks, matching Estar's grin.

"Jhesus is coming this way. He was spotted on the border of Galilee and Samaria. He should be here by tomorrow or the next day."

"Do you think he'll stop in Sychar?"

"He'd better. I've been telling everyone in town."

"Well, you are certainly good at that," Zarus says.

"Mother, do you think he can spend the night with us at the manor?" Devorah asks.

"Have you met Jhesus?"

"Indeed, we have. Remember when we came up here last year for a few days rest and to just get away out of the heat?"

"Of course, I do. I wanted to come with you, but had already invited a lot of ladies to come to the next showing of my tunic designs and couldn't change the date."

"Anyway, we invited Jhesus and his twelve aides to come spend the night here. There is plenty of room. They were comfortable."

"And tell her what else happened that night."

"Mother, Zarus and I were baptized. Amram too. He is the best man you will ever meet. He is the prophet Moses said would come after him."

"I guess I need to meet this young man."

"Zarus and Devorah, after you left, I was baptized too," Estar says pleased.

Everyone smiles, but Avigail. *Just who is this young man, Jhesus?*

Tomorrow, let's all go to the city square to watch for Jhesus. We want to be ahead of the crowd.

Outskirts of Sychar, Province of Samaria

Their trek down the mountain is slow. The lepers help each other the best they can. Mostly they are quiet. Deep in thought. Deep in wonder.

What if Jhesus can't do it? What if I make a fool of myself? It'll be worth it. I must try everything. It's been proven he can heal. Will he heal me?

Silently they each pray. *God, help Jhesus heal me. Please, God.*

They arrive in town. The city square is just ahead. It is empty except for the normal number of people this time of day. They go to a side street and wait. Wait for Jhesus. They've waited all their lives.

The impossible appears. The impossible walks in through the gates of the Sychar. A small group accompanies him.

"Jhesus, you came." It is Zarus. "Welcome once again to the city. We have wonderful memories of your last visit and hope you can stay longer this time."

"I want to stay in the city square for a while. Many people pass by here during the day. That's what I want. Not just one family, but the entire city."

Jhesus squats on the ground, and his twelve aides squat with him. So Zarus and his family do the same.

"Son," Zarus whispers to Amram, "now is your chance. He can heal you."

"No, Father. My happiness does not depend on my foot."

"Hello, young man," Jhesus says to Amram, sitting near him.

"Hello, sir." I am fourteen years old now, and I was wondering if I could be your aide when I am eighteen. That's just four more years. I want to help you spread peace in our nation."

"I'm afraid I won't be around much longer, so you won't be able to travel with my physically. But you can travel places I would go if I were still here, and tell people my message. Go into all the world for me. Teach the good news. Would you do that for me, Amram?"

The boy grins widely. "Would I? I would go anywhere for you!"

"Even with your foot?"

"Even with my foot. Maybe especially with my foot. It helps me get people's attention."

"You have great faith, my son."

They look up. There is a small crowd of dirty, ragged men coming in Jhesus' direction.

Jhesus stands. "I believe I am needed now."

Everyone with him stands too, and watches. Everyone knows something out of this world is about to happen. Such things always happen around Jhesus.

But what?

Now they hear the ragged men as they draw closer.

"It's him. It's Jhesus. Come quickly, everyone," Yigal calls out.

"It's Jhesus himself, our next priest-king," Kalman says.

"He's on his way to Jherusalem to take over," Yona surmises.

The group of ten desperates stands separate still, not sure what to do next.

At last, Nashum calls out. "Master! Master!"

Jhesus looks in their direction. He does not turn away. Is there hope?

They shuffle forward. Closer to facing Jhesus. Closer to knowing for sure. Closer to a new life. If he can just carry it off.

Their collective hearts beat faster. All weak from the trip down the mountain. But determined. Stubborn. Jhesus has to do it. Jhesus has to heal them. *Please Jhesus. Please, God.*

Tears in some of their eyes. Laughter on some of their lips. Hope in all of their hearts. Their last chance. Jhesus or die.

Oh God, help Jhesus heal us.

"Jhesus!" they call out in waves of desperate passion.

He waits still.

"Take pity on us!"

"Yes, please have compassion on us. Jhesus, we're dying."

"Please, save us. Save our lives."

The crowd around Jhesus scrambles. They recognize lepers when they see them, whether or not they call out the required, "Unclean! Unclean!"

Shuffling where the panicking people were moments ago. Shuffling in helplessness. All dying.

Tears in their eyes. Hope. Waiting. What will the moment bring?

Jhesus looks at each and indeed does take pity on them. How can Satan keep doing this to people? Then convince people God caused it? Jhesus, with the soul of God, reaches out to them with his spirit, his spirit of healing.

"Go back to your priests. Get the proof you need that the disease is gone. You've been healed."

Jhesus can heal ten people at once?

The crowd, still well within listening distance, is unimpressed. No one got healed. Jhesus is a fraud.

But the lepers. They continue to hope. They must hope. Jhesus is their last hope.

Eitan had previously lived in Sychar. "There is a synagogue here. This way," he shouts.

They shuffle down the street. *Please, God, heal me. Heal me, God. Please,* Kalman begs.

"Your hands! Look at them," Chaanoch tells Kalman.

They stop.

"Take off your head cloth! Your nose, "Yigal tells Nashum. "It's whole! Your eyelashes are long!"

"Look at my hands. And my feet!" Yona announces.

They dance around each other.

They break out into a run toward the synagogue. Running in ecstasy. Quickly they must find a priest. Then they can legally return home. Home. Family. A day-to-day job. Normal.

One old man stops. He does not go with them. Nashum is a Samaritan. He turns and walks back toward the crowd. He sees Jhesus still standing where he was. Motionless. Wordless.

Nashum rushes toward his healer. "Oh, thank you!" he calls out as he runs. "Praise God for what he has done through you. Thank you. Thank you, Jhesus!"

Nashum falls to his knees in front of his Savior near the people around him. Not ashamed. Only ashamed of his sins. Not self-important with pride that he has been selected for healing. Only pride that he is in the presence of God's crowned one. God's holy crowned one.

"Where are the others?" Jhesus asks Nashum, knowing the answer, but wanting it to sink into the crowd's hard hearts. "Where are the other nine?"

Nashum has no answer. He remains kneeling but saying nothing.

Jhesus turns to the crowd. "Did no one else want to return and give proper thanks to God except this Samaritan?"

Jhesus reaches down for Nachum's hand. "Stand up and go. Your body is whole. Your soul is whole."

Zarus and his family stand nearby, stunned. *I knew Jhesus could perform miracles, but I never saw a miracle before. Amazing. He is more than a man.*

Avigail is with them. Estar is next to her.

"Zarus," Avigail says. "Invite that young man to spend the night with us."

On Road between Jhericho, Palestine, and Eilat, Idumea

"I'm so sorry, Zarus, but I am entertaining several priests right now, some of whom will probably stay until tomorrow," Priest Caalev says.

He closes the door, and Zarus turns to his family.

"Children, we had good luck on our trip up to Samaria. But we may not have as good luck returning home."

"What do you mean, Father?" Amram asks.

"I am a Samaritan. Your mother is Jewish. That makes you

half Samaritan. Many Jews in the southern province of Jhudea are very prejudiced against Samaritans. It's not as bad up in the northern province of Galilee; Jhesus, for example, is from Galilee."

"What your father is trying to say is that we may have trouble finding a place to stay tonight," Devorah continues. "We may have to put up a small tent, and all sleep in it tonight, and take our chances."

"Now, remember, no matter what names people may call you, you are loved by God. And, of course, you know that Jhesus loves you because he said so. Hold your head up. And no tears. All I want are smiles."

"I'm going to throw rocks at anyone who says bad things about us," Ithamar pronounces.

"No, you won't, Son. Jhesus said we are to love our enemies, and that is exactly what we will do. Now we are going to go to an inn in Jhericho and see if the proprietor will let us spend the night."

Zarus and his family lead their animals through the streets carefully and without speaking. They arrive at an inn.

"Wait here," he tells them.

He enters, is gone for several moments, and comes back out.

"They said they are full, but there is another inn in town, and we can try there."

The little group follows Zarus slowly and quietly. Once again, Zarus goes in, stays a few moments, and comes back out.

"This inn is full too."

"They can't be. There isn't that much traffic, and there are no holidays going on. They're lying to us." It is Amram.

"We will go to the city square and set up a tent there," Zarus says. The road going out of town is too dangerous.

It is dark by the time they arrive at the city square. People do not pay any attention to them. They set up their tent to sleep. In the morning, they head toward Jherusalem.

Small talk among the family members resumes until then.

"Now children," Devorah says as they approach Jherusalem, "we are going to be going past the great temple. You will want to see it. But we won't stop. We will keep going."

"Hopefully, we can make it as far as Malatha by tonight," Zarus explains.

They do get that far. But the city rejects them.

"How do they know we're Samaritans?" Amram asks.

"Because the innkeepers ask me where I was born and where I live now."

"You don't have to tell them, Papa," Ithamar says.

"That would be lying. I used to lie sometimes, but since meeting Jhesus, I know we must never lie."

They go to an inn at Malatha and are rejected. They go to the other inn in town and are accepted.

"Children, we are now in the province of Idumea, which is not as prejudiced against Samaritans. We will be okay the rest of the way home."

Once inside the inn and their assigned room, Devorah whispers to her husband.

"Sweetheart, you look so tired."

"You and I are united though Jhesus' teachings. Do you think his influence will ever reach to the rest of the world?"

"I don't know, husband. Let's get our rest now. We should be home tomorrow."

"I wonder how my investment went."

Now on his way to Jherusalem, Jhesus traveled along the border between Samaria and Galilee. As he was going into a village, ten men who had leprosy met him. They stood at a distance and called out in a loud voice, "Jhesus, Master, have pity on us!"

When he saw them, he said, "Go, show yourselves to the priests." And as they went, they were cleansed.

One of them, when he saw he was healed, came back, praising God in a loud voice. He threw himself at Jhesus' feet and thanked him—and he was a Samaritan.

Jhesus asked, "Were not all ten cleansed? Where are the other nine? Has no one returned to give praise to God except this foreigner?" Then he said to him, "Rise and go; your faith has made you well." (Luke 17:11-19) (Not a parable.)

26 ~ THE ACCOUNTING

AD 28
Eilat, Port City on Red Sea, Arabah Desert, Idumea

*T*he recent conversation with Zarus' before leaving on his trip is still fresh on the three officers' minds.

"This is a lot of money, sir," Noach had told Zarus.

"I've never seen so much money in all my life," Wajid had said.

"Thank you for your confidence in us, sir," Saabhu had said.

"Remember, you have to invest my gold bouillon and bring me a profit by the time I am back from my trip. I won't be gone for years, so you'll have to find something with a quick return."

"But why us?" Noach had asked.

"You have been with me the longest. Well, Wajid hasn't been with me quite the full twenty years, but it is close. You are the most experienced. I need to branch out into other investments besides copper. See what you can do. Goodbye, and good luck."

Zarus had just now left the *officium* tent.

Alone now, the three men bring over three cushions from a larger meeting area, put them in front of the bouillon, and sit. They stare at it. No one speaks.

Finally, Noach looks out the tent flap and sees the sun going down.

"Well, I guess we need to take them home for safekeeping until we decide what to do with them."

"We will meet back here tomorrow morning before everyone else comes in, to decide how to get started," says Saabhu.

"Good idea. And in the meantime, God might send us a dream to tell us what to do. You never know."

The other two men look at Wajid with skepticism but are used to his different ideas.

Saabhu and Noach go home, tell their wives what is happening, and hide their bouillon. Wajid, unmarried, goes to his tent in the Timna Valley, hides his bouillon under the camel-hair floor of his tent, and prays for God to give him a vision.

The next morning, the three are back at the mine's *officium* tent and resume their seats on the cushions.

"Well, do we have any ideas?" Saabhu asks.

"We could pool our funds and invest in a new smelting operation," Noach suggests, "but it would take too long to see a return on it."

They think a while.

"We could go to Phoenicia and offer to install copper sheeting on the bottom of their ships to keep them from collecting seaweed and other things that rot the hull," Saabhu says. "But it would take too long to refine, smelt, and form the copper into sheets, then transport them to the Great Sea for installation."

They think again.

"We could grind the copper into powder that the physicians can use for salves and elixirs. It's very good medicine. We could make the rounds of all the alchemists and physicians here and in Anatolia, Greece, Italy, Egypt, and Britannia. We'd be known as the saviors of mankind," Wajid says with a distant look in his eyes. "But, I don't think we could sell enough to make a profit."

The three sit and think in silence once again.

They hear a bang and yelling and run out of the *officium* to see what is going on.

"Nothing but another wagon tipped over, and the copper spilled," Noach says. "Let's go back inside."

They settle back down and think again. After a while, Saabhu speaks up.

"He didn't say the investment had to be in copper. In fact, he said he would like to invest in something else to give his investments some variety," Saabhu recalls.

"In that case," he continues, "it seems to me that it is only big landowners who are rich. We could go to Jherusalem, Caesarea or some other big city, buy land, put in an access road, and sell lots. Or we could even keep the lots, build on them, then sell both."

No one says anything.

"Well, maybe not. It would take too long to get a return on our money

They sit on their cushions. Wajid takes a swig from his waterskin, Noach scratches his head, Saabhu pulls out a knife and cleans his fingernails.

"We have enough money to hire mercenaries, attack a small country, and get the land for ourselves. Then we could exact tax money from them," Noach suggests. "However," he adds, "Zarus wouldn't approve of it.

"Well, if we can't think of anything, we could always sell passes to go to the moon. Ha, ha." Wajid says. The others smile but make creases between their eyebrows and shake their head.

Back to the thinking.

"Okay," Noach says. "I think we need to split up. I'm thinking of investing my share in silk from China."

"Well, I've been thinking of investing in pearls from India," says Saabhu. "What about you, Wajid?"

"I've been waiting for a vision. I need God to tell me what to do. I know it will come if I am patient enough."

"Don't be patient too long, Wajid or Zarus will be back before you even begin your investment," Saabhu replies.

"My thinking," Saabhu continues, "is for us to spend two weeks buying whatever merchandise we want to sell, then two weeks onboard a ship making the rounds of whichever seaports our ship—or ships—stops at. In each port, we could contact dealers in whatever product we choose, and sell to them. What do you think?"

"It sounds reasonable to me," Noach says. "So is it agreed that we meet back here in two weeks?"

The others agree. "We can choose the ship making the most ports as soon as we get back here," says Saabhu.

"I'm sure God will speak to me by then," Wajid says.

That afternoon, Saabhu and Noach go down to the ports and talk to sea captains about the best places they would need to go to retrieve their chosen commodities. It does not take long.

They go home, retrieve one of their gold bouillon bricks, and go to their usual banks. The rest of the day is spent with the bankers coming up with enough silver coins to cover the value. They cannot, so list on clay tablets what they hold in account for each man for the balance of the bouillon value. Both men scratch onto the tablets their signatures.

Loaded with silver coins, they return home, give the coins to their wives, who then sew them into hems and various other places in ample tunics and cloaks. They keep some out for their money belts.

The maids bake enough bread to satisfy them for five days and put them in a satchel along with dried dates and figs, and an ample wedge of cheese.

———

Early the next morning, Saabhu and Noach say goodbye to their wives and meet at the docks.

"Well, Saabhu, what did you find out yesterday? Do we need separate ships, or can we sail together for a while?"

"The ship *Evimería* is headed to the northern coast of China. How about you?"

"I learned that the *Grigori* is headed for the southern tip of India, and the ship *Thesaurus* is headed for Thailand."

"Well, to get to China, they have to go around the southern tip of India, and that's where I want to go," Saabhu says. "Why don't we both get a ticket for the *Evimería,* and we can spend a day or two together before parting."

"I wholeheartedly agree," Noach says. "It's docked down there where all the activity is. My guess is that it is preparing to set sail right now. We're just in time."

The two men walk as fast as Noach can go considering his sixty years.

"I'm ten years younger than you," Saabhu says. "Why don't I go on ahead of you to make sure the ship doesn't leave without us. I'll pay for both of our tickets, and you can pay me back when you get on board. I'll meet you at the top of the plank."

Both onboard and just before hauling in the chains from the dock and the anchor below, the ship's second mate shows the two investors to a camel's hair canopy on the main deck. "Stay here. You will be out of everyone's way, and it will be cool for you. I hope you brought food. We do not provide it. It's best that you brought your own water, at least until it runs out."

They are quiet for a while. At last, Noach speaks up. "I wonder if Wajid has his vision yet." They both smile. Most of the trip, they are quiet, each trying to figure up how much they will have to spend on merchandise as well as paying people to get the merchandise to them and on board a ship back to Eilat.

The following day, they dock at Ceylon across from the southern tip of mainland India.

Ceylon, Laccadive Sea

"Here is where I get off," Saabhu says. "Good luck to you."

"And luck to you, my old friend."

As soon as the ship docks, Saabhu disembarks. On his way off the ship, he asks the first mate when the ship will be returning.

Two weeks," he is told.

"Perfect. Here is money for my return passage. I will be here waiting for you. Where can I go to hire a translator?"

The first mate points straight ahead toward a wood building with animal-skin flaps for window coverings and surrounded by ferns and other tropical vegetation.

After a wait of about two hours, Saabhu is introduced to a young man who says he is available for two weeks. Without flinching, he tells Saabhu what his rate will be plus all lodging and food, and, although the price seems high, Saabhu is in a hurry.

"Here is half now, Rajiv. You will receive the other half at the end."

"Thank you, *Sahib*. Now, where do you want to go first?"

"I want to buy pearls."

"They are very hard to find, *Sahib*, unless someone dives for them for you."

"Yes, yes. I understand that. Do you know any divers?"

"I know one, *Sahib*."

"That's a start. Take me to him."

The two walk about an hour.

"It is very beautiful here, no?"

"Yes, it is very beautiful here. Where I come from, it is mostly desert."

"Ah, and hot."

"I don't think any hotter than here, Rajiv."

After a pause, Saabhu adds, "I have two children, but they are both grown."

"Ah. A boy and a girl?"

"Yes, we were lucky: A boy and a girl. The girl is married to a goldsmith, and the boy is being educated in Memphis, Egypt, my homeland, in mine engineering."

They arrive at a grass hut by the bay.

"Prabhu, are you at home?" Rajiv calls out.

Soon a very thin young man comes out of the hut. The two Indians talk in their native tongue.

"He says he will dive for you. He also has a brother and some cousins that are looking for work. The best one of them can dive down over one hundred feet and hold his breath long enough to pick up a full net of oyster shells.

"How much is their charge?"

Rajiv speaks to the young man again, they chuckle, then he tells Saabhu what their charge is.

"I'll bet I could get divers for half the price," Saabhu objects.

"Ah, *Sahib*, but you just have two weeks. It will take a thousand shells to find three or four pearls."

"I would like to take fifty pearls back with me. If they will guarantee one thousand shells a day, they are hired."

Rajiv once again speaks in his native tongue to the young diver. Once again, they chuckle.

"*Sahib*, they not only will bring you one thousand shells, but their sisters will search through the shells for the pearls for you."

"For how much more?"

Rajiv gives the price, and without haggling, Saabhu agrees.

"They start right now."

"But..."

"No buts. He has ten moments to round up his brother and cousins and start diving. He can bring the sisters tomorrow to start searching for pearls in the shells."

"Ah, yes, *Sahib*. He will start right now."

Huzhou, Zhejiang Province, China

Three days later, Noach goes ashore at Huzhou. As had Saabhu, he asks when the ship will be leaving on its return voyage.

"We have to go over to Korea and Japan next. We will be back here in ten days," the first mate tells him. Would you like to rejoin us then? If so, the return fare would be the same, sir."

"Here is your money," Noach says, reaching into his money belt and hoping against hope that no one on shore is watching him.

"Now, where do I find a translator?"

"There is a building painted blue on the docks. They will have everything you need. The Chinese are very efficient."

Noach disembarks and walks to the blue building. He finds himself towering over everyone else and weighing twice as much as anyone he sees.

"Translator?" he says upon entering.

Everyone working there sits on a silk cushion. Those needing their services stand and wait their turn. Noach does not understand anything being said, so watches each intently, hoping to detect when a service is concluded. When one seems available, he goes over and repeats, "Translator?"

The petite but pretty lady with slanted eyes and ivory complexion points to one of the men who was standing when he first arrived. Noach bows in the manner he had seen others do.

"Do you translate?" he asks the man.

"Yes, I do. I have been half the day waiting for someone needing my services. Sometimes I wait all day, but today I am lucky. My name is Chen."

"What is your charge?"

Noach does not understand the currency, so brings a silver coin out of his money belt and shows it to the translator. Chen takes it.

"I will require one each day."

"Fair enough, Noach says. Now, I need you to show me your silk makers. I want to visit each one. How many are there in Huzhou?"

"There are thirteen, *Géxià.*"

"I am going to need a wagon or wagons to hold all the bolts of silk they have, and whatever you use here to pull wagons. I will also need reed mats to wrap them in and keep them safe on board ship."

"Yes, *Géxià.*"

"Do you think each silk maker will have enough on hand to fill one wagon?"

"No, not all of them. Some are very small shops."

"Okay. Right now, I want you to rent a wagon. Then we will go to whatever shop makes reed mats, and I want to buy them all."

"Yes, Pengyou." Chen says with a broad grin. "There is a place where we can rent a wagon right here on the docks. Let us go now."

Noach walks behind Chen, watching him take short scuffing steps. *I wonder how these people ever get anywhere. I'm sixty years old and can walk faster than that.*

Once a wagon is rented, Noach insists that Chen sit on the wagon to guide the oxen. *Oxen go faster than Chinese men do, even when they are ambling.*

Noach and Chen spend the afternoon going to three shops. The first two have hardly any bolts of silk woven and dyed ahead of time. The third one is much larger and finishes filling the wagon.

Chen helps Noach wrap each bolt in a protective mat, careful not to snag the delicate fabric with their rough fingers.

By the end of the third day, Noach has purchased every bolt of silk in the city.

"Tomorrow, we must go north to Suzhou to get their silk. We

are far short of what we need. I need to rent a small warehouse on the docks. Now, how will we get to Suzhou?"

"There are the sampans. We can board one and be in Suzhou in four hours."

"How often does one leave?"

"They leave when they get full."

"Fine, see if one is ready to leave now."

"But, it is almost dark."

"Then, we shall ride in the dark."

Chen leads Noach to a row of green buildings along the waterfront. He goes in the one on the end, then comes out. "Their rent is one silver coin each day."

"That's very expensive."

"They say the rest are full."

"Okay, give him these five silver coins so we can go ahead and unload the wagon and turn it in."

It is dark by the time they are through unloading the wagon and delivering it back to its owner.

"Pengyou, it is too late to get a sampan now. There is a boarding house at the end of the docks. We can spend the night there. And they serve very good food. One silver coin for each of us for the bed, and one for each of us for a meal." Chen smiles.

Why didn't I wear ragged clothes? They are all taking advantage of me. Well, I don't have time to haggle with them. "Here, Chen, are four silver coins for our beds and meals."

Suzhou, Zhejiang Province, China

The next morning, Noach and Chen board a sampan to Suzhou. By noon, they are in the city and renting a wagon and oxen. There are twenty-three makers and sellers of silk here. By the end of the day, Noach has purchased enough to fill two wagons and has rented a warehouse to store them in.

The next day, they fill three wagons. On the third day, they fill three wagons again.

"Tomorrow, we will have to hire a sampan large enough to take all the silk back down to Jiangsu."

"That will be hard to do, but I will look very much, Pengyou, until I find the sampan just right for you."

They spend a good night at the boarding house and find sleep easily, despite the snoring on the other side of the room.

The next day Chen is able to find a large sampan, and Noach pays dock laborers to unload the contents of the warehouse into it.

Progress is slow going back down the coast. The boat is deep in the water. Though his merchandise is under a canopy, Noach prays it does not rain.

Huzhou, Zhejiang Province, China

They arrive back in Huzhou that evening, too late to do anything other than unload the bolts of silk into his warehouse on the dock.

The next day the ship back to the Red Sea has not arrived yet, so Noach walks through the city to the shops he had seen a few days earlier to see if any have managed to make enough silk for one more bolt. One of the thirteen has, so he carries it in his arms.

The next day he walks down to the docks and inquires about his ship. He is told it should be back sometime during the day. It does arrive, and Noach arranges with the second mate to bring his goods on board. He pays for their transport.

It takes all day for the ship to unload.

It takes all the next day for the ship to load its new cargo.

Finally, the ship is ready to leave. Noach says goodbye to his translator and watches him shuffle with his short steps back to the blue building.

Eilat, Port City on Red Sea, Arabah Desert, Idumea

Noach, having met up with Saabhu in Ceylon, disembarks from the ship with his friend, each with their sought-for cargo of pearls and silk.

"We have used up our two weeks. Before we leave the docks, we must find a ship going to as many ports around the Great Sea as possible and as fast as possible. You go this way, and I will go that way. Whoever finds a ship meeting our requirements, meet back here, and wait for the other." It is Saabhu.

Two hours later, they meet.

"I gave up. There are no ships stopping at each port going along the Great Sea," Noach says.

"The ship *Stello* is leaving in two days and will stop at most of the ports north and then west of here."

"Does it have room for my silks?"

"I forgot to ask."

Saabhu leads Noach to the *Stello.* They talk to the captain and are assured he has room for the silk. Noach pays for his passage and storage for the silk, then hires a wagon to take his silk out of the warehouse and to the ship.

That done, the two men head into town and their homes. On their way, they wonder aloud about Wajid. "Do you think he ever got his vision?" Noah asks. Saabhu grunts.

AD 29
The Great Sea

Without looking for Wajid, Saabhu and Noach board the ship *Stello.*

"I used up the last of my money on passage. How about you?" Noach asks.

"I've got enough left that I can get us through an emergency, but not enough left for passage back home once we sell our merchandise. If we sell our merchandise."

Port after port, the two men disembark, find directions to the nearest fabric shops and jewelers and make their sales. Noach always makes arrangements before leaving the ship for someone to distribute the silk according to the clay tile receipt they show the second mate.

Caesarea, Tyre, Tarsus, Myra, Ephesus, Troas, Athens, Corinth.

"We need to head back," Noach tells Saabhu. "Have you sold all your pearls?"

"All but one. How about you?"

"I've run out of silk. Could have brought more, but there was no more to be bought."

"Well, I think I will save that last pearl for my wife," Saabhu says.

Eilat, Port City on Red Sea, Arabah Desert, Idumea

"Where are Saabhu and Noach?" Zarus asks Wajid. "The three of you were to be ready for me by the time I arrived."

"They probably made some bad investments with your gold bouillon and now have gone into hiding somewhere down in Africa."

"Did you hear them talk about going to Africa?"

"No, I didn't, sir. Maybe if you wait until tomorrow or the next day, they will show up. I hope they didn't lose the entire seven bricks of bouillon you gave them. You don't deserve that."

"Yes, I will wait one more day, but that is all."

"What will be their punishment for losing all your money, sir?"

"Wajid, I need to do some work. Why don't you go out and survey the benches on the pit sides to see if any need shored up."

"Yes, sir."

An hour later, Zarus hears a familiar voice.

"Did you have a nice trip, Zarus, sir?" It is Saabhu.

Zarus rises and steps quickly to his old friend. Noach is with him. Zarus notices right away that both men are smiling. That is a good sign.

"Do you have news for me?"

"Indeed we do," Noach says for them both.

"Saabhu, would you go get Wajid?"

"So, tell me about your trip with your family," Noach says. Did you have a nice vacation?"

"Indeed, we did. It was good in every way. Well, at least in most ways. It turned out better than I had hoped. What is keeping Saabhu and Wajid?"

"Sir," Saabhu says, returning to the *officium* tent. "Wajid says he needs to go home to get what you entrusted to him."

"Well, tell me about your success with what I gave you. Saabhu, you go first."

"Sir, at my home right now are ten gold bouillon bricks."

"Well done, Saabhu. How did you do it?"

"Pearls, sir. I went to Ceylon and hired young men to dive for me. Then I toured the Great Sea ports and sold them."

"I'm proud of you, friend," Zarus says, patting him on the back. "I am going to make you an official junior partner, and you will have shares in my mine so you can reap of the profits."

"And you, Noach? How did you do?"

At my home are four gold bouillon bricks, twice as much as what you gave me."

"Good for you, Noach. How did you do it?"

"I went to China."

"China? What an adventure that must have been."

"Yes, sir. I bought silk from every silk maker and seller in the two major seaports where silk is a specialization."

"You'll have to tell me all about your trip. So, then, how did you resell it all?"

"Saabhu and I went on the same ship and stopped at every seaport along the Great Sea until we ran out. We could have sold more. And here we are."

"Noach, I am going to make you an junior partner, and you will have shares in my mine so you can reap of the profits."

"You really knew what you were doing, Noach. Did you save any back for your wife?"

"Well, no."

"We'll have to fix that the next time a ship arrives from China."

Zarus puts his hands behind his head and grins. "I cannot tell you how proud I am of the two of you. Now, where is Wajid?"

"He should be here soon," Saabhu says.

"And here I am," Wajid says with a pack on his back.

"Okay, tell me how you doubled my investment."

"Oh, I didn't take so many chances like Noach and Saabhu did. I was very careful with mine. They must have cashed theirs in and spent it all. But I did not."

Zarus leans forward. "Then what did you do?"

"I buried mine."

Zarus' expression changes. He rises and paces.

"You did what?"

"I buried mine."

"I knew how demanding you were. And, well, frankly, sir, you use all of us who mine for you. We all work hard all day, and you get the profit. There is never anything in it for us."

"Wajid, that's not true. You get good wages."

"Well, I deserve it. But I deserve more. I deserve part of the profit from the mine."

"But you aren't putting any of your money into it for equipment and to pay everyone's wages," Noach says.

"I don't care. I deserve part of the profits, and his highness, Zarus, here won't give it to me."

Zarus continues to fume. He thinks back over the twenty years he has put into the mining business and his endless work and sacrifice.

Wajid takes off the pack from his back, sets it on the camel-skin floor, and pulls out his gold bouillon.

"Here, sir, even though you've always been unfair, is your bouillon back safe and sound."

"But you could have at least invested it so I would earn some interest from it. You didn't even do that?"

"No, sir. I don't trust bankers. Here's your gold back."

Zarus stares at Wajid. Saabhu and Noach remain quiet. After a moment of silence, Zarus points to the flap of the tent.

"Out," he says. "Out. And do not ever come back."

"Again, it will be like a man going on a journey, who called his servants and entrusted his wealth to them. To one he gave five bags of gold, to another two bags, and to another one bag, each according to his ability. Then he went on his journey. The man who had received five bags of gold went at once and put his money to work and gained five bags more. So also, the one with two bags of gold gained two more. But the man who had received one bag went off, dug a hole in the ground and hid his master's money.

"After a long time the master of those servants returned and settled accounts with them. The man who had received five bags of gold brought the other five. 'Master,' he said, 'you entrusted me with five bags of gold. See, I have gained five more.'

"His master replied, 'Well done, good and faithful servant! You have been faithful with a few things; I will put you in charge of many things. Come and share your master's happiness!'

"The man with two bags of gold also came. 'Master,' he said, 'you entrusted me with two bags of gold; see, I have gained two more.'

"His master replied, 'Well done, good and faithful servant! You have been faithful with a few things; I will put you in charge of many things. Come and share your master's happiness!'

"Then the man who had received one bag of gold came. 'Master,' he said, 'I knew that you are a hard man, harvesting where you have not sown and gathering where you have not scattered seed. [25] So I was afraid and went out and hid your gold in the ground. See, here is what belongs to you.'

"His master replied, 'You wicked, lazy servant! So you knew that I harvest where I have not sown and gather where I have not scattered seed? Well then, you should have put my money on deposit with the bankers, so that when I returned I would have received it back with interest.

"'So take the bag of gold from him and give it to the one who has ten bags. For whoever has will be given more, and they will have an abundance. Whoever does not have, even what they have will be taken from them. And throw that worthless servant outside, into the darkness, where there will be weeping and gnashing of teeth.' (Matthew 25:14-30)

27 ~ DANGER ABROAD

AD 30
Road between Jherusalem and Jhericho, Province of Jhudea, Palestine

A man's form drops from the cliff above and crashes down on the unsuspecting merchant.

"What? Oaf!"

Simeon falls to the ground, and lets go of his donkey's reins.

Heavy. The man on me is heavy. Can't breathe. Get off me.

A rod finds its mark on his head. Simeon tries to get his hands up to protect his head, but the attacker grabs them, holds them down, and puts his knees on them.

Another blow to his head.

"How I hate you," the attacker growls. "Stand up and fight like a man."

The pressure on his back is released, and Simeon is pulled to his feet. He turns around to see who is attacking him.

"Why? What did I ever do to you?"

Jherusalem, Province of Jhudea

"I am seventy years old, and still have not been invited to be on the Sanhedrin, even though I now own a gold mine," Caalev tells a fellow priest his same age."

"You're too old now. You should have retired five years ago. Me too. But I guess it's hard to give up what has been part of you for so long."

"But I've dedicated my life to the temple. I never married. I was a missionary to Italy and Samaria. I am sent requests to speak at feasts and synagogues, but the Sanhedrin pays no attention to me."

"You're just too good for the Sanhedrin, Caalev."

"Recently, I changed my affiliation from Pharisee to Sadducee because that is mostly who rules the Sanhedrin. My family doesn't know, of course. Denying people come back to life after death is serious business. Denying the prophets is too."

"Looks like there is nothing left you can do."

"Well, recently I have started writing opinions on the Torah in hopes they will become part of the Talmud. Then the Sanhedrin will recognize me."

Road between Jherusalem and Jhericho, Province of Jhudea

"What did you do wrong? You are alive, that's what. You make the money I deserve to have. You deserve nothing."

With that, the highwayman shoves his iron fist into Simeon's middle.

"Oaf. No. Ugghh."

Again and again.

"I want you to suffer like I've suffered."

"But I don't know..."

"That's right. You don't know."

Another punch, this time to Simeon's jaw.

"Ugghh."

Simeon is knocked back onto the ground. His donkey stomps in place, then sideways, braying incessantly. The highwayman turns to the donkey and socks it in the nose, followed by a blow from the rod in his other hand. The donkey raises up on its hind legs, then back down.

Jherusalem, Province of Jhudea

"Elii, is that you?"

Zarus is in Jherusalem on his way to Jhericho to visit his mother-in-law, who is becoming weak and feeble.

Elii stands and stares at Zarus a moment. Finally, "Zarus?"

"Yes, it's me. It's been a long time. Twenty years I guess."

"A lot of life has been lived in that time. So, you're the one who took the love of my life from me. Well, maybe it was for the best."

"Yeah, I guess I did. So, how has your life been? I hope it has been a good one."

"It's been good. I married later to a quiet woman who loves the Lord and is a good mother to my children."

Hey, why don't I take you over to the inn to eat? You always did look like you could put on a few pounds."

"Well, I don't know, you being a Samaritan and all. You know how it is down here in Jhudea?"

"Have you heard of Jhesus? Devorah and I are now followers of him. We have no religious differences anymore."

I've heard him,, and I think I like him. Well, okay. There is an inn down at the end of the block."

Once settled at a table, Zarus tells Elii, "Order whatever you want. I can afford it. I know a Levite's salary isn't the greatest, but you are providing a good service, one that does not go unappreciated."

"Actually, I just have time for something to drink. Then I have to go back to work."

"Okay. I have some business to take care of before I leave Jherusalem anyway."

Road between Jherusalem and Jhericho, Province of Jhudea

Simeon takes advantage of the diversion and leaps on the back of the highwayman, a giant compared to the merchant. The highwayman grabs Simeon's arms and turns in circles, trying to get him off. The donkey continues to bray incessantly, and the highwayman lowers his head, pulls harder on Simeon's arms, then bucks.

Simeon lands on his back.

"Oafff."

Simeon struggles to get to his feet, but his attacker pounces on him, landing with his knees on Simeon's middle.

Stop. No. I can't breathe. Stop. No.

With both fists, he hits Simeon on the jaw, in the eyes, in the ears.

No!

Blood coming from Simeon's nose, his ears, his lips.

Still the punches. Right. Left. Right. Left.

Simeon can no longer see straight. No longer hear right. No longer think rationally.

Jherusalem, Province of Jhudea

"Caalev, may I have a word with you?"

A member of the Sanhedrin actually wants to confide in me? Maybe at last.

"Certainly, sir. You are Elii's father, aren't you? Fine young man. Fine. Fine," Caalev says. "What can I do for you?"

I would like to take a closer look at your treatise on fasting. Some in the Sanhedrin have read it and are impressed. Could you have fifty more copies ready to distribute tomorrow morning?"

How am I going to do it? I'll stay up all night but still need help.

"Of course, sir. No problem. I have some scribe friends—*well, I have one*—who will help me. You will have them first thing in the morning."

"Good. I will see you then."

Priest Caalev turns toward the outer gate of the temple and home. *I've got to start on this immediately.*

He spots Elii just coming in.

"Well, hello there, son. How would you like to earn a little extra pay?"

"When?"

"The rest of today and all night if required."

"Oh, I have to go home to my wife as soon as I am off work. She is pregnant and expecting any day." He continues on his way.

"I will pay you one denarus per hour," Priest Caalev shouts.

Elii stops and turns back to Caalev.

"That's a day's wages for each hour."

"That's right. I'm sure you could use the extra money with the baby coming."

"What work do you have in mind?"

"I need to have fifty copies of my treatise ready to give to the Sanhedrin first thing in the morning. I have one friend in Jhericho who will help me, but I need more. Will you come to my home and help make copies?"

"I'll come as soon as I am off work."

Road between Jherusalem & Jhericho, Province of Jhudea

The donkey bucks and brays, and the merchandise on its back breaks loose. Still the bucking and shrill braying.

Another punch at Simeon's face. And another.

The highwayman pulls out a dagger. He holds it above Simeon's heart. It hovers there. Then the attacker jumps up, turns to the donkey, and thrusts the dagger into the donkey's neck.

A shrieking bray.

Another thrust of the dagger in another part of his neck.

Still the shrill braying.

Another thrust to the neck, this time slicing across from left to right.

The donkey raises up on its hind legs, stomps down, goes to its knees, brays weakly, and falls to its side.

The highwayman turns back to Simeon, who is now on his knees, crawling on the road toward his attacker, bloody eyes looking up. The two stare at each other. They both know who will win.

———

Priest Caalev leaves out the front gate of the temple and walks toward the southern gate of the city.

He is clutching a bag stuffed with fifty small scrolls and his beloved treatise on fasting.

In a basket, he has several large corked bottles of ink sitting upright to avoid spillage, and twenty pens in case of breakage.

His steps are quick.

"Let me see," he says to himself. "If I copy two treatises an hour, I could get twenty done by morning. But that doesn't account for the time necessary to walk to Jhericho and back."

He continues to mumble to himself, and passers-by do not pay attention to him, though the children giggle when they see him.

"Well, that's eighteen if I don't stop to eat. Now, if I can get my friend, Hanan, to help, he could do eighteen. So that's thirty-six."

He arrives at the gate in and out of Jherusalem and walks through it, still muttering.

"If Elii comes as soon as he is off work, he could do perhaps fourteen. Yes! Then I would have my fifty."

Caalev smiles.

The road down to Jhericho grows ever more steep.

At least I'm going down. It's so much faster than the long climb up to Jherusalem in the morning.

Caalev goes around a curve in the road.

"What's that?" he mutters.

He squints and sees up ahead a dead donkey and a man lying next to it.

There's a third man. He's scaling the cliff above it. Now he's gone.

Priest Caalev slows down. *What should I do?* He looks behind him. No one there. He looks up the cliff. *If there was someone up there, he's gone now.*

He inches closer to the injured man. Blood everywhere.

It's probably too late. Besides, what if the bad guy comes back? He'll kill me.

Caalev goes to the opposite side of the road and runs away as fast as his old legs will let him.

Run. The robber may come back. Run.

If the guy is injured that bad, he'll probably die soon anyway. Besides, all the work I have to get done tonight.

———

With the traveler gone, the highwayman jumps back down from the cliff. He is not through.

He kicks Simeon in the chest. Simeon raises his head, then collapses once again on the road.

"You think you're so good," the highwayman says as he kicks Simeon in the side.

"Ugghh."

Again and again. Kicking, kicking, kicking.

"Ugghh. Ugghh"

"Do you know why I hate you so much, swine?"

Another kick.

"Ugghh."

"I try and try to get a job, but none of you will hire me.

Another kick.

"Ugghh."

You want all your money for yourself."

"Ugghh."

He's killing me.

———

Levite Elii leaves the temple and heads in the direction of Jhericho.

I really do not want to be doing this, he thinks. *First of all, I'll have to deal with Devorah's mother. Well, maybe Caalev will keep her out of the way.*

He goes out the Jherusalem gate and heads down the steep road between it and Jhericho. His tall frame allows for long steps, and his head lurches forward like a turkey's as though his head will make the rest of his body go faster.

Why now? The baby is due any day. I am needed at home.

There are not many people on the road this time of day. People shy away from the dangerous, winding road if there is any chance of being on the road when darkness comes.

Elii stretches his head a little farther ahead of his body and lengthens his step.

He spots something in the road. His eyesight is not good. He must get closer.

His walk is cautious as he makes his way to the something, his head going ahead of his body even more. He slows his pace so he can figure out what is in his way.

He realizes one of the objects is a donkey, apparently dead. Then he sees the man lying next to it. He sees another shadow nearby and cannot tell if it is a shadow of a tree hanging over the road from the cliff above or a second man.

I don't know anything about medicine. If the man is still alive, I couldn't do anything for him. Besides, how would I carry him? On my back? Can't do that. What would people say?

———

The donkey raises its head and begins the frantic screeching, shrieking braying anew.

The highwayman turns toward the donkey, steps over to it, and plunges the dagger in its heart, leaving it in place.

"Shut up!"

Back to the merchant, his attacker picks him up by the tunic and throws him like a sack of barley. Simeon's head hits the pavement, and he grows silent.

The attacker picks him up again by his tunic and throws him onto another part of the road.

So what, if someone comes around the curve and spots me. I'll kill him too.

The highwayman lifts Simeon's torso and takes off his royal blue robe with silver threads and tassels. The man is sitting on part of it, so his attacker lifts him and throws him on his front to get the rest off.

———

Having completed his business in the city, Zarus heads out toward Jhericho. He leads a donkey with some gifts for Avigail and Priest Caalev, along with things he needs while traveling. As he makes his way down the road, he remembers how his sister was almost killed on this road a few years before, and how her husband was killed.

Dangerous road. Dangerous to walk alone.

Still, Zarus has only so many days to be away from the mine. He must go see Avigail, deliver the trinkets Devorah has sent her, and give her the letter from her adoring Amram.

As he comes to one of the curves, he looks down the drop-off where the road curves again and thinks he sees something in the road.

What's that?

He urges his donkey into a run.

If I can subdue the robber, I can perhaps save the man.

———

The highwayman turns Simeon on his back again, grabs the knife out of the donkey, and cuts the little man's tunic off, cutting Simeon's chest as he goes. He throws the tunic to the side of the road near where the turban had landed. He decides to keep them both, donning the turban onto his own head, and stuffing the torn tunic—much too small for him—in his belt.

Turning his attention to the donkey, he cuts the straps, and the goods he had been carrying spill all over the road. He unrolls an empty pack he had dropped from the cliff just before pouncing on the merchant, and stuffs it with what he can. What is too big, he throws up to the top of the cliff from whence he had come while in hiding.

Walking over what he does not want, he goes around to the back of the donkey and lifts it enough to push it to the drop-off edge of the road. And with a great heave, the donkey goes plunging to the valley below.

He turns and looks at the merchant and pulls his loincloth. He stares one last time at Simeon and mutters, "Oh, how I hate you. I hope you go to hell."

Just then, Zarus rounds the curve and sees the highwayman. He slides off his donkey and runs.

"Halt! Stop!" he shouts. His robe flies behind him. His kerchief flies off his head.

"Stop! Get away from that man!"

Zarus has not run this fast and hard in years. He becomes winded. Still, he runs.

"Stop!"

By the time he arrives, only the naked man is on the road.

Zarus rushes up to the man and takes off his cloak to cover him. He holds his ear up close to the man's chest and hears a faint heartbeat.

"Sir, I am here to help you," he whispers. *I hope the man can hear me. It will give him hope to stay alive.*

"I'll be right back," Zarus says.

He goes to his donkey, who has followed him and stopped nearby and looks through his traveling supplies. He brings out some swaddling bands and a jar of olive oil. Oil good for keeping lights aglow in the mines, and for healing.

Gently he pours the oil on all Simeon's wounds, hoping some of the dirt will float away in it. He dabs the wounds, then wraps them in bandages.

He turns Simeon on his side, and Simeon groans. "Easy there, sir." I'm just going to soothe those wounds on your back."

That done, Zarus talks again to the little merchant.

"Sir, I am going to put you on my donkey and take you the rest of the way into Jhericho so I can get more help for you. I'm sorry, but since you cannot sit up, I am going to have to put you on your stomach.

"No, you have too many wounds on your stomach. I am going to carry you over to my donkey, and your legs will straddle it.

"I'm too big for there to be two of us on the donkey. So I'm going to walk beside you. I am tall, and you can put your head on my shoulder. I will support you with my arm. I have long legs, and we will get you to Jhericho soon."

Jhericho, Province of Jhudea

Just before arriving in the city, Zarus notices the man has passed out. He listens for a heartbeat, but cannot detect one.

"You cannot go any farther. There is an inn just up ahead. I will get a room for you there."

When they arrive, Zarus puts the man in his arms and carries him into the inn. The other customers watch him.

He walks up to the innkeeper.

"Sir, this man was beaten up on the highway and left for dead.

I would like a room for him."

"I don't know. What if he dies while he's here?"

"Sir, I will pay you double. I'll stay with him tonight."

"So, you take full responsibility for him?"

"Yes, sir. I really need to get him to a bed now."

"Well, okay. As soon as you lay him down on a bed, I expect my money."

Zarus follows the innkeeper down a long hall. At the far end, a door is opened, and Zarus enters with his wounded charge. He places Simeon on the bed with the gentleness of a mother with her child and hears him groan.

Zarus smiles. "He's going to live. I am going to make sure of that."

He pulls out two denari and pays the innkeeper, closes the door, and sits on the floor next to Simeon. And prays for him.

If only Jhesus were here. He could make him well instantly. I know he could.

Zarus lays his head down on Simeon's bed sometimes and closes his eyes, but whenever he hears a groan, he returns to full awakeness.

He has a bowl of water next to the bed and occasionally sets a kerchief dipped in the cold water onto the man's forehead to try to keep fever down.

The night is long.

Zarus jerks awake.

"Where am I?" The voice is but a whisper.

Zarus takes the man's hand and whispers back to him. "You are safe. You are at an inn. My name is Zarus. Can you tell me your name?"

"Sim…Sim…eon."

"Very good, Simeon. We are going to take good care of you. I am going to leave the room for a moment to order some broth for you. Do you think you could drink it with your cut lips? Probably not. I'll get some warm goat's milk for you. I'll be right back."

Moments later, Zarus is back at Simeon's bedside with a copper bowl of milk and a wooden spoon.

"Here you go, sir. Try to sip as much of it as you can."

Simeon takes a few sips, then drifts off to sleep.

"That is good, my friend. Sleep is good. It is dawn, and I have to go on into town to see some relatives. But I will be back later. I won't desert you. I'll be back."

———

Zarus pays the innkeeper another two denari.

"Did you hear the news, sir?" the innkeeper asks Zarus. "Everyone's talking about it."

"What news?"

"They crucified Jhesus."

Zarus' head swims.

"Why? He was a good man. Everyone was following him."

"That was the problem. The Jewish leaders were losing their influence and power because of him."

"It can't be," Zarus replies. He looks up at the ceiling as though, in the process, the whole thing will disappear.

"That's what everyone said. But it happened."

He looks back at the man. "Who ordered it?"

"The Sanhedrin."

Dumbfounded, Zarus leaves the inn and heads for Caalev's house. *I wonder if Caalev approved of it.*

When he arrives, he is greeted at the gate by Avigail's maid, Sarach.

Zarus hands the reins of his donkey to the stable boy, then greets Sarach.

"I thought I heard a familiar voice." It is Avigail shuffling toward Zarus with outstretched arms. "How is Devorah? And that sweet boy of yours, Amram? Did you bring me anything?"

They hear a man's gruff voice coming out of an adjoining room. "We just now got done in time. Now we must rush back to Jherusalem and get these scrolls delivered to the Sanhedrin."

Priest Caalev stops when he notices Zarus.

"Well, how are you, my boy? Do you remember Elii here? His father is on the Sanhedrin. "

Were they both in on it? Crucifying Jhesus?

"I am fine, and, yes, I remember Elii."

"We were expecting you last night."

"I almost made it. But there was a wounded man by the side of the road. He'd been beaten up pretty badly and left for dead. But he wasn't dead. I spent the night helping him and…"

Zarus stops and looks into the shocked faces of Caalev and Elii.

But he wanted to justify himself, so he asked Jhesus, "And who is my neighbor?"

In reply Jhesus said: "A man was going down from Jherusalem to Jhericho, when he was attacked by robbers. They stripped him of his clothes, beat him and went away, leaving him half dead.

A priest happened to be going down the same road, and when he saw the man, he passed by on the other side.

So too, a Levite, when he came to the place and saw him, passed by on the other side.

But a Samaritan, as he traveled, came where the man was; and when he saw him, he took pity on him.

He went to him and bandaged his wounds, pouring on oil and wine. Then he put the man on his own donkey, brought him to an inn and took care of him.

The next day he took out two denarii[e] and gave them to the innkeeper. 'Look after him,' he said, 'and when I return, I will reimburse you for any extra expense you may have.'

"Which of these three do you think was a neighbor to the man who fell into the hands of robbers?"

The expert in the law replied, "The one who had mercy on him."

Jhesus told him, "Go and do likewise." (Luke 10:30-35)

28 ~ FOUND WANTING

AD 31
Copper Mine, Timna Valley, Arabah Desert, Idumea

"**H**udas **has been with us over a dozen years, Gersshon,**" **Zarus says as Gersshon walks into the *officium* tent.**

"Uh, yes," Gersshon says, abruptly stopping where he is and looking at his partner with his brow furrowed. "We were lucky to get him. He worked with the biggest banker in Sebaste."

It is early morning.

"How often do we pay him?" Zarus asks, staring back at Gersshon.

"He comes out once a month to audit Yair's books, and I pay him then for the whole month."

Gersshon walks over to some ore samples and picks them up for examination.

"How much do we pay him?"

What is going on with Zarus? Why suddenly all the questions?

"He receives one silver brick of bouillon for his pay every month," Gersshon says, holding the ore samples up to the light coming in through the flap.

"That's an odd way to pay him," Zarus says, watching Gersshon.

"That's the way he likes it. He has an arrangement with a local banker."

"Why did he resign from the bank up in Sebaste?"

Gersshon grits his teeth, then answers. "He didn't resign. He retired early."

Over at the doorway, Zarus notices Yair approaching the *officium* tent. Since his grown children who used to carry him back and forth to work had moved away, he had come up with another form of transportation.

Zarus looks back at Gersshon. "So, has he given Yair a hard time?"

"They seem to get along just fine."

Zarus goes over to Gersshon, takes the ore samples out of his hands, and makes Gersshon look at him.

"I never see him here."

"He does most of his auditing work at home."

Yair arrives in his horse-drawn chariot and parks it close to the flap. Zarus turns his attention to Yair, walks over to the chariot, lifts the legless man out of it, and delivers him to his work table.

He turns back and looks at Gersshon. "He does all his work at home?"

More questions. I've got to put this fire out before it spreads.

"Uh, by the way, Zarus, I have some great news," Gersshon says with a wide grin. "Hudas is going to have a feast at his house the day after tomorrow, and it is in your honor. It was supposed to be a surprise, but I guess he won't mind if I tell.

I've got to get to Hudas right now and get guests invited, and food and entertainment arranged fast.

Eilat, Port City on Red Sea, Arabah Desert

"Welcome to our home, Zarus. And this is your lovely wife, I presume, and here are your fine children," Hudas says with a broad grin.

The host is dressed in a red toga, green tunic with silver-threaded fringe, a gold chain with ruby pendant, and matching ring.

"Yes, certainly you remember my wife, Devorah. These are my children, Amram, Ithamar, and Lleah."

"How lovely. And how old are your children?"

"Amram is sixteen, Ithamar is thirteen, and Lleah is ten."

"You have a fine family. Oh, here comes my wife, Gila. Gila, come greet our guest of honor."

"Welcome to our home," Gila says, "It is so good to see you again. But you must come away from the gate as though you don't know whether to go or stay. Ha. Ha."

Gila is a small but portly woman who seems to be much younger than her husband. She is wearing a silk tunic of gold with necklace, earrings, bracelets, tiara, and rings of gold, all with topaz insets.

The couple leads Zarus and his family through the courtyard with mosaic tile depicting ships at sea, and surrounded by marble columns rising high to support rooms on the second and third floor.

They arrive at the banquet hall. There are about twenty people there, and Devorah notices servants are taking away several unused tables and couches.

"We wanted an intimate gathering in your honor," Hudas says. "Now, your place is at the head table with Gila and I, of course. We were not expecting your lovely children, but are pleased to give them the three closest tables to ours."

As Zarus and his family are seated, harpists come out and seat themselves in the back of the room. Their music flows like siren songs, exotic and alluring.

At each place is a silver plate and golden goblet.

"Attention, everyone," Hudas says above the music. "We have gifts for you. The servants will be around to your place momentarily. Each of you will receive a gold ring. And for our honored guests, Zarus receives a gold ring with ruby in it, and his lovely wife, Devorah, receives a gold ring with an opal in it."

The guests applaud, though it is almost imperceptible in such a large hall.

"Tonight we celebrate Zarus, a great man. He came here to the valley with nothing and has risen to become the richest man anywhere around. It has been a great honor to associate with him and be part of his organization. I am fortunate to call him friend."

Applause.

"Now, bring in the food."

Three days later, a message is delivered to Zarus' home. Devorah receives it.

"Dear," she says from the courtyard, reading the ornate carved clay tablet as she walks, "we have been invited to Hudas' house tomorrow for a private dinner. He would like our children to meet his children."

"What is that man up to?" Zarus says. He is in his study going over some scrolls Yair had given him that afternoon.

"I don't know," Devorah answers,"but we don't really know them very well. Perhaps we should go."

"Very well, we will go. But we cannot stay long."

Devorah calls out for the children to come to her in the

courtyard. She tells them the news. They are not receptive.

"It wouldn't hurt for you to make new friends, you know. Now go to your rooms and pick out something appropriate to wear."

The next day, Lleah comes to Devorah. "Mother, I'm not really excited about going to their house tonight."

"Why is that, Lleah?"

"He has two daughters—Mazal and Vared—and they aren't always very nice. I see them around town sometimes, and they wear, well, their clothes are, well…"

"I understand, Lleah. We really have to go since their father has worked for your father for a fairly long time. We won't stay very long. I promise."

———

"Welcome, once more, to our home," Gila says to Zarus. "I am so glad you could come," she says, looking over at Devorah. I'm so glad your children could come. Now they will have a chance to meet our children."

Once again, Gila leads the way. They go through their ornate courtyard and to a smaller side room than where they had been earlier in the week.

"This is where our family eats. We feel as though you are family, too, so you will join us here."

Hudas walks into the room leading his children.

"Welcome, friends. I see you have three children, just like we do. That is fortunate."

His children do not smile as they stay next to their father. Zarus' children do likewise.

"May I introduce my children to you," Hudas continues. "This is my oldest, Tanchum. He is twenty-five. My second is a daughter, Mazal, twenty-two. And my baby is Vared, nineteen. Isn't she beautiful? Just like your daughter is beautiful."

A servant arrives and shows Zarus' family to their places while Hudas' family goes to theirs.

Other servants bring in the food and drink.

"So, is Amram going into the copper business with you, Zarus?"

"He does not know for sure yet. He has another interest he may pursue."

"Or perhaps he can do both," Gila says.

"I would like to travel one day," Ithamar volunteers. His parents do not admonish him for speaking out.

"Did I ever tell you that, whenever we have a family vacation, we take tours of different famous places?" Hudas says.

"Yes, we have been to Alexandria, Athens, Rome," Gila adds, "and our next vacation may be to either India or Britannia; we haven't decided yet."

Dinner is eaten with the parents chatting with each other. Now and then, Devorah grabs at her chest but forces a smile. Other than Ithamar's one comment, the children do not speak.

"Well, thank you, Hudas, for the final meal. We are pleased to meet your children. Now, if you will excuse us, I still have much work to do before I retire for the night."

Everyone rises and makes their way toward the courtyard and ornate carved outer gate.

"By the way, Hudas, would you mind giving me your auditing records while I'm here?"

Hudas stops. His face turns red. He clears his throat. "Uh, well, of course, Zarus, sir. But I'll have to pick them up at the mine."

"I understand you do all your work at home. I will wait a few moments while you find them. You have a garden, I notice. We shall wait out there."

"Well, go get them, dear," Gila tells her husband, "and you children may go to your rooms."

Hudas stands still. The children leave, but Hudas does not. "I can't."

"Of course, you can," Gila says. "Now, you go get them, or I will."

"You don't understand."

"All right then, I will go get them."

"No, I will."

Copper Mine, Timna Valley, Arabah Desert

"Yair, have you gone over all the books for the past thirteen years, as I asked?"

"I have."

"And you've compared them with Hudas' auditing books?"

"Yes, sir. But there are many irregularities. I may not have the knowledge of banking that Hudas has, but I know numbers, and something is not right, sir."

"I am not surprised. His house is more resplendent than my own. Where did he get that kind of money?"

Yair hesitates.

"You can speak freely. Gersshon has gone to Persia to see if he can find a refining operation that charges less than the one in Egypt."

"I was afraid to put my findings in writing, just in case he discovers them."

"Just tell me. Then, if you can put it in writing this morning, you can give it to me without being found out by anyone else."

"Well, sir, he has been embezzling heavily. He has taken an average of forty bricks of silver bouillon as his pay each month. It amounts to one hundred and twenty million denari over the period of twelve years.

"He listed half of it as pay for miners we do not have, and the other half as his pay."

Zarus stands and paces. "I knew it. I think I have suspected it all along. But I didn't want to disturb my friendship with Gersshon. I couldn't jeopardize our partnership. Well, maybe Gersshon didn't know about it. Probably he didn't."

He stops and looks back at Yair. "I need to go find Noach. Then I will be gone the rest of the day."

Zarus goes out toward his copper pit and asks around for Noach until he finds him.

"Noach, I need twenty of your strongest men. Bring them out and tell them to clean up and put on fresh tunics. It should just take them a few moments. They will meet me by my horse."

Eilat, Port City on Red Sea, Arabah Desert

"Open up, Hudas!" Zarus shouts.

Two of the miners who had followed him into the city pound on the gate until someone comes to unfasten it.

When the gate opens, Zarus rushes in with the twenty strong miners behind him. He does not wait to be shown around. He goes from room to room until he finds Hudas.

"Grab him and chain him," Zarus orders as he walks back out into the elaborate courtyard.

He turns and stands with his arms folded, feet apart in a fighter's stance, ready to pronounce sentence.

"Oh, please, Zarus. I didn't mean to," Hudas says,

"Of course you did."

"But my children deserved the best. I grew up as a poor orphan. I couldn't put them through what I went through. Surely you understand."

"Stealing to put food on the table and clothe your children is different from stealing to give them opulence."

"My wife. She insisted on the house. She was going to leave me. She is so young and beautiful. What was I supposed to do?"

"I've heard enough. Put chains on his feet and get him to the magistrate. I am pressing charges of theft. You will have to remain in prison until you can repay me my millions."

"No!" Hudas screeches. "No!"

"And the rest of you men, I want you to go throughout the house and bring all the furniture here. It will be sold, then the house.

"But where will my wife and children live?"

"They won't have to worry about that. They will be indentured to work off your debt until it is paid back to me."

With all the commotion in the courtyard, Hudas' wife and children rush out to discover what is happening. The servants stay in the background, but they, too, wonder.

Hudas falls to his knees.

"Please, Zarus. I didn't mean to. They pressured me. And I heard you were poor one time. Surely you understand what it is like to be poor and deserted."

Zarus says nothing.

"Please, sir. I will do anything for you. I will work for you for the next twelve years free. Just give me a chance."

Still, Zarus stares at the pitiful man at his feet. He remembers back to the years of his own indenturement to win Devorah. Four years of hell.

"I am begging you with tears. Please don't send me to jail and sell my wife and children to pay off my debt. Look at them. What will they do without me? If you do not care anything about me, think about what they will go through because of my foolishness."

Zarus puts his hand through his brown and graying hair. Indeed. *How can I put them through this? Money isn't everything. What would I do with the extra millions if I did get it back?*

He turns and walks away from Hudas. He hears Hudas sobbing behind him. *Jhesus, what would you do? Would you sacrifice so much for me?*

Finally, Zarus turns back to Hudas. "All right. I forgive your debt."

Hudas rises. "Oh, thank you, Zarus. You will never regret it."

"Men," he calls out. "We're through here. Put the furniture back and unchain Hudas."

As he reaches the outer gate, Zarus turns back and looks at

Hudas. "But, you will no longer work for me."

Copper Mine, Timna Valley, Arabah Desert

"Where is Yair? I haven't seen him in two days," Zarus asks Noach.

"I don't know. I will ask around."

"I hope he is not sick."

While Zarus waits, he looks through Yair's entries in his accounting log.

Smart man. Too bad about the mining accident that got his legs. I am indebted to Devorah for finding him. He has been loyal to me since the beginning.

"Sir," Noach says, reporting back to the *officium* tent. "Yair is in prison."

"He is what?" Zarus responds, standing, his fists clenched.

"He is in prison. Debtor's prison."

"Someone, bring my horse around. I have to see him."

Eilat, Port City on Red Sea, Arabah Desert

The gate behind Zarus clangs shut and is barred. A guard leads him down several steps into a cave-like area with bars across it. It reminds Zarus of the underground mine he had worked in as a young man.

There are some fifty men on the other side. Some wear good clothes. Some wear shabby clothes.

The guard calls out. "Which one of you guys is Yair?"

No one answers.

"Sir," Zarus says, "he was in a mining accident years ago, and his legs cut off. Oh, I see him. He is over there."

Content with Zarus' recognition of whoever he has come to see, the guard opens the gate and lets Zarus in.

Zarus covers his mouth and nose with his handkerchief. The mine underground hadn't smelled much better. But that was long ago.

The prisoners watch this man with fine, though plain, tunic and robe.

"Yair, friend!" he calls out.

Zarus goes up to Yair and squats on the filthy floor next to him.

"Oh, sir, you found me."

"I did not realize you were missing until today. I thought perhaps you were ill. But let's get right to the point. Why are you here?"

"Sir, I am here because I owe someone two hundred denari."

"Who do you owe, Yair? I thought your pay was sufficient to support you in a decent manner."

"When I had to find another way to get to work. I heard of an old chariot for sale and an old horse with it. I sent word to the owner, and he said the price would be two hundred denari."

"Did you have some money put away?"

"I did, but it was being saved for something else."

"So you borrowed the money? Was it from a banker?"

"No, sir. It was from Hudas."

"Hudas?"

"Yes. People are afraid to loan money to a man in my condition. I had no choice. I had to be able to go to work and support my wife and I."

"After you told me you had actually forgiven his debt, he sent for me to come to his house. I thought, even though I was late paying him, he had decided to follow your example and forgive my debt to him."

"But he didn't. He must have been getting back at you for turning him in."

Zarus rises and calls out for a guard.

"Sir, this man owes two hundred denari." He reaches into his money belt and pulls out the required money.

"His debt is paid in full. Now, release him."

The guard unbars the door, Zarus picks up Yair in his still-strong arms, and the two leave the prison.

When they get up to the guard command center just before going out into the street, Zarus stops.

"I need two things, and I will pay for them.

First, I need a chariot to take this man to his home, wait for him while he cleans up, then take him to my mine out in the Timna Valley. The driver will be paid for his service when he is delivered at his place of work.

"Second, I need four constables to go with me. There is a man in the city who owes me millions, and it is time he pays his debt."

An hour later, Zarus is at Hudas' gate with four constables in front of him. One of the constables pounds on the gate with the brunt of his sword.

"Open up! Open up!"

They hear the rattle of the bar and step back. The moment the gate is ajar a hand span, the constables push their way in. They spread out and search the rooms. Moments later, one of them comes out with Hudas. He is chained hand and foot.

Zarus stands in the courtyard. Their eyes lock. And Zarus walks away.

"Therefore, the kingdom of heaven is like a king who wanted to settle accounts with his servants.

As he began the settlement, a man who owed him ten thousand talents was brought to him.

Since he was not able to pay, the master ordered that he and his wife and his children and all that he had be sold to repay the debt.

"The servant fell on his knees before him. 'Be patient with me,' he begged, 'and I will pay back everything.'

The servant's master took pity on him, canceled the debt and let him go.

"But when that servant went out, he found one of his fellow servants who owed him a hundred denari. He grabbed him and began to choke him. 'Pay back what you owe me!' he demanded.

"His fellow servant fell to his knees and begged him, 'Be patient with me, and I will pay you back.'

"But he refused. Instead, he went off and had the man thrown into prison until he could pay the debt.

When the other servants saw what had happened, they were greatly distressed and went and told their master everything that had happened.

"Then the master called the servant in. 'You wicked servant,' he said, 'I canceled all that debt of yours because you begged me to.

Shouldn't you have had mercy on your fellow servant just as I had on you?'

In anger, his master turned him over to the jailers to be tortured until he should pay back all he owed. (Matthew 18:23-34)

MAP OF ISRAEL &
LOCATION OF THE MINE

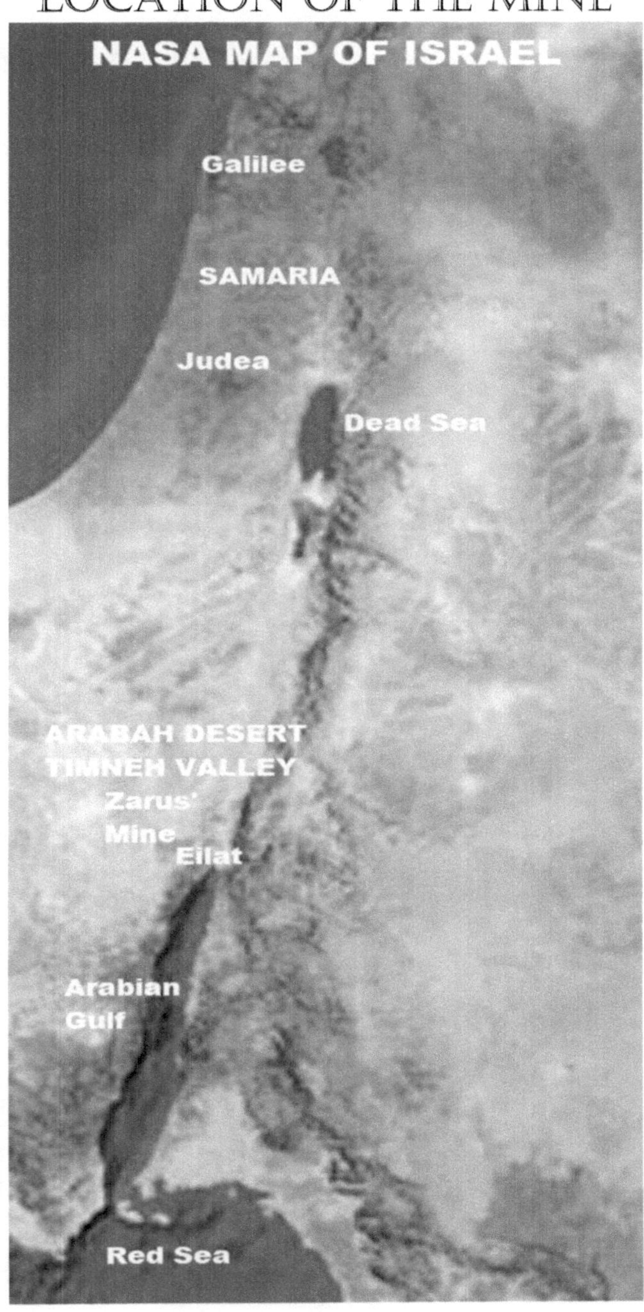

29 ~ GOOD AND BAD

AD 34
Copper Mine, Timna Valley, Arabah Desert, Idumea

"So, how are my sons doing with their apprenticeships?" Zarus asks.

Zarus, Noach, and Saabhu are sitting on three cushions in the *officium* tent, enjoying a goblet of pomegranate juice and some grapes.

"You're looking at each other like neither one wants to tell me," Zarus grins. "Well, you're going to have to. I'll find out anyway, but it would be better coming from you."

"Well, I have to say that Amram has a lot of potential," Noach begins

"Everyone does. Get specific with me."

"He's very intelligent. He takes his time learning something until he understands everything about it. I keep telling him he doesn't have to understand everything, but..."

"But that's his way," Zarus grins. "Been that way all his life. Go on. What does he insist on knowing that he doesn't have to know?"

"Scheduling. We have over four hundred men working for us now in three shifts. That's around one hundred forty men per shift. Well, your Amram wants to know how tall each man is and how much he weighs."

Zarus rares back and guffaws.

"He thinks it would be more efficient to divide the men up so that you have an equal number of men representing each height and weight in each shift. That way, production would be equal in all three shifts."

"You didn't give in to him, did you, Noach?"

"Of course not. So, what does he do? He pulls out a clay tablet and makes a note on it. Probably plotting what he will do if he ever gets good enough to take over my job.”

“Well, you’re sixty-six now, getting a little too old, and Amram is 19, still a little too young. I guess I’ll take experience over enthusiasm.”

Zarus turns to the mine engineer. “And you, Saabhu. How is young Ithamar doing?”

“Well, sir, uh, does he ever stand still?”

“Never has,” Zarus laughs. “Even when he was a year old, and we had him sitting up and surrounded by pillows, he would rock his head back and forth for hours and giggle. Once he started crawling, we had to block doorways so he would stay either in the courtyard or one of the rooms. He was faster on his knees than a cat chasing a rat. So, what have you been teaching him?”

“I wanted to show him how to calculate how far apart and how high and wide to make the benches to protect the floor of the mine from falling rocks surrounding it. When I gave him a clay tablet to write down the formula, he threw it in the air, turned, and caught it behind his back.”

“Ha, ha, ha,” Zarus responds, slapping his knee. “He has been a challenge to his tutors. They always had to make everything they taught fun, or he wouldn’t learn it. He is so much like his mother: Independent and adventuresome.”

“Then when I tried to show him how to analyze the berm to see if it needed shoring up,” Saabhu continues, “he ran to the top of it, laid down on his stomach, and looked down on the berm. He could have stayed with me and looked up at the berm. But he said his way was more fun.”

“What did I tell you, Saabhu?” Zarus chuckles. “But then, what did you expect out of a sixteen-year-old? I’m sure he will be worse when he is seventeen. It’s going to take a few years to settle him down. In the meantime, take advantage of that energy. When you need to climb something to make a safety inspection, send him.”

The men sit in silence a while. “At least you don’t have them for more than half a day each day. They still have their lessons in mathematics, reading and writing, Hebrew, and learning the Torah for me and the Prophets for Devorah.

“You believe that Jhesus came back to life, don’t you?” Saabhu asks.

“Yes, I do. Devorah showed me in the prophets how his whole life fulfilled one prophecy after another—when and where he would be born, where he would grow up, that he would perform miracles, how he would die, and that he would be the Word of God in a human for a while. No man could have fulfilled all those prophecies. Their fulfillment proved to me that he was. Indeed, God walking the earth again, just like he did with Adam and Eve at the beginning."

"In Egypt, we have many gods. I never could figure out which one to believe in. None of them made sense. Maybe I'll try your Jhesus."

"Sir," Jhoel says, standing at the flap of the tent. "Another man just collapsed. His face is red with fever."

The three grow serious, set their empty mugs on a nearby table, and head out to the mine pit.

"Where is he?"

"He's all the way down on the floor."

Zarus, being the youngest, leads the way with Saabhu right behind him, but huffing to keep up with Zarus' long strides, and Noach behind them several paces.

They spot him when they see several men huddled around the sick man. By the time they arrive, and the others step aside to let their bosses see, he is shaking with chills.

Zarus takes off the protective kerchief on his head and lays it over the man. Saabhu and Noach do the same.

"All right, carry him up to the barracks tent."

"But, sir, what if what he has is catching?"

"Okay, take him to the *officium* tent until we decide what to do."

The three walk back up the sidewall of the mine over the haul road, the same way they had come. Walking is slower this time.

"We could take him home. He lives right there in Eilat," Noach suggests.

"No. If what he has is catching, we'd better not endanger his family."

They walk in silence a little longer, careful to walk at a slow, steady pace in the desert heat and not overwork their hearts.

"Saabhu," Zarus says, "I need you to go into the city and send a doctor out. We will take any doctor that is free for now so he can come immediately."

"Noach, I need you to go into the city and see if you can find a tentmaker. This is the third man who has come down with whatever it is. They need to be isolated."

Both Saabhu and Noach leave. Zarus stays by the side of the feverish man. He sets a bowl of water and cloth on the camel-hair floor next to the man and puts it on his face to cool the fever. He finds his emergency cloak for when sand storms come up and puts that over the man to ease his chills.

Zarus stays with the man all afternoon. Sometimes he prays. And he wonders if Jhesus had ever healed a man of a fever. He decides he had.

Outside he hears the sound of horses walking in the desert heat. He goes to the tent flap and looks out. It is Saabhu with a doctor.

"Thank you for coming out on such short notice, Elchanan. The patient is right over there. I will wait outside."

The doctor kneels next to the miner and takes off all covering, including his short tunic. The patient groans and curls up to get warm.

"Sir, I need you to be patient with me a moment while I figure out what is wrong with you. I am Physician Elchanan. Now, you need to answer some questions for me. Can you do that?"

The man nods his head and opens his eyes slightly, but not for long.

"I don't see any tumors under your arm, on your neck, or in your groin. I don't see any black spots on you. How about your lungs? Can you breathe okay?"

The man groans, nods his head yes, and shakes even more.

"That is good. If you had any of these symptoms, it would mean you had the black plague, and there would be no hope for your survival. But you don't have the symptoms. So we can cover you up again. It's too hard to get your tunic back on. We'll just lay it on you and put the kerchiefs and robe on top of those. I have an extra blanket on my horse. I will go get it for you in a moment."

The patient manages a slight smile, then closes his eyes again.

"Now, I have some more questions for you. Just nod or shake your head. Sir, are you nauseated? Yes? Have you vomited at all? Yes? Do you hurt anywhere? Yes? Is it just in one spot?" No? Is it all over? Yes? Does your head hurt worse than the rest of your body? Yes?"

Elchanan takes the cloth out of the bowl of water still sitting there, and spreads it across the man's forehead, then dabs it on his cheeks and neck. He does it several times.

"I know what is wrong with you, sir. You have malaria. You seem to be a strong enough man. It takes a strong man to work in a mine. So your chances of recovery are excellent."

The patient opens his eyes briefly, smiles slightly, then closes his eyes back.

"I'm going to go out and talk to your boss. You just go to sleep."

Elchanan rises and steps outside.

"Well?" Zarus asks.

"I was afraid he had the black plague, which I heard is going around over in Egypt. He does not."

"And?"

"He has malaria. It is caused by bad air. I don't think it is air from the mine; if it were, every miner would have it.

"Bad air can be caused by stagnant water. We had one of our few rains a few days ago. Since there is solid rock not far below the surface out here in the desert, the rain didn't have any place to go. Do you know of any pools left from the rain that may be turning stagnant? That would turn the air bad."

"Yes," Saabhu says. "There are a few pools west of the mine."

"Do any of your miners go over there?"

"Some of our warehouses are over there."

"I'd like to suggest that you not use any of the warehouses close to the pool. Will that leave you enough?"

"It will be tight," Zarus replies. "We have to be ready when the ships come in for copper. Perhaps we can use some warehouses along the docks."

"Fine," Elchanan says.

"Since several of your miners have gone near that bad air over the stagnant pools, you need to be ready for future cases. Is there someplace where they can be together?"

"Like a *hospitium*?"

"Yes."

"I have sent one of my men into the city to find a tentmaker who can come out and set up a tent wherever you think best," Zarus says.

"I think east as far away from the stagnant pools would be best. Do you have room there?"

"I do. Hopefully, it will be up sometime tomorrow."

"Now, for treatment. Here is a supply of chamomile leaves. I grow them myself. Make a tea or syrup with them, and give some to every patient every hour."

"Yes, sir. I will inquire if we have a miner with any medical knowledge who can take care of the men. And thank you again, Doctor, for coming out. Here are two denari for your trouble. Can you return tomorrow and the next day until we get this under control?"

"Yes, I can, and I will."

The next day, a large tent is set up on the east border of the mine property.

Gersshon, who is absent from the mine more and more, arrives the next day. Zarus explains what has been happening.

"Is malaria catching?"

"The doctor says it isn't unless several people drank from the same contaminated water. He says bad air causes it, and sometimes the bad air gets in the water."

"What do you need me for then?"

"I'm afraid we are going to need more men. Do you think you could recruit some more off the ships like you always do?"

"Good thinking. I'll go into the city right now and see what I can do. In all fairness, I will have to admit to them that there is bad air over the mine right now, and men are getting malaria, but if they want to take a chance, we will pay them well."

"Yes, always be honest."

———

The *hospitium* tent has been up two days. More miners are coming down with the malaria.

Gersshon returns at last from the city. "Zarus, we may be in trouble. First, there are no ships where any of the hands want to be exposed to malaria. Second, the sea captains are complaining that they are not getting their required amphoras of ore to take to the smelters in Persia and Egypt. If they don't get their quota, they don't get paid."

"Well, I know where there are two men who are available. I will go home and get them," Zarus says.

Eilat, Port City on Red Sea, Arabah Desert

"Amram! Ithamar!" Zarus calls out from his rich tiled courtyard. "I need to talk to you both."

He waits for his sons to report to him. Both are wearing tunics that are short, loose, and easy to maneuver in. Sometimes they call them their house tunics.

"Yes, sir," they say in unison as they arrive in front of their father.

"You are needed at the mine. I am short-handed with the malaria going around. We can't find men down at the docks like we usually do. They're afraid of the malaria."

"Should we be afraid of it?" Amram asks.

"I'm not afraid of anything, Father. I'll go," Ithamar says.

"Good for you, Ithamar. I'm proud of you. How about you, Amram?"

"But should we be afraid to be around people with malaria? I heard it is catching."

"As far as we know, it is not catching. The doctor said it comes from bad vapors in the air. So, can I count on you?"

"Father, I'm doing my Hebrew homework. You know Hebrew is hard for me. I am just trying to make you proud of me. I want to be able to read the Talmud as well as you do. I just cannot go."

Zarus stares at his oldest son. "I'm surprised you are using the scriptures as an excuse to not do a good work by helping me."

"But Ithamar is strong and healthy. With my foot like it is, I can hardly walk without a cane. What good would I be in the mines?"

"You're just using your foot as an excuse to not help our father," Ithamar says. "You're always using it as an excuse. That's all I've heard all my life. 'Do such-and-such for Amram because of his foot.' Or 'Do so-and-so for Amram because of his foot.' So, sit home and feel sorry for yourself. I'm going to help our father."

"Amram," Zarus says, "perhaps you are right. Perhaps I was expecting too much of you with your foot and all."

He turns to Ithamar. "When can you be ready?"

"I'm ready right now."

"That's my boy. You go on. I need to take care of some business down by the docks and will be out at the mine late this afternoon."

"Yes, sir," Ithamar says while looking at his big brother and making a face.

Ithamar goes to find his mother, tells Devorah where he will be the rest of the day, and leaves. He walks down the hill where his house is, and whistles as he goes. He sees a toy wagon in the road and leaps over it easily, despite his being a hand span shorter than his brother.

"Hey, Ithamar, what are you doing?"

"Hi, Zev. I'm headed for my father's mine. He's low on men today and needs me."

"Wow! He considers you a man?"

"Yup."

"But won't you get dirty?"

"Yeah, but I've got my get-dirty clothes and my fancy clothes. I don't mix 'em. So, what are you up to?"

"I'm just trying to get away from home a while. My father is mad at me again. All the guys are having a foot race down at the warehouses. Wanna come?"

"Well, just for a few moments. Then I've gotta get over to the mine."

The boys walk down to the warehouses. There are eight others there, four of which plan to enter the race.

"Okay, men, what are your bets?"

"I've got a denarus on me," Ithamar calls out."

"And who are you betting to win?"

"Zev, of course. He's the longest, tallest boy in town."

"Okay, get ready, go!"

The race is close. Zev does not win.

"Hey, that's no fair," Ithamar declares. "Two out of three. Here's my bet, another denarus."

The guys race again.

Copper Mine, Timna Valley, Arabah Desert

"It's mid-afternoon, and Ithamar still isn't here," Zarus says. "Over the last four hours, another man has been stricken with the malaria."

"Has Ithamar done anything like this before?" Gersshon asks.

"Well, yes. He does get distracted sometimes. But never from anything this important. I need every man I can get during this malaria epidemic."

"Wait. Who's that coming?" Gersshon, standing across from the tent flap, asks.

Zarus walks around and looks outside.

"Praise God, it's Amram," Zarus replies as he walks outside.

Amram pulls up his horse and slides off.

"Amram, I'm so glad you came. What changed your mind?"

"Hello, Father. I started thinking about what Ithamar said."

Father and son walk side by side toward the mine pit.

"Anything he said was out of jealousy. You know that."

"But it was true what he said: I do use my club foot as an excuse."

"Well, let me take you down to the floor of the mine. That's where I need your help the most."

As they walk down the haul road, Zarus asks his son, "Are you sorry you never asked Jhesus to heal you?"

"No. I have so many blessings, I feel like it would be unfair of me to have a whole foot too."

"You know, what you're doing today will enhance the way

people look at you. They'll look at you with a new respect. That's important if you are going to take over the mine before I die."

"But I promised Jhesus I would spread the word about him."

"You can do both. Sometimes you will be gone to check on a smelter and can spread Jhesus there. Other times you will be here, and, with our turnover, you'll be able to tell all four hundred and fifty about Jhesus several times a year."

They arrive at the mine floor, and Zarus looks around.

"Okay, I see a hammer and chisel over there. Look around for a vein of green. That's the copper. Squat down next to it and chisel out all of it you can, and have them hauled up to our warehouse."

Zarus watches Amram get settled in.

"I wonder what happened to your brother. Is he okay? I'd better go back to town and check. He could need me."

"What do you think? There was a man who had two sons. He went to the first and said, 'Son, go and work today in the vineyard.'

" 'I will not,' he answered, but later he changed his mind and went.

"Then, the father went to the other son and said the same thing. He answered, 'I will, sir,' but he did not go.

"Which of the two did what his father wanted?" "The first," they answered. (Mathew 21:28-31)

30 ~ THE WEDDING

AD 35
Eilat, Port City on Red Sea, Arabah Desert, Idumea

"Leah, your copper jewelry is almost as beautiful as you," a customer says.

"Everyone tells me I look just like my mother."

"How old are you, Lleah?"

"Fourteen."

"I remember when your mother moved here when she was nineteen. You could have passed for twins if you had been around then."

"So, are you interested in any of my jewelry? I designed this one, this one, and that one over there."

"Your jewelry is interesting. It's bold. Most jewelry these days is delicate. You're different."

"That's something else they say I inherited from my mother: Being different," Lleah says, laughing.

"Do you have any pain in your arms? I'd like to suggest this bracelet over here. You can wear it on your upper arm or squeeze it together a little more and wear it on your wrist. If you have pain in your legs, you can pull it apart a little more and wear it on your ankle."

"How delightful, Lleah. Yes, I think I would like that bracelet."

"Leah," she hears from the back of the jewelry booth. "I need to take over a while so you can work on your designs."

"Have I thanked you lately for taking me on as an apprentice?"

Ariella laughs. "You tell me about once a week. But I never tire of it. You have been my star pupil since you first came to me two years ago. I thought you were too young, but it worked out after all. I'm very proud of you."

After a while, there is another customer.

"May I help you?" Ariella asks.

"I'm Devorah, Lleah's mother."

"Oh, I'm so embarrassed. Of course, you are. I will call her." *When did she get to be so thin? And those dark circles under her eyes….*

"There you are, Lleah," Devorah says. "I happened to be in the market and thought we could have lunch together. I brought some dates, cheese, and olives. We could eat at the city square."

Lleah looks at Ariella, and her mentor nods in approval.

"I'll be back before you know it. Ariella. Thank you."

The two walk over to the city square not far from the market. Devorah pulls out a reed mat and lays it on the ground for them.

"So, what do you want to talk about, Mother?"

"Oh, nothing in particular. I just wanted to spend some extra time with my beautiful daughter. Besides, you are the age of thinking about marriage, so I may be losing you by the end of the year."

"Mother, I'm not interested in marrying right now. I've got my jewelry designing and am very happy doing just that."

———

Just as Lleah arrives back at the front counter of the jewelry booth, a big red-headed sailor wanders by. He is wearing a short amber tunic, a black cape, high leather shoes, a gold chain, and a wide band around his head to keep his red hair tamed.

Livianus looks in her direction as he is doing with all the shops to see if he happens to spot something he likes. He does, indeed, see something he likes. A beautiful black-haired woman.

He backs up and wanders over to the jewelry booth. Once there, he holds out his cape and sweeps it across him as he bows.

Lleah giggles.

"Methinks I am dreaming. Are you real, or am I experiencing a vision? Are you a goddess, a mermaid, an angel? Do not waken me. Let me live in my vision forever."

Lleah breaks out into laughter. "I think you have been out to sea much too long, sir."

"Listen. My vision speaks."

She looks into his green eyes and sees mischief and merriment.

"Are you interested in some copper jewelry for the love of your life?"

"Who? My mother?"

"No, silly, your sweetheart, your wife."

"Indeed, I do have a mother. That's how I got here. But sadly, I have no sweetheart or wife. Would you like to marry me so I can say I have a wife?"

Lleah laughs, tipping her head back. Tears come to her eyes. "You can have my jewelry, but you cannot have me."

"And why not, my lovely?"

"Just because. I'm not interested in getting married. I am having too much fun making copper jewelry and meeting crazy customers like you."

"So, you think I am crazy, do you?"

"You need to be locked up somewhere," Lleah says, still chuckling.

"Well, your wish is my command. I do lock myself up in my ship every time we sail the sea."

"And what is your position on your ship, may I ask?"

"As though it's any of your business, I am the captain."

"Oh, my. A real captain. And how did you get to be captain, sir? By murdering the previous one, and hanging anyone in the crew that didn't follow you instead?"

"Do I detect a devious mind under that beautiful black hair? If you must know, I inherited the ship from my father."

"Prove it. Who was your father, and what is the name of your ship?"

"My father, since you insist on knowing, though I can't imagine why, is Hector, and his ship, which I inherited, is the *Celox*."

"When did he die?"

"Oh, he isn't dead. He is alive and in fair health, but he retired. I'd been sailing with him since I was twelve, so in the past eight years, I learned everything he wanted me to know about commandeering a ship."

"Okay, so I'm convinced you are a real live sea captain. But you are taking up my time. I have things to do. So off with you. Shoo. Fly away, or sail away or whatever you do."

"You're not getting rid of me that fast, my love,"

"First, I am not your love," she says with a twinkle in her eye. "Second, you are interfering with my real customers who want to see my jewelry."

"In that case, my love…"

"Stop saying that," she rebukes, finally becoming annoyed.

"In that case, my sweet, I shall become your customer. Show me which pieces you made, and I shall buy them all."

"You will not, partly because you don't have that much money—I am an artist—and partly because there would be no more selection for my regular customers until I was able to make more."

"All right. I do not want to be the one responsible for you losing your customers. Show me what you have, and I promise to buy just one thing."

"Well, I made that one, and that one, and this one over here. Oh, yes, and I just added this one this morning."

"Ah, indeed, my vision has talent. Let me see. Which is the most expensive one?"

"That copper chain with a mother-of-pearl pendant."

"Then, that is the one I want. How much is it?"

"For you, one hundred denari."

"I do believe the price just went up."

Lleah grins.

"All right, my vision, I will buy the copper chain with mother-of-pearl pendant. Here is your money."

Lleah takes the money with a smirk.

"Now, off with you," she says, flapping her hand as though shooing away a fly.

Livianus puts on the chain, grabs hold of the bottom corner of his cape, and sweeps it out around him as he bows once again.

"You are now forever next to my heart. I must go now to India and China. But I shall be back. Be ready to sell me something else when I return that is overpriced."

With that, Livianus turns and walks away, now and then leaping and clicking his heels as he goes.

———

Oh, Father," Lleah says a week later while eating at her parents' manor, "I met the most dreamy man."

"I thought you weren't interested in men right now," her mother teases.

"How can a man possibly be dreamy?" Zarus asks.

"Well, he said I was a vision, so I guess he can be dreamy."

"All right. Tell us about your man."

"Well, he is tall like Father, has red hair, green eyes..."

"You looked at his eyes? This must be serious," Devorah interjects.

"...a lot of muscles, and he's funny."

"That's a good measure of a man," Zarus says. "He's funny. So what does he do, this funny man?"

"He is a sea captain, Just inherited his ship, the *Celox*, from his father, who was a sea captain too."

Zarus drops his piece of bread and stares at his daughter.

"What ship did you say?"

"The *Celox*. Why?"

"I think I met his father a long time ago about the time your brother, Amram, was born. He said he just had a son who looked just like him. Redheaded, you say? What is his father's name? Did he mention it?"

Zarus now pushes his bowl away and continues to stare at his daughter.

"I think he said his father's name was something like Hector."

Zarus stands and looks up at the ceiling. Devorah walks over to him and puts her head on his shoulder.

"Father. What's wrong? Who is he?"

Devorah turns. "The year your brother was born was the same year your father bought the land where the mine is. He had to sell everything we owned to get the land—even our furniture. We slept and ate on the floor for a long time, and..."

"Lleah," Zarus continues, "Hector is the one who owned the land the mine is on."

"Lleah sighs, not knowing how to react.

"One other thing," her mother says. "We didn't quite have all the money he was asking. So he said he would take our horses as the final payment. Do you remember us talking about my delicate Egyptian horse, Khemoh, and Father's big Arabian horse, Shalva?"

"I inherited my prize Arabian horse from my father," Zarus explains. "Until I met your mother, he was my best and most loyal friend."

"And the way you describe your new dream man, you are practically describing his father."

"I didn't know," Leah says.

"Has his ship left?" Zarus asks.

"Yes, I think it left right after I met him. He said he had to go to China, then he'd be back."

———

"Sir, you asked me to let you know when the *Celox* came into port. It is here."

"Thank you, Leib. Did you find out how long it will be docked?"

"The sailor I talked to said he thought it would be here a week."

"Good. I cannot go today, there is so much going on at the mine. Would you deliver a message to the captain that I would like to see him in three days?"

The three days drag by like a beached sea turtle. Zarus' mind goes back to his youth when he was poor, and sacrificed everything to give him and Devorah a good home and life. But mostly he thinks about giving up Shalva.

When the day arrives, he slides up on his horse and walks it toward the docks. He is dressed in a brown tunic with silver threads at the neck, sleeve, and hem. His head kerchief is gray with copper threads on the hem. It is held in place by a leather band. He wears one of his daughter's copper bracelets on his upper arm, having been assured by her that it would help the pain he is developing in his shoulder.

"Permission to come aboard," he says from the bottom of the plank. Permission is granted, and he ties his horse up to a rail nearby.

Zarus walks up the plank, trying to remember the ship he saw so long ago when he was young. When he reaches the deck, he turns around and looks a moment at the tavern he had met Hector in and worked out a deal for the land.

"You are Zarus?" the second mate asks.

"Yes, I am."

"This way, sir."

Zarus is taken across the deck to the stern, and into a cabin, obviously reserved for the captain. The second mate opens the door for Zarus and steps aside.

"Welcome. I presume you are Zarus. I am Livianus. "

The young captain holds out his hand, and Zarus grasps it.

"Please be seated. I assume you are here about your daughter. I suppose she has told you that I saw her the day I arrived, and also yesterday. We have spent a lot of time together."

"No, she didn't tell me. She doesn't live at home. She lives with her mentor."

"Well, anyway, yesterday we went riding. She is very good with a horse."

"Yes, she is good with a horse, just like her mother was, well and is," Zarus says awkwardly. *How can I give Lleah up?*

"I remember your father," Zarus says, changing the subject. "You look a lot like him."

"Yes, that's what everyone says."

"We did business together."

"Yes, that's what Lleah said. You bought the land your mine is on from my father."

"I had to struggle to come up with that much money for raw land. He finally said he would take my horse and my wife's horse as the final payment."

"I know nothing about that. I do remember a couple of old horses in our stable. Father used to let me ride the Egyptian when I was young because it was smaller. Later he let me ride the Arabian. They were both gentle horses, as I recall. Good for children."

"I don't suppose they are alive anymore. My Arabian would be forty years old now."

"After I was grown, I didn't pay any more attention to them," Livianus says. "Yes, I suppose they are dead."

The two men sit in silence. Livianus crosses one leg, then the other. He puts his hands together, intertwines the fingers, and cracks his knuckles. He folds his arms together, then unfolds them.

"Do you love my daughter?" Zarus asks, choking the words out.

"Yes, I do, sir. I loved her from the first day I set my eyes on her. Do you understand how that can be? There was just that connection."

Zarus remembers when he had first met Devorah. He had felt the same way.

Livianus clears his throat. Zarus stares at him in silence, waiting for the young man to show he can be a man.

"She's funny."

"That's what she said about you."

"See there? We are alike."

They stare at each other once again.

"She said one of your officers went to China once. Brought back some fine silk."

"Yes, he did. Fine silk."

Livianus looks over at the wall, down at his sandals, and up at the ceiling.

"Sir, I may as well just say it. I would like to wed your daughter. She is intelligent, beautiful, adventurous, and a little bit daring. She is everything I ever wanted for a wife."

"You haven't known her long."

"I've known her long enough. Sir, I promise to take good care of her and never beat her and to allow her to have her way a lot."

Zarus smiles. "You know she will keep you guessing half the time. Women are like that."

Livianus grins. "Does that mean I have your permission, sir?"

He stands, realizes he is towering over his superior and reseats himself.

"But there is one other thing that concerns me. Livianus. She is a Christian. One of Jhesus' apostles came to this city a couple of years ago, preached that Jhesus died and came back to life to prove he was the Son of God. Now I know that is a lot for you to..."

"Sir. Sir. Stop. Say no more. I, too, am a Christian. Even though no apostle has visited our city in Greece—Corinth—that I know of, I learned about Jhesus in Caesarea when I was docked there to take on wheat. One of Jhesus' apostles, Philip, was there, and I learned from him. I was baptized and now am a Christian myself. I even went home and convinced my family to leave worship of all those gods and worship only the one true God of the universe and his Son Jhesus Christ."

Realizing he has blurted out perhaps too much information at one time before his elder, Livianus sits back in his elegant but worn chair.

Zarus pinches his lips together and looks up at the ceiling. *Oh, Jhehovah God, how can this be? You have blessed me more richly than I deserve.*

"God bless you, my son. I will send for Lleah when I arrive home. If she is in agreement, I shall draw up the betrothal papers. What will you pay for her?"

Livianus rises, walks over to a ledge with a wooden coffer on it. He brings it to Zarus and opens the lid. "I consider Lleah my pearl. I give you this pearl. When I come back, I will have more. Is that sufficient?"

Zarus takes the pearl and stands. It is sufficient for now. We will have the betrothal ceremony in two days, and you can indicate what else you would like to use to buy her."

"Sir, would you accept an Egyptian and Arabian horse for the rest of it? They wouldn't be your horses, but it would be a token of my respect for you and the brief association you had with my father."

"That is very thoughtful. Yes, that is acceptable. When do you expect to return?"

"I should be back in six months. I must travel to Alexandria, then over to Gaul, and finally to Britannia, and I cannot sail in the winter.

———

The six months go by for Lleah like a cloud ambling across the sky on a balmy spring day, but much too fast for Zarus and Devorah.

"Mother, I would like to have a party for my closest girlfriends."

"For your wedding attendants. Of course. How many would you like to invite?"

"Oh, ten or twelve."

"That's fine."

"I would like to have the party this week since Livianus' ship is due back next week. Would that be okay, Mother?"

"So, who would you like to invite?"

Lleah fetches a wax tablet on which she has etched a list of names.

"Let's see: Dafna, Aviva, Yardina, Sira, Chaya, Bina, Fruma, Maya, Ruth, Tava, Zissel, Naama, and maybe a couple others."

"All right. You will be in charge. You will have to write your own invitations, put up your own decorations, and order your own food. As a ship captain's wife, you will have to get used to entertaining."

"Oh, I love him so much, Mother. I never dreamed..."

Rather than finish her sentence, Lleah raises her eyes and her arms, and dances around the marble floor.

Devorah grabs her chest, turns her back on her daughter, cringes, breathes, turns back around, and smiles.

———

The day of the wedding arrives. Zarus and Devorah act busy in an effort to hide the anguish of giving away their daughter and perhaps not seeing her for years.

One by one Lleah's maids in waiting arrive at her house. They laugh and giggle and make over Lleah in the way that maids are supposed to. They wash her hair, then try different hairstyles until they come to one they agree with. Then they look over her dress.

"She needs to wear flowers in her hair," one of the girls says.

They all go out to the market looking for flowers. They laugh and flit from one flower booth to another. Disappointed that Lleah has not liked any she has seen, they return to Lleah's home. Smiling with laughter in her eyes, she takes them into the garden off her marble courtyard and shows them the flowers she plans to wear in her hair.

The time draws near.

Does everyone have everything you need?" Lleah asks. She is assured they do.

Finally, she dons her long yellow tunic and the long red veil that flows from her crown down her back to the floor.

The wait begins. When will her Livianus arrive to whisk her to the ship, her new home, and adventure?

It grows dark. The giggling slows.

"Perhaps you should go down to the docks and wait for the groom there," Devorah suggests to her ten maids. "Then you can show him and his friends the way to our home."

The girls in waiting agree and leave. With their ten oil lamps burning brightly and their fairly large number, they feel safe walking down toward the dock at night. There is a forum just before arriving at the dock. They decide to wait for the groom there.

"What is going on with him?" they say to each other as the hour grows later and later.

"What can he be doing so long on his wedding day?" Yardina asks.

"He's a ship's captain," Tava replies. "He probably got a late load of something and has to make sure it's all loaded before the ship leaves tomorrow morning."

The night continues on. The maids in waiting grow sleepy. They lay their heads down in their arms and fall asleep.

Naama starts awake with a noise. "It's them," she says. "It's the groom. Let's go out to meet him and lead him to Lleah's house."

"Wait," Dafna says. "The flame is going out in my lamp. I'm almost out of oil."

"Mine too," Maya says.

"Give us some of your oil, Fruma."

"I can't. If I did, there wouldn't be enough for me."

"What about you, Ruth? You brought an extra jar of oil."

"I'm the same as Fruma. I only brought enough to refill my lamp one time. I would be out by the time we got halfway to Lleah's house. You'll just have to go find some to buy."

"At midnight? There are no shops open at midnight."

"Maybe a tavern keeper has some extra you can buy from him. Good luck."

"Hello ladies," Livianus says, sitting on the shoulders of two of his friends. "Shall we go? Lead the way."

Half an hour later, the wedding party with five of Lleah's ten maids arrives at the manor of Zarus and Devorah. A servant opens the gate for them and lets them in.

Livianus slides off the shoulders of his friends, and being last, stands at the gateway without entering.

"Come in," Zarus says.

"Sir, I have the last of my payment for the bride price. Bring your wife out. They are for both of you."

"They?"

Zarus calls his wife, and he and Devorah step out into the warm night. There they see an Arabian and an Egyptian.

"Just as you promised, Livianus."

"But more," the groom says.

"I would like you to meet the grandson of your Shalva, sir, and the granddaughter of your Khemoh, ma'am."

Zarus and Devorah stare at the horses, stunned. Tears come to both of them.

Devorah is the first to walk up and pat the Egyptian on the nose. "You look just like your grandmother. I shall call you Miss Khemoh if you don't mind, my precious one."

"Zarus steps close to the Arabian. "And you, my dear boy, look just like I remember your grandfather. I think I shall follow Devorah's example and call you Master Shalva."

He looks over at his wife. "We shall go riding tomorrow, just like we used to do when we were young."

"Yes, my love. We shall go riding."

Breaking the spell, Livianus announces, "Actually, I am very anxious to see my bride, if you don't mind."

The reins are handed to Leib, the rest of the wedding party enters, and the gate is closed.

"Mother. Father. Thank you. This is the happiest day of my life. I will come back and see you as often as possible. And I shall give you many grandchildren to spoil."

Zarus looks from his daughter to his wife. *Dear pearl of mine, may it happen as she says. Please live long enough to see your grandchildren.*

"At that time the kingdom of heaven will be like ten virgins who took their lamps and went out to meet the bridegroom.

Five of them were foolish and five were wise.

The foolish ones took their lamps but did not take any oil with them.

The wise, however, took oil in jars along with their lamps.

The bridegroom was a long time in coming, and they all became drowsy and fell asleep.

"At midnight the cry rang out: 'Here's the bridegroom! Come out to meet him!'

"Then all the virgins woke up and trimmed their lamps.

The foolish ones said to the wise, 'Give us some of your oil; our lamps are going out.'

" 'No,' they replied, 'there may not be enough for both us and you. Instead, go to those who sell oil and buy some for yourselves.'

"But while they were on their way to buy the oil, the bridegroom arrived. The virgins who were ready went in with him to the wedding banquet. And the door was shut.

"Later the others also came. 'Sir! Sir!' they said. 'Open the door for us!'

"But he replied, 'I tell you the truth, I don't know you.'

"Therefore keep watch, because you do not know the day or the hour. (Matthew 25:1-13)

31 ~ GOODBYE

AD 36
Copper Mine, Timna Valley, Arabah Desert, Idumea

"Well, the deal is done," Gersshon says, coming in to work one morning."

"What deal is that?" Zarus asks without looking up from the diagrams engineer Saabhu had given him the day before.

"I have bought Hudas' house. It has been sitting empty for five years. No one could afford it."

"He went overboard on everything he did with the house. No one needs all that. Just his gold goblets cost a small fortune— the fortune that happened to belong to us."

"Don't forget the agate-lined pool he had in his garden, and flower pots with rubies and garnets embedded in them," Gersshon adds.

"He was spending our money just to be spending money. Is that what life is all about?" *And where did Gersshon get enough money to buy it? It's more elaborate than my house.*

"Well, his wife was the spender. She'd go on one of her cruises and come back with all kinds of exotic things. They even had their own menagerie. I'll be you didn't know that. They had an African lion, an Indian tiger, a couple monkeys, a zebra, a giraffe. In their garden, they had a couple of peacocks, though Hudas was getting ready to get rid of them; their squawks kept him awake at night."

"Did you get his furniture too?"

"No, the magistrate sold all that at auction. The statues and murals too. But I did get the marble columns, the mosaic-tiled floors throughout the house, the frescoes on the walls, the bath, the swimming pool, and the theater. Oh, and the music room.

"What did you do for furniture?"

"You know all those trips I made to Egypt and Persia to check on smelters? I always bought a couple pieces of furniture whenever I went. So I'm on my way. Would you and Devorah like to come over for dinner sometime?"

"I hope you're not offended, but we have some bad memories of that place," Zarus replies. "It's going to take us some time."

"How is Devorah, anyway?"

"She's having more and more trouble with her breathing. She rasps when she breathes and has to lift her chest to fill her lungs."

"I'm really sorry to hear that, Zarus. No one deserves to live like that."

"Dr. Elchanan comes to the house once a week to check on her. He provides sage for her to inhale and drink. Another one of the herbs he grows himself."

Zarus stares into nothingness a moment, then returns.

"He gives her breathing exercises, and she says they help some. But she had another attack of the pain yesterday. *Oh, God, don't let me lose her.*

"Sometimes, we ride down to the waterfront. She says the salty air from the sea helps her," Zarus continues.

"So how is it working out, riding the grandchildren of your Arabian and Egyptian?"

Zarus' eyes brighten. "We love them. It's almost like having Shalva and Khemoh back. I think they know that. They nuzzle us before we mount them like their forbearers used to do.

"Well, I want to go down to see what Noach is doing," Gersshon says. "He's been talking about creating a fourth shift, so the men do not have to work so long."

"They don't work long now. Most miners work twelve-hour shifts, and ours work eight-hour shifts.

"All I know is what he told me. But I'm probably going to tell him to stay with things the way they are."

"Yair, good morning," Gersshon says as he leaves the *officium* tent.

"Good morning, sir. How about a helping hand?"

Gersshon keeps on walking.

Zarus looks up from the diagrams, sets them down, and walks out to the chariot. He picks up legless Yair and takes him to his workspace. It is a low table, and Yair sits on a cushion on the camel-skin floor.

"Did you notice my new chariot?" he asks Zarus.

His employer takes two strides, looks outside, and grins. "Well, look at that. When did you get the new one?"

"Well, it's not completely new, but it is better than the one I had. The spokes were falling off the wheels, and the bronze plating was rusting away. Got a new horse in the deal too."

"Yair, I have to hand it to you. You seem to have spent your salary well all these years," Zarus says.

"The annual pay raise you give me always helps. I try to keep my spending the same every year and save the extra for when I need to buy something unexpectedly. How is your wife, by the way?"

"Her weight keeps going down. The tunics that used to fit her perfectly are getting looser and looser. She has had to take off the rings she used to wear because they kept falling off. She lost a couple of them at the market. Luckily the others fell off at home where she could retrieve them."

"But, I'll bet she is still beautiful, sir."

"That, indeed, she is. She will always be beautiful."

He pauses and looks outside. *But when I embrace her, her bones stick out. She is looking more like a skeleton.*

"How are things with the books these days?" Zarus asks.

"I'm glad you asked. They have gone back to not making sense again."

"In what way?"

The payroll keeps going up. Seems like we're paying more people than actually work for us."

"Have you asked Gersshon about it?"

"Yes. He said there is so much turnover, it's hard to keep up. Sometimes a man comes and works two weeks, then quits. So he hires someone else the same day. It looks like two people when it is actually one."

"That's how he explains it?"

"Yes, sir. Did you say your wife goes for walks sometimes?"

"She used to. But she has gotten so that she can only take small steps."

The day goes by slowly as do most days now. Zarus continually worries about the mine and his wife. He knows he has to always worry at least a little about the mine to keep it productive. But Devorah?

I wonder what she's doing right now. Sitting in the garden? Writing poetry? Eating a couple of grapes? Singing? Or perhaps she is napping so she will be fresh for me when I arrive home from work?

Oh, my darling pearl. Don't you leave me.

The day is over, and he heads for home.

Eilat, Port City on Red Sea, Arabah Desert

Zarus takes out his key, but a servant opens the ornate gate for him.

"Welcome back, sir," Peretz says.

"Thank you. Where is my wife?"

"In the garden, sir."

Zarus takes long strides across his marble-tiled courtyard and enters the garden. He sees the love of his life seated on a pillowed concrete bench near the lily pond and is soon at her side.

He does not expect her to stand as in years gone by. Seated next to her, they embrace and kiss. Her eyes are glassy.

"What's wrong, my love?"

"I have pain in my legs, especially my left one. It is hard for me to walk."

"My darling pearl. I would take that pain away from you if I could. Please don't be in pain. Please, my pearl."

"Oh, Zarus, my sweet. I don't hurt that much. It's okay. It will probably go away. Don't weep for me. Things will get better."

Zarus sits on the bench with his arm around his wife, they put their heads together and stare into the pond, each with their own thoughts. Their hearts touch, and they are one.

"Master, it is time to eat," old Penina says. "Would you like me to bring it out here to the garden?"

"Yes, if you would, that would be fine," says Zarus.

Shortly, Peretz brings out a table and sets it in front of the couple. Penina follows with a tray of goat cheese, bread, grapes, and olives. Peretz disappears and shortly reappears with a pitcher of pomegranate juice and two goblets.

Zarus picks up a grape and puts it in Devorah's mouth.

"What are you trying to do? Choke me?" she says, giggling.

Glad to hear her laughter, Zarus dangles a grape above his head, then drops it into his mouth.

"Now your turn," he says. "You eat an olive, then I eat an olive."

He puts one in her mouth, then dangles another one over his head and drops it down into his mouth.

"Deeelicious," he pronounces. "Now, a bite of cheese."

He breaks off a bite for her, holds it up to her mouth, and sees that she has fallen asleep. Keeping one arm around his wife, he pushes the table out of the way with his foot. Then, putting his other arm under her knees, he lifts Devorah. *She is so light.* He walks with her out of the garden, across the courtyard, up the stairs, and toward their bedroom.

Penina sees what is happening and hurries ahead to turn her covers down.

Zarus lays his frail wife on her bed with tenderness, covers her up, and pulls a chair close. He sits and stares at her. And remembers.

"We've been through a lot together, you and me," he whispers. "We started out so poor, and look where we are now. But I'd give it all up to have you back the way you were even two years ago."

He lays his head down next to hers until it is dark. He hears Amram downstairs and rises.

"I'll be back after a while, my pearl."

He goes down and greets his son. "How has your day been?"

"I've been interviewing the miners, Father."

"Why would you do that? They're all hard workers and earn their pay. And we pay them well."

"That's not what they say."

"Let's talk about this another time," Zarus says.

"How is Mother today?" Amram asks, not willing to upset his father about the slavery problem any more than he is upset now.

"About the same."

They grow quiet and sit with each other in the courtyard.

Zarus becomes tired and retires. In bed, he leans over and gently kisses his beautiful Devorah, envelopes her in his arms, and closes his eyes.

The sun rises. Zarus wakens and notices Devorah is not in the bed next to him.

"Good morning, my love."

Zarus looks around the room and sees Devorah sitting on a chair at the foot of the bed.

"Did you have a good night?" she asks.

"Well, look who got up before me."

"Did you know you snore?"

"You've been telling me that for years. But I'll have you know I do not snore."

"Then, you've got some sort of loud-sounding demon in you at night."

"Ha, ha."

Zarus rises, steps to his wife, leans over, gives her a morning kiss, then kneels. "What would you like to do today?" he asks. "Do you feel like going for a horse ride with our 'grandchildren'? It wouldn't have to be long."

"Well, maybe. If you let me ride your Arabian for once."

"You mean both of us on him?"

"Yes," she says with a grin.

"At the same time?"

"Yes." She says while pulling him toward her by the beard, he had let grow long and planting another kiss on him."

"For that, my dear, you get anything you want."

"Then, after breakfast, we go. I'm starved," she says.

Zarus quickly dresses, helps Devorah on with her own tunic, sweeps her into his arms, and carries her down to the courtyard. In his heart, he feels a painful happiness. *How many moments like this are left for us?*

Penina hears them coming and brings their breakfast.

Zarus sets Devorah on one couch, and he reclines on the other.

"Jhehovah God. We thank you for all our blessings. Bless this food that it may bless us. May we do your will today. Thank you for our children and for each other, and most of all, thank you for Jhesus Christ, your Son."

Devorah whispers amen and reaches for a date.

"I see you have your appetite back, my pearl.

"Penina, would you ask Leib to get my Arabian ready? We're going for a little ride this morning."

Penina smiles broadly. "Yes, master."

Zarus and Devorah eat their breakfast, Zarus careful not to urge her to eat more than she can handle.

"Now, where would you like to go?"

"You pick. I like surprises."

"Like when we got our Egyptian and Arabian horses back through their grandchildren? Wasn't that a surprise?"

"A wonderful one."

"Ready?" Zarus stands, lifts Devorah into his strong arms, and takes her out to the stable.

Master Shalva stands ready, with Leib holding the reins.

"Steady there, ole boy," Zarus whispers.

With care, he swings Devorah up onto the horse so that her legs are on one side. Without letting go of her, he swings his own body up. He cradles her with one arm and guides the horse with the other.

"With you in front of me, I can whisper love thoughts into your ear," he says.

Leib pretends not to hear.

The gentle horse takes the couple out into the street in front of their house. It turns to go down the hill. They go down the street a block.

"Is that enough, for now, my pearl?"

"Yes. It was a good ride. I enjoyed it."

In silence, they ride back to the stable, Leib takes the reins again, Zarus slides off the horse, then slides Devorah toward him far enough she is once again in his arms.

"We'll have to do that again," he says.

"Zarus, I'd like to lie down a while now."

"Where?"

"I think on the couches where we eat. That way, I'm around all the activity of the family."

"Good thinking," Zarus says.

Once settled, Devorah closes her eyes, and Zarus goes out to the courtyard.

Just as he arrives, the gate opens, and Ithamar walks in. He stops and stares at his father.

"What's going on, Ithamar? Where have you been all night? I thought you were up in your room."

"I was just out. That's all."

"You're eighteen years old. You still answer to me."

"All right. I spent the night with Zev. I don't understand all the angles Saabhu is telling me about at the mine, and Zev explained it all to me."

"Very well, Son. I'm sorry I was short with you. It's just that, with your mother..."

"I know. It's hard watching her like this. I don't want her to be sick."

"Me neither, Son. Me neither."

Ithamar turns to go to his room just as Amram comes down the stairs.

"Going to the mine?"

"Yes, sir."

"Would you give a message to Gersshon or Noach for me? Tell them I won't be in today, but if they have an emergency they need my help with, just send for me."

"Yes, sir. I hope Mother feels a little better today."

"Me too."

The house is quiet now except for Penina in the kitchen and Peretz bringing in a pail of water for the plants in the garden.

Zarus goes to Devorah, sits on the floor next to her, watches her sleep, and recalls times when they were young.

There is a knock on the gate. Peretz hears and answers it.

"Who is calling, madam?"

"Tell them it is Estar."

Zarus hears the familiar voice and hurries to the courtyard.

"Estar. What a pleasant surprise," he says, taking his long strides to his sister.

They embrace, then pull apart.

"I came to help with Devorah."

"How did you know?" Zarus asks.

"Penina wrote me."

"Dear Penina. She is resting on a couch in the dining room. Give Peretz your case and come in to see Devorah.

He walks with her arm in arm. When Estar sees her sister-in-law, tears come to her eyes.

"Oh, Devorah, what has happened to you?"

"Dr. Elchanan says it is her heart. As it grows weaker, the rest of her body becomes weaker."

Estar walks over to Devorah and touches her arm. Devorah opens her eyes.

"Hi, Estar," she says with a weak smile. "When did you get here?"

"Just a moment ago. I'm sorry you're not feeling well. Would you mind if I nursed you a while to make myself feel useful?"

"I'm sure Penina can use your help," she whispers.

"Penina is still around? She helped raise you, didn't she?"

"That she did," Devorah responds with a whisper.

"If you would like to put your things away," Zarus interjects, "Peretz will carry them to your room and bring you some water to freshen up."

As soon as Estar is gone, Zarus sits once more at his spot on the floor next to his beloved.

"Now, where was I? Oh, yes, when I went to your father to ask if you could marry me. I was so scared. He knew I was, and looking back, I think he was amused at it. Well, I wasn't amused. I was so scared, I nearly forgot my own name."

"Still talking to yourself, I see," Estar says, re-entering the room.

She seats herself over to one side, so she is not distracting, and watches her brother cling to his wife. Oh, how she remembers doing that with her husbands. Why did they have to die? Why did her life have to turn out as it did?

They say nothing more.

"Would you like a few bites to eat for lunch?" Penina asks Estar.

"I am so sorry, Penina. I forgot to go help you. How have you been doing?"

"Pretty good, Estar. Pretty good."

"Well, I would like some figs if you don't mind."

Devorah wakens and looks over at Estar.

"I had such a nice morning," she says. "We went for a ride, and I had a very good nap. Zarus, sweetheart, would you help me sit up?"

"Of course. Anything else you would like?"

"I'd like to go for a little walk."

"Are you sure?"

"Of course, I'm sure. As soon as I eat a fig, I'll be ready for my walk."

"And where would you like to walk to, my pearl?"

"I think out to the garden. I like it out there."

"I know you do, and you shall have your walk."

Fig consumed, Zarus takes his wife's elbow with one hand and puts his other arm around her. He lifts her to her feet and pauses.

"You okay?"

"So far so good," she replies.

Devorah takes a step forward and smiles. One step at a time, she makes it across the courtyard and into the garden.

Zarus guides her to the cushioned concrete bench, and she sits on it. He sits next to her and puts his arm around her. She lays her head on his shoulder.

"Don't you love the little fish in the pond? They're so active and wiggly like we used to be in the old days."

"Well, I'm not sure I would call us wiggly, but we were active."

"You were so strong, lifting those boulders all by yourself."

"Now look at me. I'm going to be fifty years old next year."

"I miss my father, you know. He always understood me. He died too young."

"Yes, he was a good and honest man."

"I miss my mother too." Devorah takes a raspy breath. "She was a unique woman. No one else in the world was like her." She looks up at her husband with a weak smile. "Mother sure took to Amram, didn't she?"

"Amram loved her. Truly loved her."

Devorah lays her head back on Zarus' shoulder.

"Sometimes, I think about the terrible way my brother treated you. I knew he beat you and starved you. But I didn't have any way of stopping him.”

“Well, I lived through it and got you as my prize. I would do it all over again.”

“Zarus?”

“What, my pearl?”

“Would you go get the pearls? You know, the one my grandmother left me that you bought back for me, and the one we got for giving our little Lleah away to that sea captain.”

“Certainly. I’ll be right back.”

Estar, who has been sitting nearby, but not close enough to interfere with their time together, comes over. “I’ll sit with her until you get back,” she whispers to her brother.

A few moments later, Zarus is back with two small coffers: One made of acacia wood and the other made of alabaster. Estar gradually stands, and Zarus takes his place again next to his beloved.

He opens the alabaster box and hands her the pearl from her grandmother.

Devorah’s hands are in her lap. She opens one and accepts the pearl. She looks at it a while in silence.

“I used to sit and stare into this pearl for hours at a time. So beautiful and pure,” she whispers.

He opens the wood box and hands her the pearl from Livianus for their daughter. He puts it in Devorah’s other hand, also in her lap.

“You always called me your pearl, but she was my pearl.”

She leans on Zarus’ shoulder again. He gently leans his head over on hers, and they dream together.

Zarus wakes with a start. The sun is rosy in the western sky, and Estar is gone.

“Sweetheart, it is time to go to bed.”

Devorah rouses, groans a gentle ascent, and looks at him as she once had. “Your eyes were always so blue. They still are.”

Zarus takes her into his still-strong arms and, with his usual long strides, takes her out of the garden, across the courtyard, and up to their room.

With tenderness, he lays her on her bed and sits on the floor next to her. Once again, he lays his head down next to hers.

“Remember when Amram was born? We were so poor. But we were happy. I was so excited when it turned out that he looked just like me.

“The club foot never bothered me. I was always proud of our son. And he grew up to be such a loving, intelligent, and honest young man.”

Estar stands in the doorway. "Would you like anything, Zarus? You did not eat any supper."

"No, thank you," Zarus says softly.

"Well, at least let me bring you some apple juice. You need something."

"Okay, Estar. I'll take some apple juice."

He lays his head back down next to his beloved. "Remember when our little Ithamar was born? He never slept through the night like Amram usually did. He was never still. He still isn't. He kept us hopping, but he was good for us. I guess Amram was a little boring compared with Ithamar. Then there was little Lleah. Everyone loved her."

Estar arrives with the apple juice. Zarus sits up and looks at his sister. His eyes are swollen. The richest man in Eilat and probably all of Idumea has been weeping.

"Thank you, Estar," he whispers.

He drinks it in one swallow, and she takes the mug from him. "Do you need anything else before I go to bed?"

"No, we'll be fine. And, Estar..."

"Yes?"

"Thank you for coming."

Alone again with the one he has loved for twenty-seven years.

Oh, Jhesus, if I cannot keep her, take her into your arms. And let me be with her again someday.

Another knock on the door. Zarus is stiff. He rises, answers it, and realizes it is morning.

When he stands, Devorah rouses. "Good morning, my love," she whispers. "You were naughty and did not come to bed."

"I guess I forgot," he says, smiling.

"I don't think I'll get up just yet. We had a big day yesterday, didn't we, horseback riding and all like we used to do?"

"Yes, we did."

"Could I see my boys?"

Zarus dresses and goes to Amram's and Ithamar's rooms. "You need to come visit with your mother," he tells them both.

He returns to his and Devorah's room and sits on a chair in the corner. Soon Ithamar comes in, followed by Amram.

"Come here, my children," Devorah says. "Sit here with me."

The two sit on each side of the bed. They hold back their tears, though Amram is more successful at it than Ithamar.

"You've always been good boys. I was always so proud of you both."

She pauses, looks over at Zarus, smiles, then back to her children. "I have always been by your side through everything, and I want you to know I will be by your side forever."

"Yes, Mother. I love you, Mother," Ithamar says, his lips trembling.

"I love you too, Mother," Amram says. "Don't die."

"When you get married, would you mind marrying someone like me? That would honor me. It would thrill me."

"Yes, Mother, we will," Amram says. "We promise."

"And we'll name our first daughter after you," Ithamar adds.

Devorah smiles weakly, then closes her eyes.

The boys look over at their father. He gives them a faint smile, holding one fist in his other one in an effort to maintain control.

Amram and Ithamar kiss their mother on her cheek and move to the foot of her bed.

Zarus returns to his spot next to her.

Her breathing is labored.

Heavy-hearted, the boys, leave the room.

Zarus climbs in bed beside her and embraces his beloved. They dream together as they have lived together.

Times passes in its own mysterious way, bringing with it new shadows.

Later that day, Devorah opens her eyes and whispers, "I have always loved you."

"Yes, I know, my pearl. And I have loved you more than life itself."

"Zarus. Thank you for the life you gave me."

These are the last words Devorah speaks.

Later, when preparations are made for her funeral, they open her hand, and in it is the pearl Zarus had bought back for her. Her sacrificial pearl.

32 ~ THE VAGABOND

AD 39
Eilat, Port City on Red Sea, Arabah Desert, Idumea

"Father, Ithamar is not reporting to work at the mine like he's supposed to," Amram says. "He hasn't been there in two weeks."

"Why hasn't Saabhu told me this?"

"I guess he doesn't want to get Ithamar in trouble with you."

Amram has just joined his father in his study, where he keeps most of his charts of the mine.

"Be patient with him," he says, looking up from one of the scrolls. "He's really upset about his mother's death."

"I'm upset about Mother's death too, but I go to work every day, and you go to work every day."

"Each person handles their grief in their own way," Zarus replies. "He'll come around."

"I think he's getting worse. He won't talk to me anymore, and he hardly talks to you. All he wants to do is go down to the tavern with Zev and drink all day and night."

"I'll speak with him."

They hear a rattle at the gate.

"I'll bet that's him now," Zarus says as he stands to greet whoever has arrived. Out of curiosity, Amram follows him.

"Hi, Father. Hi, Amram. It's a beautiful day, isn't it?"

"Yes, it is," Zarus sputters.

Ithamar is dressed in a dark green tunic with fringe on the sleeves and hem and a matching kerchief to protect his head from the desert sun. He is wearing four copper chains. The tunic has smudges all over the front.

"Well, well. And what black hole did you crawl out from?"

Amram responds. "Surely not the mine."

Ithamar continues. "I've decided to go to China."

"What are you talking about, Son? You have work to do at the mine. Saabhu is growing old, and he needs your help. It takes time to learn his job."

"Maybe I will someday, Father. But I'm still young. I want to do things and go places while I don't have any obligations. I can settle down to the mine after that."

"Where did you get such a fool idea?" Amram asks.

"I've been talking to Noach."

"You've actually shown your face at the mine?"

"Be quiet," Zarus admonished. "Let's all go into the garden. Then let your brother talk."

In the garden, Zarus glances at Devorah's favorite bench and her last days there and sighs. The men seat themselves on three of four individual concrete benches facing each other with a small pool between them.

"Now, Ithamar, continue."

"Noach has been telling me all about China. He was there and saw everything in person. He says it's an enchanted land. While I am young, I intend to go."

"But, Son, you're only nineteen years old."

"I'm nearly as tall as you, Father. I am strong and have a lot of energy. I'm even intelligent; you said so yourself. What more do I need to get along in the world?"

"What you need, little brother, is money. How are you going to get there?" Amram counters with a smug glare.

"I've thought of that." He turns from his brother to his father. He clears his throat.

"Uh, well, Father. I would like my share of my inheritance. Mother is gone, and, well, you aren't in the best of health. You could even be suddenly killed at the mine. I think it is only reasonable that I receive my share now."

Zarus' eyes squint, and he puts his head forward as though to hear better.

"You what?" Amram says.

"I'm serious, Father," Ithamar answers, though not looking at his brother.

"Well, what did you have in mind?"

"I know, as the oldest, Amram gets most of the inheritance, and Lleah doesn't get anything because she's a female. But, I thought, well, if I could have the manor, I could sell it and all the furniture, and come out with a decent amount."

Zarus stands and walks around the garden. He walks over to Devorah's bench and sits. *What should I do, Devorah? He's too young. But we were adventurous at that age. We met when I was but a little more than his age, and I went to work in a mine when I was twenty to earn you. We ended up pretty good.*

Zarus walks back over to where his two sons wait for him.

"I tell you what I'll do, Ithamar. I will put a mortgage on the manor and all the furniture in it. That way, you can have the money without Amram and I having to move. Fair enough?"

"Yes, Father. More than fair. That means I can go to China sooner than I thought. Thank you, Father. Wait till I tell Zev. He's going with me; I'm paying his way."

Ithamar stands, embraces his father, and rushes out through the garden, the courtyard, and the outside gate. It clangs shut as he leaves.

———

"Okay, while we're onboard the ship, we've got to learn some Chinese."

Ithamar is wearing a special tunic. It is long with a large hem in it. He also wears a long cloak with a large hem in it. Sewn up in the hems are silver and gold coins. He has already paid the ship captain and has kept what he believes he will need to rent a room for them and buy some food once they reach China.

"We can't speak common Greek all the time there. Zev, you're quick with languages. Why don't you find a Chinaman on the ship and get him to teach you? Then you can teach me. I'll pay him.

"Noach said the women are beautiful in China," Ithamar continues. "They are tiny and delicate like dewdrops in the morning. And some of the men are big and ferocious and wrestle with each other like we have at our Olympic games. We are going to have so much fun in China. Aren't you glad I talked you into coming with me?"

"Yeah, Ithamar. Wherever you go, I go. We're pals. We're a team."

Daily, the two nineteen-year-olds have their lessons in Chinese. Zev learns it easily, as Ithamar had known he would. Ithamar is not as successful. "Oh, well, I can depend on you to translate for me, Zev."

The cruise is uneventful except for one squall they go through at the southern tip of India.

Shanghai, Province of Jiangsu, China

As Ithamar and Zev disembark from their ship, they look around at all the activity going on at the docks. Black-headed men scuttle instead of walk to and from their duties. Bamboo wagons are everywhere, often pulled by the Chinese themselves rather than animals.

Beautiful girls stand around with red bow lips, white faces, silk robes, and delicate hands. They smile at all the men passing them.

"Man, look at that. I'm going to get me one of them after we get settled. We are in heaven, Zev!"

Once they are away from the docks, they look for a market with food.

"I'm starved," Ithamar says. "We didn't bring along enough food with us when we left Eilat. Didn't account for squalls at sea to slow us down."

"I haven't eaten in two days."

"Okay, look around for something good to eat. I've got the money for whatever you want."

They load up on cheese and fruit.

"Now to find a room to rent. Zev, go back and ask some of the people in the market where we can find a room nearby. Remember, money is not an issue. We get nothing but the best."

"Okay," Zev answers, and wanders away while Ithamar leans against a palm tree to eat.

Shortly, Zev is back. "Let's go. They told me about a place where even their emperor slept on a trip to their city one time. It's called the Imperial Boarding House."

When the door is opened to their room, they stare at the opulence. Round teakwood latticework separates parts of the room into bedroom, eating room, and receiving room. Along the walls are silk tapestries. The floor is Mahogany but mostly covered with carpets designed with intricate patterns and many colors.

There is a low table in the eating room with silk cushions on each side. There are other, higher tables nearby for the servants to set the food on before serving it to each guest. There are intricate ivory carvings on some of the tables.

In the sleeping room is a bed with rosewood posts at each corner and silk tapestry hanging behind and over it. Jade statues of various Chinese gods decorate the rest of the room

In the receiving room are chairs with silk cushions and tables on which sit opulent vases, some decorated with mother of pearl.

"Perfect. We need to put our clothes away, but I can't leave my cloak behind with all the money in it. Would you mind wearing it sometimes? You're taller than me, and the hem won't drag the ground and tear with you wearing it."

"Anything you want," Zev replies, still turning in circles standing in place, observing the rooms where they will actually live.

"Now, it's fun time," Ithamar announces.

As they leave through the front gate of the Imperial Boarding House, they stand and look around in order to catch the attention of anyone who might want to be envious of them.

They turn left and head up the street strutting. But the farther they go, the more opulent the houses go, mostly private homes. They turn around, go past their boarding house, and head in the direction of the dock.

They do not have to go far before they see a tea house and tavern. They go in and are seated on cushions at low tables. Zev asks what they have to drink. He turns to Ithamar and says, "They have rice wine, grape wine, hawthorn wine, and honey wine. Which do we want?"

They make their selection and look around for something to do. They see men rise from their table, escorted by genteel women, and disappear into a back room.

"I wonder what's back there—women or gambling. I think we should find out. Zev, call a waiter to come escort us back there."

They do and are taken to a room where a few men are drinking tea, and others are smoking. They are seated and asked if they prefer to drink their cannabis or smoke it. The waitress explains that the effects are faster when smoking but more intense when drinking it.

"We'll drink it," Ithamar says with a grin.

"What did I tell you, Zev? We're having more fun than we'd have in a lifetime in the Timna Valley."

Their cannabis tea is brought to them, and it is explained that it may be an hour before it takes effect, but be patient. Before the tea is served, they must pay. Silver coins are acceptable. Ithamar pulls out two silver coins for the two of them. The waitress waits.

"More? Okay, here are four silver coins for the two of us."

Zev sips his. Ithamar blows on his to cool it down, then gulps it. They are escorted to some cushions to wait.

"Hey, I'm floating."

"Look at me. I've turned into a lion."

"I just thought of Amram's club foot. It is the ugliest thing you ever saw. Ha, ha, ha."

"Look at your hands. They have turned to spikes like they use at the mine." Ha, ha, ha.

"What did you say the Chinese word for fun is?"

"Hanyu pinyin. Ha, ha, ha."

"Hanyu pinyin, everybody. Hanyu pinyin. Ha, ha, ha."

"Hey, where'd everyone go? There are just cats in here. Black-haired cats. I don't like cats. Send them away. Go away cats. Shooo."

Ithamar stands and begins to hit the other guests on the head. "Go away. Shoo!" he shouts.

A big man comes out from one side of the room, grabs Ithamar's arms, and pins them behind his back.

"Oh, do you want to dance?" Ithamar laughs.

The man opens a back door and shoves Ithamar out into an alley.

Ithamar stands, looking around him. "Hey, Zev, where are you? Oh, I left him in there with all the cats." He turns around, opens the door back up, sticks his head in, and calls out, "Zev. Ohhhh Zev. Wherrrre are you, Zev? Come out where ever you are, Zev my Zev."

Soon, Zev stumbles over the other men who he thinks are sticks, laughs, and joins Ithamar.

Back out in the alley, they turn toward a street and stumble their way to it.

Once at the street, they manage to ask a stranger where the Imperial Boarding House is. He points them in the right direction, they laugh, and work their way down the street, one of them slapping the air, the other leaping in circles. Upon their arrival, a guard at the front gate lets them in, and another man helps them find their rooms.

They spend the next two days crawling out from the effects of cannabis.

"Whew. That was fun," Ithamar says. "Today, we look for women, but not at the waterfront. We want classy ladies. Zev, go to the proprietor and discretely ask if any classy women come here to service the men."

Shortly, Zev returns with the information. Yes, there are prostitutes in the boarding house. Yes, there are two available right now, though they do not speak Greek. And the cost is two hundred silver coins each.

"Okay. It's only money. Go pay them. You take the sitting room, and I'll take the bedroom."

An hour later, Ithamar is ready for more excitement. "Wake up, Zev. There's too much to do besides sleep. Let's go to a tavern and see if there are any games going."

Zev wakens, puts on Ithamar's long, heavy cloak with the money sewn in its hem, and follows his friend out the door. "Whatever you say, Ithamar. It's hard to keep up with you, but I'm trying."

"You're doing just fine, Zev. I'm very glad you came with me."

They walk toward the docks and check several tea and wine houses. At each one, Ithamar shows the proprietor—whichever one Zev points out as the proprietor—a hand full of money. Finally, Zev is told gambling is not for the poor but for the rich.

The two young men make their way back to the boarding house and ask the proprietor if he knows of any rich games going on at the moment. They are sent through an elaborately-carved teakwood door. On the other side are groups of men in huddles. Some are playing with cards, some with dice, and some with sticks.

"What's that stick game?" he asks through Zev. Zev explains they need to get as many sticks uncrossed from each other as possible.

"That sounds boring. I see they are playing with dice in that group over there. I wonder if they'd let us join them."

Ithamar leads Zev over to that group and holds out a hand full of gold coins. The men smile and move over so the two young men can join them. While they are not looking, the older men wink at each other.

The game begins, and Ithamar wins time after time.

"Hey, this is fun. These guys don't know what they're doing. But I have the golden touch," Ithamar says.

At last, someone comes over to their group and indicates the game is over.

Ithamar is given a pouch into which to pour his winnings.

"You know well how to play that," Zev says as they return to their room.

"Yeah. And tomorrow we start all over again. The food, the wine, the women, and the games. This is living!"

Indeed, the next few weeks are filled with all that Ithamar promised. All goes well except with the games.

"What's wrong with me? I've been losing all week. I can't keep losing like this. I can't go broke. It's impossible."

The men he is playing with feign sadness for their playing partner and indicate he will win next time.

"Maybe we should go to another city and start over," Zev suggests. "I haven't eaten since yesterday."

"I'm no coward. I know I've got the golden touch. I just need to bet them one more time, and I'll get all my money back," Ithamar replies. "Take the robe off. I want to get the rest of my money out." With that, he returns to the gambling room.

"Okay, guys. Here it is. All of it," he announces, sitting down with his gaming buddies.

The dice are thrown. Again and again. With each throw, Ithamar loses until he has nothing left.

He stands and takes off his chains and rings, and puts them on the low table in front of everyone.

Once again, the rolling of the dice. It does not take long to lose that too.

The big man in charge of the gambling room has been watching. He now comes over and motions for Ithamar and Zev to accompany him outside.

"No, wait! I own a ship out in the harbor. I will bet you the ship against anything you have. What do you say?"

"Ithamar, don't do this," Zev cautions under his breath. "These can be dangerous men."

Ithamar loses. The men at the table stand.

"They are demanding the deed to the ship," Zev interprets.

"What'll I do, Zev? I don't have a deed. I don't have anything. Run!"

Ithamar dashes toward the outside door, Zev right behind him. They run through the outside gate of the Imperial Boarding House and down the street toward the docks.

Behind them are thugs, kept on standby at the game room. They have daggers, swords, and nets, and they are shouting.

"Run, Zev. Run."

Though Zev has longer legs, he has less agility. Ithamar sees a scalable wall ahead of him and climbs it. Just as he hops over to the other side, he catches sight of them nabbing Zev. He huddles on the ground on the other side of the wall, crying.

What has gone wrong? Zev? Zev? No!

He hears a netherworld scream. Then another one that makes the night air quake. The thugs leave. *I must check on Zev. But what if one of them stays behind? I've got to wait until dark.*

When darkness arrives, Ithamar scales the wall and jumps down to the street side. There he sees Zev. He has been stabbed, and his hands cut off. His body lies still against the wall, his eyes lifeless but horror-filled.

Ithamar takes off down the street, running as fast as he can.

He makes it to the docks and sleeps beside a warehouse. When morning arrives, he sees he has blood—Zev's—all over his hands and clothes. He takes off his tunic and dips it in the ocean water to get the stains out, then puts it back on wet.

He goes to several men, indicating he needs work. He mimes digging, chopping, hammering, and sweating. Finally, one taking pigs out of his cart on leashes and leading them up the gangplank returns to his empty cart. He motions to Ithamar.

Encouraged, Ithamar climbs into the bed of the wagon, and the man urges his oxen to turn around. They head through the city, out the city gate, and into the countryside.

Eventually, they arrive at what looks to be a farmhouse. Ithamar climbs out and waits for his new employer. He looks around and sees the man's crops have turned brown. He mimes rain, and the man puts out six fingers. He does not know if that means it has been six months since it rained or six years, but either way, it is bad for farmers.

The stranger leads Ithamar to a barren section of his farm. There, behind fencing, are what seems to be a thousand pigs.

The farmer shows Ithamar how to load a basket of stalks from a dry pile beside the barn and shows how the stalks are to be thrown to the pigs so they can eat.

He hands the basket full of stalks to Ithamar and walks away.

Ithamar stands on the outside of the fence and throws the stalks as far as he can as he walks along the fence. Most, but not all, of the pigs amble over to the center where the stalks land and eat their fill.

But those in the back of the area are crowded out. Ithamar climbs the fence, walks among the pigs to the back, and throws stalks to them. As he does, some of the pigs bump up against him.

Some of the older boars lower their heads, ready to charge with their tusks curled away from their snouts. Ithamar drops his basket and runs until he reaches the outer fence. He leaps over it and watches as the boars attack the fence.

He sits on the ground, observing the pigs and falls asleep. He is awakened by a kick in his side. The sun is on the other side of the horizon.

The farmer motions for him to refill the basket and feed the pigs again.

Ithamar figures out a system. He will feed the ones in front first. Then, while they are busy eating, he will work his way to the back and more dangerous ones. He will throw stalks to them, then when he empties his basket, run for the fence. He will refill his basket and repeat the process until all thousand pigs are fed.

That done, he sits on the ground, watches the pigs, and once more falls asleep. Once more, he is kicked in the side. The sun is coming up in the east. The farmer motions for him to get up and get to work.

Ithamar motions that he is hungry. He mimes, eating something invisible. The farmer rears back and laughs heartily. He calls into the house, and soon his wife and ten children come out. They are all skinny with bloated stomachs. They, too, are hungry.

Ithamar refills his basket with stalks and once again throws them to the pigs.

Mother used to call me her pearl in hiding, not yet discovered. Well, it's worse than that, Mother. I'm your pearl who has been thrown to the pigs.

One basket after another, he throws to the dirty animals. They snort and grunt and get their fill.

Father, I'm sorry. I did things you would be ashamed of. I'm sorry, Father. You will never forgive me. I'm so lonely. No friends. I'm not even worthy to be called your son.

More thrown in the back and a dash to the fence to get out of their way.

I may as well let those boars get me and die right here. They are treated better than me. The farmer is going to let me starve. Oh, Mother, why did you have to die?

Jhesus continued: "There was a man who had two sons.

The younger one said to his father, 'Father, give me my share of the estate.' So he divided his property between them.

"Not long after that, the younger son got together all he had, set off for a distant country and there squandered his wealth in wild living.

After he had spent everything, there was a severe famine in that whole country, and he began to be in need.

So he went and hired himself out to a citizen of that country, who sent him to his fields to feed pigs.

He longed to fill his stomach with the pods that the pigs were eating, but no one gave him anything.

"When he came to his senses, he said, 'How many of my father's hired men have food to spare, and here I am starving to death! (Luke 15:11-17)

"Do not give dogs what is sacred; do not throw your pearls to pigs. If you do, they may trample them under their feet, and then turn and tear you to pieces. (Matthew 7:6)

33 ~ ROOTS

AD 40
Shanghai, Province of Jiangsu, China

*O*nce again, at the close of day, Ithamar lies down outside the fence and sleeps. He dreams he is home, and the well-fed servants are bringing him, his brother, and their parents a meal of more than they could ever consume.

He wakes with a start. It is still dark.

Penina, Peretz, Leib, and the other servants have plenty to eat. The miners eat a lot better than me. I could have been their boss right now if I'd not run away to have my fun. Instead, I've become a nobody in a country where everyone probably hates me. God probably hates me too.

Ithamar looks up at the full moon, the same moon that looks down on his father and Amram. He stands.

"Father!" he calls up into the sky. "Can you hear me? Please, God, make him hear. I'm sorry, God. Father, I'm sorry."

He raises his arms toward the heavens and spreads his fingers wide. "I have become a nobody and a nothing. I don't deserve to be called your son. Hire me on as one of your miners. I'll work hard, Father. I promise. Please."

I must escape here. I've got to get home. Home is the only place anyone really loves me. Please, God. Help me find a way to go home.

In the shadows of night, Ithamar walks toward the city the way the farmer had brought him that day. *Surely it is not all that far. I will walk the rest of the night if I have to.*

He arrives at the gate into Shanghai and waits for it to be opened. He walks with his head down in case the hoods are looking for him. He must find out which way the docks are. He stops someone, mimes ships on the sea, and they point. He hopes they understood and walks in that direction.

By the time he reaches the docks, everyone is up and busy. He stops to rest. His weakness is increasing. He watches the crewmen on the various ships and looks for the name of their ship on the side. He eliminates those with oriental features and lettering on their ships. He sees one with a Greek name and goes to the plank.

He calls up. "Kind sir, I need passage back to Eilat. Is there someone I can talk to?"

"You can talk to me. The fare is ten silver coins."

"May I please talk to the captain. My father is Zarus of Eilat. He is the richest man in all of Idumea. He will pay three times my passage if you will take me there."

"Wait here," the officer says.

Ithamar sits on the dock, dangles his aching feet in the soothing saltwater, and closes his eyes. He wakes with a start when someone yells at him. He is slumping over and about to fall into the sea. He straightens up, stands, and steps back over to the plank.

The officer returns and calls him to come up.

"We accept. But your father will have to pay five times the normal passage."

"Agreed," Ithamar says. "Where do you want me?"

"You are to go below. When you see barrels of wine, you are to sit among them."

Ithamar agrees and goes below. It does not take him long, once his eyes adjust to the blackness, to find the barrels of wine. He sits among them, feels a rat run across his foot, and cries.

Copper Mine, Timna Valley, Arabah Desert, Idumea

Zarus is already at work when Yair arrives.

"Sir, how long have you been here?" he asks.

"Well, it wasn't daylight yet. But I may as well be here. I can't sleep."

"Haven't heard back from Ithamar yet? I'm sorry, sir. Truly I am."

"I don't understand it. He promised to send me word when he arrived."

"Maybe he still will, sir. We have to keep hoping."

"Yes. Hoping and praying."

Zarus finishes up his paperwork and goes out to the mine. He walks along the edge and thinks about how large it has grown in the twenty years since Ithamar was born.

He remembers back to the day he made his appearance into the world. Someone had to come get him to go home. Devorah hadn't been in labor nearly as long as she had been with Amram. By the time Zarus got home, Ithamar had arrived.

Always in a hurry, my Ithamar. Had to be first everywhere he went, everything he did. Once he accomplished that, he couldn't wait to be first at something else. What a boy. But now a man. A lost man. Will I ever see my son again?

"Good morning, Zarus ole boy." It is Gersshon. "What do you think? Will we be ready for the next shipment?"

"What? Oh. Sure. Yes. Both Saabhu and Noach assure me we will."

"Heard from the boy yet?"

Zarus sighs. "No, not yet."

"Think he's run into some kind of danger?"

"I don't know, Gersshon. All I can do is pray that he hasn't."

"Too bad if he has. We may never know what happened to him. *That would be one down and two to go.*

"Excuse me, Gersshon. I see Noach over there. I need to talk to him."

Zarus takes his usual long strides over toward the warehouses. Still strong on the outside. Collapsing on the inside.

"Good morning, Zarus, sir," Noach calls out.

"I do have your assurances that the order will be filled by tomorrow."

"Oh, yes. We've got everything under control. All production is on schedule."

The two men stand side by side in silence.

"Have you heard anything from Ithamar?"

"No, I haven't, Noach, and it is gradually killing me."

"He's smart. If he's having any kind of problem, he will work it out. Always did."

"If he's been inducted into a foreign army, I may never hear from him again," Zarus replies. "What if he's dead on an obscure battlefield somewhere? What if he's never buried?"

Old Noach lays his hand on Zarus' shoulder. "He's a survivor. He can survive anything. He'll find a way to come home someday. He always loved you."

"I pray you are right, Noach. Thank you for the encouragement. Well, if you're sure the shipment will be ready tomorrow, then I don't have to worry about it," Zarus says.

They stand side by side a little longer, saying nothing. Quietly, Zarus steps away as though drifting in the sands of an enigma.

He approaches the haul road and starts down. He sees Saabhu about halfway down the pit, looking up at a berm.

Saabhu waves. "Hello there, Zarus, sir," he calls out. "I'm a little worried about this berm. I think it needs shored up. Does it look like it's leaning forward to you?"

Zarus looks at it, moves a little to view it from a different angle, then to yet another location. "Wouldn't hurt to put some chains up there."

"That's what I was thinking, sir."

They are quiet a moment, looking up at the berm.

"Heard from Ithamar?"

Zarus sighs. He knows everyone means well, but they are intruding into his agony. Answers? He has no answers.

"No, I'm afraid I haven't, Saabhu."

"You will. I'm sure you will. Whenever he worked for me, he was always asking questions and jumping around like the pit was his playground. Now that he's grown, he considers the world his playground. He'll be back someday, and oh, the stories he will have to tell."

Zarus forces a smile, and Saabhu pats him on the back.

"I know I'm right. I have a gut feeling about that boy, and my gut isn't often wrong."

"You're very kind to say so. I'm sure you're right. I pray you are right."

Zarus progresses down to the floor of the pit. He walks around watching the men humpbacked, crouching over their work with a chisel and hammer.

"Good work," he says to one miner, patting him on the head.

"Good job," he says to another miner, patting him on the shoulder.

"Good, good," he says to yet another. "You're doing a fine job."

As he makes the rounds, they look up at their boss. They are the envy of every miner in the Timna Valley to have a boss like Zarus.

They all know about his missing son. Word gets around. They feel sorry for him. No father should have to go through what he has been going through.

"I'm praying for you, sir," one of them says, "and your son."

"Thank you. I appreciate that," Zarus replies.

He jerks around to start back up the haul road, hoping no one had seen the tears coming back to his eyes. Always so close to the surface. Tears that are never satisfied. Searching tears. Wondering tears. Agonizing tears.

Work progresses through the day as it has for the past twenty-three years since he and Devorah had sacrificed everything to purchase the land.

Oh, Devorah, what am I going to do? Our son has been gone a year. No one has heard from him. Must I lose you and then lose our son?

Late afternoon Zarus decides to return home, though he does not know why. Nothing at home but agony. Hollow agony. He slides up onto Master Shalva and urges him into a slow walk toward the city.

Eilat, Port City on Red Sea, Arabah Desert

At home, Zarus hands the reins of his Arabian to Leib and goes into his manor.

He walks around in the empty mansion. Mosaic tile floors. What for? Marble columns. What for? A garden—Devorah's garden—garnished with every possible desert flower there is. What for?

He goes out to the garden and sits on Devorah's favorite bench. He touches the place where she had always sat and tries to feel her presence as he had for nearly thirty years.

He rises, walks back to the courtyard, and climbs the stairs. He does not go to his room—his and Devorah's. Instead, he turns down the hall and goes to Ithamar's room. He opens the door.

Everything the way his youngest had left it over a year earlier. The dirty tunic he had taken off after following Noach around the mine half the day, asking him questions about China. The work sandals that would not be necessary in an exotic land.

He sits on Ithamar's bed and picks up his son's clay tablet with notes on it about the city he should go to, what the people looked like, a reminder to take Zev along, how much he thought the house was worth.

He always took too many chances. He always tried to outdo other people, thereby making enemies for himself.

Zarus rises and steps over to some pegs on the wall with Ithamar's favorite tunic and cloak on them.

What if he got into a tavern brawl and was stabbed to death? What if he got into a gang that was too wild even for him, and couldn't get out? What if he was kidnapped and made a slave the rest of his life? What if...

"There you are, Father," Amram says. "You spend too much time in Ithamar's room. He's gone and probably will never return. He never cared anything about the rest of us. He'd stay out all night and not care if you worried. He never cared about anyone but himself. Quit tearing yourself apart for him. You've still got me. Isn't that enough?"

Zarus shakes his head "Amram, I can't believe you are speaking like that about your own brother. How can you? I never heard you speak about anyone like this before. What's different? You've become mean since your brother left."

"He spent his whole life making fun of my club foot. He resented me for being born first and being taller than him. There was nothing about me he liked. Why would I want to worry about him now that we have rid of him?"

Zarus rushes past Amram and down the hall. He goes to his bedroom and closes the door. He kneels next to his bed.

"Holy Father God in heaven. You know where my Ithamar is. Watch over him. Put your protective hand over him, and don't let him come to any harm. And bring him home. No matter what he has done, bring him home so we can love him again—Amram and I."

Zarus stays on his knees but does not know how long. All he knows is that the sun is in a different place in the sky now.

He rises, gets control of himself, comes out of his room, and walks down the stairs to the courtyard. There he grabs a chair, goes out the gate with it, and sets the chair down. From this place, Zarus can see all the way down the hill. From this place, Zarus can see him coming.

He sits in his chair the rest of the day. When night comes, he brings his chair in. But at sunrise, he is back in his chair watching for Ithamar.

"Please, God, keep him safe and bring him back home to us. Take my strength and give it to my son."

All day he sits. He no longer goes out to the mine. The only time he goes into the manor is to eat a little and pretend to sleep. Then he is back. Sitting in his chair. Straining to see his son walking up the hill toward home.

A week. Two weeks. A month. Zarus has lost interest in everything else but keeping his son alive so he can come home.

Sometimes he walks down to the docks and asks around.

"Has anyone seen a dark-haired young man, twenty years old now, a little shorter than me? Anyone? Anyone at all?"

Then back home to his manor on the hill and his chair.
Sitting.
Waiting.
Longing.
 "Don't be dead, Ithamar. Don't be dead."
Praying.
Groaning.
"Come back, my son. Come back."
Morning again. Back to his chair, eyes, and heart straining.
Hoping.
Begging.
He sees a young man. Always he prays, "Let it be him." It never is. Why hope?
But this time...
Is it possible?
Zarus stands. He watches.
That's Ithamar's walk...
That's the way Ithamar holds his head...
That's Ithamar's hair...
Zarus dares to walk a little way down the hill.
Could it be?
Is it?
Perhaps?
It is.
It is Ithamar!
Zarus runs. Arms held out. Running toward his wayward son.
The young man looks up, recognizes his father coming toward him, and he too runs.
Father running toward son.
Son running toward father.
And into each other's arms.
"Oh, my son, Ithamar. My son. You're alive. My son. My son. I thought you were dead."
Zarus dares not let go. What if it is a vision? He cannot let go of his vision.
But Ithamar struggles loose and steps back. Zarus is confused.
Slowly Ithamar lowers himself to his knees in the middle of the street.
"Son, what are you doing?"
"Forgive me. You were right. I was wrong. If you can forgive me, then make me one of your miners. I will work in the most dangerous part of the mine. I am not even worthy to do that much,

but if you will forgive me just a little…”

Zarus takes his son's elbows and raises him back to his feet.

“Ithamar, you are my son. You have always been and always will be.”

Ithamar is crying. Zarus is crying. Once more, they embrace and comfort each other. Father comforting son. Son comforting father.

“Come on, the rest of the way home, Son.”

Walking side by side now, their arms across each other's shoulders, they walk on up the hill and to home. Both with tears, but new tears.

When they arrive at the gate, Zarus opens it, escorts his son in, and shouts, “He's home! He's home!”

Penina hurries from the kitchen. “Oh, Lord, you brought him home.”

Peretz comes rushing from upstairs. “Oh, master, you're home.”

Leib comes running in from the stables. “Praise God, you're home.”

Zarus stands next to Ithamar with tears of gladness, finding their way down his cheeks and into his graying beard as the servants gather around them to welcome the young man home.

When they leave to resume their duties, Zarus holds Ithamar out in front of him. Now he sees him with clearer eyes.

“What has happened to you? You weigh hardly anything. Have you been eating? Look at your clothes? Is that all you have left?”

“I don't even have any of the money left,” Ithamar whispers. “I wasted it all.”

“Don't worry about the money. Let's get some food in you, a bath, and clean clothes. Your room is the way you left it. Everything is the way you remember it.”

“Penina, whatever you have in the kitchen that can be eaten right now, bring it out for Ithamar. He is starving.”

As Ithamar eats, Zarus gets an idea.

“We're going to have a feast. I will tell Leib to go to the market and find a fat calf to eat. Help me remember your friends so I can invite them to celebrate your homecoming with us.”

“Can I do that after I clean up, Father?”

“Of course you can. You go on, and I'll get things started down here. Oh, and I'll have a barber here for you by then. You need a trim.”

Ithamar finishes his meal, then looks long at his father.

“Father, I am talking about a different kind of cleaning up. Before anything else happens, I need to tell you something.”

Zarus, who had been pacing near his son, sits back down. "Certainly, Son. What is it?

"Zev is dead. It could have been me. Those times when I thought I was going to die, I was really scared. I had always thought I would die an old man after doing all the living I wanted to do."

Zarus stares into his son's eyes. "All young men think that."

"Well, I suddenly realized I could die at any time, and I wasn't ready to meet God. I realized that, if God gave me as much attention as I have given him, it would be hardly any. In all my sinning, I sinned against God. I was following the devil right to hell. Father, I was so afraid. I still am. I don't want to go to hell."

"Son, Jhesus paid our punishment for us. But we have to become his follower. Is that what you want to do?"

"Yes, Father. I want to be baptized."

"Do you understand that baptism is to imitate Jhesus' death for our sins, burial, and rising up out of his grave as our Savior? You'd be dying to your old sins, burying your old kind of life, then rising up out of the water a reborn saved one."

"That's what I want, Father. Could you baptize me? Our pool in the garden is deep enough. Please, baptize me. Otherwise, I can never face dying."

"There is no one else around here to baptize you, so I would be proud to help you."

Father and son walk out to the garden, and Zarus baptizes his son.

They embrace.

"Two homecomings in one day. Home to Eilat, and someday home to heaven," Zarus says.

He recites some sayings of Jhesus, and they are quiet together for a long time.

"Well, Father, now that I am a new man, maybe I need to change my clothes. But I will remember this day the rest of my life."

"Me too," Zarus says. "Me too."

When Ithamar leaves, Zarus stays out in the garden and stands before Devorah's bench. "He's home, my pearl. Our son is safe, and he is home. I know you would throw a party for him, so I'm doing it for you. I wish you could be with us to celebrate. Well, maybe you are."

When Ithamar returns downstairs, the barber is there waiting with Zarus. Both are beaming. "Welcome home, Master," he says.

As the barber sets to work, Zarus pulls out a wax tablet and says, "Okay, give me the names and locations of your friends."

"Are you sure you want to do this, Father?"

"I'm sure. Now out with it. Give me a list of your friends so I can send Peretz to invite them all. We will start cooking the calf tonight, and you will have your welcome-home celebration tomorrow."

Nighttime comes. Everyone has been extra busy. Now everyone is tired and ready for bed earlier than usual.

"Welcome home, Son," Zarus says one last time before going into his own bedroom. For the first time in over a year, he will sleep all night.

Later in the evening, when everyone is in bed, Amram comes home. All is quiet. *Probably father is in his room crying. I won't disturb him. I need to be back at the mine early in the morning. Noach and I need to make sure that shipment gets to the docks and ready to load onto the ship.*

Morning. Zarus rises, smiles, goes down to Ithamar's room, opens the door slightly, peeks in, and retains his smile. It hadn't been a dream. His son is still home.

Soon he hears Penina stirring in the kitchen.

"If you need more fresh vegetables and fruit," he tells her, "send one of the other servants to the market to buy them. I need you here to make bread and sweets."

He checks with Peretz. Yes, he delivered all the invitations just before dark the day before. "Everyone will be here at noon," he assured Zarus.

"Oh, and I want musicians. What's a party without music?"

Ithamar sleeps until late into the morning. Zarus wonders what has happened to make him so exhausted. Time for that later. If Ithamar chooses to tell him, fine. If he chooses not to, perhaps not knowing would be even better.

When Ithamar rises, his father has a brand new outfit for him to wear at his party. As he dons it, he still feels overwhelmed, thinking about what he had been doing a month earlier. *How can Father forgive me so easily after all I have done to sully his name?*

Noon comes, and so does Ithamar's old Eilat friends. One at a time, they arrive and welcome Ithamar back home. "How was China?" they ask.

"Beautiful place," Ithamar always answers, "but home is better."

The calf has been roasted. Vegetables and fruit are scattered around tables. The musicians arrive. The celebrating in full begins: Eating, singing, line dancing.

Late that afternoon, someone else comes to the gate. Zarus

rushes to it himself. It is Amram.

"Oh, Son, I didn't hear you come in last night. Wonderful news. God has answered our prayers. Your brother is home. He arrived about this time yesterday. Isn't it wonderful?

"And you're giving him a party?" Amram replies. "I'll bet he is out of money. Just came home to get more so he can go running to prostitutes again. That's what he used all his money on, isn't it?"

Zarus is shocked. "But he is your brother. We had begun to think he was dead. But now he is alive again."

"Father, I've worked hard all these years at the mine, and what did I ever get out of it? Did you ever invite my friends over so we could eat even a skinny goat? No, of course not. You take me for granted with never a reward, but reward my brother for being bad. What kind of justice is that?"

"Not justice. Mercy. Forgiveness. Can you ever bring yourself to forgive your brother?"

"You mean, for being given the party you never gave me?"

"Son, you are my oldest and will inherit the mine and everything else I own. And you begrudge your brother a party?"

I will set out and go back to my father and say to him: Father, I have sinned against heaven and against you.

I am no longer worthy to be called your son; make me like one of your hired men.'

So he got up and went to his father. "But while he was still a long way off, his father saw him and was filled with compassion for him; he ran to his son, threw his arms around him and kissed him.

"The son said to him, 'Father, I have sinned against heaven and against you. I am no longer worthy to be called your son. '

"But the father said to his servants, 'Quick! Bring the best robe and put it on him. Put a ring on his finger and sandals on his feet.

Bring the fattened calf and kill it. Let's have a feast and celebrate.

For this son of mine was dead and is alive again; he was lost and is found.' So they began to celebrate.

"Meanwhile, the older son was in the field. When he came near the house, he heard music and dancing.

So he called one of the servants and asked him what was going on.

'Your brother has come,' he replied, 'and your father has killed the fattened calf because he has him back safe and sound.'

"The older brother became angry and refused to go in. So his father went out and pleaded with him.

But he answered his father, 'Look! All these years I've been slaving for you and never disobeyed your orders. Yet you never gave me even a young goat so I could celebrate with my friends.

But when this son of yours who has squandered your property with prostitutes comes home, you kill the fattened calf for him!'

" 'My son,' the father said, 'you are always with me, and everything I have is yours.

But we had to celebrate and be glad because this brother of yours was dead and is alive again; he was lost and is found.' " (Luke 15:18-32)

34 ~ PERSIA

AD 41
Copper Mine, Timna Valley, Arabah Desert, Idumea

"Do we have any more ideas on who is breaking into our warehouses at night?" Zarus asks his long-time partner.

"After a year of investigating, I think I'm close," Gersshon replies.

They are walking along the perimeter of the mine toward the warehouses. Things have been tense between them of late. Zarus keeps asking questions.

"I think it's been going on a lot longer than a year, and I do not understand why it would take you a year to find the culprits when all you have to do is set up surveillance at night."

"It's more complicated than that," Gersshon retorts.

"How could it be complicated?

"Well, I'm hearing different stories from my spies. One tells me he saw this person sneak in at night, and another says he saw that person sneak in at night. Their stories do not coincide."

"Then it is obvious, some of our spies are in on it."

"As soon as I interrogate a spy about my suspicions of him, he disappears. So I still don't have enough proof to take them before a magistrate."

Zarus stops and faces Gersshon.

"Maybe I should take over the investigation," Zarus says.

Gersshon steps back, and his eyes squint briefly. He switches to a smile.

"But you're going to Persia, ole boy."

"No, I'm not." Zarus puts his hands on his waist. "I'm not going anywhere, especially with Ithamar home such a short time. He needs me. And I don't want to be away from Amram either."

"Amram has his own house now. You don't see him as much

now anyway."

"I see him every day here at work."

"Take your boys with you. Or at least take Amram, and I'll watch over Ithamar."

"Why would I go to Persia? You were just there."

"As you know, I always make arrangements at the smelters for them to buy our copper. I've come to a conclusion: We need to build our own smelter."

"That's a big step."

"That's why you need to go. I did some negotiating with Tirham, but he wants to meet the other partner—you."

"I don't know."

"You should also take Noach and Saabhu with you."

"Well, that would help me come to a proper conclusion."

"That's right: The co-owner, the owner's son, and our two most trusted officers should make an impression on Tirham" *and get him out of my hair.*

"No, now isn't the time," Zarus says.

They resume walking.

"I promise, I'll have the culprits who are stealing from our warehouses by the time you are back."

"You're that close?"

"That close."

"Well. You sure you'll keep close watch on Ithamar? Then I'd better call a meeting of my officers."

They turn away from the warehouses. Zarus stops a messenger boy.

"Would you find Noach, Saabhu, and Amram, my son, and tell them to meet me in the *officium* as soon as possible?"

The men arrive one at a time, Noach being the first. Later comes Saabhu, and finally, Amram. They sit in a circle on cushions laid on fine carpet.

"Men, it has come to my attention that we need to go to Persia."

"Persia?" Amram repeats. "That's always been a dream of mine."

All the men smile except Noach, who complains he is too old to travel so far in the desert.

"I need you, Noach. I need all of you. I need your expertise on setting up our own smelter. I also need my son because I think I want to put him in charge of it."

"So, when do we leave?" Saabhu asks.

"As soon as we can line up the camels and get our personal

things ready. No use putting it off. The sooner we leave, the sooner we get back."

Gersshon, who has been standing in a corner looking over a diagram of the entire mine operation, hides a smile.

"I'll hire two guards to go with us," Zarus says. "So, there will be camels for each of us, two for supplies and gifts, one for my servant, Peretz, and two for the guards—nine in all. Will you take care of that, Saabhu?"

"We will be traveling through Nabadea, Arabia, and Mesopotamia to get there. I estimate it could take as long as three months."

"We will meet here at the mine just before daylight in the morning. Now everyone needs to go home and prepare."

Gersshon smiles still.

Road between Idumea and Persia

The travel is slow. They must not wear out the camels on such a long trip. Kalam leads the way, and the other guard, Varja, brings up the rear.

As always, the desert is hot. But as they work their way northeast, they find gradual relief from the inferno usually experienced back in the Timna Valley.

After a week out and everyone knows the routine, Amram brings his camel up next to his father.

"Father, I have been wanting to tell you something about what is going on at the mine. I found out when Mother was so sick and tried to tell you, but decided to wait. Once you were doing better after her death, Ithamar left. It's been going on for twenty years, and I think you need to know."

"What is it, Son? It sounds serious."

"Father, remember when I was interviewing all the miners who work for us?"

"Yes. I don't know what you hoped to learn, but I do remember."

"Well, the ones who have been with you the longest never had a choice to leave. That's why they've been with you the longest."

"What do you mean, they didn't have a choice? Of course, they did."

"Father, they are slaves."

Zarus pulls in on the reins of his camel and stops. Amram does also.

"They say Gersshon bought them off ships twenty years ago. They think they were traded for copper."

Zarus squints his eyes and presses in on his lips. "That cannot be. I have known Gersshon most of my life."

"They said Gersshon promised to have them killed if they ever told. Father, were there any miners who were paid as a group instead of individually?"

"Well, yes, there was one group. I would pay Gersshon, and he passed the money out to…"

Zarus becomes silent. "No. That cannot be. Gersshon wouldn't do that. He has been a little bit shady in some of his dealings through the years, but nothing that bad. No."

Amram remains quiet.

"That would mean he has stolen millions over the years." He looks away from his son, then toward a distant mountain. "I shall investigate when we get back. "Finally, looking at his son again, "But I am sure you will find those miners were mistaken."

He whips his camel into a trot in order to catch up with the others and distance himself from the atrocious news.

Night comes. Another day, another week.

They pass through Nabadea and Arabia.

"Father, I wanted to tell people of other lands about Jhesus whom we serve. I have my chance now and have done so at every oasis and public well we stop at."

"What has been their reception?"

"Last night, while you were asleep, I baptized one man and his wife into Christ Jhesus, and they became Christians."

"That's wonderful, Son. How did you communicate with them?"

"Well, I only know Hebrew, Aramaic, and Greek. They spoke Greek."

"I'm proud of you, Amram."

They arrive in Mesopotamia and the Zagros mountain range. They pulls out their wool robes and long leather boots to stay warm.

"What's that white stuff, Father?" Amram asks.

Zarus smiles. "That, my son, is snow."

"It is so beautiful. I shall write a poem about it. Snow."

They go down the other side of the range and know they are now in Persia. They continue northeast.

"Sialk is not too far away now," Zarus explains. "Just a few more days."

"Sir, Zarus," Kalam, one of the guards, says one of their last evenings before arriving at their destination.

"Yes, Kalam. You have done a fine job protecting us."

"I have grown to respect you, sir. I just wanted you to know that your partner, Gersshon, has been hiring some of the other guards to do special jobs for him on and off the past few years. They don't tell me what they are hired to do, but I do not think it is good."

"Thank you, Kalam. I'm sure it wasn't anything too bad. Gersshon is basically a good man."

"As you say, sir."

Sialk, Kashan District, Persia

"Tirham, it is an honor to meet you. The people of my country salute the people of your country,"

Zarus is wearing a long green tunic, matching kerchief on his head, and a robe of red.

"May I introduce myself," he continues. "I am Zarus, formerly of Samaria in Palestine, but long time of Idumea. This is my mine superintendent, Noach of Idumea."

"I admire you, Noach, for making such a long, arduous journey. I do not think I would have the courage to try it," Tirham says.

"I wholeheartedly agree with you, sir," Noach replies. "I am seventy-two years old now, and too old to be running up and down mountains."

"This is my mine engineer, Saabhu of Egypt," Zarus continues.

"I hear great things of the mining and smelting down in Egypt. Is everything I hear true?"

"My father was an engineer many years, and I grew up around it," Saabhu says. "I think what you have heard may be true. But what Egypt has accomplished does not come near to what your country has."

"Finally, Tirham, this is my eldest son, Amram. If we decide to buy the plans from you to build our own smelting plant, Amram will be put in charge of it."

"Such ambition for such a young man, but a strong young man, I must say," Tirham replies, smiling up at Amram now taller than his father."

"I think I look young for my age. I am twenty-six years old," Amram replies.

"I am sure you are a very smart twenty-six," Tirham says.

Tomorrow, I shall take you on your first tour. But now you

need to freshen up and rest. If you did not bring your own tent, I can provide accommodations for you."

"We do have our tent. It can be divided into several rooms so we can confer about the copper business together."

"Fine. You will want to set it up over there by the Zayandeh River. I will send a servant to get you in the morning.

————

"What did you think of the tour, Zarus?" Tirham asks.

"I was impressed. However, my engineer, Saabhu, has some questions for you, as does Superintendent Noach. But first, come to my tent. I sent my servant, Peretz, into town this morning to buy fruit so we can have a refreshing drink while we talk. He also bought cheese, grapes, and bread. Please be my guest," Zarus says. "We have pomegranate and apple juice, whichever you prefer."

The following four hours are taken up with questions about materials and methods in making the giant kilns, storage after smelting, how to guard against accidents, and transportation. Also, they talk about contracts with local copper craftsmen as well as working with tin mines to make bronze.

They take another tour of the smelter to help answer their numerous questions.

"Your men well know what they are doing, or they wouldn't be asking so many intelligent questions. But they have worn me out, and perhaps even you. After we all rest, I would like to invite you to my house tonight for a reception."

"You are most gracious, Tirham. I accept. We will be there."

————

Tirham's house is one of the largest the men from Idumea have ever seen. What they do not realize is that its walls are eight feet thick to keep out the desert sun and enemies. The outside is plain with no windows for the same reason.

They enter through a high arch into a small foyer, then on to the main reception area. The ceiling in the reception area is the height of eight men. The walls are of stucco that have been formed into geometric motifs and dyed red and gold. The floors are stucco also but covered with numerous carpets, also with geometric patterns as well as flowering tree branches and birds of every color imaginable.

"Forgive us for staring, Tirham," Zarus says. "Your home is

more than we ever imagined."

"You have not seen my paradise yet."

Tirham leads the group of five men out to his garden, dominated by a pool as long as the house ceiling is high. Surrounding the pool are trees of pomegranates and figs, and along the walls are grapevines.

"Amazing," Saabhu, the engineer, says.

"Out of this world," Noach says.

"I want a garden like this someday," Amram says.

"Now, we eat. Let us adjourn to the banquet hall. They are ready for us."

Tirham leads the men to their tables, low to the floor, and surrounded by cushions.

Their host is dressed in a short tunic over a long skirt. The tunic is blue, and the skirt is red. He is wearing three chains of copper, silver, and gold, with a pearl attached to each one.

They eat and laugh and enjoy the entertainment—flute players. Zarus teaches Tirham a Samaritan song, and Tirham teaches Zarus and his company a Persian song.

At the end of the meal, Zarus asks for his guards to be admitted.

"Tirham, for your hospitality, may my son and I present you with an ivory and jade statue imported from Sheba. Also, copper jewelry designed by my daughter, Lleah, with inlaid peridot and mother of pearl."

Saabhu stands. "I would like to present you with a mahogany statue of an elephant from India."

"As for me," says Noach, "I would like to present to you ten bolts of the finest silk from China."

"Such a wonderful evening, gentlemen. I am so glad you came our way," Tirham says. "Now for dessert. "I assume you have heard of baklava. We serve it with honey tea."

"Well done, Tirham. It is our favorite," Zarus says with a grin.

"I am afraid I must leave tomorrow," Noach says. "We have been gone longer than expected. Zarus believes I must check to see if things are running smoothly. I heartily agree with him. Therefore I will be cutting my visit with you short, with my regrets."

"I am sorry you are leaving so soon, Noach. Have you found a caravan to travel with?"

"Indeed, I have. I will be safe, and look forward to being home again."

Copper Mine, Timna Valley, Arabah Desert, Idumea

"Noach, what are you doing here?" Gersshon says. "What a surprise. Where are Zarus and Saabhu?"

"They are not with me," Noach replies. "We were taking longer than expected, so I thought I'd come back to see how things were."

"Oh. Is that so?" Gersshon replies.

"I arrived home yesterday, so am ready to go back to work today," Noach says. "By the way, where is Yair? I didn't see him."

"He started riding his chariot around the warehouses and had an accident. He's laid up for a few days."

"I'd like to see the warehouses."

"You're still tired, Noach. Why don't you do it tomorrow?"

"I don't want to do it tomorrow. I plan to do it right now."

"Are you sure?"

"Of course, I'm sure."

"Well, have it your way. I have to run into the city. Take your time," Gersshon says.

Noach makes his way to the warehouses. He enters the first one and sees that it is empty.

What? This warehouse has never been empty. What's going on?

He walks along the walls. He checks for trap doors in the bottom. He does not find any clues as to what happened to the copper.

Noach walks to the second warehouse, his stomach-churning. He opens the tall, wide door, and finds it the same. Empty. Again he walks around the walls and checks for trap doors in the floor. He finds none.

Back outside, he walks to the third warehouse. It is full, just like it had been when he left. He hears a sound behind the pile. He walks around to it.

"What are you doing here," Noach says sternly.

He hardly has time after spotting the dagger to turn and attempt a crippling getaway.

A second assailant grabs him from behind and stabs him in the heart.

Noach is dead.

Late that afternoon, Gersshon returns to the mine.

"Gersshon, sir, something terrible has happened," one of the miners says.

"What? Did we have a landslide?"

"No, but come with me. It's at the warehouse."

Gersshon runs to keep up with the miner."

"We came here to deposit more copper, and he was lying there dead."

Gersshon kneels beside Noach's body, listens to his chest, then rises.

"This is a tragedy. Did anyone see who did it?"

"No, sir."

"Well, tomorrow we will dedicate to Noach's memory. He was with us twenty years. I am just devastated. Everyone will be. I will go back into the city and notify his family. Tomorrow we will have a reading of the beginning of the Torah in his honor."

"Yes, sir."

"What a tragedy. What a terrible tragedy. Something must be done."

AD 42
Sialk, Kashan District, Persia

It is an extra warm night. Zarus decides to take a walk.

Oh, my Devorah. You would have loved it here. The people are so colorful. Their music is unique. And they are so inventive. You always liked new and different things. You missed out by going away from me. How I miss you, my pearl.

He hears a noise behind the tent but does not pay any mind to it. *It's probably Saabhu.*

Zarus continues his walk. He looks at the stars. *Is that you looking down on me, my darling? Or is that one over there you? My heart is touching your heart right now. Save a place for me. I will be there someday.*

He hears the noise again. He turns and looks behind him. All goes black.

———

"Where am I?"

"You are in my tent," Razak replies, taking the sack off Zarus' head."You'd better get used to it. You're going to be here a while."

"Guards! Guards! We have invaders."

"Sorry, Zarus, or whatever your name is, but you are the invader, and the guards are mine."

"What are you talking about?"

Zarus tries to lift his head, but it is heavy with ache.

"You'll get over it. I'm going to leave for a while now. There is no way for you to escape. Well, unless you pay."

"Pay what?"

"Your ransom, of course."

"Where am I?" Zarus asks again.

"You are still in Sialk. Well, outside of Sialk. Don't think you can escape, though. I have guards on each side of this tent. No one enters without my permission. And the only way they are going to get my permission is to make arrangements for the ransom."

"Can you get word to my son?"

"Don't worry. We already have. Well, kind of. We left a message with your host, Tirham. Now get some sleep. That's what I intend to do."

Razak leaves the tent and closes the flap. Before he does, Zarus spots the guard standing at attention next to it.

"How much is the ransom?" Zarus calls out.

"Two hundred thousand denari," comes the answer from outside the tent.

Zarus lays his head back down on the mat, puts his hands over his eyes, and prays. "No one knows me here, God. Why would anyone kidnap me? God, help me be strong."

Morning comes. Razak is back.

"Good morning. Got a headache? We haven't heard from anyone yet about your ransom, but we expect to soon."

Indeed, Saabhu comes.

"What did I tell you? They're already working on it," Razak says, coming into the tent.

Saabhu enters behind him.

"I shall leave the two of you to figure out how to get the money to us."

Saabhu sits on the floor of the tent across from Zarus. "How are you feeling, sir? Did they hurt you?"

"Well, I have a knot on my head. Other than that, I'm still in one piece."

"Tell me what I can do to get you out of here."

"I need you to go back to Timna and tell Gersshon that I need two hundred thousand denari. Also, I need you to check on Noach. I expected to hear back from him by now. Can you do that?"

"Yes, sir."

"And my son. How is Amram doing?"

"He's frightened for you. But Peretz is right there with him giving him courage."

"Yes. Good. Tell Peretz he is doing the right thing. And the guards we hired: Are they still here?"

"Yes, sir. But their time you paid them for is running out."

"Tell them I will pay them double to stay here and protect my son."

"Yes, sir. They like you. They trust you and believe you will come up with the money to pay for your ransom. I think they'll do it."

"Tell my guards to never let my son out of their sight, night or day.

"I will. And I'll prepare to leave with the next caravan. God bless you, Zarus. And Jhesus Christ, his Son."

"Thank you, Saabhu. That means a lot to hear you say that. Goodbye again, Saabhu, my good friend. God go with you."

Copper Mine, Timna Valley, Arabah Desert, Idumea

"Well, well, well. If it isn't Saabhu," Gersshon says. When did you arrive?"

"I came right here. I haven't even been home yet."

"What's the hurry? You're here, aren't you? The hard part of the trip is over."

"Something bad has happened to Zarus. He has been kidnapped by a gang of nomads led by a criminal named Razak."

"Is that so? That's terrible. How did it happen? I thought he took guards along with him."

"He only took two guards. Anyway, the ransom is two hundred thousand denari. I need it right away so I can return and free Zarus."

"That's a lot of money. However, it must be done. It will take me a couple of days to gather up that many denari from the bankers," Gersshon says. "I hope Zarus is all right."

"Did Noach ever arrive?" Saabhu asks.

"He did, but he took sick and died. We had a nice funeral for him."

"Oh, I'm sorry to hear that. He was a good man. Well, then, while I wait for the ransom money, I want to inspect the warehouses."

"I can't imagine why. They are doing the job for which they were built."

"I still want to inspect them. Zarus asked me to."

"Well, okay. But wait here. I need to tell Yair something. Then we can walk over together."

As Saabhu waits, he notices that Gersshon is nearly running to the *officium*. With Gersshon's growing middle, it must be hard to do. In fact, he has never seen Gersshon run, especially out in this heat. Still, Gersshon runs.

Saabhu squats on the ground and waits. Several moments later, Gersshon returns. He is winded.

"I guess we'd better take it slow going over to the warehouses," Saabhu admonishes.

"Good idea."

"So, what were you in such a hurry for?"

"Just business, Saabhu. Just business."

Several moments later, they arrive at the warehouse.

"Be my guest, Saabhu. Go on in ahead of me."

Saabhu enters the first warehouse. It is mostly empty except for a group of men. At the feet of each one are ten or twelve copper-and-stone rocks. The first one hits Saabhu in the head and knocks him over.

Another stone finds its mark in his chest. He turns over on his stomach and puts his hands up over his head. The next stone hits his hands. Another lands on his lower back. His hands and arms slide away to his side. Another hits his head again. Then his shoulders, his legs, his arms, his back, his head.

"Stop," Gersshon shouts. "I want to see if he is still alive."

Gersshon turns Saabhu over on his back and listens to his chest. "May as well finish him off."

"You know what to do then."

After disposing of all their rocks on and around Saabhu's body, they throw him in the bottom of a wagon. Two men stay and watch for the next wagon load of copper to come up from the mine floor. When it arrives, they take the copper out of that wagon and throw it on top of Saabhu in the other wagon.

That done, the two men bring over two oxen, which they hitch up and drive down to the docks. Once they arrive, they wait for their turn. Chains are lowered from the hull of an awaiting ship. The two men loosen the wagon bed from the axle and attach the end of the ship's chains to the bed. It is pulled up. A man at the bronze tripod suspending the wagon bed orders his men to swing it around. That done, the wagon bed with Saabhu at its bottom is lowered down into the belly of the ship. And Saabhu is never heard from again.

"Listen to another parable: There was a landowner who planted a vineyard. He put a wall around it, dug a winepress in it, and built a watchtower. Then he rented the vineyard to some farmers and went away on a journey.

When the harvest time approached, he sent his servants to the tenants to collect his fruit.

"The tenants seized his servants; they beat one, killed another, and stoned a third. (Matthew 21:33-35).

35 ~ RANSOM

AD 43
Sialk, Kashan District, Persia

"I do not know what has happened to Noach and Saabhu. Both of them should have been back here by now."

Zarus is still confined to the tent with the four guards on each side to prevent escape. Amram is with him, as is his daily habit.

"Father, I am worried too. What are we going to do?"

Both men have grown thin, Zarus because he is not fed much, and Amram because he worries so much, his appetite is mostly gone.

"When are you going to start taking care of yourself?" Zarus asks. "You've got to start eating. You need your strength, and I don't need to be worrying about you."

"That's what Peretz says, Father," Amram answers, smiling.

"Well, do what he tells you."

"I will try, Father. But I can't stand to see you in here."

"Do you have the plans for the smelter that Noach and Saabhu came up with before they left?"

"No, they took them with them so they could line up some men to get started on it while they returned to you with their report."

"You've worked with them both a long time. Do you think you could duplicate their plans?"

"Not exactly. I think I could Noach's, but not Saabhu's. That's Ithamar's specialty."

"Do what you can. It will keep you busy while we wait for them to return. Now, go back to our tent. I want to take a nap."

The days continue to blend one into one another. Still, neither Noach nor Saabhu show up. On Amram's next visit, Zarus tells him of his decision.

"Something is very wrong at the mine. They should have been back long ago. I'm going to send you back to the mine. They are just officers. Perhaps they need more authority. You are that authority."

"Me?"

"Yes. When you go back, you put on my best tunic and robe and go out there. They will connect you to me more. Demand my ransom money. Don't ask. You are equal to me. They will listen to you. And find Noach and Saabhu. I'm afraid they have run into some serious trouble on their way back. Can you do that?"

"Yes, sir. I will do my best."

"No, you won't do your best. You will do my best. You will become me in their eyes. Stand strong, my son. Stand strong. And go with Jhesus Christ, whom we serve."

"Yes, sir. And may Jhesus Christ keep you safe until our return."

Father and son embrace as though they will never do so again.

Eilat, Port City on Red Sea, Arabah Desert, Idumea

"Greetings, Ithamar," Amram says, entering the manor house.

"Well, if it isn't big brother. Have you been to your own house yet? Where's Father? I thought you'd be back in town a long time ago."

"We ran into a lot of trouble."

"On your way?"

"No, after we got there. Father was kidnapped by Persian nomads and is being held for ransom."

"No. Not father. He is too strong for that to happen to him."

"We don't know how it happened. They are demanding two hundred thousand denari. It's as though they knew Father was rich enough he could pay the ransom."

"That's a lot of money, even for Father. What are we going to do?" Ithamar asks.

"I am going to the mine tomorrow and get the money. Also, I have to find Noach and Saabhu. Father sent them back here for the money, and they never returned. I didn't hear anything on my way back that anyone was killed in the past year along the highway."

"I don't trust that, Gersshon. I never have. I've had friends like him. They pretend they're your friend while robbing you," Ithamar says.

"Have you seen Saabhu? You normally work with him."

"Actually, I've been spending a lot of time in Ceylon. I'm

learning to dive for pearls. I think I'm going to go into the pearl business. I never was much interested in the mine."

"Well, what is important right now is to get Father freed. First thing in the morning, I am going to the bank to get the money."

"Will they give it to you?"

"Father gave me full authority to speak in his name before I left Persia. He made me full partner in the mine. I have the scroll with me. I'll take it to the bank tomorrow."

Morning comes. Amram leaves his house, goes back over to his father's manor, and puts on his father's best clothes as a sign of his authority. Though he is now taller than his father and most other people he knows, he decides it will look fine on him anyway.

Amram goes to the bank and shows his partnership papers. The banker checks the mine's account.

"It's empty, Master Amram. Someone must have moved it to another bank. I am truly sorry. I need to find out what happened."

"I need to also. I will be back in a few hours. It is imperative that I have the money. My father's life depends on it."

"Zarus? What is going on?"

"I cannot explain right now."

"Good luck out at the mine. That is where you are going now, isn't it?"

"Yes."

Copper Mine, Timna Valley, Arabah Desert, Idumea

"Is that Master Zarus back from Persia?" the miners at the floor of the pit ask each other.

"Looks like him. It's about time. He's been gone forever, it seems."

Amram slides off his father's Arabian and enters the *officium*.

"Where is Gersshon, Yair?"

Yair looks up, and his eyes widen. "I thought that was your father riding up on his Arabian."

"No, Father has been kidnapped by Persian nomads and is being held for ransom. I came back to get the money. It's two hundred thousand denari. It should be in the bank, but isn't."

"I guess he transferred it to another bank before he left," Yair replies, looking down at the floor, and biting the inside of his lower lip.

"No. He specifically told me which bank to go to. He did not move the money. And where are Noach and Saabhu? Father sent them back to get the money, but they never returned. What's going on?"

"Well, uh…"

"They never arrived," Gersshon says, standing in the doorway to the *officium* tent.

"What do you mean, they never arrived? They traveled in reliable and safe caravans. Of course, they arrived."

"I'm just telling you what I know, Amram."

"And another thing: Where is the money in the bank account?"

"Well, I transferred it to a different bank. This one was not providing the service I needed."

"Father never said anything about transferring the money. He told me which bank to go to. It is the same bank he has always used."

"He must have forgotten because I transferred it before he left. Listen, Amram, I need to take you for a little ride. It's not too far. I think I found a new vein of copper. We could start a second open-pit mine. It's right on the desert floor, just like this one was when we first discovered it."

"Don't change the subject, Gersshon. You're not talking to my father now. You're talking to me, and I know you are up to something. Now I need two hundred thousand denari immediately so I can take it back to Persia to free my father."

"What do you mean, free him?"

"As though you don't know. My father is being held by Persian nomads for two hundred thousand denari. Give it to me now. And I mean now! Do you hear me? No more stalling."

Amram's face is red. He holds out a fist and thrusts it in front of Gersshon's eyes.

Gersshon smiles.

"You'll get your money just as soon as we get back. I want to show you that new vein so you can take the good news back to your father. Don't you think he deserves some good news?"

"As soon as we get back, you will get me the money. I am not letting you out of my sight until you do. Is that clear?

"You'll get it. You'll get it."

Gersshon mounts his horse and waits for Amram to slide astride his father's Arabian. The horses' gait is slow, as usual, because of the heat. They ride west until the mine is out of sight.

"It's right over there between those two boulders," Gersshon says.

The two ride over, and Gersshon dismounts.

"Come on. It's right over here."

Amram slides off his father's horse and follows Gersshon.

"Now look down here. You have to look closely to see it. Look closer."

Amram puts his head down, Gersshon picks up a rock, and slams it hard down onto Amram's head. Amram falls to his knees then onto his back. He looks up at Gersshon.

"Why?"

"Because I hate your father. I have always hated him. Now I'm going to take from him a little of what he took from me. And with you, the heir gone, nothing will be in my way."

With that, Gersshon slams the rock again onto Amram. Amram stares straight ahead, whispers, "Mother," and dies.

Sialk, Kashan District, Persia

Peretz sits in the tent with Zarus.

"What is keeping everyone, Peretz?" Zarus asks. Something is wrong. I've got to figure out a new strategy. Noach has been gone a year and a half. Saabhu has been gone a year. And Amram has been gone over six months. They all should be back by now."

Peretz does not say anything.

Zarus' weight continues to go down. His beard is now completely gray. Sometimes his hands tremble.

"Sir, I sneaked in some extra food. You need your strength."

"I've got to figure out a way to pay the ransom myself."

"Do you think you can, sir?"

"Bring me a scroll or clay tablet with stylus so I can send Tirham a message. Can you do that?"

"I'm certain I can, sir. I will bring it to you as soon as I find one."

Zarus waits the rest of the morning. At noon Peretz returns.

"Sir, here is a clay tablet for you."

"Wait for me to write out my offer and take it to Tirham. Stay with him while he reads it. I don't know if he can read Greek. You may have to translate for him."

As Peretz waits, he thinks back on Zarus when he had all three children at home and Devorah skittering around the house, being busy with so many things. What a lovely family, now all in the past.

"Okay, here it is. Take it to Tirham, then return and tell me what he said."

Zarus waits, and while he does, he thinks about the warehouse problem back at the mine. *What's going on?*

Peretz returns with a smile on his face.

"Do you have good news for me?" Zarus asks.

"Yes, Tirham said it was agreeable with him. All he needs is for you to sign a bill of sale on this new clay tablet for twice as much copper ore needed to pay for your ransom and pay him back."

"Good. And when can he pay the ransom?"

"He did not say."

"Regardless, I will be out of here soon, and we can return home."

Zarus etches out the bill of sale on the clay tablet and hands it to Peretz. Peretz leaves, and Zarus prays.

"Jhesus, where are they? Get me home now so I can find them. Especially my son. Especially my son. And would you say hello to Devorah for me?"

Late that afternoon, Peretz returns to the prison tent with Razak.

"Well, I see you made your payment. Very good, Zarus. You are now free to go. It's been fun getting to know you. You understand it was nothing personal. Actually, I kind of like you."

Zarus stands and holds out his hand to Razak. "God bless you."

Razak is taken aback but clasps Zarus hand and smiles. "You're a little strange, but I like you."

He leaves, and Peretz explains what he has arranged.

"There is a caravan leaving in the morning. In three months, we should be home."

AD 44
Copper Mine, Timna Valley, Arabah Desert, Idumea

"I need to go straight to the mine," Zarus tells Peretz. "Help me get there. I have to find out what happened to my son. And to Noach and Saabhu."

"Sir, you are weak."

"I won't be much stronger tomorrow. Help me get there."

The two men ride their camels into the mine complex.

They arrive at the *officium*, their camels kneel, and Peretz helps Zarus off. They notice Yair's chariot next to the tent flap entrance.

"What is Shalva doing hitched to Yair's chariot?" He asks.

The two men enter the tent. Yair drops his pen.

"Master. You're back. I'm so glad you're back. Everything has fallen apart since you left.

"My horse…"

"I wanted to take care of him for you. This was the best way I knew to give him the exercise he needed."

"And, what of my son. Where is Amram, Yair? Where is he? Tell me!"

Tears come to Yair's eyes. He presses his lips together to maintain some control.

"I'm sorry, Master. I'm so very sorry."

"No. No. No! Where is he? Where is Gersshon?"

Zarus lunges out of the tent and yells down into the pit.

"Where is Gersshon?" he bellows. "Tell me where Gersshon is, or you're all fired!"

One of the miners nearby comes running up to Zarus.

"Zarus, sir. We did not recognize you. Gersshon is down on the mine floor. Shall I go get him for you?"

"Yes," Zarus says with all the force he can muster in his weakened condition. "He is to come to me now."

The miner scurries down the haul road into the mine and down to the floor. Zarus stands at the top, alternately looking down at Gersshon and up at the sky. He sees Gersshon look up at him and head up the haul road to the surface.

When Gersshon is within hearing, he breaks into a run. "Oh, Zarus. Something terrible has happened. Zarus, my friend."

By now, Gersshon is in tears. He falls on Zarus' neck and weeps. The two boyhood friends lean on each other and weep for Zarus' child.

"I couldn't get control of them. The thugs who were stealing out of the warehouse must have felt threatened when Noach came back. Someone stabbed him. We delivered his body to his family and had a nice funeral. The next day was dedicated to the memory of Noach."

"And what happened to Saabhu? Was he stabbed too?"

"We don't know. He never arrived. He just disappeared."

Zarus does not want to ask the next question. He does not want to hear the answer. But he must know. He must ask it. He takes a deep breath, bites the inside of his lower lips, then says it half in a whisper and half in a groan.

"What about my son? Where is Amram?"

Gersshon's eyes well up with tears once again. He looks at

Zarus, then up at the sky, then toward the *officium*.

"He's gone."

"Gone how?" Zarus demands. "Tell me, Gersshon!"

"He insisted on going out into the desert to see if he could find a new vein of copper so he could have his own mine. I warned him not to go so far out alone, but he insisted. We looked for him for days and never found him. All we found was your Arabian and his cloak full of blood. That is all that was left of him. We brought the Arabian back.

"I am so sorry, Zarus. He was such a fine young man. He was so much like you. You were so lucky to have a son like him."

Gersshon once again falls on Zarus' neck, and the two men weep openly. Some of the miners stare, though many do not out of embarrassment for their bosses.

Gersshon breaks away, puts his arm on Zarus' shoulder, and guides him toward the *officium*.

"Why don't you take some time off? Let me take care of business while you mourn and take care of any legalities you must see to."

Zarus does not answer.

"Come, friend. Your mind is overloaded with sorrow."

———

Zarus returns home on his Arabian, which Peretz had unhitched for him. They ride at a slow pace together. Peretz rides one of the camels and leads the other to drop off at the place where they had rented them over two years earlier.

Now at his gate, Zarus slides off his horse, and Leib comes out to take care of it.

"Master. You're home. But home to such sadness. Ithamar will be glad to see you. You can comfort each other."

Penina hears voices and opens the front gate. She looks at Zarus and falls into his arms.

"Oh, my master. What has happened to this family? Such sorrow. Poor Devorah. Then Ithamar for a little while. And now, Amram. Oh, my master."

Zarus returns old Penina's embrace. A few moments later, they break away from each other, both in tears.

"Is Ithamar here?"

"No, but he should be home shortly."

"I want to go to the cemetery."

"Only Devorah is there, Master."

"I know. But I need to talk to her."

Zarus turns and goes back out the gate. "Leib, if you have not unhitched Shalva, I'd like to take him to the cemetery."

"He's pretty tired, sir. Would you like to take the Egyptian? Khemoh could take you."

"Devorah's horse would be fine," Zarus whispers.

She is brought out, and Zarus easily slides up to mount her.

Slowly he rides her through town to the cemetery. Once there, he goes to her grave.

"Devorah, our son is gone. Oh, why did I have to take him with me? He was too young. I'm so sorry I didn't take better care of him, my pearl. I have let you down. I have let everyone down."

Zarus sits on the ground at the foot of the crypt. He looks down and sobs. "How am I going to keep on living? I have lost you, and now I have lost Amram."

He says nothing for a while. Then, "Yes, I still have our Ithamar. I must live for him. He is so much like you. He has your black hair and eyes and even your nose. He is doing better now, you know. He is twenty-seven years old. You should see him. He has become so strong. But he still has your sense of adventure. And he loves people, even strangers, just like you always did. You would be so proud of him, my love."

The sun begins to go down. "You know, I need to have a crypt made for Amram right here next to you. No one knows what happened to his body, but we can pretend he is here.

"Be sure and tell him for me, won't you? Tell Amram I love him. I love you too, my dear. I always have. How lucky I was to meet you and for your father to give his consent for you to marry a lowly Samaritan. I liked your father, you know. Your mother too.

"By the way, I brought your Khemoh to see you. She's been well taken care of. I wonder what I should do with her. Maybe I'll give her to Ithamar. He would like that. If not, I could give her to Estar. She always admired your horse. The two of you were good friends, weren't you?

"Well, love of my life, I must go. But I will be back tomorrow, and we will talk again."

Zarus stands. It is nearly dark. He takes the reins of delicate Khemoh, and together they walk toward home.

"Ithamar. Will he be there? I hope so."

"The tenants seized his servants; they beat one, killed another, and stoned a third.

[Then he sent other servants to them, more than the first time, and the tenants treated them the same way.]

Last of all, he sent his son to them. 'They will respect my son,' he said.

"But when the tenants saw the son, they said to each other, 'This is the heir. Come, let's kill him and take his inheritance.'

So they took him and threw him out of the vineyard and killed him. (Matthew 21:35-39)

36 ~ THE PEARL

AD 45
Eilat, Port City on Red Sea, Arabah Desert, Idumea

"Father," Ithamar says one evening while they sit together on the roof of the manor, "I have decided to go into the pearl business."

Zarus does not respond right away. He looks up at the sky, down at his feet, and finally at his son.

"Didn't you get adventure out of your system when you went to China?"

"You know, Father, that while you were in Persia, I went to Ceylon at the tip of India to learn pearl diving and who to sell them to."

"Yes, I forgot about that."

"I am ready to go into the business."

"Did you bring any pearls back with you?"

"Well, I did find one. That may not sound like much to you, but we have to dive and collect a full amphora of clams from the bottom of the sea in order to find three or four pearls. That's a lot of deep dives. Your average ship holds twenty amphoras."

"My pearl was valuable, but small. I used it to buy passage back home from India and a chariot.

"You bought what? Why did you buy a chariot?"

"I thought you saw it in the stables."

"I never go in there anymore."

"The reason I bought the chariot is because of all Mother's stories about her father being a chariot racer. I've been taking lessons."

"So, basically, your pearl is gone."

"Basically, yes."

"So how are you going to start a pearl business with no pearls?"

"I saw one down at the docks. The man with it said he would hold it for me."

"So, how much does he want for it?"

"Seven million denari."

"That's impossible. Find yourself another trade if you don't like mining, but one that is within reach."

Penina comes up the steps to the roof with a pitcher of apple juice and a few bites of cheese.

"I thought you could use a little refreshment," she says.

"Penina, you shouldn't be climbing the stairs with a load like that," Zarus admonishes.

"I'll have you know I am eighty years old, not dead."

The men both smile.

"Thank you, Penina. You are very thoughtful. Now take the rest of the evening off. If we want something, we'll get it ourselves."

"Yes, Master."

"Well, Father, I have worked out a way I think I can buy it."

"Even if you could, what good is one pearl?"

"Father, I know you've been gone a long time, but surely you know pearls are the most valuable gem in the world now. Did you know that, whenever the wives of statesmen give state banquets, they don pearls, not diamonds or emeralds? Caesar decorates his horse with a necklace of pearls, and his slippers are full of pearls? The interior of the temple of Venus is decorated with pearls? Even the rich will give a year's wages for one pearl."

"Okay, I know one pearl is worth more than you have. So, how are you going to get that pearl you have your eye on?"

"Well, Father, I don't want to sound crass, but Amram is gone. If you would give me his house and furniture, I could sell it and buy the pearl."

"That's way more than the value of your mother's pearls."

"That was a long time ago. The value has jumped up over a thousand times more than they were when you were my age."

Zarus walks over to the table and refills his goblet. *He may be right. I bought my field in the desert for one hundred thousand denari. I guess the same undeveloped field would sell for one million denari today.*

He looks out over the street below, then up at the sky. *Devorah, what would you do?*

Ithamar sits quietly, watching his father. His father looks over at him, Ithamar says as meekly as he knows how, "Please," and his father looks away again.

Zarus sits on a bench at the far side of the rooftop and looks at his feet. He stands and walks back to the edge, then over to his chair next to his son.

"I've been wondering what to do with his house. Your brother did love you, you know. I think, well, I think he'd like for you to have it."

"Thank you, Father," Ithamar says, jumping up. "You'll never regret it."

With that, he jumps down the stairs. He calls up to his father, "Going to bed early. Gotta get an early start in the morning looking for a buyer."

Zarus remains where he is. Alone again. Solitude again. *I used to like the quiet here at home after the noise of the mine all day. But, Devorah, now it's too quiet. Ithamar is going to go away again. He's loud, but he's all I have left.* "Jhesus, don't let him go away from me."

———

"You will notice, the marble columns surrounding the courtyard. Also, the colorful tiles on the floor portraying the finest designs from India."

"They are very nice, but I wanted sailing ships portrayed on the floor. These are just geometrics."

"Well, our religion forbids making images of anything, lest people begin to worship them. You know how it is."

"Too bad. I liked the house otherwise. Maybe you will find someone else."

Ithamar smiles but does not want to. His prospective customer leaves, and Ithamar follows him out the gate. He goes to visit a friend.

"Do you know of anyone wanting to buy a nice house?"

"Whose house? Your father's?"

"No, my brother, Amram's. Father gave it to me."

"He didn't give it to you so you could turn right around and sell it."

"Actually, that's what he did. I am selling it with his blessing."

"Well, maybe I'd be interested. I've been in the house before. How much do you want for it?"

"Seven million denari."

"No, I couldn't go that high. I would give you five million, but that's as high as I can go."

"Sorry, friend," Ithamar says. "I have to have seven. If you hear of anyone else wanting one of the best houses in the city, let me know."

"Of course."

Ithamar leaves his friend's house and goes over to the city square to sit and think He spots an empty concrete bench, so he doesn't have to squat in his good clothes. He is wearing a white tunic with blue kerchief on his head to keep the hot sun off.

Who else can I find? I know. I'll go over to the forum and see if one of the city magistrates or other officer would like to buy it. It would give them status.

"Sir, might you be interested in buying a splendid manor that is befitting your station in life?"

"What did you say, young man?"

The gray-haired magistrate stares at Ithamar with curiosity in his eyes.

"I have the perfect house for you that would make you the envy of all your colleagues."

The magistrate stares at Ithamar longer but says nothing. Ithamar waits.

"Is it here in the city?"

"It is not only here, but it is in the best part of the city on a hill."

"I tell you what. I will talk to my wife about it, and if she is interested, we will be at the house first thing tomorrow for you to show us around. How do I find it?"

"It's on Banner Street. Just go to the highest hill in town and walk or ride on it until you are three-fourths of the way up to the top. It has unique engraved copper gates on it. You can't miss it."

"Don't count on us. There is only a slight chance my wife will be interested. She doesn't like change."

"Yes, sir. Tell her she will be able to throw the most amazing banquets at her new home, and everyone will be talking about them."

Ithamar turns back toward home. He has walked into the city rather than bring a horse. To him, horses in the city are like pigs among pearls.

Lacking anything else to do the rest of the day, Ithamar stops by the homes of a few friends and invites them to Amram's manor to gamble. He stops at the market to pick up a few refreshments.

That night sleep does not come for very long at a time in Amram's bed. Ithamar prays that God will help him sell the house for the full price he needs to buy the exceptionally large and beautiful pearl he wants. "And God, I'm sorry I was so mean to Amram all those times. I was just jealous of him. Would you tell him for me?"

Morning, and he dons one of Amram's finest tunics—one of the short ones since Amram was a handspan taller than him. He also puts on a gold chain that had belonged to Amram and a matching armband.

Since there are no servants here, when someone knocks at the gate, he answers it himself.

"Is this the house for sale? My wife said she would like to look at it if it is all you say it is."

"Yes, come in, sir. Come in, madam. Look at whatever you like."

This time, Ithamar decides to remain silent and let them look around on their own. He stays nearby in case they have questions. They do not.

After viewing all the rooms, the roof, and the garden, the magistrate makes an offer. "I'll give you four million for it."

"I have to have seven million."

"Young man, just because you have to have seven million denari for whatever it is you want to buy, it doesn't mean we are going to donate three million more than the house is worth."

Ithamar is taken aback. *I never thought of it like that.* "Would you give six million for it?"

"I might give you four and a half, but that is the most I will give."

Ithamar thinks. *What would my father do?* The magistrate gives him time.

"Okay. I will take four and a half million."

"And that includes the furnishings," the magistrate adds.

"Agreed," Ithamar responds.

"I will have a deed drawn up, and you can sign it tomorrow." The two men shake hands, and the magistrate leaves.

Ithamar seats himself in the courtyard. *Where am I going to come up with the last two and a half million denari?*

He walks around the house. He looks in each room. *I have already sold all the furnishings. All that is left is what Amram wore.*

Ithamar looks in each of Amram's coffers. *Jewelry. That's it. He's got gold, silver, and copper jewelry, some with semi-precious stones in them. I should be able to get the last two and a half million from them.*

Ithamar sets up a booth at the market in the jewelry and precious stones section. His brother's taste is popular. He sells out by the end of the day but has only earned another quarter million.

He goes to his father's house and to his room.

"Hello, Father. How have you been doing?"

"Fine, Son. I've been doing fine. Did you come to have dinner with me?"

"No, I won't be long. I just need all my jewelry."

Soon, Ithamar is out the gate, leaving his father alone.

That day he manages to sell all his jewelry for the same amount he got for his brother's the day before.

He returns to his father's manor that evening.

"Sir, can we talk?"

"Certainly, Son. What would you like to talk about?"

"Well, that big pearl."

"Have you raised your seven million denari yet?" Zarus says, walking out to the garden and to Devorah's bench.

Ithamar follows him and sits on a nearby bench.

"Father, uh, well, you have two pearls. They're not big or anything, but I'll bet I could sell them for the balance of what I am short."

"How short are you?" Zarus asks, sighing.

"Two million denari. I'm sure I could get two million for that pearl of Mother's, and the one Lucianus gave you for Lleah's hand."

Zarus squints his eyes at his son. *He wants to take the last thing of value I have of Devorah's?*

"I don't think so."

"Well, if not that one, what about Lleah's? She's my sister and would want me to have it if it helped me."

Zarus stands, walks around to where the four smaller seats are facing each other elsewhere in the garden. He sits on one but says nothing.

Ithamar knows his father's habits whenever he ponders and waits.

Finally, Zarus returns to where his son is seated in the garden.

"You can have Lleah's, but not your mother's. And that's it. I have nothing else to give you. I've mortgaged my house for you. I have nothing else."

Ithamar does not mention the Arabian and Egyptian out in the stable.

"Thank you, sir. You won't regret it."

He waits while his father slowly climbs the stairs to the second floor, goes into his bedroom, closes the door, finally opens it again, and brings down a small coffer.

"Here is your sister's pearl." It brought happiness to her. May it bring happiness to you. And may we be able to see her again someday soon."

Ithamar does not want to be rude, so he stays seated, though he wants to rush out in the street, down to the market, and sell it.

After a decent amount of time, he rises, gives his father a bear hug, and leaves.

That afternoon, he sells the pearl for one million denari.

I have six million now. Where will I get the last million? If I don't get it all, I cannot buy the pearl.

He returns to his father's manor. "I'm not here to ask for anything, Father. So don't worry. I just need to think."

They go up on the roof. Though Zarus prefers the garden, Ithamar likes to look out over the city and see the ships down at the docks.

"Father, I am one million denari short. What am I going to do? I just have to have that rare pearl to start my new business and have a good reputation for quality."

"Perhaps you need to sell you instead of a thing."

"You mean how you sold yourself to be a slave in the mine for four years? No, thanks."

"You wouldn't have to sell your freedom. What are things you know how to do well?"

"I'm a good talker."

"That you are, Son," Zarus says, laughing. "You could talk an archer out of his last arrows. What else are you good at?"

"I can dive for pearls, though not very well yet. I don't think I could find another pearl of the size and quality that ship captain has."

"He may wait for you to come up with the money, but not that long. So what else? What else can you do?"

They sit in silence.

A new thought comes to Zarus' mind. "Didn't you say you have a chariot now and have learned to race it?"

"Yes, but not enough to enter a race against other drivers."

"You take after your mother, and your mother took after her father. They were both adventurous like you. They also took chances. After all, she took a chance on me, a Samaritan."

"Are you saying, Father, I should enter a race to win my last million denari?"

"It's up to you. Are you willing to risk it all for one pearl, as fine as it is? Are you willing to lose it all and have to start all over again with nothing and a father with nothing left to give you?"

"I don't know, Father."

"Ithamar, you've been asking people to take chances on you all your life. Are you willing to take a chance on yourself?"

"Do you think I'm that good?"

"I have no idea how good you are. That's up to you to judge for yourself. Why don't you go down to the circus tomorrow and find out when the next races are, and who has entered them? Then it will be your decision. All or nothing."

"Can I spend the night here in my old room, Father?"

Zarus smiles. "Indeed you may, and I'll ask Penina to fix your favorite breakfast." Zarus' eyes sparkle with delight.

After Ithamar retires for the night, Zarus goes back to the garden and sits on Devorah's bench. *Sweetheart, he wants to be a merchant. He can't make anything worth selling, so he'll have to travel to get what he wants to sell. I'm afraid we are losing him like we lost Lleah. I wonder where Lleah is right now.*

The next morning, Ithamar comes downstairs refreshed and humming.

"So you've found a solution, huh?"

"I'm just not good enough at chariot racing. What I am good at is diving. I'm going to go down to the docks and see if I can find a rich and reckless sea captain willing to wager I can dive ten man-lengths and bring up whatever he ties to the bottom of a chain."

"Are you sure, Son? That sounds very dangerous."

"It is if you don't know what you are doing. I've developed my lungs and know how to control them. Would you like to go along?"

"Indeed, I would. The mine will have to wait."

"Breakfast will too. Can't eat and dive."

The two men ride their horses—father on his Arabian, son on his mother's Egyptian—down to the docks.

Zarus sits on a bench near a warehouse and waits while Ithamar makes the rounds of the shops and taverns. As he watches his son, he tries to etch into his memory his mannerisms—his swagger when he walks, the way he tilts his head when he talks to strangers, the way he is always picking lint off his clothes, the way he bites the inside of his cheek when he thinks deeply.

After a while, Ithamar returns to his father. He is smiling. "I found someone willing to bet one million denari that I cannot dive twenty man-lengths, get what's on the bottom of a chain, and return to the surface.

"Father, this is Phoenix. Phoenix, this is my father, Zarus. Now, Phoenix, I have my million denari on me, and you can see I am handing it to my father. You do the same."

"No, I brought my first mate over. He will hold my million denari. Now, give me a few moments to get a chain in the water with something on the end that you can take off. How would a wool cloth tied to it work for you, Master Ithamar?"

"That sounds fair. Now, while you're doing that, I have some breathing exercises I need to do."

The four men walk toward the water.

"Are you sure this is what you want to do, Ithamar?" Zarus asks. "It sounds very dangerous."

"Not any more dangerous than a chariot that could turn over on me and kill me. This is safe. I've done it many times."

Soon the ship captain comes back with the chain and piece of wool fabric tied securely around it. The chain is lowered.

Ithamar no longer looks at anyone around him. He looks into the water as though it is beckoning him to it. He takes several more deep breaths, then plunges into the blackness.

Deeper and deeper, he goes. Holding his breath, legs kicking steadily, arms waving and thrashing, back and forth.

The water beckons Ithamar deeper and deeper into the unknown. No more sun, no more heat, no more sand, and people and laughter and tears. No more of life on earth or the sky above. Deeper now. Streaming through a liquid nothingness that challenges and wants to swallow. Down farther. Into the jaws of an awaiting liquid mass. Farther, deeper. Mysterious. Another world that wants to keep whatever enters it. A world flowing and yawning and searching for intruders. Deeper. Deeper.

Ithamar becomes lightheaded. But he knows he is almost there. Indeed, as he stretches his arms ahead of him, and feels now for the end of the chain, he finds it.

He turns and struggles to untie the wool cloth. It will not budge. He struggles still. Get it untied. But it does not untie. He pulls out a knife he uses in case he is attacked by an unwanted species underwater, or gets tangled in anything, and cuts the cloth loose.

Up on the dock, the captain, the first mate, and Zarus look into the black water, watching for signs of the young man. Time passes. Zarus' heart speeds up. *I shouldn't have let him do this. Ithamar, come back to me. The pearl isn't worth it. Just come back to me alive.*

Down in the blackness, the young man puts the wool in a bag tied around his waist that he had used to collect clams at the bottom of the Gulf of Manaar.

Now, with his arms above his head and legs almost straight,

he kicks and makes his way to the surface. Not too fast. Relax. The air will come later. Easy. Stay calm. Soothe the lungs for what it craves and will have shortly. Steadily gliding out of the abyss. Slipping from the clutches of a watery womb yet one more time.

Time now for rebirth. He looks up and sees light. Light is close. Air is close. A new life is close. A little closer. And closer. Nearly there. Don't breathe yet. It will come. Near to the world he had left behind. Near to his fortune and his pearl. His pearl of great price.

His hands break through the surface first. Then his head and torso. He breathes. Deeply. Evenly. Steadily. Ithamar looks up at his father, and their smiles touch.

Zarus stoops to help his son out of the water. Both men face the captain.

"Well, did you get it or not? You didn't, did you? I knew you couldn't do it."

Ithamar opens up his bag and pulls out the wool cloth. "It was tied on pretty tight, but I got it loose. Here is your wool. Now, may I have my million denari?"

Captain Phoenix frowns, then smiles. "Hey, how would you like to sail with me? I'll take bets on you in every port we go to."

"Sorry, I have other plans," Ithamar says. "But if I ever run into you in my travels, sure. I'd be happy to help you out. Well, for half the take."

"It's a deal. I'll be looking out for you."

The men part company. Zarus, still holding on to the reins of their horses, gives a little boost for his son to get back on the Egyptian. He looks up at Ithamar.

"I'm proud of you, Son."

They arrive home, and Penina still has breakfast out for them.

"Thanks, Penina. I appreciate it," says Ithamar. "But I need to rest just a little. Then I shall make that breakfast of yours disappear so fast, you will wonder what happened." He leans down and kisses her on the cheek.

Father and son sit in the courtyard.

"Now what, Ithamar?"

"As soon as we eat, I will go back down to the docks and pay for the pearl."

"I shall go with you."

"I still have the chariot. I will sell it for my passage. Then I will sell the pearl in Rome where I can get the best price for it. With that, I will probably go back to Ceylon, where I will do a little diving. But, since I'm not a professional, I will pay the best guys in the world to dive for me. I should be able to come away from there with hopefully twenty pearls. Then my pearl business will be off and running."

"When do you plan to leave?" Zarus asks.

"I hope tomorrow."

"But the weather is bad on the open sea this time of year. Don't you want to wait?"

———

Ithamar boards the ship *Ursus* the next day with his pearl. Zarus embraces his son as though for the last time.

The ship slides down to the southern tip of the Arabian Peninsula, then up to Egypt. There, it connects with a canal to the Nile River. It works its way up to Alexandria, then out into the Great Sea, and on its way to Rome.

There is a storm. It is fierce. It rocks the ship, its cargo, and passengers. It begins to break apart. The sailors struggle to save it. They throw cargo overboard in vain. They throw straps under the hull in vain. They cry out to their gods in vain.

Ithamar cries out to Jhesus to save his soul. The mast he is clinging to breaks, a large wave slams up to him, grabs him, and drags him off what little is left of the ship *Ursus*. Ithamar and his pearl of great price go to the bottom of the sea.

"Again, the kingdom of heaven is like a merchant looking for fine pearls.

When he found one of great value, he went away and sold everything he had and bought it. (Matthew 13:45-46)

37 ~ DREAMING

AD 46
Eilat, Port City on Red Sea, Arabah Desert, Idumea

It has been a year, and still, Zarus has not heard from Ithamar. Every morning he goes down to the docks and inquires about the *Ursus.* No one ever knows.

Then one day, someone does know. "I heard it went down and sank in the Great Sea about a year ago."

"Are you sure?" Zarus asks.

"Almost sure. I haven't seen the *Ursus* around in a long time."

Not again. Both sons. My wife. This cannot be. Please, God, turn back the years and let me start over again. Oh, Ithamar. Ithamar. My son. Now all I have left is Lleah. She's been gone so long. Can I at least have Lleah back, God?

The old sailor turns to leave.

"What about the *Celox.* Do you ever hear anything about the *Celox*? It used to go to Britannia all the time, but I heard it goes to China now."

"So the *Celox* is still plying the seas. It's an old ship."

Zarus takes out a silver coin and gives it to the sailor.

He remounts his Arabian and wends his way up the hill away from the Red Sea that has been both his friend and his enemy. How can it be both? But it is. Just like people can be.

Is Lleah still on it sailing around the world with her husband? Is Livianus good to her? Does she know about her brothers? Lleah is all I have left in the world, and I do not know where she is.

Zarus draws close to his manor and changes his mind. He directs his horse in another direction.

How can this be? Just a few short years ago, there were five of us happily living together in my house. Now I rattle around in it alone. What has my life been for?

Zarus rides to the cemetery. He slides off his Arabian and squats at the foot of Devorah's crypt. Next to her on one side is a crypt for Amram, though his body was never found.

"Sweetheart," he says. "We've lost Ithamar now. The impossible has happened. How can I lose you and our sons both? Devorah, I am growing tired. I am sixty years old now. I am so tired. If only God would call me home to you and our sons. I am ready to go. How I miss you all. How I long to hold you in my arms.

"Did I tell you your Miss Khemoh had a colt a few months ago? She is beautiful. I sold her to a family with a little girl. Well, I guess she's not a girl anymore. She's sixteen, the same age you were when you were betrothed to me. The happiest day of my life. Well, up to then. Our wedding day was even happier. We were lucky, weren't we?

"I guess, even though he won't really be there, I need to get a crypt made for Ithamar. I will put him next to Amram. The place next to you is reserved for me."

"If you see Ithamar, tell him I am proud of him. Amram already knew it. I didn't tell Ithamar enough.

"Goodbye, for now, my love."

Zarus remounts his horse heads out of the cemetery, out of the city, into the desert, and toward the mine.

It's time I go back to work. I need to stay busy with the mine. It was a mistake to take time off after Amram died. Things have not been the same since then. I can't quite figure it out.

Copper Mine, Timna Valley, Arabah Desert

Zarus arrives at the *officium* tent and does not see Yair's chariot. He finds it curious. He notices the flap covering the entrance is down. *What's going on?* He turns toward the pit, walks over to the edge and looks down. Everyone is busy at their jobs as usual. He walks back over to the *officium* tent and enters.

He stops abruptly. "What?"

In baskets scattered around the floor are all of Zarus' belongings: The extra outfit of clean clothes in case they have an important visitor; his scrolls with notes on them about mining accidents; his scrolls from ship captains; his supply of blank clay tablets along with several styluses; an extra pair of sandals in case the strap on his breaks in all the walking over rocks; even his cushion he sits on at his work table.

Zarus stares, looks around the tent, then at the work table. He is stunned. Gersshon has moved his own things onto it.

"No! I will not allow it. Where is he? Gersshon!"

Maybe it wasn't Gersshon. Stop. Think. Maybe it's a prank. Whoever played such a prank is guilty of subordination and will be fired.

Zarus rushes out of the tent. "Gersshon!" No answer. His heart is pounding.

He finds Yuval, the new mine engineer. He does not know where Gersshon is. He finds Uziel, the new mine superintendent. Neither does he know where Gersshon is.

Zarus slides up onto his Arabian and checks the far reaches of the mine, including the warehouses. "Gersshon, where are you?" he continues to bellow.

His face red with exertion and fury. With a jerk of the reins, he heads toward the city.

Eilat, Port City on Red Sea, Arabah Desert

Zarus goes to Gersshon's house and pounds on the gate. A servant answers it. "I need to see Gersshon right away."

"He's not here, sir."

"Gersshon!" Zarus shouts into the courtyard. "You'd better not be here because I'll find you where ever you are!" He glares at the servant and leaves.

He remounts his horse and heads toward the three taverns that are Gersshon's favorites. He finds his partner in the second one. He stomps heavily up to Gersshon's table and pounds on it.

"Okay, Gersshon, what's going on?"

"Hey, don't disturb my friends. We're celebrating."

The veins bulge on Zarus' forehead and neck. Steel gray hair is down in his eyes, he glares at his partner as though hurling knives at him. "Outside, Gersshon. Now."

Gersshon laughs toward his friends, takes another drink, and does not move from his place. "Ha, ha, ha."

Zarus grabs him by the front of his tunic and pulls him up out of his chair. He pushes him toward the exit. "I said outside."

Gersshon laughs. "Ha, ha, ha."

They stumble through the gate as though they are drunk

friends. They're not.

Zarus pushes Gersshon up against the wall. Gersshon laughs even louder.

"Ha, ha, ha."

Pedestrians stretch to see what is going on.

Zarus takes hold of the reins of his horse with one hand and pushes laughing Gersshon down the street with his other. He takes a rope off his horse's neck and throws it over Gersshon, pinning his arms to his side. He leaps up onto his horse and pulls his partner toward the edge of town.

"Hey, don't be so mad. It's your own fault," Gersshon calls up to Zarus, still laughing deliriously. "Ha, ha, ha."

They go through the city gate and a little way into the desert. Zarus climbs down off his horse, lets go of the rope, and attacks his boyhood friend with his fists.

Gersshon, no longer laughing, grits his teeth, slides out of the rope, and hits Zarus in the stomach.

The men get into a clinch, Zarus pulls free and hits Gersshon on the jaw. Gersshon returns the punch with one in Zarus' eye.

They clinch again and this time fall to the floor of the desert.

Passersby come closer to watch.

"Aren't they the richest men in town? What's going on?"

The two get to their knees. Gersshon grabs Zarus around the throat and squeezes. Zarus, the taller, pushes Gersshon's arms away, stands, and kicks him in the chest.

Zarus gets the better of Gersshon and throws him onto his back, then lands on him with his knees, pinning Gersshon's hands and arms to the ground.

"You're going to tell me what is going on," Zarus shouts between labored breaths.

"Well, if you'll let me up and quit beating on me, I'll be more than happy to tell you, ole boy."

Zarus cautiously lets Gersshon up as he catches his breath. Gersshon wipes dirt off his tunic.

"Okay," Gersshon says. "You forfeited your half of the business."

"Absolutely not! Now tell me what is going on."

"I just did, ole pal. Remember the contract we signed at the beginning?"

Zarus does not reply.

"Well, it says that, if either partner is gone more than two years without any messages, he will be assumed dead. Therefore, the surviving partner becomes sole owner."

Zarus squints his eyes, sets his jaw, and clenches his teeth.

"There is no such statement in our contract."

"Why don't you go back to the mine and check it yourself. I left you my extra copy in one of those baskets of your stuff. I dare you. Go back and look."

Acid rises to Zarus mouth. He grinds his teeth. He lowers his brows and glares at his old friend. He leaps up onto his Arabian and heads to the mine.

Copper Mine, Timna Valley, Arabah Desert

When Zarus arrives, he notices some of the men at the top of the pit looking in his direction and talking to each other.

He goes into the *officium*, looks through his stuff on the camel-skin floor, throwing everything aside but the scrolls. With shaking hands, he opens each scroll, then throws it aside.

He spots the contract. He scrolls through it, scanning. Then he sees it. Gersshon has underlined it. It reads as he had said.

Zarus rolls all the way through the scroll until he gets to the signatures. The signatures are correct: The way Zarus signed his name and Gersshon signed his so long ago in their youth.

He sits now, the scroll in his lap. He rocks back and forth, sometimes pounding the leather floor with a fist.

"No!"

Gersshon arrives, enters the *officium* tent, and leans against a pole, arms folded and grinning.

"You cannot stay in your house, you know, ole pal. I paid off your mortgage. It is now my house. But I am not completely ruthless. You can stay in the stable."

"You scoundrel. You planned the whole thing. It was you who hired those Persian nomads to kidnap me. All those trips you made to Persia, you would know who to hire."

"You can't prove it. It's just guesswork. You'll never be able to prove it."

"But why?"

"Simple. Because I have always hated you."

"What?"

"You always thought you were better than me, so I went along for the ride. But things did not always turn out right.

"Back when we were working on the road together, you're the

one who got Devorah. Then, later, when I fell in love with your sister, Estar, you made sure she didn't marry me. Having her husband killed on the road to Jhericho did me no good. She just married someone else. You built that fancy house and had a family. Of course, without Estar, I had no family. She should have cooperated and loved me.

"When Baaruch's mine shaft collapsed, you're the one who bossed everyone around. I was as smart as you. Then you tried to humiliate me for eating rat to survive."

"The slaves. Is it true what Amram said, that you were using slaves?"

"Not all of them, but at the beginning they were. How else were we supposed to have a crew of miners?"

"You had to buy them. How did you manage that?"

"I sold stock in our company…"

"But we didn't have any stock."

"Exactly. By the time the slavers discovered the 'mistake' we had enough copper, I could pay them with that."

"You hedged on the price? You told me you sold our copper for one price, but it was really for more?"

"That's right, old pal. And you were so dumb, you never noticed it."

"So, you killed Amram."

"Had to be done. He had discovered too much. Besides, after getting rid of Saabhu and Noach, it was only logical. I eliminated all my competition. I knew Ithamar wasn't interested in the mine, so it got down to just you and me."

"How did you get the contract changed?"

"Oh, I didn't. It really was a part of our contract. Good thing. I didn't remember it myself. Just happened to be re-reading it just before I convinced you to go to Persia. I sent a man on ahead of you to arrange for your kidnapping. Nice touch, wasn't it?"

Silence.

Both of them know Zarus cannot prove any of it before a magistrate.

"How could you? We've been friends since we were boys."

"Well, you must admit we had our good times. So it wasn't all for naught."

"How could you pretend for so long?"

"After a while, you get used to it. Besides, you were always so naïve. So trusting. You were easy to fool. Now about your house: Did I tell you that I'll let you stay in the stable? I'm not completely heartless. Oh, and if you plan to go to your sister, she seems to have disappeared. Poor dear. She was very beautiful at one time. She should have chosen me.

"I'm going to go back to the tavern now, and resume my celebration."

Zarus sits on the floor, stunned. Hoping he will wake up, but knowing he never will. He hears Gersshon leave and walks out of the *officium*.

The miners have all come up from the pit and are standing at the top, lined up in rows. He looks over at them. They know. A few at first, but then all of them raise their dirty, scratched, calloused hands and salute Zarus.

He stands still and salutes them back. Then he walks over to them and passes each man, looking them in the eye and shaking their hand or putting his hands on their shoulder.

Nearly five hundred of them. Steadily, he walks. The men stand in place, not willing to leave until everyone has had a chance to give their Zarus their final wish for him.

"You were always a good boss," one tells him, "considering you are a Samaritan."

Zarus smiles. "That's a fine compliment."

"Would you like us to sabotage the mine? A bunch of us know how."

"No. It would cut off the supply for copper needed in other parts of the world. We do not punish them for our problem."

"Would you like us to take care of him when he gets back? He could disappear just like your son did."

"No. Jhesus said to love your enemies."

"Zarus, sir. You are the finest man I have ever known. I even named my son after you. A lot of us did."

An hour later, Zarus walks away from his men and into the *officium* tent, looks through the things Gersshon packed for him, and takes them all outside. Uziel, the new superintendent, and Yuval, the new engineer, are standing nearby.

"You can have these things," Zarus says quietly as his world falls apart. "And see if you can get my wife's Egyptian horse in my stable. Give her to Yair."

"What about those charts Amram made one time?"

"They won't bring him back to me."

Still in his dream, Zarus walks away from the *officium*, takes one last look at the mine pit and the warehouses in the back of the operation, climbs on his Arabian, and rides away.

Eilat, Port City on Red Sea, Arabah Desert

Back in the city, Zarus rides to the cemetery.

"Sweetheart," he says, kneeling at Devorah's crypt, "I've got to go away. I've got to start over somewhere."

He chokes out his words, then remembers he must be brave for his beloved.

"You may think I'm too old to start over, and maybe I am. But Jhesus will be with me."

He falls quiet again as he remembers back to the beginning. "Things were impossible when we first started out, you know." He pauses. "But they became possible after all."

He looks over at Amram's and Ithamar's crypts, then back at Devorah's. "You've been gone ten years now, my beloved. A lot has happened. I've lost both our sons. Losing the mine, well, I'll figure out something. But losing your pearl that I thought was safe in the house... And losing my family...

"Oh, my beloved. My life was wrapped up in you. You were my everything. You still are and always will be."

Zarus' eyes are red. His gray hair is matted from the fistfight. His clothes are torn. They will tear more.

"Goodbye, my love. Goodbye, my sons. I promise to stay close to Jhesus, and we will see each other again someday. I keep my promises. Some day. Some day."

Zarus stands, leads Master Shalva out of the cemetery, slides up onto his Arabian, and goes out through the city gate.

He does not look back. There is nothing left to see. Only that which is important exists any more, and that is being protected within his heart.

He rides slowly north through the desert. As always, the sun is hot. As always, he will have to pace himself. As always, he will have to keep close watch for oases. Everything else is so dry. Dry like Zarus' out-of-control life. *What is life for anyway?*

At his first stop, he lets his horse drink first. Shalva has done all the work. He fills his water skin and looks around at the other travelers, some laughing among themselves, some in small caravans.

Back on Shalva, as protective and as much of a friend as his grandfather, the original Shalva, he takes his master farther north, a little at a time out of the desert and into the cooler hills.

Jherusalem. Jherusalem the holy. Zarus thinks about visiting the temple. But his clothes are in too bad shape; he would not be admitted at the gate. Besides, Jhesus had said no one needs to worship in Jherusalem any more, for worship will be in spirit and in truth.

What is truth? he wonders. *Is it my truth? Gersshon's truth? It must be Jhesus' truth. How can we rely on ourselves to determine truth?*

On to Jhericho. Slow. Steady. In a dream world. A world of nightmares and everything collapsing in on itself. Zarus remembers his mother-in-law, Avigail, and her uncle, the Priest Caalev, both long gone. He wonders if Caalev ever got on the Sanhedrin as he had longed and worked for most of his life.

Avigail. So much like her son. Zarus cringes when he remembers that agonizing trip Benyamin took him on, prodding him with a rope all the way from Samaria to Baaruch's mine at the bottom of the desert.

And the four years that followed. Beaten. Hungry. Worked beyond endurance. *But I lived through it. I won my Devorah. To see her once more, can I do it again?* On he goes, plodding, trudging, heaving through his dream.

Now past the Dead Sea. The sea with no more life in it than what is in Zarus' present and his future. Only what is in his heart lives on, despite the challenges of death.

Now the Jordan River. The river of baptisms and new life.

He stops at public wells along the road. It is harvest time. Sometimes he goes into a field and picks three ears of corn—two for Shalva and one for him, or picks several stalks of wheat, rubs them in his hand, gives three hands full to Shalva and one to himself.

"Good boy, Shalva. You are being brave. You deserve more than this. When we get home, I promise to treat you. They have apples on the farm."

When Zarus stops for the night, he notices an open sore on his lower leg. *It'll probably be gone by the time I arrive home.*

Farther north. Farther into the hills. Further toward the mountains of Samaria.

As long as I'm careful with the money I had with me when I left, we should arrive without starving.

Then what?

38 ~ THE ABYSS

AD 47
Sebaste, Province of Samaria, Palestine

At least, when I visited my brothers last time, they accepted me. How happy we were then.

Zarus draws closer to Sebaste. He goes around the city and directly to the family farm.

It comes within sight.

"At last, Shalva. Home at last. This is where your grandfather was born. This is where I grew up."

He breaks Shalva into a trot. It is as though Shalva knows. With one last burst of energy, Shalva breaks into a gallop.

"Atta boy, Shalva! We're home. We're home."

They draw closer.

Things look different.

Zarus draws Shalva back into a trot, and then a complete stop.

Nearly out of breath, Shalva paws the ground in anticipation. Home. He sniffs toward the stable. He knows.

His rider slides off his back, dusts off his clothes, takes off his torn cloak to hide on Shalva, and reties the kerchief on his head.

Zarus walks up to the familiar embossed copper gate and knocks. His smile is broad. He is home.

The gate opens. "Hi, there! I have decided to…"

He looks at the stranger. "Oh, you must be a new servant. Or are you one of my nieces? Anyway, tell my brothers I am home."

"And who are you?"

"Oh, I forgot. You wouldn't know that. I am Zarus," he says, smiling.

The young girl disappears. A man appears at the gate. Zarus

does not know him. His smile becomes shaky.

"Sir, you must have the wrong house. There is no one here who knows you."

"Don't joke around with me. Call my brothers out."

"I am very sorry, but there is only my wife and I here. We bought this farm a year ago."

Zarus takes control of his emotions before they can control him.

"But what about my three brothers? Do you know where they are?"

"There were only two brothers that I bought the farm from. Perhaps one of them died. I do not know where they are now. I am sorry. Good luck to you, sir."

The stranger closes the door, and Zarus stands still, looking at the familiar gate with the unfamiliar people inside. He turns, looks over at the stable, and then at Shalva.

Still holding the reins, he turns Shalva, and they walk toward a tree out at the road. Zarus squats, leans on the tree, and lets Shalva's reins go. He is free to go where he wills.

Straighten up, Zarus. You can't let this get to you. God has better plans for you than you thought. Go to Sychar and find out what they are.

Shalva grazes nearby. Zarus goes up to him and takes the reins. "Thank you for your loyalty, big boy. You've had a little respite. We'll head out and go as far as we can before dark. The road between here and Sychar isn't too dangerous. We'll be okay, friend. We'll be okay."

As he lay down on his blanket that night, he notices another open sore on his leg. They are growing toward each other and are beginning to be painful.

I have nothing to treat them with. Maybe they'll go away on their own.

Sychar, Province of Samaria

"Sir, could you tell me where Moshe lives?"

"Yes, he's up this street. Go until you get to a cedar gate. He may not be there, though. He is just finishing up an impressive house on the highest hill in town. You can't miss it. If you miss him, his newest building project is at the bottom of the same hill."

"Thank you, sir."

Zarus takes the reins of his Arabian and starts walking up the hill. He sees the house just being started, but Moshe is not there. He continues on.

He spots the mansion at the top of the hill. As he draws closer, he spots a figure that looks all too familiar. The man is wearing a tunic of the rare color of purple.

"I wondered when you were going to show up," Gersshon says. "I would have thought two weeks, but it took you three. What were you doing all that time? Oh, yeah. I forgot. You left without your wealth; well, actually, it was my wealth. Looks like you lost a little weight. Oh, and you need to trim your beard; you look like an old man."

Zarus walks up to Gersshon. His face is barely a hand span away from Gersshon's.

"You," Zarus' voice rumbles, "will not win." From deep in his throat, he growls, "You must repent. You have created disaster and tragedy in every life you have ever touched. You portray yourself as an angel, but your father is the devil himself."

"Ha!" Gersshon replies, stepping aside. "At least I don't have a weak God like your Jhesus. I am on top of the world, and you are in a valley of shadows. I am even on top of Sychar."

Zarus turns to face Gersshon again. "Take this as a warning because you once were my friend: This is not stable land. Everyone in Sychar knows it. That is why no one else has built here."

"You're wrong, Zarus. You're always wrong."

———

After making his way to the bottom of the hill, Zarus turns and leaves out the back gate of the city. Though weak from lack of adequate food, Zarus' long strides take him to the estate of Baaruch, where Devorah had grown up.

The old manor is boarded up. He walks over to where Baaruch used to practice racing his chariots with his Egyptian horses. A house has been built on it. He closes his eyes, remembers it as it was, and envisions racing around the track with Devorah the first time they were ever alone.

How they had laughed, talking horses and the scriptures and teasing each other. First true love for both of them. So young. So full of hope and dreams and visions of a glorious life. A life together.

He looks around and sees that the stables are still there.

"Well, friend," he says to Shalva III. "I boarded your grandfather here when I was falling in love. I think I shall be boarding you here too if no one minds."

He walks Shalva into the stable and looks for a stall with no boards broken down in it. "Here you are. There's plenty of hay here, though I don't know how old it is. Eat what you can. I'll be back tonight."

With his heart full of the past, Zarus walks back into the city and to the market. He looks around for someone he had known in the old days.

"Hey, Avi. How are you? I'm Zarus. Remember Zarus, who used to work on the road to Sebaste out here?"

"Is that you, Zarus? You've gotten old."

"So have you, my old friend. We both have," Zarus laughs. "Hey, uh, I have done pretty well in my life, but suddenly have hit some very hard times. Might you have a job for me? Just a little for now?"

Avi looks down at Zarus' dirty, torn clothes, then back up to his eyes. "Sorry, friend. We've been having a little bit of a drought around here, and I'm not doing so well myself."

"That's okay, friend. You and I will both do better soon."

Avi tries to smile. *How can he say that when he looks so bad?*

Zarus wanders down the narrow alleys of the market, looking at people, hoping to run into another merchant he used to know.

"Hey, Tzurial. How have you been? It's me, Zarus. Remember, the guy who helped build the road out here?"

"That was at least a hundred years ago. Is that really you, Zarus?" Tzurial answers, keeping his eyes on Zarus to make sure he is who he says he is.

"Yeah, it's me. I'm in the midst of a little bit of a hard time. I'll pull out of it, I'm sure. But for now, might you have a little bit of work? I don't need much," Zarus replies, forcing a smile.

"Well, there are a couple weeks worth of picking out at my olive grove. You'd be perfect for it, you're so tall. But are you sure this is what you want to do?"

"Nothing like working with the common man to stay in touch with the world, Tzurial."

"Okay," the merchant says. "To get to my orchard, go back out this gate, then left, and you'll see it on your right. Someone will be there to tell you where to go."

"Thank you, friend. I won't forget you."

The rest of the day goes by in slow motion. He is paid for the day and walks over to the market to buy something for his evening and morning meal. "Oh, and I want a couple of apples for a friend of mine."

He goes back out of town, to Baaruch's estate, to the stable, and gives Shalva his two apples.

He hears whimpering. "What?" He looks around in the other stalls until he finds it: Four half-grown puppies, all cuddled up next to their mother. The mother looks up at Zarus as though to say, "I must take care of my children."

"Of course, you do," he says, then returns to the stall closest to his Arabian. There he forms a mattress of hay, wraps his tattered cloak around himself, and falls asleep.

The next morning, he feels something on his leg. He looks down and sees his sores have grown together into one large ulcer and getting worse. One of the puppies has come over and is licking it.

He stands and does the same thing he had done the day before—picking olives, buying enough food for the day, sharing a few crumbs with the puppies and their mother, giving an apple to Shalva, and going to sleep in Baaruch's stable.

His last day of work comes. His old friend had only promised him two weeks. It is now the end.

He is given his pay and goes into the market to buy enough food for tonight and tomorrow. Then there will be no more.

He walks slowly out the back gate of the city and once more to Baaruch's stable. As he walks, he blanks out the house on the former raceway, and once again sees Devorah and himself in their youth. He looks over at the manor and remembers their betrothal day.

How lucky I have been. Thank you, Jhehovah God, for giving Devorah to me. So blessed. So very blessed.

Zarus goes back into the stable and beds down for the night. He feels something else on his leg. Another ulcer. This night is a little cooler. He sleeps. After a while, he feels something furry against is legs. He opens his eyes, sees the puppies and their mother snuggled against them, then goes back to sleep.

The next day he wanders around outside, reliving the past. His life in slavery for his beloved. His life with the underground mine and its collapse. His life selling everything to buy that copper treasure on the land. His life with the two boys she gave him. Then saying goodbye to them all. All but little Lleah. *I hope, where ever she is, she is happy.*

Once again, he is out of food. Even Shalva is growing too lean. He walks his Arabian over to the spent olive grove and lets him eat among the grass and discarded olives below the trees.

The puppies and their mother follow them to the grove and back again.

A day of wandering and dreaming and remembering. Nighttime.

That night, Zarus realizes the ulcer on his leg is growing. Both wider and deeper, He is careful not to sleep in such a way that anything touches it. Sometimes, however, one of the puppies licks it, and it feels a little better.

The next morning, Zarus walks back into town and in the direction of the hill with the rich houses on it. His step is not as sure. At the bottom of the hill is the most recent house Moshe has been building. Moshe is there.

"Good morning, friend," Zarus calls out in a weakly-disguised jovial voice.

Moshe stares a moment at the tall man with the dirty, tattered tunic, sandals with a broken strap, and scraggly gray hair.

"Zarus, is that you?"

Zarus walks up to him and whispers, "I'm afraid so."

"What has happened to you, my friend? Sit here with me. Tell me what is going on with you."

The two longtime friends, one ten years older than the other, sit on a pile of clay bricks.

"Moshe, I've lost everything. Well, everything but my faith."

"What do you mean? Are the boys okay?"

"I lost Lleah when she married a sea captain and have had no idea where she is for years. Then I lost Devorah. Amram was murdered, and Ithamar apparently drowned at sea."

"Murdered? Who murdered Amram?"

"The man you were working for a couple weeks ago."

"I wasn't working for anyone who would murder. I was working for...for..."

Zarus looks Moshe in the eyes and freezes.

"Gersshon? Why would he do such a terrible thing?"

"I don't know. He's been bitter since he was a boy, and I guess was more successful at hiding it than any of us realized. Well, you may as well know the rest of it. He also murdered Noach and Saabhu, then took the mine from me."

Moshe jumps up and stares at Zarus.

"No! He can't do that."

"Even though he got half the profits as equal partner, he stole from my half by not accounting for all the ore we sold."

"No! He can't get by with it."

"Well, this isn't what I came to talk to you about. Moshe, I've got to eat. Can I work for you on this house?"

"You're not going to do manual labor for me, Zarus. It's not right. You've suffered enough. Besides, you're getting old like me. This is my last house. I'm going to retire after this one. I'm seventy-eight years old. I can do no more.

"I tell you what I'll do, Zarus. You can be my superintendent. I sometimes stay home because I overworked the day before. These are the diagrams I made of all the details of the house. Look around and see if you have any questions. Then I'll go home and take a rest."

The old friends shake hands. Moshe tells his crew Zarus is their new boss and not to pay attention to his clothes because he has one of the most brilliant minds he has ever known anyone to have.

The rest of the day, Zarus spends getting to know the crew and studying the plans.

He goes back to the stables that night content but limping more. *I have to choose between eating and a doctor. I guess I'll have to choose eating. After all, I now have seven mouths to feed.* As he nears, the four puppies and their mother come running out to greet him. Shalva neighs.

Zarus is more tired than ever, even though he had not stood this day as much as he had at the orchard. *That leg is sapping the energy out of me.*

That night he dreams of his house back in Eilat and that Gersshon comes along and swallows it. He wakes with a start. His leg is burning. He goes outside a moment where the moon is full. He sits and examines his legs. Another open sore has started on his other leg. It stings.

Morning. He limps back into the city and Moshe's house. Moshe is there.

"Zarus, you're limping. Are you okay?"

"Yeah. It's nothing. It'll go away in a few days."

Zarus busies himself with the next phase of getting the house up. He is enjoying his work. It takes his mind off everything else. For a while.

The next day Zarus is late arriving.

"I'm truly sorry, Moshe. I guess these ulcers on my legs are getting to me."

"So that's why you've been limping. I thought it was because your joints were hurting."

"I wish that were the case. The first ulcer has dug itself into my leg so far I think I can see bone."

"Let me see it," Moshe says.

Zarus lifts up his tunic and Moshe gasps.

"Did you know I had leprosy while you were gone?"

"No, I didn't know that."

"It had eaten away at my hands and feet, and I could hardly walk." He flexes his fingers. "But they are all back, thanks to Jhesus, who healed me."

"Amazing, Moshe. But I believe you. I met Jhesus myself, and truly believe he was the Son of God. He had to be."

"Well," Moshe continues, "I thought maybe you might have some sores on you that were the beginning of leprosy like I had, but your sores are not at all like mine. You don't seem to have any other symptoms like lumps on your face. I don't believe you have leprosy. But I still don't like what I'm seeing. I'm surprised you can walk at all."

"Moshe, I can still walk. I can still do the work."

"I know you can. That's why I am keeping you on. It has been a relief to me."

That day after work, as usual, Zarus walks through the city past the market and buys his food for the next day, along with two apples for Shalva and a calf bone for the dog.

He sits outside the stables and eats while dreaming. Dreaming of the days of his youth when he was strong and healthy. Now he grows weak, and the pain in his legs is becoming almost unbearable. One of his ulcers is now as large as a man's hand and going deeper.

He takes the reins of Shalva and limps over to the olive grove for his evening meal. While there, he sees a strong branch on the ground. He tests it. Yes. It will do. He breaks off the shoots and walks back to the stables with his new cane.

He thinks of Amram, who needed a cane his whole life. *If you were here, Son, we could go for walks together. If we had a race, I have no doubts you would win.*

He nears the stable. *I don't know how much longer I can work. This leg is killing me.*

39 ~ HOME

AD 48
Sychar, Province of Samaria, Palestine

"Moshe, you do not know how much I appreciate you letting me work for you over the past two months," Zarus says. "But you have carried me without me doing much work for the past week. You cannot afford to do that. My guess is that you have just barely enough to take care of your wife and yourself once you retire when this house is completed. I can no longer be a burden to you."

"No, Zarus," Moshe says, alarmed and with a little moisture coming to his eyes. "Please, don't leave me."

"I must, Moshe. My legs are killing me a little at a time, especially the one with the largest ulcer. It is now the size of two hand spans and is eating away at my bone. I can no longer function."

"You can sit and direct the men."

"No, I can't. I cannot think straight anymore. The pain is controlling my mind. I need to wait somewhere and then die."

"You're not going to die, my friend. You are only...you are how old? You're not seventy yet. You've still got a few years left in you. What if I give you some extra money so you can go to a physician?"

"It's too late. The ulcers are too deep and spreading. It is not only eating my flesh, it is eating my bones. And this morning, I found a new ulcer right under my beard. It is only a matter of time before it eats away at half my face."

"No, Zarus. This cannot be happening to you. You are one of the kindest and smartest men I have ever known. You do not deserve this. No, Zarus. Oh, no..."

Moshe stops. Tears fill his eyes for his old friend, and his lips tremble. He leans over and puts his head on Zarus' shoulder. "No, Zarus. No..."

The crew notices what is going on. Some are embarrassed for the two old men and look away out of respect. Others stare and sympathize, hoping their lives will not end like this.

"Well, Moshe, I guess this is goodbye," Zarus says. "I am going back to Baaruch's stables..."

"Is that where you have been staying? I should have asked. I'm sorry..."

"I'm going back to Baaruch's stables and sleep. Tomorrow morning I will get my Arabian horse and bring him to you. If you are not here, I will just hitch him to one these house posts, and it will be here for you when you arrive."

"Zarus..."

"Don't try to change my mind. You have been very kind to me for a very long time, and especially now. You deserve it. You should be able to sell him for a lot of money. Use that to help support you and your wife."

"Zarus..."

Zarus stands, and once again, the old men fall on each other's necks.

"Be careful," Zarus says, smiling through his own tears. "Embrace me on the other side where there is no sore. I do not know if it is contagious. I've never seen anything like it."

"How can I say goodbye to you?"

"Like we've said goodbye to so many other loved ones in our years. If you are a Christian, I will see you on the other side."

"I am, and so we will."

"Until then."

"Until then."

———

The next morning Zarus rises and wishes he hadn't. As long as he is dreaming, he has no pain.

He looks around. *What was it all for? Everything and everyone gone. Was my whole life wasted?*

He stands and limps heavily over to Shalva.

"You and I are going for a long walk this morning," he says, patting him on the nose and then the side. Shalva nudges Zarus under the chin, and Zarus smiles.

"Yes, we have been through a lot together. But, just because I suffer, it does not mean you have to. You will like Moshe. He isn't as tall as me and won't be able to mount you as easily as I can, but be patient with him." He pauses.

"I wish I could mount you one last time and ride you to your new home, but my leg is barely there anymore. You and I will have to walk. Ready?" He looks around.

"Where's my cloak? There it is. It's colder out there at night. I'll need it. Will you carry it for me?" He throws it over Shalva's back and picks up the watering bowl to attach to the horse's harness.

With his cane in one hand and Shalva's reins in the other, Zarus looks over at the manor one last time. "Goodbye, my love. Goodbye."

Slowly, taking steps no longer than a hand span, he makes his way toward the gate of the city.

"Sorry, I can't take you to the orchard today. But Moshe will feed you well. Just you wait and see."

Arriving on the other side of the gate, Zarus looks around the city square and sees a bench. He limps over to it and sits. It is a relief to take the weight of his entire body off what is left of his legs.

His mind thinks of nothing, and he dozes. When he wakes, he knows what he must do.

He stands, adjusts to the pain, and resumes his walk. It is then that he realizes he has company. The mother with her four puppies have followed them into the city.

She knows. That little mother knows. But what she doesn't know is that I cannot feed her any longer.

"Come along, little ones, if you insist."

Zarus leaves the city square and resumes his walk up the street toward the hill. He reaches Moshe's last house before Moshe arrives.

This is best.

He walks over to a post and ties Shalva to it. He sits a while on a pile of bricks and rests.

Don't stop now.

He rises, steps over to Shalva, puts his head on the horse's cheek, and the horse nuzzles Zarus.

"Have a good life, my friend."

Zarus takes his robe and a torn reed mat off the horse's back, along with the old watering bowl, turns and resumes his walk up the hill. The dogs follow.

He hears a neigh behind him but does not look back.

The pain grabs hold of him and will not let go. He becomes nauseated. He stops in the street and puts both hands on the top of his olive-grove cane to steady himself. Moments later, he resumes.

If I stop now, I will never get there. Keep going, ole boy. Keep going.

A few more steps. And a few more. One step at a time. Sliding, shuffling, scuttling.

Don't look around. Don't look at the houses. Don't look at the people. Don't look.

One step. Then another. And another.

He looks up at the sky. *I'm coming.*

Closer, he comes to his destination: The top of the hill. Closer. Still closer. *Do not give up. Keep going. Keep going.*

Zarus stops and closes his eyes. He feels himself leaning to one side.

Can't fall. Start walking again.

Still, he strives. Strives for the top and a successful mission.

Step after step. Creeping. Edging.

At last, he reaches his destination.

Zarus looks up at the magnificent castle-like manor. He surveys the columns rising like sentries reaching toward the sky, opulent use of copper décor like a grand lady in all her adornment, and the steps leading up to the front gate like the allure of a veil.

He sets the old reed mat on the ground, lowers himself to his knees, turns, and settles into a sitting position. Zarus puts the old watering bowl in front of him, and says, "Alms. Alms for the poor."

As night comes, he grows cold. He puts his tattered cloak around him, lies down, and falls asleep. He dreams Gersshon has slammed his fist into a ship, and it sinks in the deep with Ithamar on board.

The next morning, he sits up with his bowl. "Alms. Alms for the poor," he says again.

Job. I'm just like Job, Zarus thinks. *He lost all his wealth, all his children, and his health. Had sores everywhere. Well, Job, you have company. How did you do it? You were younger than me. You got your wealth, your children, and your health back—or at least substitutes for what you lost. How did you handle it, Job? All the pain and isolation? No one there but so-called friends to taunt you? How did you do it?*

"Hey, Zarus, ole boy! Where did you come from?" It is Gersshon. "What brings you to this part of town? And what's that sitting there with you? A beggar's bowl? Oh, my. Isn't that beneath your dignity, oh great one who thinks he knows it all, owns it all, and controls it all?" He snortles.

"You are so much a nothing," Gersshon continues. "You would

have been if it hadn't been for me. I always had to watch out for you. You have to watch out for yourself now. Of course, look where it's getting you." He shakes his head.

"Well, Zarus, my friend, I've got to go inside now. It is breakfast time. And you ought to see all the women I now have serving me. Oh, but you only had eyes for Devorah. How boring. Anyway, ta ta."

Periodically through the day, a servant going into town walks near Zarus to see if he needs anything.

"You've only got a few copper denari in your bowl. Not many people come up here. Can I get anything for you?"

"A piece of bread will be fine, thank you," Zarus always says.

Days go by. The ulcers on both legs have now eaten away to the bone and beyond. The one on his chin expanding. He can barely eat without touching the raw place that is now so close to his lower lip.

———

The weather grows colder. Zarus no longer reserves his cloak for nights. He keeps it wrapped around him. The cloak that used to be royal blue. The colorful threads in it shredded and coming loose everywhere. His tunic that he wore leaving Eilat that day he last visited Devorah's crypt is tattered and nearly falling off of him.

More days and nights. The mother and her puppies continue to snuggle up to Zarus. When he is asleep, they lick his wounds. He lets them do it. It soothes him.

More days. Today is especially cold. The wind shifts and swirls overhead along with the churning clouds that are growing grayer and more menacing.

Life has been hard. Oh, there were good days, but there were many hard ones too. Why? What was it all for? I got wealth and lost it all. I got a wife and children and lost them all. Why was I even born?

"Hey, Zarus, ole boy," the familiar voice calls out from his portico at the top of the expansive steps. Once again, he is wearing the rare purple, now his favorite color.

"What are you going to do if it rains? Oh, I know. You will jump up and run for shelter. Bring a tent along? Of course, you didn't. You are such an idiot, sitting out there like that day after day. Expect me to feel sorry for you? Not on your life. Not considering all the things you did to me. How I hate you."

The rain begins, and Gersshon goes back into his manor. Zarus imagines him watching from an opulent balcony.

The rain becomes a downpour. The wind whips around, the lightning flashes, the thunder rumbles.

Still, the rain. Coming down like the rocks of a mine collapse. Unrelenting. Caring not what is below it. Or who.

Pounding.

Hammering.

Beating.

On and on it comes.

Penetrating.

Piercing.

Trenching.

A rumble. Not a thunder's rumble. Something else. Zarus looks up at the house. One side is leaning. Farther, it leans. Then begins a slide. The sand in front and to one side. Sliding. The house sliding with it.

Get out of the way, Zarus!

Get out of the way!

Zarus!

No!

With a growl and roar and an unearthly screech, the house leaves its foundation and slips closer and closer to Zarus.

Zarus begins to tumble.

But the mud, it is so soothing.

He turns over onto his head and then his back.

Can't stop.

Over and over.

Still soothing

Can't see.

And over.

Can't breathe...

———

"Hello there, Zarus. Are you ready?"

Zarus looks up and sees a bright being. "Who are you?"

"I am your guardian angel. We really went through some bad times lately, you and me. But now I'm ready to take you home."

"Home?" Zarus asks.

"Everyone is waiting for you."

Zarus is bewildered, but only a brief moment.

Then comes understanding. Realization. Comprehension.

"Yes. Take me home. Take me with you. I'm ready."

Zarus is now hovering. Now floating. Now flying. Soaring higher and higher. He looks down and sees little lights flickering where he had been moments earlier. He sees Baaruch's manor house, and Sychar, and the mine in the desert all growing smaller and smaller.

He looks up. The stars. So bright. Coming closer.

Soaring through the universe. Stars and galaxies and worlds.

Now something bright beyond it all. Drawing, pulling, inviting.

Closer.

Closer.

Then he sees it. A pearl. A great pearl. Greater than any on earth. Greater than any imagined. The pearl has a gate in it. The gate opens for Zarus, and on the other side, he sees a very old man. The man speaks.

"Hello, there, and welcome."

Zarus does not know what to say.

"By the way, I am Avrahaam. I fathered you about two thousand years ago. Well, I didn't actually father you myself, but one of my grandsons did. Welcome, my son."

Zarus realizes he is no longer in pain. He is no longer dirty. No longer with unkempt hair and grimy hands and torn clothes.

"We've been waiting for you."

"Who's been waiting for me?"

"The crowd in the throne room has been waiting for you. Hear them shouting?"

> *Praise and glory*
> *And wisdom and thanks and honor*
> *And power and strength*
> *Be to our God forever and ever!*

"Now they're singing. Hear their voices?"

> *To him who sits on the throne*
> *And to the Lamb*
> *Be praise and honor and glory and power*
> *Forever and ever!*

"Go ahead. He is watching for you."

"Who?" Zarus asks. "I don't know anyone here."

"Yes, you do. It is God."

Zarus walks forward. The crowd parts for him. There before him is the throne of God. Almost too brilliant to look upon. The throne is jasper, and above God is a red glow, and above that is an emerald rainbow.

He falls on his face worshiping and trembling before the Creator of the universe. Love. He feels love. Love like never before.

Someone else calling his name now. A familiar voice. He looks up, and stepping down from the throne is the Jhesus he had met at the well so long ago. He is holding out his hands. They still have scars in the middle of them. Nail scars.

"They really did crucify you," he whispers.

Once again, Zarus falls to his knees.

And worships.

At that moment, all else is enveloped in glory.

"Lord, he whispers. My Lord Jhesus and my God."

That's what it was all about, Zarus thinks. *It was just a journey. I have arrived. My destination. This is what life there was all for.*

The light reduces itself. He hears the voice again.

"Rise and smile," Jhesus says. "You made it, Zarus. Your journey is over. You have maintained your faith in me the whole time. It hasn't always been easy. But you stayed the course. I am proud of you."

Jhesus reaches down his hands, the scarred hands, and lifts Zarus to his feet.

"Now, I don't want you to feel you are all alone here. There are some people who have been waiting a long time for you to join them."

"Hello, my darling."

Zarus turns and sees his beloved Devorah looking as young as the day they had met in their youth. He embraces her.

"Oh, my pearl. How I have missed you."

"My darling, I missed you too. But for me, it was just a few moments in timelessness."

Did you hear me all those times I talked to you after you left?"

"Sometimes I did," Devorah replies. "But God only let me hear the good things you told me. He sheltered me from any sadness, for there are no tears here. He said he would personally help you get through your hard times."

"He did, my pearl. He gave me strength I did not know I had."

"Come see our children," she whispers, smiling.

"Hi, Father."

Zarus looks over and sees Amram. He no longer has a club foot and is walking without a cane.

"Amram. How I've missed you," he says, stepping over to his

oldest son. "I see you are doing well here."

"Indeed, I am, Father. Heaven is everything you said it would be, but more. Much more. I am happy here. I have made friends with so many people, and even quite a few angels. Well, the angels are our servants, but we are friends, anyway."

"You have no idea how great it is to see you again, Amram," Zarus says.

"Don't forget my brother. Ithamar is here too."

"Hello, Father," Ithamar says.

"My! How fine you look, Son. So, how do you like it here? Enough excitement for you?"

"God keeps us busy doing amazing things. Plus, I've learned to sing a lot better than I used to. And did you see that pearl when you arrived?"

"I did see it."

"There are eleven others just like it—twelve in all, and all turned into gates. What I sacrificed so much for on earth was trash compared to what is here."

Zarus embraces his sons, takes Devorah's hand, then looks back over at Jhesus, who is beaming more broadly than anyone.

"I am glad all of you accepted my offer to take your punishment for your sins. Hell is a horrid place. But I conquered it for you—well, for anyone who accepts my offer. Not everyone does, you know. But enough of that. I have built something for you, Zarus."

"You built something for me, Jhesus?"

"Of course. Why be so surprised? I was a carpenter on earth, you know. Follow me. Oh, and bring your family with you."

Jhesus leads them down a golden street until they come to a mansion more grand than any Zarus had ever seen in his travels on earth.

"It's yours. Here's the key."

Zarus opens the door into his mansion, and his family follows him in. He looks at its magnificence with wonder in his eyes and an overwhelming sense of God's love in his heart.

"How do you like it, sweetheart?" Devorah says. "I live right next door."

"You can look around some more later," Jhesus says. "But first, it is meal time. Zarus, I understand you have been pretty hungry lately. I have a feast prepared for you."

Jhesus leads Zarus and his family, all arm in arm, farther down the golden street.

"Look over there," Jhesus says, motioning with his scarred

hand. "I've prepared your meal in that green pasture. Come and dine with me."

Zarus thinks about everything Jhesus had done for him while on earth.

"I lifted a lot of boulders in my life down there," Zarus says. "You were there all along, helping me lift them, weren't you?"

"There was a rich man who was dressed in purple and fine linen and lived in luxury every day.

At his gate was laid a beggar named Lazarus, covered with sores

And longing to eat what fell from the rich man's table. Even the dogs came and licked his sores (Matthew 13:19-21).

But everyone who hears these words of mine and does not put them into practice is like a foolish man who built his house on sand.

The rain came down, the streams rose, and the winds blew and beat against that house, and it fell with a great crash." (Matthew 7:26-27)

"The time came when the beggar died and the angels carried him to Abraham's side.

"There was a rich man who was dressed in purple and fine linen and lived in luxury every day.

At his gate was laid a beggar named Lazarus, covered with sores and longing to eat what fell from the rich man's table. Even the dogs came and licked his sores.

"The time came when the beggar died and the angels carried him to Abraham's side. The rich man also died and was buried.

In Hades, where he was in torment, he looked up and saw Abraham far away, with Lazarus by his side. So he called to him, 'Father Abraham, have pity on me and send Lazarus to dip the tip of his finger in water and cool my tongue, because I am in agony in this fire.'

(Matthew 13:22-24) (To some this is a parable; to others it really happened.)

EPILOGUE

AD 49
Eilat, Seaport on the Red Sea, Province of Idumea

*D*uring the thirteen years that Lleah and Livianus were at sea, they spread the good news about Jhesus Christ to China and India to the East, and Gaul and Britannia to the west. Everywhere they went, people were "baptized into Christ."

Zarus' and Devorah's daughter, Lleah, returned to Eilat a year after her father's death to visit her parents, only to learn they had both died.

Not knowing that Gersshon had taken over complete control of the mine, she went to the magistrates to see if her father had left a will. Of course, he had. In the will, he left the mine to his daughter and her husband.

Asking around the city about the whereabouts of her father's partner, she learned he had died also. Therefore, the mine reverted to the nearest relative. Since Gersshon did not have any children, the mine reverted to Lleah.

Lleah decided it was time to settle down. The bank through whom Zarus had mortgaged the house in order to help her brother, Ithamar, had been paid but remortgaged by Gersshon. She paid it off and moved into the house where she had grown up.

Lleah was now twenty-seven. Her husband, Livianus, was thirty-three, the same age as her other brother, Amram, had he lived.

Livianus loved the sea life and was not ready to give it up yet. Lleah decided to run the mine herself. By asking around, she was able to locate its last engineer, Yuval, and the last superintendent, Uziel. They agreed to return to work at the mine under the condition that they receive the first proceeds once the mine got under operation.

Of the five hundred men who had to leave their jobs upon the death of Gersshon, one hundred and thirty-three came back. Were they hesitant to work under a woman? If it was Zarus' daughter, they knew she would be as smart and fair as him.

And so it was that the son of the man from whom Zarus had bought the land with the copper on it—Hector's son Livianus—became owner of the land once again. And the daughter of the man to whom Hector had sold the land—Lleah—became owner of the mine once again.

She had a crypt made for her father and placed it next to her mother. Of the four, the bodies of none of them were ever located except for her mother's.

Still, Lleah went to the cemetery on each of their birthdays. She would always take flowers and tell them, "Wait for me. I'm coming."

THANK YOU

Thanks for reading my book! I'm so honored that you chose to spend your precious time with my characters. You are appreciated. I'm an independent author who relies on my readers to help spread the word about stories you enjoy.

Would you take a few minutes to let your friends know on Facebook, Pinterest...wherever you hang out online? Also, each honest review at online retailers means a lot to me and helps other readers know if this is a book they might enjoy.

I welcome contact from readers. At my website (below), you can do so. You can also sign up for my monthly newsletter (below) for half-price paper and 99c ebooks for the whole family - novels, non-fiction, storybooks and first peek at my newest release.

GET ALL 8 BOOKS IN THE HISTORICAL SERIES
INTREPID MEN OF GOD

Novel 1 ~ Lazarus: The Samaritan
Novel 2 ~ Paul: The Unstoppable
Novel 3 ~ Luke: Slave & Physician
Novel 4 ~ Mefiboset: Crippled Prince
Novel 5 ~ Joseph: The Other Father
Novel 6 ~ Michel: The Fourth Wise Man
Novel 7 ~ Stephen: Unlikely Martyr
Novel 8 ~ Titus: The Aristocrat

HISTORICAL & SCIENTIFIC BACKGROUND

DNA: Several hundred Samaritans still exist today. Their male chromosomes center around Ashkenazi, Cohen (priestly) and Danfi family clusters, which are all very close to the Jewish DNA. On the other hand, the female chromosomes cluster closely with Iraqis (where Assyria was located at that time) and Jews. It seems when the Assyrians sent some of their people to repopulate Samaria, they apparently sent mostly women, a "mail-order bride" kind of arrangement.

Samaritans today stay closer to the Law of Moses than Jews do. For example, on the Passover, they slaughter lambs for sacrifice, something modern Jews do not do. Actually, Samaritans call themselves the "true Israelites".

Although most Jews hated Samaritans to some degree, it did not exist as much in the northern province of Galilee. Examples in the Bible show that mostly Jews in the ruling province of Judea in Jhesus' time hated Samaritans. The same hateful Jews readily declared nothing good could come out of Galilee, the province just north of Samaria.

ORIGINAL RIVALRY. Joseph's brothers had always been jealous of him. Then, when Joseph's two sons, Ephraim and Manasseh, were born, both sides of the new generation were still jealous of each other.

Eventually, the tribes (descendants) of Ephraim and Manasseh were given by far the largest amount of land in the new Promised Land, thus promoting jealousies and distrust. Disagreements continued so much, that eventually the northern kingdom of the Jews and the southern kingdom of the Jews split. The northern kingdom became known as Israel, while the southern kingdom became Judah. Much later, the northern kingdom itself had a split, and its far north province of Galilee went with Judah, and the middle of the country remained in the old Israel.

Despite all this, we still have some examples of Samaritans from the tribes of Ephraim and Manasseh among the "remnant of Israel" helping the Jews in Jerusalem when they contributed to repairing the temple in King Josiah's time (II Chronicles

34:9f). The prophet Jeremiah referred to people from Sebaste, Shiloh, and Samaria (later renamed Sebaste) bringing offerings to Jherusalem (Jeremiah 4:1-5).

King Asa assembled people from Ephraim and Manasseh (later known as Samaria) and they swore an oath along with the Jews in the territories of Judah and Benyamin to follow God, not pagan idols (II Chronicles 15:9-15).

King Hezekiah invited the Ephraimites and Manassites in the territory later called Samaria, to come to Jerusalem for the Passover (II Chronicles 30:1, 11-14) and at that time, they removed the pagan altars throughout Jerusalem.

Isaiah prophesied that the exiles of Israel assembled with the exiles of Judah, and that the Ephraimites (a large portion of Samaritans) and Judaites would no longer be jealous of each other (Isaiah 11:12-13).

All of this shows that not everyone who lived in the Province of Samaria were pagans. Many remained true to the Law of Moses. In fact, today, the Samaritans, who still speak Hebrew and offer sacrificial lambs at Passover every year, call themselves the true Israelites.

It might be noted here that the two main differences in the non-pagan Samaritans and Jews is that the Samaritans worshiped God in Mt,.Gerizim instead of Jerusalem, and the Samaritans did not believe in the Prophets section of the Old Testament. But keep in mind that the Sadducees, a sect of Judaism, did not believe in the Prophets either, yet many were on the Jewish ruling Sanhedrin in Jerusalem.

SYNAGOGUES IN SAMARIA. We know Jews did have synagogues in the province of Samaria because, when Jhesus healed the ten lepers (Luke 17:14), he told them to go show themselves to the priests, something required in the Law of Moses when someone had open sores, etc. They had to be pronounced clean so they could resume worshiping in their synagogues and at the temple.

HEBREW spellings of names are from **http://www.20000-names.com/**

ROMAN ROADS were so well constructed, many still exist today and are in use. Before beginning, they moved obstructions out of the way to prepare a smooth roadbed. The 1st layer was 1" of mortar. The 2nd was four layers of masonry. The 3rd layer was 1' of stones held together by cement or clay. The 4th layer was

10" of rammed concrete. The 5th layer was 18" successively laid
rolled layers of concrete. The 6th layer stones cut to fit snugly
together smoothed with concrete.

SHALVA is Hebrew for peaceful.

KHEMOH is Hebrew for shelter.

LATRONES was a first-century board game. There are red granite pieces on
one side and white granite pieces on the other side. The men on one
side try to bump the men on the other side off the board,"

SYCHOR AND SEBASTE are about ten miles apart.

IDUMEA was Edom founded by Esau, son of Isaac. Edom means "red"
Jacob's son had red hair. The rocks were red. In one location, red
rock cliffs were carved into temples later and renamed the city of
Petra in Jordan.

EILAT is a port city at the northern tip of the Red Sea. It still exists today
and often visited by tourists who enjoy its beaches.

TIMNEH VALLEY IN ARABIAN DESERT. The Timney Valley in the Arava
Desert below the Dead Sea and near the Red Sea holds over 10,000
mining shafts. A movie called "Solomon's Mines" was made in that
area.

QUESTORS for governments were in charge of maintaining public treasury,
both taking in funds and deciding who to pay them to. Questors in the
military were in charge of the spoils and how to distribute them.

JACOB'S WELL at Sychar was nearly 8 feet across and 135 feet deep. In
1935. The bottom is solid limestone and the interior was, at one time,
lined with mortar.

SILK was discovered by Roman legions fighting the Parthians who had
purchased it from China. Around 30 BC, regular commerce of silk
between China and Rome began. The oldest surviving silk products
were found at Qianshanyang Site in Huzhou, Zhejiang Province in
1950.

PEARLS were rare and outlandishly expensive in the first century. In In
order to find enough pearl oysters, free-divers were often forced to
descend to depths of over 100 feet on a single breath, Divers manually
pulled oysters from ocean floors. It took an average of one ton of
oysters to find one oyster with a perfect pearl inside.

JEWISH SECTS were primarily two, and that is how the Sanhedrin
ruling body was divided up. The Pharisees were like the House
of Commons or the House of Representatives. The Sadducees
were like the House of Lords or the Senate. The Pharisees
identified themselves with the commoners. The Sadducees
were fewer but rich, and ruled the Sanhedrin. They only
believed in the first five books of the Bible. They did not believe

in any of the prophets or in life after death.

THE TORAH sometimes refers only to the first five books of the Bible, and sometimes to those plus the remaining history of the Jews.

THE TALMUD contains the teachings and opinions of thousands of rabbis concerning the Talmud and life applications thereof.

ROAD TO JERICHO from Jerusalem was 15 miles and a steep descent of 3700 feet ~ almost 250 feet per mile. It was a winding road with cliffs on one side and drop-offs on the other side.

KUSHAN in Persia was a center for iron mining and smelting beginning the first century BC and continuing for three hundred years. Sialk was an important metal production center A significant amount of metallurgical remains are there including large amounts of slag pieces, litharge cakes, and crucibles and molds.

PEARLS: Until the twentieth century, pearls were rare and highly expensive. The only way to find them was for humans to dive often to a depth of one hundred feet and back in one breath. It took on average a ton of oyster shells to find three or four quality pearls.

ZARUS' DISEASE is called "Desert Sore" found primarily in North Africa and the Middle East. It is also called "Varicose Ulcer". Some believe it was the most common ulcer in Bible times, seen principally on the legs. Occasionally it was so severe it consumed the flesh all the way to the bone. Pictures I have seen of it show it to be similar to "Flesh-Eating Disease". It was believed lack of adequate protein and uncleanliness plus impaired local circulation were primary causes.

BUY YOUR NEXT BOOK NOW
Check out what they are about and a buy link.

HISTORICAL NOVELS FOR ADULTS

THEY MET JESUS Series of 8
http://bit.ly/TheyMetJesus

INTREPID MEN OF GOD Series of 8
http://bit.ly/IntrepidMen

HISTORICAL STORYBOOKS FOR CHILDREN

A CHILD'S LIFE OF CHRIST Series of 8
(Parallels Adult *They Met Jesus*)
http://bit.ly/ChildsLifeOfChristSet

A CHILD'S BIBLE HEROES Series of 10
http://bit.ly/Bible-Heroes

A CHILD'S BIBLE KIDS Series of 8
http://bit.ly/bible-kids

A CHILD'S BIBLE LADIES Series of 10
http://bit.ly/BibleLadies

DISCUSSION QUESTIONS

CHAPTER 1: Recall a time when you thought you knew more than someone else, let it be known that you did, then it turned out you were wrong. How did it make you feel?

CHAPTER 2: Did anyone ever treat you badly because they were jealous of you? Or perhaps you were that jealous person. How can the jealousy be neutralized?

CHAPTER 3: What is it like to be in a love triangle? If you've been part of one, how did it turn out?

CHAPTER 4: What are some things you absolutely refuse to compromise on? Why?

CHAPTER 5: Tell about a time when you had to get something done, but could not, no matter how hard you tried. Did anyone step in to help you finish it? Or perhaps you are the one who helped someone else.

CHAPTER 6: Have you ever been wrongly accused? How did you feel during the punishment? Were you glad you could take the punishment for someone else? Did anyone step in to defend you?

CHAPTER 7: Throughout history, people have been given the wonderful opportunity to become Christians so they could go to heaven instead of hell. How would you handle it if you were persecuted for being a Christian and had to go through "a living hell" first?

CHAPTER 8: There are some people in the world nearly impossible to get along with. Do you know anyone who managed to get along with even the unloving? Jesus said if we do not forgive our enemies, God will not forgive us. Talk about forgiveness.

CHAPTER 9: What is the most surprising gift you have ever been given? Share it.

CHAPTER 10: Do you belong to an organization that gives food to the needy? Perhaps clothing also? How is it handled? Or, what national or worldwide organizations do this? Which ones? How do they handle it?

CHAPTER 11: Have you ever thought of giving a party (perhaps a Thanksgiving meal or other celebration) and going down to the park or street corner or wherever the homeless normally are, and inviting them? How would you go about it?

CHAPTER 12: Do you know anyone who died just before or right after their dream came true? What is your dream? If you lost your dream, how do you think you might face it?

CHAPTER 13: What is it like to search for survivors of a catastrophe? If you have never done this, how do you think you would feel if called upon?

CHAPTER 14: Did you ever pray fervently for something and never get it? Then later you get something better? Tell about it.

CHAPTER 15: Tell about a time you entered into a project knowing it would be hard, but half way through you gave up because it was too hard? Did anyone continue after you quit? Why do you think they did?

CHAPTER 16: Have you ever lost something, then found it a year or years later when you weren't expecting to? Tell about it.

CHAPTER 17: If you started a new project and had it all figured out, then someone came along and tried to push you aside, how could you handle it?

CHAPTER 18: Can you think of something that is good and godly and are determined to pray for it the rest of your life? What would it be?

CHAPTER 19: Life is hard. What kind of rock do you base your life on so you can face those hard times? Is there more than one rock for you?

CHAPTER 20: Do you have anything valuable that has been handed down by past generations to you or someone in your family? Why is it valuable to you?

CHAPTER 21: Think about the last responders where you live?

Do you know any first responders yourself? Can you write a letter to the editor praising them or write a letter directly to them?

CHAPTER 22: Have you ever believed you should be honored for something, but someone else was honored instead? How have you been able to handle it?

CHAPTER 23: Most people think the woman at the well just had six live-ins, even though the Bible said five were her husbands. Do you know someone who has been misjudged and gossiped about? How can you help that person's reputation?

CHAPTER 24: What talents do you have? Perhaps it's a hobby. Have you ever thought of using them to bring someone else joy? How can you do it now?

CHAPTER 25: Have you heard of someone people were prejudiced against but were actually more intelligent or talented than most people were? In what ways could you honor that person, whether dead or alive?

CHAPTER 26: Did you ever go to a foreign country alone and needed someone to help orient you? Were they fair to you? Were they honest? Did they go out of their way to help or not help you?

CHAPTER 27: Do people tend to not steal big things, but they steal little things? Name some little things people commonly steal and say, "No one will ever notice?".

CHAPTER 28: What is forgiveness? Some people may be against you for reasons that do not exist? Is forgiveness condoning the way they act around you?

CHAPTER 29: There are some people who act holy on Sunday mornings, and get up front and perform or speak or usher, but, when there is a good work that needs to be done, they never show up. Then, there are those who quietly do their good works all the time, but others in a congregation don't know them? Who do we normally praise? Should we?

CHAPTER 30: How can a person have a savings account if their income barely meets their expenses? Think about the "widow's mite" or the widow Elijah helped. What about you? Do you have any money set aside for an emergency? How do you think you will handle that emergency when it happens?

CHAPTER 31: Think about a person whose loved one dies unexpectedly and one whose loved one dies a little at a time. Which way, to you, would saying goodbye to the loved one be easier or harder?

CHAPTER 32: What is the worse mistake you ever made? You may not want to tell about it. But, if you do, is there some way you could have avoided it? Did anyone try to tell you not to do it? Or are you trying to help someone else right now on the verge of making a terrible decision?

CHAPTER 33: Often, when siblings fight all the time growing up, they quit fighting and become good friends once they are grown. Why do you think that is?

CHAPTER 34: The world is full of injustice. If a terrible injustice were done to you, what could you do it be able to accept it and move on with your life?

CHAPTER 35: Have you known anyone who faced one tragedy after another but was able to keep smiling? How do you think that person was able to do it?

CHAPTER 36: Sending a son or daughter or husband or wife off to war, not knowing if you will ever see them again is hard. How can you best handle your time apart not knowing?

CHAPTER 37: Have you ever lost everything or known someone who did? Perhaps their house was destroyed and they had no insurance. Perhaps they lost their job and could not keep up payments on their house? Some people commit suicide. How do you think you would handle it?

CHAPTER 38: At times in your life, have you ever felt completely alone? Perhaps no one knew of your devastation because you did not tell it. How low did you get? What finally pulled you out of it?

CHAPTER 39: Although there are no tears in heaven, how do you think you would look back over your life on earth and all its problems, knowing what you do now (being in heaven)?

ABOUT THE AUTHOR

Katheryn Maddox Haddad spends an average of 300 hours researching before writing a historical novel—ancient historians such as Josephus, archaeological digs so she can know the layout of cities, their language, culture, and politics.

She grew up in the northern United States and now lives in Arizona where she doesn't have to shovel sunshine. She basks in 100-degree weather, palm trees, cacti, and a computer with most of the letters worn off.

She is author of 77 books, both non-fiction and fiction. Her newspaper column appeared for several years in newspapers in Texas and North Carolina ~ *Little Known Facts About the Bible* ~ and she has written for numerous Christian publications. For over twenty years, she has been sending out every morning a daily scripture and short inspirational thought to some 30,000 people around the world.

She spends half her day writing, and the other half teaching English over the internet worldwide using the Bible as textbook. She has taught some 7000 Muslims through World English Institute. Students she has converted to Christianity are in hiding in Afghanistan, Iran, Iraq, Yemen, Uzbekistan, Somalia, Jordan, Tajikistan, Sierra Leone, Pakistan, Indonesia, and Palestine. "They are my heroes," she declares.

With a bachelor's degree in English, Bible and social science from Harding University and part of a master's degree in Bible, including Greek, from the Harding Graduate School of Theology, she also has a master's degree in management and human relations from Abilene University. She is a member of American Christian Fiction Writers, Historical Novel Society, International Screen Writers Association, and is also an energetic public speaker who can touch the hearts of audiences.

CONNECT WITH
KATHERYN MADDOX HADDAD

Website: **https://inspirationsbykatheryn.com**

Facebook: **bit.ly/FacebooksKatherynMaddoxHaddad**

Linkedin: **http://bit.ly/KatherynLinkedin**

Twitter: **https://twitter.com/KatherynHaddad**

Pinterest: **https://www.pinterest.com/haddad1940/**

Goodreads: **https://www.goodreads.com/katherynmaddoxhaddad**

GET A FREE BOOK

Sign up for Katheryn's monthly newsletter with half-price books for the whole family and insider tips on what's coming next.
http://bit.ly/katheryn

JOIN MY DREAM TEAM

Members get the first peek at my newest book and have fun offering me advice sometimes. I have a point system of rewards for helping me get the word out. Check it out here: **http://bit.ly/KatherynsDreamTeam**

www.ingramcontent.com/pod-product-compliance
Lightning Source LLC
Chambersburg PA
CBHW031735180726
48283CB00005B/1514